TRAIL OF DEAD

TRAIL OF DEAD

A SCARLETT BERNARD NOVEL

MELISSA F. OLSON

47N☰RTH

Text copyright © 2013 Melissa F. Olson
All rights reserved.
Printed in the United States of America.
No part of this book may be reproduced, or stored in a retrieval system, or
transmitted in any form or by any means, electronic, mechanical, photocopying,
recording, or otherwise, without
express written permission of the publisher.

Published by 47 North
PO Box 400818
Las Vegas, NV 89140

ISBN-13: 9781612183121
ISBN-10: 1612183123
Library of Congress Control Number: 2013930531

For my husband, Tyler. You know why.

Prologue

The call had come anonymously from one of the witches, not their new leader, Kirsten. That was unusual, which aroused the cleaner's interest, and on a whim she decided not to call Kirsten herself until she'd arrived at the crime scene.

She followed the directions to a building on Olympic in East LA, a small, dingy theater that had been closed for years. The building exterior—including the weathered For Sale sign out front—was covered in graffiti, and the decorative climbing vines now seemed to be swallowing the structure whole, like a snake devouring a mouse. Squinting against the dim street lighting, she spotted the side door and parked right in front. She pushed aside a stray vine and pulled on the door handle.

It opened straight into the main theater, to an aisle alongside the shabby seating that ran all the way to the stage. The only light came from the few remaining emergency bulbs that lined both aisles. The cleaner immediately saw that witches had been using this building for a while—spell-casting paraphernalia was scattered throughout the seating area. She picked her way past burned-out candles, crumpled paper, pencil nubs, and piles of chalk dust, down the aisle toward the raised stage, which was the darkest area of the room. Squinting against the gloom, the cleaner reached into her large canvas bag and pulled out a heavy-duty flashlight. She switched it on, following the beam up the little set of stairs leading onto the stage itself.

She saw the pentacle right away. One of the witches had spray-painted it directly onto the stage floor, and the white paint looked scuffed and worn around the edges. Whatever they'd been doing here, this wasn't the first time. The cleaner's flashlight caught a smear of red, standing out against the white of the pentacle, and she crouched down and touched one gloved finger to the stain. Blood. She followed the direction of the smear a few feet, expecting a body, but instead her flashlight caught a big pile of...something. Dirt? Clay? The pile was the size of a kitchen stove, and as the cleaner stared at it, the dirt... trembled. She gasped, but in surprise rather than fear, and bent closer.

"Help me."

Startled, the cleaner whirled and zigzagged her flashlight beam around the stage, alighting on a pile of ancient books, the tiny corpse of a long-dead dove—and something else. Minding the blood smear, she stepped forward.

"Help me." The voice was plaintive and forlorn, begging. The flashlight found a pile of charred clothes. The cleaner crossed the stage carefully, keeping on one side of the blood smears, and approached. It took her a long moment to realize that the clothes were moving slightly, and then longer to understand that they weren't just a pile of burned clothes, but an entire burned person who was still managing to breathe.

She crouched down. The woman—the witch—was small and twisted, her right leg bent in an awkward direction. The cleaner ignored this and played the flashlight around the woman's exposed skin. What was left of it. A long section of her skin, from chin to hip, was black and flaking. The top part of her face was untouched, and her hazel eyes were fixed on the cleaner, pleading.

"This is third degree, maybe fourth," the cleaner observed calmly, looking closely at the witch's stomach. She moved the light back to the woman's face. "You're going to die."

"No," the woman whispered, tears sliding from the corners of her eyes down into her glossy hair. She spoke without moving her chin, but the cleaner could understand. "You have to help me."

The cleaner cocked her head back in the direction of the blood smear, toward the pile of dirt. "Is that what I think it is?"

Something new flashed in the burned woman's eyes. Pride. "Yes."

"Interesting," the cleaner said thoughtfully. "A rare specialty. It absorbed most of the impact?"

"Yes."

"You must have been trying for something big." The cleaner stood up, brushing off her pants. "But you're still going to die."

"Take me…"

"Where, to the hospital?" The cleaner chuckled down at the desperate woman. "They'll give you the good drugs, true, but the journey there will be agonizing, and if that's third degree you shouldn't be in too much pain right now." She glanced around. "If you want, I could find something heavy, put you out of your misery…"

She took a few steps back, playing the flashlight beam around the stage. Sometimes the spells required a knife…Before she'd made it more than a few steps, though, she heard the voice whisper at her back. "I have money."

The cleaner froze and turned slowly back toward the burned witch, raising an eyebrow. "How much money?"

"Old money," the witch said simply. "And I know a healer. Get me there."

The cleaner looked at the burned witch for a long moment, weighing her options and enjoying the woman's panicked stare. Finally, she gave an elegant little shrug. Why not? "Perhaps we can work something out," Olivia said.

Chapter 1

"Miss? He sent another drink."

The flight attendant gave me a somewhat disapproving look as she set out a little square napkin and topped it with my second plastic flute of champagne. "Just so you know?" she whispered, leaning over so her age-dappled cleavage surged toward my face. "He's wearing a wedding ring."

"Oh, we're not together," I said lamely. "He's my...uncle."

"Mmm-hmm." She gave me one more condemning glare and turned on her sensible heel, back up the aisle to her post.

I sighed and picked up the champagne, trying to ignore my seatmates, a middle-aged couple who stared at me with identical "what am I missing" expressions. We were on our way to Los Angeles, so they probably figured I was an actress or something. I wasn't about to correct them—after all, I couldn't exactly explain that the werewolf in first class wasn't interested in dating me, or even getting his membership card in the mile-high club. He was just delighted to have me aboard, simple as that.

Well, maybe not quite that simple. The guy was relieved—literally. Ordinarily, the magic that infects werewolves never lets them really relax: the wolf part itches away at their psyches, making most werewolves restless and quick-tempered, especially in a small, enclosed area like an airplane...unless they're around me. I'm a null, one of the very rare humans who neutralizes all the magic in a given area—which means that as long as they stay within around ten feet of me, vampires and werewolves become human again. Witches aren't able to channel any magic. The werewolf in first class was just grateful to get some peace on the five-hour flight from New York to LA. He probably didn't realize he was making me look like a bit of a whore.

When we finally got off the plane at LAX, I kept my head down and avoided eye contact with the other passengers as the herd moved en masse toward baggage claim. It was late, especially for those of us still on East Coast time, and we were all staggering zombie-style through the terminal, which was decorated with cheerful red-and-green-tinsel garlands. The touristy shops in Terminal 4 informed us, with festively threatening signs, that there were only seven more shopping days until Christmas.

I hadn't checked a bag, which allowed me to break away from most of the group and head straight for the exit. I felt sort of a *tug* as the werewolf left my radius. He felt it too, and stopped his migration, pivoting to face me. He turned out to be a white-haired black guy, which probably explained why the uncle thing hadn't worked. He looked like he was in his fifties, but the wolves age slower than humans do, so he may have actually been much older. I stood still for a second, unsure if I should go talk to him, but he just gave me a polite smile and a nod and was on his way again. I shrugged to myself. You're welcome, I guess.

I had almost made my escape into the night when I heard my name. "Scarlett?" I lifted my eyes to see Detective Jesse Cruz leaning against a concrete pillar near the sliding doors. I froze, a mixture of happiness and anxiety further polluting my tired brain. Cruz worked with LA's Southwest Homicide Division, and it didn't look like he'd come just in case I needed a ride home. When our eyes met, he pushed off and took the few steps toward me.

"Who did she kill?" I said immediately. "Her doctor? One of her friends?"

A couple of my fellow passengers glanced at me, and I was suddenly very aware of the tinny rendition of "Jingle Bells" playing on the overhead speaker. Oops. Jesse took my carry-on in one hand and my arm in the other and led me toward the automatic doors. "It's not Olivia," he said quietly. "I've been watching for the names on your list, but there's been no movement."

The cool LA night hit my face like a splash of water. There might have been snow in New York, but even at this hour LA was a balmy fifty degrees. "Oh," I said lamely, oddly deflated. I didn't want anyone else to get hurt, but I was sick of waiting for Olivia to come for me.

Once upon a time, Olivia had been my mentor. She was also a null, and had persuaded me to get involved in the Old World in the first place. It took me a long time to find out that she had done some terrible things, and by the time I did she was dying of cancer. Somehow, though, Olivia found a way to turn herself into a vampire—and then had made a couple of terrifying appearances back in my life. But no one had heard anything from her since September, though Jesse kept an eye out within the police department.

"If you're not here because of Olivia, why are you here?" I asked. "And how did you know when I'd be back?"

"Molly gave me your itinerary," he said shortly, without looking at me. "I need to show you something."

"It's almost midnight."

"This can't wait."

Without another word, Jesse opened the sedan door for me, and I actually saw his hand twitch up for a second, as though he was about to guide my head into the car, perp-style, but he managed to suppress it. When we were situated on the on-ramp for the 405 North, I looked over at him, trying to adjust to the sudden turn of my night. A couple of months earlier, I had helped Jesse solve a murder case that connected back to the supernatural world, which calls itself the Old World. Afterward Jesse had made it known that he was interested in being, as the kids say, more than friends, but we'd gone on just one date that ended in enough of a disaster that I wasn't exactly thrilled to be trapped in a car with him. And he definitely didn't seem thrilled to be trapped in a car with me.

"So where are we going?" I finally asked.

"Crime scene."

That got my attention. "What do you mean? A murder?"

He didn't answer me, which wasn't like him. Why was he taking me to a crime scene? And why the snappishness? At this point I probably should have just kept my mouth shut and let it play out, but I'm not known for my subtlety. Or my manners. "Dude. Have I done something to piss you off in the *five minutes* I've been back in the state?"

The line of his mouth quivered into a frown. I may have forgotten to mention that even in a town full of movie stars, Jesse is alarmingly gorgeous, with dark Latino good looks on a muscled frame. He makes those perpetually topless Abercrombie & Fitch guys look like homely wannabes.

I had been at least half kidding, but he took the question seriously. "I'm not sure, but I think so."

Great. His tone said *don't ask*, and for once, I listened to my inner Dr. Phil and didn't. I was just too tired for this. Instead, I just stared out at the city lights. Some of the towers were lit up with red and green lights for the holidays. Presumably, someone from the Old World had been killed, though I didn't know why Jesse would necessarily call me in for that. I make my living working for the three heads of the LA Old World community—the witches, the vampires, and the werewolves—cleaning up supernatural crime scenes before the police can get there. If a vampire spills blood somewhere, or a werewolf accidentally murders a neighbor's chickens, I get called in to hide all the evidence. I almost always make it in time, and Dashiell, the city's master vampire, pulls strings to cover it up if I can't.

The system works because, despite being the second-largest city in the country, Los Angeles has just never had much of a supernatural population. The wolves don't like being two hours of unpredictable traffic away from good natural areas, and most of the out-of-state vampires I've met think living in LA is…tacky. Basically, most of the Old World's attitude about LA is sort of the equivalent of most of the humans' attitude about, say, Boise: sure, it's *there*, but who the hell cares?

So yeah, I'd helped Jesse on a case before, but I still couldn't figure out why he was bringing me to a crime scene now: If he was already officially on the case, then the police knew about it, so what would be the point in bringing me in? It was now up to Dashiell to pull some strings with the higher-ups. I gave up on trying to logic it out and settled for yawning and resting my head against the cool glass of the window.

I dozed off after Jesse got on the 101 on-ramp, but snapped awake when the car finally stopped. Blinking, I peered in the direction of the nearest major street: Ventura Boulevard. We were in Studio City. Jesse was out of the car before I had my seat belt undone, so I had to scramble to catch up as he strode toward the front door of a dingy stucco apartment building. A half-assed attempt had been made to throw Christmas lights on the tree-shaped shrub next to the front door. It probably would have looked better if they had forgone the Christmas lights entirely.

Jesse ushered me into a little vestibule with beige paint and a couple of neglected-looking potted plants. No lights for them. He made a beeline for the call box, stabbing the button for apartment 313 with an index finger. He identified himself to the female voice on the other end and marched us through the buzzing interior door—all without saying a word to me. I clenched my jaw. Fine. I was too tired and travel-worn to try to apologize for whatever it was I had allegedly done to piss him off. If Jesse wanted to play the quiet game, I could hold my own.

He led me up two flights of stairs, down a very long, very beige hallway, and to the last door on the right, the only one with a cheerful welcome mat and a plastic wreath adorning the door. Jesse rang the bell and held his badge up to the peephole.

After a moment, the door creaked open a few inches and two large, red-rimmed brown eyes appeared in the space. The girl was maybe a couple of years younger than me, college aged, with gorgeous dark-brown skin. She had a crumpled washcloth in her visible hand and that wrung-out look of someone who's been crying for hours.

"Ms. Jackson?" Jesse asked. "I'm sorry for the late hour, but I did want to have the specialist here as quickly as possible."

Her voice was soft and grave, with a slight Southern accent. "Of course, please come in." The door swung all the way open, and she stepped back to let us in. I looked around. The apartment was very small, but the space had been used with efficiency and color in mind. It had a whole Urban Outfitters dorm room kind of feel to it. Not exactly my thing, but not terrible, either.

Cruz made the introductions. "Jubilee Jackson, this is Scarlett Bernard. Scarlett is the crime-scene specialist I told you about."

"Uh, hi," I said. She was plump, but in a natural, self-confident way. She wore a summery yellow top with dark-green pajama pants and those long, stripy wool slippers that go halfway to your knee. She held out a hand, which I shook, and then I glanced over to Cruz, waiting for my next cue.

"Could we have a moment alone in the room, please, Ms. Jackson?" he asked.

"Of course," she said, waving her hands absently toward a hall. "I need to call Erin's mom back, anyway. They're flying in later this morning." She sniffled, dabbing at her nose with the washcloth.

I followed the two of them through the entryway and down a long hall, completely bewildered. Jubilee stopped in front of a door. "I haven't touched anything, like you said," she told Jesse, her worried eyes lingering puppy-style on his face. "I'll just be in my room if you need me." She nodded to the door across the hall.

"Thanks, Ms. Jackson. We'll let you know when we're finished," Jesse said, in the soothing "it'll be okay" voice you use with broken people. He reached out to touch her arm, and she nodded trustingly. Jeez. I was glad that Jesse used his hotness powers for good.

When Jubilee's door had closed, Jesse opened the door in front of us and flicked on a light switch. "Go ahead," he said, tilting his head. "I want to hear your impressions."

I should have been angry that he'd dragged me out here only to give me the silent treatment, but he was beginning to really freak me out. I straightened up and stepped forward, looking around the small bedroom. I saw the enormous bloodstain on the carpet right away, and glanced back at Jesse. His arms were folded in front of him, face expressionless. No help there. I squatted down for a closer look. The stain ran almost the length of the room, maybe five or six feet. It had to be at least a few hours old—I figured Jesse's crime scene guys had come and gone already—but it still looked soaking wet. It was also much longer than it was wide—vaguely person shaped, I guess, but more like a snow angel than a chalk outline. I deal with blood all the time, but usually it's just little spatters. The vampires, of course, don't waste much blood, and the werewolves usually start healing before it gets this bad. The only other time I'd seen this much blood in one place was during the massacre in La Brea Park in September. I shuddered. Turning to look at Jesse, I spotted a framed picture on the wall of a young woman, twenty or so, smiling arm in arm with Jubilee. She had light-brown hair, an easy smile, and a hint of something secretive in her eyes. Erin, I presumed.

"Is this…Erin's blood?"

"We think so. Blood type matches, though it'll take a while for DNA."

"Did your experts think...can she still be alive?" I asked, keeping my voice low.

"No. With that much blood loss, unless she'd basically been *at* the hospital...she's dead."

I sidestepped the pool and continued around the room. The girl who lived here was a student, judging from the textbooks that were stacked on the small bookshelf above the computer table and the backpack tossed against the wall just inside the doorway. All of her belongings also had this look like they'd been purchased separately over time. The curtain and bedspread were a matching purple-and-green pattern, but the desk and desk drawer were a different green that didn't quite match. The desk lamp was from a completely different style...genre, I guess. I'd seen the same thing when my brother Jack was in college; it happens when you move a lot.

I turned in a circle, and finally figured out what was bothering me. The entire room was fairly neat, especially by my own low standards, but the half with the desk and the bed was slightly tousled. Books were stacked haphazardly on the shelf instead of lined up, and the pillow and covers were thrown across the bed, like someone had shaken them out without smoothing them down. In a hurry. That could have just been Erin's style, except that the opposite half of the room was pristine.

And the window...Erin's window was standing open, and had no screen or bars. When I stepped closer I realized why—the whole apartment building was like a big hollow box, with a little courtyard in the middle, containing a few picnic tables and a small spa pool. This window faced inward, with a straight thirty-foot drop to the courtyard below. Cool air drifted into the room, and I shivered in my wool peacoat, which had seemed too warm only a few minutes ago.

"We found the window screen floating in the spa," Jesse's voice said behind me. Reading my mind. I pulled my head in and turned around.

"Did your guys find anything else?"

He gave me a little *not much* shrug. "There was some gray dirt on the floor. The roommate says they were both pretty careful about tracking mud in, so we'll try to match it to a pair of her shoes to see if it's related."

I went back to the bloodstain and crouched down, automatically tucking the bottom of my jacket against my body so it wouldn't drift into the blood. There was just something wrong with the bloodstain, and in spite of the hour and the travel and the cryptic detective beside me, I was getting interested. I ran through a grisly list of injuries in my head, things I'd seen or heard about: gunshot, stabbing, decapitation, dismemberment, throat cutting. Nothing seemed to fit. If Erin had died from straightforward blood loss—a stab wound, for example—there would be a smeared end where the body had lain, and then the rest of the stain would be circular, if the floor was even, or all misshapen and wispy on carpeting like Erin's. If she'd died from a cut artery, there would be blood spray everywhere. This wasn't right. I looked up at Jesse. "It's too...neat."

He nodded, and his voice had an edge. "Techs said the blood is nearly the same depth over the whole stain."

Huh. "What causes that?"

"My crime-scene people had one theory, but only in a half-joking kind of way, because it was so out there."

I froze.

"They said it looked like she'd been crushed. Slowly." He gave me a pointed look, and I finally understood why I was here. It wasn't for my expert opinion. It was an accusation.

The crime scene had been cleaned. Professionally.

Chapter 2

"I don't know anything about it, Jesse. I just got off a plane, remember?" As I said it, I was really wishing that I'd gotten a chance to check my messages before Jesse had grabbed me in baggage claim. Eli, my apprentice/former sex buddy, had been in charge of the cleanup business while I was in New York. He would definitely have called about a complete body; those were rare. Jesse didn't know that Eli was the one covering for me, though, and since what we do is technically illegal, I wasn't about to tell him.

He took another step toward me, looking angry. "I know you did. But someone was filling in for you while you were out of town, right? I mean, the Old World doesn't stop making messes just because you aren't here to clean them up. Look around—someone tampered with this room."

I rolled my eyes. "You're right. No human being could stack books that way."

He didn't smile. "This is serious, Scarlett," he snapped. "Ordinary murders don't look like this. And the only reason to take the body but leave the blood is to hide what was done to the body, which just screams Old World. So who cleaned the room?"

Now I was starting to get mad. "Are you kidding me? You of all people should understand that even if this is an Old World thing— which I have absolutely no idea about, by the way, because *I just got here*—there's no way the police can get involved."

"Look where you are right now," he hissed, not backing down an inch. "This room belongs to a twenty-year-old kid whose room-mate is devastated. Her parents are catching the first flight out of Michigan, and I have to tell them something when they get here. Maybe you don't know—yet. But you're involved, or you're going to be. So who's been covering for you?"

Dammit. Jesse hadn't just grabbed me at the airport to get to the crime scene faster: he had picked me up instead of calling or com-ing to my house because he hadn't wanted to give me a chance to get my story straight with someone. That was so...cop-like. I rubbed my eyes, which were stinging with tiredness, and thought about it for a second. If Jesse knew that Eli worked for me, it would put Eli in legal danger and be yet another way for Jesse to mess around in Old World affairs. Dangerous for everyone. "I can't, Jesse. But if I hear anything that I think would be useful to you, I'll pass it on."

"That's not good enough," he said heatedly, switching tactics. "What if I just go over your head? I could stop at that bar and ask the werewolves. Hell, I know where Dashiell lives. How about I go knock on his door and see what he says?"

Jesse started to push past me, toward the door, and I skittered sideways, trying to block his path and still avoid the blood. "Stop! Are you *trying* to get dead? You know better than to screw around with these people, Jesse. You don't want to so much as remind Dashiell that you're *alive*, much less start poking around in Old World business again. Last time you almost got—" I stopped, but we both knew what I had been about to say: *got yourself killed*. Dashiell had threatened Jesse's life, and only his good behavior and silence had kept him alive. And it hadn't hurt that I'd just saved Dashiell's wife, Beatrice, from being killed for good.

"So help me." He folded his arms and stared at me defiantly.

My mouth dropped open. "*This* is your plan? You're going to bet your life that I care enough about you to keep you from getting killed? You're an idiot."

He took the last step toward me, the one that put him all the way in my personal space and forced me to turn my head up to see him. His dark eyes searched my own, and I felt heat flutter in my stomach. "I'm still right, though, aren't I?" he said quietly.

I glared at him. "I hate you." I took a step back, putting more space between us. "You could have just asked for my help, you know."

His smile turned sad. "I was hoping that when you saw her room...you'd offer."

Ah. I'd failed another of his little morality tests. I felt the old gulf between us settle back into place. Jesse still believed in always doing the right thing. I believed in survival on whatever terms necessary. I wouldn't say that there were no lines I wouldn't cross, but in Jesse's eyes I was willing to do a lot of things that were neither legal nor ethical. Like not get involved with this case. Jesse, on the other hand, still practically radiated integrity and goodness. Maybe it was proof that I was just a soft touch, but I *would* get involved for him. And he knew it, the bastard.

"I'll make a couple of calls," I allowed.

He smiled at me, for the first time that night. Then the smile faded, and he cleared his throat. "Listen, um...there's something else I should tell you. I'm sort of seeing someone."

I blinked. "Oh," I said stupidly. I don't know why I was surprised. Jesse was a kind, cheerful, gorgeous man living in Los Angeles. Women had to be throwing themselves at him every day. I tried to keep the sting off my face.

"Yeah, well, it's only been a couple of dates, but she's...very sweet. Gentle."

Ouch. I knew that probably hadn't been a direct shot at me, but sweet and gentle were definitely two things that I wasn't. I pushed the thought away. Jesse had paused, looking at me nervously.

"What?" I said finally.

"Are you still going to help me?"

I rolled my eyes. "Yes, Captain Ego. You're still my friend. Or whatever." He had the decency to look embarrassed.

I checked my watch. It was almost 5:00 a.m. in New York, and a half-assed catnap on the plane wasn't enough to clear my head for thinking. "Okay, look, you have to give me some time to make some inquiries. Can we get together for lunch?"

His eyebrows furrowed with irritation. "Breakfast."

"Jesse…" I said. Okay, maybe it was more of a whine.

"I'll pick you up for brunch at ten. Final offer."

"Ugh. Fine."

"And I want the body," he pressed.

I shook my head. "I can't do that."

He was fuming. "Knock it off, Scarlett. This isn't the time to be cute."

"No, I mean, I literally can't do it. If—again, *if*—this is really my kind of thing, the body is gone. Like, *gone* gone." If Eli had cleaned the scene, he would have gone straight to my incinerator guy in Van Nuys. Jesse's sudden glare was full of ferocity and something like betrayal. "Jesse, it was gone before I got off the plane. Giving me the stink-eye isn't going to change anything."

Jesse sighed, and the glare collapsed into something sadder. "Sometimes…I just don't know how you do what you do."

I couldn't help it. I flinched.

We got back on the freeway, and Jesse dropped me off at Molly's house in West Hollywood less than twenty minutes later. It's amazing how fast you can get around LA at two in the morning.

Molly, my landlady, roommate, and pseudofriend, is also a vampire. She and I have a deal: she lets me live there practically free, and I help her age. Molly was turned in Victorian Wales at only seventeen, and although she was considered an adult when she was alive, in the twenty-first century she couldn't legally vote, have sex, drink, etc. When she's around me, Molly becomes human again, and ages like any normal person. She also has to use the bathroom, sleep, and eat while she's near me, which is a constant source of wonder and amusement for her, since apparently toilet habits have changed in the century since she was alive. At this point she looks like a college student, about twenty, and I've often wondered what age she wants to get to before she'll kick me out. I love her house, which is old and cute and filled with carefully chosen things, but I've never really thought of it as my home.

"Scarlett!" Molly squealed, and ran up to hug me. Molly is surprisingly touchy-feely for a vampire. I usually beg off the hugging, but it had been a while since we'd seen each other, so I allowed myself to be enveloped. She was wearing supertight jeans that probably cost more than all the clothes in my suitcase, and a T-shirt with a skull and crossbones. Only the skull had a little pink bow where its hair would have been. She also had on one of those fancy phone headsets, the kind where the microphone wraps around to be in front of your mouth.

"Hi," I said when she'd let go. She paused to straighten the headset around her hair, which had recently been dyed blonde and cut into sort of a long bob. I have no idea why vampires' hair continues to grow. Chalk it up to magic. "What are you up to?" I asked cautiously.

She pointed toward the laptop that had been plopped on the couch. "Online gaming."

"Oh, Molly."

"What?" she said, defensive. "Geeks are in now, remember? And it's soooo addicting."

"I remember. Last time you started that stuff I barely spoke to you."

She shrugged. "You were gone for like a *month*. I got bored." She crossed her legs. "Besides, they've got this new one that's all about vampires, see?" She pointed to the little screen, where an avatar woman with tight jeans and a black T-shirt was frozen, waiting for her real-life counterpart. Sure enough, she had comically long fangs pointing out of her mouth and a little wooden stake in one hand.

I rolled my eyes and picked up a stack of my mail that Molly had deposited on a side table. "I wonder what Dashiell would think of this."

"He'd probably love it. Well, not 'love,' exactly, but he would find it amusing. I think he likes when American pop culture makes fun of vampires. It makes it all the less likely for anyone to actually believe in us."

This was true. I've often wondered if there are vampires working in Hollywood, actually setting up the schmaltzy stuff to make the existence of vampires seem all the more ridiculous. I know that in the past they've started rumors about themselves—the whole "vampires fear religious objects," for example, is bullshit designed to help real vampires pass as human—so that kind of modern PR blitz doesn't seem unlikely.

I flicked through envelopes. "Except for maybe a coalition of teenage girls, who are of course known for their discerning intelligence," I said absently, then looked up in time to see Molly's face darken with sudden memory. I winced. Oops. "Sorry, Molls, exhaustion has reunited my foot and my mouth."

She shrugged again and sat back down on the couch. "Did you learn anything in New York?"

"Yes and no. I learned a couple of new tricks, but not...what I was looking for."

This was a somewhat dangerous subject. New York had been a fact-finding mission, though Molly didn't actually know the whole story behind my going. A few months earlier, the first time I'd helped Jesse with an investigation, I had accidentally turned a vampire named Ariadne back into a human—permanently. Until it had happened, I hadn't even known it was possible, and I was keeping it under wraps: so far only Dashiell knew what I had done.

But the whole thing had made me realize that I didn't know much about what I was. Hence the trip to meet the only other known null on this continent. Unfortunately, he had never heard of a permanent turn, either.

"What was the other null like? Was he yummy?"

"Molly! He's nineteen years old!" But I thought of Jameson, and may have blushed just a teensy bit.

"Yeah, yeah." She gave me a smirk. "You're twenty-three, Scarlett. It's not exactly May–December. Maybe May–late June."

I pretended to stare at the ceiling, whistling innocently, until Molly laughed. "Fine. Be that way. Are you off to bed?"

"I wish. I have to go see Eli to, uh, get my van back," I said. So smooth, Scarlett. Theoretically, I could just call Eli and ask about the Studio City scene, but I'm extremely paranoid about discussing certain things on the phone. And besides, I really did need to get my van back.

"Tonight? Now?" Her eyes sparkled. Molly didn't really know how involved Eli and I had become, but she at least knew I had slept with him. "And perhaps get a little something-something else?" *Laid*, she mouthed, with a smug nod. Molly likes to pretend our lives are more *Sex and the City* and less Bram Stoker's *Dracula*. The book, not the atrocious Keanu Reeves movie.

I rolled my eyes good-naturedly. "It's not like that. I'm officially back on duty, is all." I turned to go, but stopped and looked back at Molly, who had unpaused her video game. "Uh, Molls? You didn't hear anything else from Olivia, did you?"

The last time I'd seen her, Olivia had stalked me outside the hospital, shortly after I'd turned the vampire human again. For whatever reason, the effort to turn Ariadne had almost killed me— and resulted in me temporarily losing my radius. That moment outside the hospital was the perfect opportunity for Olivia to kill me, but she hadn't done it—which made me believe she wanted to toy with me first. Trying to get to Molly would be just her style.

"Nope," she said cheerfully, her little vampire avatar leapfrogging over what appeared to be an undead bodybuilder. "Besides, I don't think she'd mess with me. I've got a lot of years on her. And I'm scrappy."

"Yeah, I know…thanks. You gonna be around later?"

"Nah," she said, and gave me one of her wicked, not-human smiles, which she managed to pull off even though she was currently human. "I'm probably gonna go check out the after-hours scene." Ugh. Feeding. Molly had more than enough control to keep from killing her food, and as far as I knew she always left them happy and satisfied, pressing their minds so they would believe whatever story she wanted. I suppose there are worse things in the world, but it still leaves me feeling sort of icky.

I left her there and rounded the corner toward the stairs. "Hey, you put up the tree," I called back to her. There was a modest four-footer in a little alcove next to the stairs.

"Yup. Did you see the new ornaments?" came Molly's voice from the living room. I bent closer, squinting past the thick colored bulbs that Molly preferred to see what she'd used for decorations. The long, pointy-looking things weren't icicles, as I'd originally thought, but tiny wooden stakes dipped in red nail polish to look like blood. In addition to the *Nightmare Before Christmas* line she'd brought out last year, she also had the Hallmark Keepsake versions of Dracula and Edward Cullen. I shook my head at them. "eBay!" she yelled before I could ask.

Rounding the tree, I dragged my suitcase up the stairs to the bedroom I use. Then I dropped the peacoat on the bed, unbound my long, almost-black hair, and tugged a brush through it. I pulled on fresh jeans and a T-shirt and got out my toiletry bag, heading into the bathroom across the hall to brush my teeth. As I raised the toothbrush to my face, though, I paused, caught off guard by my reflection in the medicine cabinet mirror. With my hair down I looked more and more like my mother every year.

The old grief burrowed back into my chest like a hungry tick. My parents had been killed five years earlier, when Olivia had tampered with the brakes on their Jeep. In a dark, twisted way, she'd wanted me for her surrogate daughter, and my mom and dad had been in the way of her dream. They were dead, and it was always going to be my fault. Seeing my mother's face in the mirror was the least I deserved.

Knock it off, Scarlett. I dropped the toothbrush in a plastic cup and tugged at the mirror, popping the medicine cabinet open at an angle so I was no longer reflected. Then I took off, rolling my hair into a bun as I walked. I pulled my favorite canvas jacket out of the closet—well, off the floor of the closet—and deposited keys, phone, and wallet in its various pockets. It was a lot warmer than New York, but still only fifty degrees, so I wore a hoodie underneath the jacket. Ready. Well, as ready as I was going to get.

Chapter 3

I usually drive an enormous white van, which Molly has affectionately nicknamed "the White Whale." It's equipped with all my cleanup stuff—solvents, sponges, ziplock baggies that are big enough to hold body parts, a mop, et cetera—as well as a whole assortment of random stuff that had been handy at crime scenes in the past—a bag of dirt, air freshener, extra light bulbs. There's even a refrigerated section for when I have to transport dead bodies. While I was gone, however, Eli had been driving the van, so it was missing from my usual spot in the parking garage down the street from Molly's. Instead I had Eli's battered blue pickup truck. I retrieved the spare key from one of the tire wells and turned the engine over. Success. I backed out of my spot and turned the truck's nose south.

On the way, I finally checked my voice mail. Sure enough, there was one from Eli, sounding panicked and rushed. "Scar, it's me. I had a really tough job tonight and I'm worried about the results. Call me when you get this, okay? Please?"

That worried me. It wasn't like Eli to sound so frantic. He's had a lot of practice in controlling his demeanor. Eli struggles pretty hard with his inner werewolf's Call of the Wild. For a long time I thought he was only interested in me because being around me is so calming, but he's proved more than once that it's deeper than that. Still, our relationship is complicated, partly because of Jesse.

And partly because Eli was technically my employee, until I found a more permanent replacement. Finding an apprentice had not been at the top of my priority list the last couple of months.

I drove straight for Hair of the Dog, the bar where Eli works. It was just after 2:00 a.m. on a Wednesday, so the place would be closed, but only just. The bar is owned by a werewolf named Will Carling, who's the alpha here in LA. Will is one of the few Old World creatures that I fully respect: he's a good man, and a good leader. Werewolf movies always make it seem like a pack is all about dominance and submission—the pecking order—but in the wild, most wolf packs and werewolf packs are led by an alpha male and female (who are almost always a couple) who solve disputes, keep the wolves in line, and organize full moon activities. Basically, they're like parents. Will doesn't have an alpha mate yet, so his pack has a beta, a second-in-command. And that's Eli. Poor guy has to deal with pack business, holding a full-time job, *and* being my apprentice. Good thing he has easy access to liquor.

Hair of the Dog is on a little commercial stretch of West Pico, near a children's bookstore and a dry cleaner's. At this time of night, with even the bar closed, I got truly phenomenal parking. I climbed down from the pickup and trudged over to the bar entrance, trying not to notice how dark and silent the street felt. I pounded on the smoked glass door for a solid two minutes until I felt something enter my radius from the other side. I shivered. It's always weird when I neutralize someone I can't see.

For a null, having a supernatural creature step into your radius is kind of like having someone brush their hand against your hair without touching your head: you don't *feel* it, but you feel that it's happening, if that makes any sense. I can usually tell if the creature in question is a vampire, werewolf, or witch, and I get a general sense of how powerful they are. And most of them know that they've gotten close to me—the wolves lose their edginess and near invulnerability, and the vamps have to start breathing again, which often results in a series of amusing facial expressions. Witches, who always have the ability to channel magic but aren't always using it, are the only ones who sometimes don't realize they've entered my area.

The bolt on the door made a loud *snick*, and Eli tugged it open, gathering me into his arms so fast I was breathless. I smelled the sea in his dark-blond hair. He was wearing jeans and a ribbed tank that showed off the lean surfer's muscles on his arms and chest. An annoying little voice that came from somewhere lower than my head went *mmmmm*. For just a second I let myself hug him back.

"Hey," he said quietly, voice filled with relief. He released me and took my face in his hands, fingers curling in the loose strands of my hair.

"Hey, yourself," I said, taking an uneasy step back. "I got your message. What happened?"

His face tightened a little. "Straight to business, then." Tension rippled between us. Eli and I had slept together a few times, but then during the La Brea Park investigation, a witch had used Eli to power a locating spell to find me—which meant that in some magical, romantic way, he *belonged* to me. Naturally that completely freaked me out. Since then, whenever he tried to start a conversation that wasn't directly related to the job, I tended to babble until I could run away. For the most part, he had stopped trying, and it seemed like our relationship got a little more businesslike every time we spoke. I wondered if I still "owned" him.

And if I wanted to.

The moment passed, and he held the door wide. "Well, come on in. There's someone here who'd probably like to talk to you." He bolted the door after I'd passed through, and I followed him through the little alcove into the main bar area. The whole place is pretty much one big room. There's a square bar in the middle, *Cheers*-style, and a small hallway in the back that leads to Will's office, bathrooms, and a janitor's closet. The walls are covered top to bottom in kitschy dog stuff—pictures, old calendars, framed cartoons, and so on. Someone—probably Will's assistant, Caroline—had gone around and scotch-taped little Santa hats on most of the puppies. I couldn't help but smile at that. Then I saw the occupied barstool and felt a familiar hum of power enter my radius. One that had no business being in a werewolf bar after hours.

"Kirsten?"

She looked up blearily, and I almost reared back in surprise. Kirsten Harms-Dickerson is the most powerful magically talented human in Los Angeles, as far as I know, and the leader of the informal witches' union. Usually she looks like a blonde Swedish angel and has always reminded me of Samantha on *Bewitched*. Tonight, though, there were circles under her eyes, and more fine, blonde hair had escaped her ponytail than hadn't. She looked worse off than Jubilee Jackson. A pile of shredded cardboard coasters squatted on the bar in front of her, and she was working on tearing at a new one. "Hey, Scarlett."

"What are you doing here?" I said. The different Old World groups don't mix much—they have a few hundred years of tension that tends to get in the way of a good time—and of pretty much everyone I know, Kirsten has the most normal life. She has a day job and everything, which made her presence here more than a little out of the norm.

"Erin" was all she said, but it was enough for pieces to fall into place. The one thing that Dashiell, Will, and Kirsten all have in common is concern for their people's safety.

"She was one of yours?" I asked, crossing the room to drop onto the stool next to her.

Kirsten nodded, keeping her red eyes focused on the coaster, which she'd folded over and over until it looked like a sliced pizza. She started pulling the slices apart. I was opening my mouth to start another question, but Eli raised his eyebrows meaningfully, telling me not to push it. Despite their inherent differences, he and

Kirsten had developed sort of a mutual respect when they'd teamed up to save my life. "You want a drink?" he asked me, walking back behind the bar. I dropped onto a stool, hesitating, but finally shook my head. I needed to be clear.

"Not just now," I said.

We sat there for a few minutes without talking. When the last coaster slice had been torn off and ripped in half again, Kirsten spoke. "Erin called me tonight from campus begging for help. We made plans to meet up at a coffee shop halfway between her school and my home, but Erin never came. After last fall I collected a few hairs from each of my witches in case someone targeted the Old World again. I did a locator spell, and another, and another. Erin... wasn't anywhere." She abandoned the coaster and leaned forward, burying her head in her arms.

Before I could ask, Eli explained. "Meaning she was dead. Or inside your radius, but you were out of town."

I looked from one to the other. I've always suspected that Kirsten's power comes from her inherent serenity—even when she was using combat magic against a serial killer last fall, her composure had never wavered. This was scary. I raised my eyebrows at Eli, who picked up the story.

"Kirsten went to the campus, and called me to go to her apartment," he said quietly. "She thought...there was probably a crime scene to clean up somewhere."

"Was there a body?"

He nodded. "I could smell it before I got off the elevator."

I winced. Meat and blood smells can drive the werewolves kind of crazy, sometimes even forcing them to change. Eli's tolerance is better than most (for some reason the inner wolf bothers him, but blood doesn't bother his inner wolf, which just goes to show how much sense magic makes), which is why he's able to do this job at all, but it must have been rough to be in that room. "Go on."

Eli's eyes became distant as he remembered. His hands, which had been doing little closing-up tasks as he spoke, went still on the bar. "There had been some kind of fight. That girl...I could hardly tell she'd been a person. It looked like she'd been *liquefied.*"

"Crushed?" I said.

He pointed a finger at me, nodding.

"What did you smell?" I asked. Eli's werewolf senses have been helpful on more than one occasion.

"Mostly just the blood, and the other...body stuff. But there was a little bit of dirt there too. Odd smell." He shrugged.

Jesse had said the forensics team had found dirt. "What made it odd?"

"It smelled...I don't know, processed? I can't really explain why, but it made me think of industrial buildings."

"And it didn't rain last night?"

"Nope."

Hmm. No reason for Erin's shoes to be muddy. "So you took the body," I prompted. I would have too. If a person has clearly died of something explainable—gunshots or a heart attack or a car accident—I leave the body alone, even if someone from the Old World might have been involved. Basically, if there was a reasonable human explanation, I stay out of it. But a crushed body in a tiny third-floor bedroom would bring up too many questions.

"Yeah, and I cleaned up as fast as I could, but I heard the roommate coming. I grabbed the bag with the body, waited until she went into her own bedroom, and made a run for it. You said always deal with the body first, right?" He looked directly at me, and I realized what he was asking. In his quiet, pragmatic way, Eli wanted to know if he'd handled it right.

"Yes," I replied, but a second too late.

"What? What else should I have done?"

This is what I liked about Eli—his tone wasn't defensive or angry. He simply wanted to know. I felt awkward about correcting him in front of someone who was essentially our boss, but what the hell, Kirsten knew he was still training. "Taken the carpet," I replied. "There's a carpet knife in the bag, just for that kind of thing. With a bloodstain that big and that wet, they know they're looking for a dead body. If you take the carpet, all they have is a missing girl who's maybe in trouble, or maybe just ran away with her rug. It changes the story."

"So I should have picked taking the carpet over straightening the room," he said thoughtfully.

"Yes." I shrugged to say *not that it matters now*.

Looking troubled, Eli excused himself to the back office to count the till and lock up. Kirsten finally looked at me. "If Erin's roommate came home, I'm assuming the police have gotten involved by now?"

"Yeah." I filled her in on my own evening, starting when Jesse picked me up at the airport. "But he doesn't know that Erin was a witch," I finished.

"There's something else he doesn't know," Kirsten said suddenly. She reached up, making a weak attempt to smooth down her hair. "Erin wasn't the first witch to be murdered this week. She was the second."

Chapter 4

"*Two* dead witches?" I asked, startled. "Eli didn't mention another body."

"No, he wouldn't have. This one was out of our hands. The woman was thrown off the Santa Monica Pier."

"Okay, wait," I said, and my mind was clearing now. "Can you start at the beginning please?"

"Yes, of course. I'm sorry." Kirsten straightened her back, obviously trying to rally. With her makeup wiped off and her hair a lopsided cloud around her face, I was struck by how young she looked. How old *was* Kirsten? Thirty? Thirty-five? It seemed awfully young to have so much power and so many people counting on you. Granted, I was only twenty-three, but I had the opposite of power, and nobody counted on me.

"Last Friday, I got a call from one of my witches," she began. "Her name is—was—Denise Godfry, although she worked under a different name. Anyway, she asked to meet with me, in person, to discuss a problem. I agreed, of course, but I had meetings that night. We were supposed to have brunch in Santa Monica the next morning, but Denise never showed. I called and called, and finally went down there. There was a policeman at her apartment." Kirsten began victimizing a new coaster, and I noticed that her manicure was chipped to shit. A very bad sign.

"She was dead," I prompted.

"Yes. The police said she had killed herself," Kirsten said, with a bitter little emphasis on the word *police*. "Her body was found in Santa Monica, right up on the damned beach. It even made the *Times*, though you probably didn't see it in New York."

I tried to remember if I had ever heard her swear. "No."

"Anyway, I was very worried. I tried explaining to the policemen that it couldn't have been a suicide, but none of them would listen to me. Then last night it was the same thing all over again, with Erin."

"I don't mean to be insensitive, but how do you know Denise didn't just fall? Or, um…jump?"

She was shaking her head. "Denise was hydrophobic. Deeply afraid of the ocean. She told me once that she'd seen that movie *Jaws* when she was a little girl, and she still couldn't stand to be *over* water, much less in it. She would *never* have been on the pier. And if she were going to kill herself, it wouldn't be like that." The coaster in her hands was viciously ripped in half. "I told the policeman that too, for all the good it did me."

I raised my eyebrows, surprised. "You told the police?" It wasn't like her to involve the police in Old World affairs.

But Kirsten said, "At the time I was thinking Denise's death didn't have anything to do with her being a witch. I thought maybe it was an ordinary murder. If there is such a thing."

I understood. This was Los Angeles, after all, and young women who are out alone in the middle of the night do disappear for "ordinary" human reasons. "But then Erin died too, and you figured it was an Old World connection," I surmised. She nodded at her coaster pieces. "Aside from being witches, was there anything that Erin and Denise had in common?"

"Well…neither of them had much ability, I'm afraid. What you would call power."

I nodded. When I paid attention to my radius, I experienced both Kirsten's and Eli's power as two distinctive hits on my null radar: Eli as sort of a low throbbing and Kirsten as a steady buzz that flickered if she flexed her magic. A witch with less power would register as a much lesser buzz. "So you think someone may be killing...what, minor-league witches?"

She hesitated. "Maybe. It might not be that simple, though. In terms of magical ability, Erin and Denise had something else in common. They both dealt with the future."

"Fortune-tellers?" I said, unable to keep the skepticism out of my voice.

She held one hand out flat and teetered it from side to side in a "kind of" gesture. "Both women were active in our society"—the witches' word for their union—"but like many witches, both of them were really only talented with one thing: in this case, predictions. Denise read tarot cards on the Third Street Promenade, a block from the pier. She was very successful at it, but that was all she could do. Erin had even less natural magic. She got...feelings, about the future. But they were very vague."

"What do you mean, vague?"

Her eyes searched the ceiling above my head, as if she might read off an example. "She worked as a loan officer at a bank, and she would sometimes get a feeling about the people who applied. That they were going to be successful, or that they would fail miserably."

"Was she right?"

"Always, as far as she knew. But she never knew why or how something was going to happen, just sort of a general sense. I remember another witch, Stella, telling me that Erin had called and told her to keep her kids home from day care that day. Erin had no idea if that meant that the building would explode, or one of the kids would fall off the swing set, or what. She just told Stella not to let the kids go."

"What happened?"

Kirsten smiled a little. "Stella kept the girls home, and that day there was a pinkeye outbreak. It wouldn't have been fun, but it wasn't exactly life threatening, either. You can see how it was sometimes frustrating for Erin." She sighed. "And now they're both dead, and I'm just…so…" Her fists clenched over the pile of coaster bits .

Premonitions, suspicious deaths, magical theory…yep, I was way out of my depth. There was an obvious answer here: Jesse wanted to know more about the Old World's connection to Erin's death, and Kirsten wanted to figure out who'd killed Erin. It was a match made in heaven—if I could convince Kirsten to participate. "Kirsten, I'm sorry. But I'm not an investigator. Would you be willing to talk to Jesse about all this? Detective Cruz, I mean."

She looked at me as though I'd just suggested that she mow her lawn naked. "Absolutely not," she said firmly. "We don't involve the police, Scarlett."

"This is different. He already knows about the Old World, and Dashiell already knows about him. Jesse can *help* you."

"I'm not concerned with Dashiell and the vampires. Detective Cruz is with the human police. Do you have any idea the things that have happened whenever authorities got involved with witches?"

I suppressed the urge to roll my eyes at that. "Kirsten, come on. We're talking about LAPD, not the Spanish Inquisition. There are no witch hunts anymore."

"Do you know how hard we worked, how many of us died, to get it this way?" she countered, her voice rising. "The second you invite an officer of the law into our problems, you're opening a door that we might not be able to close again."

I blinked. I would bet every penny in my meager savings account that Kirsten votes for the far left, spends more than $100 on a haircut, and eats sushi at least once a week. This old-fashioned hell-and-brimstone outlook came out of nowhere.

She saw the look on my face and sighed, dropping her current mangled coaster. "I'm sorry. It's been an awful day."

"No worries."

"You don't know much about me, Scarlett, but I come from many generations of witches. There were witch hunts in Sweden a century before the trials here in Salem, so there's a certain attitude about the police that has been sort of…ingrained in me, you could say. I know Detective Cruz did good work in helping you find that man who killed the vampires, but I will *not* bring the police into witch affairs."

"Look, I promise I understand where you're coming from," I said. "But last fall, when I got cornered into working with Jesse, he really proved himself. And he hasn't shown any interest in persecuting the Old World since then." This was true. After some initial shock, and excluding this current problem with his crime scene, Jesse seemed to view the Old World the way other people view tigers at the zoo: fascinating, exotic, and interesting to look at from a distance, but you wouldn't want to go prying and poking into their business. For the last few months, he'd kept a respectful distance from Old World affairs. I very much approved of this attitude.

Kirsten sighed. "Maybe he hasn't. I'm not so prejudiced as to assume all police detectives are ignorant and hateful. But look at it this way: he still has to follow rules and uphold laws, and you know those very rarely mesh with our need for containment. What happens if the killer is Old World?"

I sat back, thinking it over. It was a fair objection. Jesse believed in law and order. If the search led to a vampire or a were-wolf, he might decide to just arrest them and damn the consequences. And there would be consequences.

I had spent less than three hours in this time zone, but I already had myself a classic rock/hard-spot scenario. If I didn't give Jesse something, he'd go to Dashiell, which could get him killed. On the other hand, if I told him about the witches without Kirsten's permission, I would probably lose my job—and maybe worse.

Christmas in New York was sounding pretty good right about now.

"Kirsten," I began again. "Two witches being murdered in a week can't be a coincidence, can it?"

"No."

"And there is every possibility that whoever is doing this will kill again."

"Yes." She stared morosely at a broken coaster, then picked up one-half and started to bend it again. "I've done what I can. I've told all my witches about Denise and Erin, and I've canceled the Solstice Party."

That surprised me. I don't really socialize with the witches, but even I had heard of the Solstice Party. Every year, Kirsten throws a blowout celebration for the witches on the night of the winter solstice, usually December 21. It's sort of like any other holiday party, as I understand it, but has a lot to do with the significance of the solstice to witchcraft, something I didn't know much about. Okay, didn't know anything about.

I pressed on. "Then you must know that you need help. Jesse is a trained investigator, and I trust him. I don't know what will happen when he catches the person, but if you don't ask him for help, someone else might die."

That was harsh, but I knew all about having the death of loved ones on my conscience, and it wasn't something I'd wish on Kirsten.

A long minute ticked by on the clock above the door, while Kirsten chewed on her lower lip and weighed what I'd said. Finally, she asked, "You'll work with him? Keep him from exposing us, and keep him safe from magical attack? I don't want any more deaths, especially a member of the police." From the tone of her voice it was clear she was worried less about Jesse's personal safety and more about getting the wrong kind of attention.

Now it was my turn to hesitate. Setting Jesse up with Kirsten had seemed like the perfect way to get him off my back, but I hadn't planned on being involved any further. Running around with Jesse didn't seem to pay very well, and we were a long way away from my actual job description.

When I didn't answer right away Kirsten looked over at me, disappointment written all over her face. "What do you need," she asked tiredly, "to care that my witches are dying?" Before I could answer, she had picked up her purse and rifled for a moment, finally pulling out a worn photo. She slid it along the bar, not forcing me to look but definitely inviting me. I picked it up.

It was a group shot, a dozen or so women at what looked like a Halloween party, though this particular group might have dressed up just about any time of the year. They were wearing long black dresses and black pointy hats, grinning at the camera. I spotted Erin in the front row, with a shy, happy smile that showed none of the nervous secretiveness I'd seen in the picture at the apartment. Kirsten leaned over and tapped her finger on the shoulder of another woman, a slightly heavy caramel blonde in the back row. She was laughing, opening her mouth so that the toddler in her arms could shove in a piece of candy. The little girl had her mother's blonde hair and a tiny witch hat of her own. Her face was smeared with chocolate, joy lighting it up like a firecracker.

"Denise?" I whispered.

Kirsten nodded. "And her daughter, Grace. Gracie. Who will now grow up without a mother. Is that enough, or shall I start pulling out cash?"

I turned the picture facedown on the bar, shame washing over me. Kirsten had risked her life to save me, and I'd just forced her to practically beg for my help. "No. It's enough."

And it was.

I arranged for Kirsten to join Jesse and me at brunch the next morning, and finally headed back to Molly's. By the time I got to the house, it was after three, and I was swaying on my feet. I locked the door carefully behind me and went straight for the stairs up to my bedroom. I didn't bother turning on the light, just transferred the contents of my pockets to my nightstand and allowed myself to tilt onto the bed, clothes, jacket, and all. I kicked off my shoes, pulling the corners of my quilt over my shoulders and snuggling in. At the last moment I remembered to set my alarm clock for nine.

The phone rang.

I looked at the clock in my hands, wondering if I had fallen asleep so fast I hadn't even noticed, but no, the time still said 3:32. I picked up my cell phone and peered at the caller ID, my eyes protesting against the bright flash of the screen. I flipped open the phone.

"Jesse, I agreed to meet up at ten. You've got to—"

"Scarlett," he interrupted. "Stop. It's not about that." I went silent. "Do the names Sara and Liam Reed mean anything to you?"

"Never met 'em." I yawned hard enough to bring tears to my eyes.

"Are you sure?"

"Yes. I'd remember 'cause Sara and Liam were my parents' names."

There was a terrible, pregnant silence. Goose bumps broke out on my biceps. "Jesse?" I said uncertainly. "Are you still there?"

When he spoke again, his voice had cop detachment. "A couple named Sara and Liam Reed were found dead in a stolen Jeep over by Laurel Canyon. It'll be a while before they can do the autopsies, but the cause of death is probably cutting wounds to the wrists. Only there's no blood in the car."

When I remembered how to breathe I said, "Cuts, not bite marks? Is there a chance it's *not* Olivia?"

His voice was steady, but the detachment was gone when he said, "I don't think so. There was no blood *inside* the car, but she used some of it to write on the outside of the windshield." His voice trailed off, and I had to work not to snap at him. He shouldn't be sparing me. This was my fault.

"Just tell me," I said through my teeth.

He sighed, long and sad. "It said *Welcome home.*"

Chapter 5

I tried to talk Jesse into letting me come to the crime scene, but he was adamant that I stay put. I told him that I had probably seen way more crime scenes than he had and would know how to spot anything out of the ordinary. He pointed out that Olivia might just be trying to lure me out into the open so she could kill me. The argument ended when Jesse said I'd be arrested if I got within fifty feet of the Jeep, and I tossed the phone on the bed next to me and stared at my bedroom ceiling.

I felt torn in half. A big part of me—hell, maybe the majority—wanted to just curl up in a ball and sob, for Liam and Sara Reed, for their families, for myself. Then there was the part of me that seethed with frustration. Why was she doing this? Was she trying to make me crazy too? And if so…was it working? Unable to hold still, I put on my running shoes and went into Molly's room to pound away on her treadmill for a while. After only a few minutes, though, the adrenaline was burning its way out, and I could already feel the edges of the queasy emptiness that would replace it.

Over the hum of the treadmill, I thought I heard something chime. I climbed onto the side rails and pulled the emergency clip in one movement, freezing in place. The doorbell rang again. Scrambling off the machine, I raced back into my room and grabbed my Taser off the charging station, cursing myself for not carrying it with me in the first place. I sped down the stairs and paused a few feet from the door, panting. Should I look in the peephole? I'd seen a movie where a guy had gotten shot in the eye that way. But Olivia wouldn't use a gun, would she? Then again, who knew what Olivia would do—

"Scarlett? It's Eli."

I mentally slapped myself in the head. You couldn't just yell, "Who is it," could you, Scarlett? I stepped close to the door and closed my eyes, concentrating on my radius. Yup, a werewolf, and no other supernatural creatures with him. I opened the door.

He was leaning into the doorway, arms on each side of the frame, wearing the same jeans and tank from the bar. Werewolves don't really need jackets, even in December. He took one look at me and said, "Cruz didn't tell you I was coming, did he?"

"Uh, no."

He raised an eyebrow. "Are you planning to Tase me?"

"Oh." I looked at the Taser in my hand and stuffed it into the pocket of my jacket, which I was still wearing for some reason. "Come on in."

He stepped through the doorway, and I had a surreal moment of wishing I'd picked up the place. Molly and I aren't particularly tidy, and rejected outfits were flipped over the back of most of the furniture. But it wasn't really the time. "I don't need protection," I began automatically. "If Jesse told you to bodyguard me, I'm doing just fine by myself. It's not like she can get near me, and—"

"Stop, stop." He held up his hands. "Cut the crap, Scarlett. Olivia is crazy, and you don't know what she might think to do to you. I'm staying until the morning."

Now it was my turn to raise an eyebrow. He actually blushed. "On the couch. Or on the back porch, if you prefer." He gave me a tentative grin. "If you really want to get rid of me you'll have to have me arrested, and Cruz already said he'd bail me out."

"No," I said stubbornly. "I don't need help. You're not a werewolf around me, remember? You're just a guy. What can you do that I can't?"

His eyes hardened, but he didn't rise to the bait. "If it helps, don't think of it as me protecting you. Think of it as me helping you protect yourself."

"I can handle it without you," I said, looking away.

"But you don't have to."

I shook my head, unable to think of a thing to say.

"Scarlett," he said softly, stepping closer. "What happened with us? You've barely looked at me since the basement."

Ah, yes. The basement where a mass murderer had chained me to the floor and felt me up, until Eli had literally dropped into the room to rescue me. That basement. "I've looked at you," I protested feebly. "We talk almost every day."

"We talk about work stuff. But things aren't the same between us. Even Caroline has noticed." Will's assistant, Caroline, had recently become a friend. She's also a werewolf, and the pack's sigma, its weakest member. I think that makes her sensitive to other people's moods. Or maybe that's just Caroline. "Is it Cruz? Are you guys together?"

"No."

"Are you in love with him?"

Oh, jeez. I shied away from the question and the door. "I don't know how I feel about Jesse." I swallowed. "Look, if you want to sleep on the porch I can't stop you. Just leave me alone."

This was usually the moment when Eli backed off, gave me space, and my hand was already moving toward the doorknob. But this time he surprised me. With no warning he bent from the waist and scooped me up, throwing me over one shoulder and marching into the living room. Werewolf or not, he was *strong*. "Hey!" I sputtered. "Knock it off! This is not a John Wayne movie!"

He sat down on the sofa, swinging me easily to straddle his lap so we were face-to-face. "Do you want it to be?" he said, grinning again. "I could kiss you, and you could beat your tiny fists against my chest until you're just too overwhelmed with love to resist."

"That's not funny," I said, annoyed.

"Talk to me," he said firmly, the smile gone. "Talk to me, and I'll head to the porch. And if you tell me you never want us to be more than colleagues, I promise you I'll respect that. But this evasion thing has got to stop."

I stared at him, openmouthed. Eli was always gentle, quiet. "Tonight? You're picking *tonight* to throw ultimatums at me? This is bullshit." I leaned back, trying to wiggle off his lap without dumping myself on my head.

Eli caught my wrists, very gently, and held me in place. "Scarlett," he began, but I didn't hear what he said next. I felt a sharp rush of panic, and salt water stung my eyes. I couldn't take his hands off my wrists. Eli's fingers were warm, but they still made me think of the cold silver handcuffs in Jared Hess's basement.

"Let go," I whispered. "Please let me go."

He followed my gaze and immediately released my wrists, looking stricken. "I'm sorry," he said quietly. "I didn't think."

I scrambled off his lap, nearly tripping over the coffee table, and dropped into the opposing armchair. I pulled my knees to my chin and hugged them, hating the gesture but unable to stop. "It's fine. It's fine." Good Lord. My body chemistry couldn't take much more of this night.

"No, it's not." He leaned forward, resting his elbows on his knees and scrubbing at his eyes with the heels of his hands. "I'm sorry, Scarlett." He looked so tired. All of a sudden I felt like a terrible person.

"Look," I began haltingly, "I know I'm not—good at this. The talking stuff." He looked at me. "I do, um, care about you. But you deserve someone who can do the talking stuff." He opened his mouth, and I held up a hand, shaking my head. "No, please don't. Not tonight, okay? Tonight could you just drop it and...come to bed with me? To sleep," I added hurriedly. "For sleeping." Stop talking, Scarlett.

He stood up slowly, so I could see him coming, and came around the coffee table to take my hand. I let him pull me up. He studied my face, but when I kept my eyes trained over his shoulder he just kissed my forehead. I led him up to my room.

Eli flipped on the light switch and took hold of my jacket so I could twist out of it. I pulled down the covers and crawled onto the bed, unbuttoning my jeans, which he tugged down my legs, depositing them on the floor. He pulled off his own shoes and jeans, exposing blue cotton boxers that I'd never seen before. He lay down beside me on the bed, lifting his arm so I could snuggle under. I marveled again at how easily Eli and I fit together.

He fussed with my hair, picking loose strands off my face and smoothing them back toward the bun. Suddenly my hair felt too tight on my head. I reached back and pulled out the rubber band, and he made a soft noise of pleasure, winding his long fingers in my hair, spiraling it around and around. I looked up at him, tensing for a kiss, but he just planted a quick smooch on my nose and said, "Tell me about New York."

I relaxed onto his chest. New York...was I really there just a few hours before? "It was cold. Very cold. And everything is decorated all to hell for Christmas. It was like being inside a snow globe." He made a "go on" noise. "The New York null is nice. His name is Jameson, and he works mostly for the city's master vampire."

"Malcolm."

"Yeah." I tilted my head up at him. "How did you know that?"

"I met him," Eli said soberly. "I moved here from New York, remember?"

"Oh. Right. Well, Jameson goes to a lot of daytime business meetings with him. I went along, got to know some of the vampires. There, um, weren't a lot of werewolves."

"No," Eli said with some bitterness. "Malcolm doesn't care for us. He forces the wolves out of the city."

Which explained why Eli had moved to LA. Not that I'd ever thought to just ask. I felt like an idiot. Two minutes of trying to have a real, no-drama conversation, and I'd brought up a sore subject. "Sorry."

"It's not your fault."

I sometimes forget that for all the tension between Will, Dashiell, and Kirsten, we're actually pretty lucky in LA. Most major cities are run by one group or another, and everyone else is encouraged to get the hell out of town. LA is the only city I know of where all three groups are welcome to live in peace, minus the occasional skirmish over who insulted whom.

It wasn't always this way. Witches, werewolves, and vampires all evolved from the same group of people, thousands of years ago. For a long time, they'd all interacted more or less in peace, even helping each other out occasionally. Then there was an Inquisition or five, which was hard on all three groups, but particularly on the witches. Their leaders went to the vampires and werewolves and begged for help, but both groups turned them away, for different reasons. The desperate witches tried to strengthen their magic, and made an inadvertent discovery that changed everything—and led to even more tension. Four hundred-some years of fighting later, a werewolf gets kicked out of New York and begins tending bar in LA.

"Did you learn anything new?" Eli asked, changing the subject.

I shifted around, trying to buy time. Eli knew that I went to New York to find out more about nulls and what they could do, but he didn't know about my apparent ability to permanently change a vampire back into a human. Unfortunately, when I'd hinted around during theoretical discussions, Jameson had been completely clueless.

I had to make sure Eli stayed that way too. It wasn't that I didn't trust him to keep it quiet, but if he knew about my newfound ability he could be at risk too. Besides, if I could permanently turn a vampire, wouldn't it be theoretically possible to change a werewolf back too? Things between Eli and me were complicated enough without something that big between us. Eli hated being a werewolf (the majority of them did), and part of him would always be hoping I would change him back.

"Sort of," I said at last. "Jameson didn't know much more than I did about the history of nulls. But I did pick up a new trick."

"What trick?"

I rolled off him and sat up, folding my legs. "Go stand in the hall."

He looked at me quizzically, but I just nodded. Shrugging, he got up and stood out in the hall. Still in my radius. "Farther," I said. He backed up a few feet. "A little farther." Realizing what I wanted, he backed up until he left my radius. "Okay, hold still."

I closed my eyes and concentrated on my breathing. When I was sure I was calm, I felt for the edges of my circle, or rather, my sphere, the same way you can focus on the feeling in one part of your body. I traced the edge of my circle all the way around, until I could hold the whole thing in my head. Then I exhaled and concentrated on the word *expand*. I felt the circle stretch.

"Whoa," said Eli from the hall. He returned to my room. "You figured out how to make it bigger."

Opening my eyes, I shrugged. "Null circles generally expand when we get really emotional or upset. I just learned how to do it without freaking out first. It's not a big deal."

"It's totally a big deal," he argued, and I felt a little pleased. It had taken me a while to learn it. Meditation techniques don't exactly come easily to me. For some reason.

He came back to bed, wrapping me up in his arms and the covers. "Very cool," he pronounced, and he kissed the top of my head. "Get some sleep."

But I lay still for a few more minutes, listening to his heart and the way he breathed. "Eli?"

"Mm."

"I don't want to be a victim," I whispered. "I don't want to be *her* victim. Or her prize, or whatever. I don't want to be a piece in a game."

He loosened his arms, scooting his body down in the bed so his eyes could meet mine. He kissed me on the lips, but a warm, chaste kiss with no need to it. "You won't be."

Chapter 6

After he'd hung up with Scarlett, Jesse Cruz had turned back to face the bustling activity at the crime scene. The Jeep was an early 2000s model, painted an unfortunate dark red that set off the blood on the windshield. It was standing upright, but looked crumpled, as though it had been rolled like a boiled egg. Which was more or less what had happened. Inside the car, the Reeds still sat upright, pinned in place by their seat belts. Liam Reed was a middle-aged business type with a sharp salt-and-pepper haircut. Sara Reed was a decade younger, with tan skin and laugh lines around her mouth and eyes. She was wearing a navy cashmere sweater with a snowman stitched into the chest. The only visible blood on either of them was a small dark circle that turned the snowman red.

The driver and passenger doors had been opened and the crime-scene photographer, Runa, was snapping shots of the bodies, completely focused on the digital camera. The two uniformed cops who had responded to the call were interviewing, separately, the couple who had discovered the body. A forensic investigator named Walter Benson was crouched next to the Jeep, collecting a sample of leaked oil. The other forensic technician saw that Jesse was off the phone and trotted over, clipboard clutched to her chest.

Gloria "Glory" Sherman was one of the nighttime forensic pathology technicians and the only other human Jesse knew who was aware of the Old World. Generally, Glory was a lab rat, but budget cuts had forced more and more of the lab technicians to spend part of their time in the field. Which had worked out in his favor tonight, because she had placed the call to get him here.

"Sorry about that," Jesse said. "What do we know?"

The night was fairly warm, but she hugged the clipboard against her body, shoulders clenched up to her ears with worry. The silver streaks in her short, ash-blonde hair seemed to stand out against the Jeep's single remaining headlight. "Well, the physics guys will do a little calculating, but it looks like the car flipped off the embankment and landed upside down. Windows and one headlight were crushed. Then something"—she swallowed, and took a step closer, eyes darting—"flipped it back over sideways." He followed her to the passenger side of the Jeep, where she pointed at two hand-sized dents at the bottom of the window, pinching closed the seam where the glass used to be. "The two driver's-side wheels popped with the impact."

Jesse glanced at Benson, a stocky black man in his midfifties with an unlit cigarette tucked behind one ear and an excited expression on his face, like he'd woken up to an early Christmas. He had torn Runa's attention from the camera and was pointing at the marks on the victims' wrists, gesturing wildly. "He knows about the bodies, I take it?" Jesse asked. "The lack of blood?"

Glory nodded. "He's the one who told me. I...recognized the signs." Glory had met Dashiell years earlier, when the master vampire had shown up to collect a newly turned vampire. Over the years he'd occasionally asked her to drop a beaker or lose a sample, always right after making polite inquiries about Glory's two children. "Listen, Jesse, I did something—"

"Hey, guys."

Jesse and Glory both jumped as the petite photographer appeared beside them. She had white-blonde hair tied in shoulder-length pigtails and three different cameras and bags strapped onto her slim shoulders. "Whoa," Runa said, laughing a little at their shock. "Just wanted to see if you needed any other shots. Oh, hey, we haven't actually met." She held her hand out toward Glory, and Jesse remembered his manners.

"Oh, sorry. Glory Sherman, this is Runa Vore, the new night-shift photographer. Runa, this is Glory." The two women shook hands, and Glory shot him an anxious look. *Does she know?* He shook his head imperceptibly.

"Sorry to interrupt," Runa continued, "but I've got all the initial shots. Did you want anything from the surrounding area?"

"Uh, sure. Why don't you do some perspective shots from the car to the witnesses' house. And, um, whatever else you can think of. Go crazy."

Runa gave him a funny look, but she turned back to the Jeep.

"Go crazy?" Glory said, the second Runa was out of earshot.

"Shut up."

"That's the girl you're dating?" Glory's eyebrows were raised to her hairline. "She's pretty."

"How did you—never mind. Stupid office grapevine."

"Hey. We're the cops. We're nosy by nature. Do you think she overheard us?"

"I'll find out later. What were you going to say?"

"Oh, right." Glory straightened her back, drawing up to her full five foot one. "When I saw the car and the blood"—she tilted her head to the writing on the windshield—"I called you first, but then I...did something."

"Spit it out, Glory."

She sighed. "He gave me this number, for emergencies. I called it."

"Who ga—"

But before he even finished the word, Jesse saw the black Bentley parked on the hill across from the crime scene; a blandly handsome fortyish man stepped out from the driver's side and sauntered toward the Jeep. His suit was expensive and fit like it had come into existence only for him, but there was something not quite modern about it too. The closest uniformed cop jogged toward him, waving a hand, but the driver just smiled, touching the cop's shoulder and looking straight into his eyes. Jesse watched as the driver spoke a few words and continued walking toward the Jeep, while the uniform stood slack and staring forward, like a marionette hung on a peg. The driver approached the little knot of witnesses and the other uniform, speaking to them in the same calm, reassuring manner. Jesse looked away, an icy thrill of fear spreading through his chest. This was Dashiell, the master vampire of Los Angeles, and he was pressing the minds of everyone on site. Jesse had never been near him without Scarlett around for protection. He felt a flare of irritation at Glory for calling the vampire, but at the same time he could hardly blame her—Dashiell had threatened her kids. He himself wouldn't have done any different, under the circumstances.

"Look down," he muttered to Glory. The vampire could probably hear him, but that was a risk Jesse had to take. "When he comes close, don't look him directly in the eyes, understand?" She nodded, hugging her clipboard even tighter.

Jesse looked around for Runa, but the photographer was on the far side of the Jeep, shielded from Dashiell. He couldn't call to her without exposing her position, so Jesse just prayed she'd stay put.

When he was done speaking to the witnesses, Dashiell continued toward Jesse, the smile still tacked onto his face. The couple turned at a ninety-degree angle and marched back toward their home in eerie synch. The uniformed cop who had been interviewing them strode to his partner, herding him toward the patrol car. By then Dashiell was in earshot, fifteen feet away by the Jeep. "Excuse me," he said to Benson, who looked up, surprised. Jesse had to tear his eyes away from what Dashiell was doing. He clenched his fists, but there was nothing he could do to stop the vampire, short of emptying his clip into Dashiell's chest. Even if Jesse did succeed in destroying the vampire heart with a gun, though, he would have been left with a lot of explaining to do.

Beside him, Jesse felt Glory shiver. "This was a simple car accident," Dashiell was saying, his voice warm and practically visible, it was so potent. With his peripheral vision Jesse saw Benson nodding mechanically. "There was nothing unusual about the bodies. You will take them directly to the morgue, where you will begin the paperwork to have them cremated." He named a crematorium on the West Side. Dashiell paused, maybe to make sure the command had hit home, and then concluded, "You may go now."

Jesse thought of his threat to Scarlett earlier that night. Would he really have gone through with knocking on this creature's door? Suddenly he doubted it. As Benson stumbled away, Dashiell finally made it to Jesse.

"Detective Cruz," Dashiell said cordially. "How nice to see you again."

Jesse swallowed. He could have sworn he felt waves of power radiating off Dashiell, but that was probably his imagination. "Wish I could say the same," he said, eyes on Dashiell's loafers. He had been to enough Hollywood parties to recognize Prada. "But it does seem like there are more dead bodies when you're around."

There was a little surprise in Dashiell's laugh. "Think of it as job security. Thank you for your call, Ms. Sherman." Glory nodded again, keeping her eyes down.

"You suspect Olivia?" Dashiell asked Jesse, as though he were leading the detective toward the obvious answer.

"Yes," Jesse said, fighting to keep an automatic "sir" out of his voice. However scary Dashiell was, Jesse still didn't have to answer to him. At least, he hoped not. "Aside from the message, the victim's first names were the same as Scarlett's parents'. And the Jeep was flipped by hand." He pointed to the dents. He was burning to look at Runa, to make sure she stayed back, but didn't want to give her away, either. Surely Dashiell had heard her moving around the far side of the Jeep? Or were the traffic sounds enough to drown out any noise? He prayed that she wasn't about to use the camera's flash.

"I see," Dashiell said thoughtfully. He pulled a cell phone out of his pocket and began tapping the screen so quickly that Jesse half expected it to start smoking. He risked a glance over at Runa, now visible on the far side of the Jeep. She had been packing up her gear. She hoisted her camera bag onto her shoulder and glanced his way. She must have figured he was interviewing a witness, because she just mouthed, "Anything else?" He shook his head, fast and tight. She smiled and gave a little wave and a head tilt to say *see you at the station*.

As Runa stood, Jesse tried to think of something to say to mask the sound of her footsteps. "What happens now?" he blurted. "I mean, do we investigate the crime as usual, or what do you want me to do? I'm guessing I probably can't just file a regular report, right?"

Dashiell looked up with a bemused expression, and Jesse dropped his eyes back down. "No," Dashiell said mildly. He pocketed the phone. "It's all arranged. This file is being closed as a simple car accident." He turned back to Glory. "I assume you can file any additional paperwork? You'll receive full cooperation with the medical examiner's office."

"Uh, yes, sir."

"Wonderful." He held out a business card. "My tow services will take care of the vehicle personally. They'll be here within the hour." Glory took the card. "Thank you, Ms. Sherman. If you would give me a moment with Detective Cruz?"

Without another word, the forensics specialist scurried toward her department-issued van, and Jesse risked a look at where Runa had been. The photographer was gone. "And Olivia?" Jesse prodded.

"Yes. Olivia. I'm afraid you've suffered quite a loss, Detective."

"*What?*"

Dashiell stepped over to the car, examining the dents on the window. He placed one hand in either corner of the window and pulled outward, snapping the handprint out of the metal with a flick of his wrists. "Your grandmother in San Bernardino has just passed away," he continued, and Jesse relaxed an inch. His last surviving grandparent had died in Mexico three years earlier. "You've been given a week of bereavement leave with full pay. A little generous for the department, I admit, but your supervisors were feeling quite sympathetic."

"Oh," Jesse said lamely. He felt suddenly like Dashiell was pitching baseballs at his chest, and Jesse was dropping every one.

"Use the week to find Olivia. Whether you destroy her personally or call me to destroy her is up to you, but I suggest you bring Scarlett Bernard along. She can help protect you, and she knows Olivia better than anyone."

"I'm not just going to *destroy* her—" Jesse began.

There was a deep chuckle. "Please. You plan to, what, arrest her politely? Have Scarlett stand next to her while Olivia is tried, convicted, and imprisoned? Maybe they could share a cell."

"I—I hadn't really gotten that far," Jesse sputtered.

Another white card appeared in Dashiell's hand, which was suddenly extended toward Jesse. "My number. If you don't have the stomach to kill her, just call." He raised a bemused eyebrow. "You do *know* how to kill a vampire?"

Goddammit, Jesse thought. Cardinal vampire or not, why was he letting this guy fluster him? "Scarlett...explained it to me," Jesse said finally.

"Wonderful. I'll be expecting your call, either way. I will also be expecting you and Scarlett at the mansion tomorrow evening at six. We're all going to discuss what has been happening." Jesse understood that "we" meant the Old World leaders: Kirsten, Dashiell, and Will.

"I know Scarlett works for you, but I don't," Jesse said, trying to sound firm. "You can't just summon me places."

Dashiell just arched an eyebrow, and Jesse had to look away from his eyes as quickly as he could. "Can't I?"

Jesse couldn't think of a thing to say, so he just shoved the card in his jeans pocket. "Look, I'm on another case right now, anyway—"

Dashiell's voice hardened. "The witch in Studio City, yes, I know. This comes first."

Witch. Erin was a witch? But Jesse couldn't follow that thought very far, because he was working to keep a grip on his temper. He reminded himself that without Scarlett here he was outclassed: Dashiell had just taken control of an LAPD-run murder scene with *one text message.* Disappearing a homicide detective would be child's play. After a breath, Jesse said, "Why me? You must have tons of vampire...lackeys, who are more powerful than Olivia."

"Yes." Dashiell's voice darkened. "But one of my *lackeys* has already been compromised. I believe you met Albert?"

"The guard?"

"Yes. He disappeared nearly a month ago, and the two of them have been seen together. I do not know if anyone else is working with Olivia, but given your feelings for our Ms. Bernard, I trust you'll be motivated to catch her."

"I'm also a cop, and Olivia is killing people," Jesse pointed out, a little irritated. Had his feelings for Scarlett been that obvious?

"Well, there you have it," Dashiell said, smiling congenially. Avoiding his eyes, Jesse stared at the vampire's teeth. The canines weren't exactly fang material, but was it his imagination, or were they extra pointy? "Either way, the job is yours."

Dashiell gave a modest little bow and turned away. He was at the Bentley before Jesse could think of another thing to say.

He was still standing there like an idiot when Glory made it back, without her clipboard now. "Doesn't leave a whole lot of room for negotiation, does he?" she said quietly.

"No, he doesn't." Jesse's eyes fell on the Jeep again. "What's going to happen to your evidence?" he asked.

She shrugged. "I'll log it as usual, but this is an accident scene now."

"Did you find much?"

"Not really. The usual LA litter, nothing that looked fresh. The ground's too hard for footprints. There are fingerprints everywhere, but they won't be processed now. Even if they were, unless this Olivia was arrested when she was alive, I don't know that they'd do any good. Best case, they'd confirm that it was her."

He sighed. "Anything that would give me a location? Anything at all?"

She frowned. "The only weird thing was a tiny bit of mud we found on the floor of the Jeep. It doesn't look like it was on either of the Reeds' shoes. But the Jeep was stolen from a rental lot, so who knows how well the rental company cleaned it."

Jesse felt like he'd just taken a shot of adrenaline. "Wait, what made it weird?"

"Two things," she replied. "First, there was a really distinctive smell to it. Like...a factory." She shrugged.

"And second?"

"The color. Soil analysis isn't my area of specialization, but I've never seen dirt that was so...gray."

"Get it analyzed, okay?"

Glory squinted up at him, bemused. "Well, duh."

Jesse banged on Scarlett's door at ten on the dot, half expecting her to answer the door in her pajamas. He felt a little guilty for pushing her so hard at Erin's, especially in light of Olivia's attack. But Erin's death—and the swiftness with which the Old World had made it disappear—ate away at him. He resolved to be a little nicer anyway.

To his surprise, though, the door was opened by Eli, wearing boxer shorts and a sleeveless T-shirt. "Oh...hey..." Jesse said lamely. Of course Eli had spent the night. Jesse tried to ignore a stab of jealousy. *You have a girlfriend*, he told himself. *It's none of your business.*

"Hey," Eli said, yawning. "She's in the shower." He backed up, making room for Jesse to slip past him into the house. Guy was so damned tall. "Thanks for calling last night."

"No problem." There was an awkward pause. Jesse and Eli had met during the La Brea Park investigation—when Scarlett had been in the hospital, unable to protect herself, the two of them had taken shifts to stay with her. Jesse was pretty sure that Eli was in love with her. Hell, maybe Scarlett was in love with him too. It irritated Jesse that this thought bothered him so much.

"How is she doing?" he asked finally.

Eli shrugged, closing the door. "Oh, you know," he said with a small smile. "It'd take a direct hit."

"That's kind of what I'm worried about."

Before Eli could respond, Scarlett trotted down the stairs, her feet bare and her hair pulled into a wet bun. She wore jeans and a green T-shirt that had damp spots where her hair had dripped, and was pulling on a jacket. "I'm ready, I'm ready," she said breathlessly.

"Shoes?" Jesse said, raising an eyebrow.

"They're right—oh, no, they're not." She scrambled back upstairs. Jesse shook his head, amused.

"You really think Olivia will come after her?" Eli said quietly. He hadn't taken his eyes off the stairs.

"Seems like it. But I never met Olivia."

"I only saw her once or twice. She was...I don't know. Regal. Commanding."

"Nuts?"

"Well, yeah. But not so you'd notice right away."

Scarlett came running down the stairs, socks and boots in her hand. "I thought you'd be dragging ass. What's the rush?" Jesse asked.

"We're meeting Kirsten," she told him. "And you need to be on your *best* behavior."

Chapter 7

We stepped out of Molly's house into my favorite kind of LA weather: cool and sunny. Sometime during the night, the wind had blown off a layer of smog, so it was even clear outside. We walked down the block to Jesse's parking spot, and I noticed one of Molly's neighbors had recently gone with the ultimate tacky Christmas decoration: four inches of cotton laid down over the grass to serve as snow. The scene was complete with Styrofoam snowmen and a gaudily decorated Christmas tree. Molly would love it.

On the way to the restaurant, Jesse told me about being approached by Dashiell and the meeting at his house that night, and I filled him in on what Kirsten had told me about Erin's and Denise's deaths: the frantic calls to Kirsten, the fact that both witches predicted the future. "So Kirsten and I think the two deaths have to be connected," I finished.

"It's not two deaths anymore. Now it's four," Jesse said grimly.

"Wait. What?"

"I'm not sure, and I can't prove it, but I think the Reed car accident is related to all this. Remember I told you about that weird dirt that forensics found at Erin's? Well, I think I found the same kind of mud inside the car last night. My friend in forensics is analyzing it for me."

"But the car thing was Olivia. We still think that was Olivia, right?"

"Yes."

I thought that over. "So you think Olivia killed the witches too?"
He hesitated. I glanced over. "What?" I asked.

"Is it possible that Olivia has...special powers? Like, since she was a null who turned, maybe she can go out in the sun or something?"

"No," I said. This was something I'd thought about a *lot*. "Other nulls feel...different. In my radius. Olivia *used* to feel like that, but that day that I saw her at the hospital, she just felt like your garden-variety baby vampire."

"Okay," Jesse said. "Then she couldn't have killed the witches by herself. The sun was still up during Erin's time of death."

It took a second for that to register with me. There was another possibility, besides Olivia working with a partner. Nulls, like me, were very rare—maybe six in the world, that we knew about. But I still wasn't the only null in Los Angeles.

"Oh, God." I checked the mirror and cut off an Audi on my right, screeching across two lanes to make the next exit.

"Scarlett," Jesse yelped, reaching to grab what my older brother always called the "oh shit" handle. "What the hell?"

"Gas station. I need a big gas station, maybe a convenience store..." I scanned the street, but the neighborhood seemed mostly residential.

"Stop," he ordered. "Pull over." He used a very big cop voice, and I found myself wrenching the wheel to bring the van to a stop at the curb.

Jesse leaned forward and flipped on my hazard lights. He looked at me. "What is it?" he asked softly.

I met his eyes. *Corry*, I mouthed, and understanding struck his face. "I need a disposable cell phone," I said, as calmly as I could manage. "Where can we get one?"

During our last case together, Jesse and I had encountered another null living in LA—only she was fifteen and had been forced into several dangerous situations by a psychopathic serial killer. We had gotten her out of the mess, and since then I'd done everything I could think of to keep her away from the Old World. But if Olivia had found out about Corry...all bets were off.

Jesse started to speak, and I shook my head. I knew I was being paranoid. The odds that anyone had bugged my phone or my van in hopes that I'd mention Corry were tiny. But my job— my life—is all about paranoia. Most of the crime scenes I clean up wouldn't even appear suspicious to normal people, but there's always the chance that somebody will be just bored or rich or angry enough to ask a lot of questions and make a lot of noise. I live on paranoia. And if there was even a tiny chance that being paranoid would keep Corry safe, well, sign me up for my tin hat.

After a moment, Jesse nodded, and his face relaxed in understanding. He had met Corry, briefly, and knew how I felt about keeping her safe. He pointed left. "There's a Target a couple of blocks that way."

I left everything in the van except my keys and some cash. Just in case.

A few minutes later we sat down in the little café area with an instrumental version of "O Little Town of Bethlehem" pealing out over the loudspeakers. Jesse showed me how to get the phone working, and I dialed a number I knew by heart. It wasn't until the phone was ringing that I realized she might be in school.

But Corry answered. "Hello?"

"Hey, it's Scarlett," I said.

"Hi," she said cautiously. "I, um, thought you weren't going to be calling me."

The last time we'd spoken, I'd made it clear to Corry that she needed to stay away from me, for her own good. It had come out a lot harsher than I'd intended at the time, but she'd gotten the message. "There's sort of a...situation...happening in my world right now. Is everything okay with you?"

"Yeah, of course," she replied. "We're on holiday break, so my brother's driving me nuts, but other than that I'm good. Why do you ask?"

I relaxed and let out a breath. "She's fine," I whispered to Jesse. To Corry, I said, "Do you guys stay in town for the holidays?"

"We have to. My dad's a minister; he has services to conduct."

I thought that over. "Listen, I don't think anyone will involve you, but just…keep an eye out, okay?" Then I added, "Especially for a female vampire with long, dark hair, looks to be in her forties."

"What do I do if I see her?"

"Get your family, keep them inside your radius, and get into a private house. Stay away from the windows and doors. If she gets inside your radius, scream your head off and call me."

"Call you while screaming my head off?" she asked, amusement in her voice.

I took a deep breath. "This particular vampire is extremely bad news, Corry. When I said I couldn't see you anymore because it was too dangerous, this is one of the people I was talking about."

Sobered, Corry agreed. As we hung up, I felt guilty for scaring a teenager, especially one who had been through as much as Corry had already. But it was better to have her scared and alive than relaxed and dead.

In the parking lot, Jesse said, "So if she's not a part of this, then someone else must be helping Olivia."

"You think she's working with a human?"

"That's my guess."

"Wow, I feel like we're in a detective novel in the forties." He gave me a puzzled look. "Oh, come on. The PI takes on two cases, and at the end it turns out that they're the same case!"

"Except that we're not at the end, Scarlett. If she—they—really killed those witches to hide their actions, we're just at the beginning of something."

Well, that was alarming. "Huh. But Kirsten said both Erin and Denise could only predict the futures of people they came into contact with. So does that mean they both knew Olivia?"

"I don't know." He sounded tired. "Maybe they both knew the accomplice. But I'm *officially* assigned to investigate all of it." His voice sounded a little bitter on the word *officially*, and I knew he was annoyed at the way Dashiell had pulled his strings. I could sympathize. "And I could really use your help.

"Will your girlfriend be okay with that?" I sounded a little sour, even to me.

"Will Eli?" he countered.

I had nothing to say to that, so we drove the rest of the way in silence.

Recipedia is a little place on La Cienega that started as an Internet café, back before everyone had their own laptops and smart phones. When people started carrying their own devices, the owner got rid of the computers and found a new gimmick: a different food special every day. There was always a full coffee menu, but each day just one food: a pastry, a sandwich, a soup—it could be anything, but it was always beyond delicious, thanks to a rotation of guest chefs wanting to show off their best items. You wouldn't think a business could survive with only one menu item per day, but somehow Recipedia made it work. Maybe they had an underground casino in the back or something.

The place was pretty packed, but I spotted Kirsten's angelic blonde bun in a booth near the back window.

"Listen," I said to Jesse, "she's nervous about meeting you. She thinks you're going to try to bust her for...I don't know, being a witch."

He gave me a skeptical look. "Come on. This isn't the Dark Ages. Half this town goes to Kabbalah meetings."

"Whatever. Magical talent is hereditary in humans, and Kirsten's from a long line. There's history that you...that most people don't know about." I was skirting dangerously close to an outright lie here because there was a part of Old World history that I had personally chosen to keep from Jesse. There are things that are dangerous to know. "I'm not going to get into it, but believe me, it's a sore spot for her. So try not to act like too much of a cop, okay?"

Jesse rolled his eyes, but nodded at me. I turned and threaded us through the tables. "Hey, Kirsten. Sorry we're late." She looked up. Her eyes were clearer than they were last night, but she still looked tired.

"Hello, Scarlett."

"Kirsten, this is Detective Jesse Cruz. Jesse, this is Kirsten." They shook hands. Kirsten's face remained cool, but she looked at me and widened her eyes just a little, the international girl code for *whoa*. Sometimes I forget how gorgeous Jesse is. I sent her back a look that said *I know, right?*

"It's very nice to meet you, ma'am," Jesse said. I glared at him. "Can I call you Kirsten?" he added.

She gave him a wary nod. She was too well-bred to be openly hostile, but I could feel tension coming off her as she looked at Jesse.

A waitress wearing one of those headbands with reindeer antlers hustled up to get our drink orders. I asked for two orders of onion rings, today's food specialty. When she went to get them, both Kirsten and Jesse looked a little amused. "What?" I said. "I haven't eaten since lunch in New York. Yesterday. And it's entirely possible that I'll share."

It took just a moment for Reindeer Headband to return with our drinks and my rings—this is one of the benefits of having only one menu item. While she walked out of earshot, I inhaled my first onion ring, "forgetting" to offer any to Jesse and Kirsten. When it was obvious they were both waiting for me to begin the conversation, I swallowed and said, "Okay. Kirsten, did you hear about a car accident last night? With a Jeep?"

She looked from my face to Jesse's and back. "No. Why?"

Jesse spoke up. "Last night, Olivia killed a couple named Liam and Sara Reed. They were in a stolen Jeep." Kirsten looked at me, reaching over to squeeze my hand. She'd remembered my parents' names? Surprised, I squeezed back. "Some of the same physical evidence that was found at Erin's apartment was found at the accident scene." He told her about our suspicion that Olivia wanted to hide her plans by killing the witches. "Did either Erin or Denise know Olivia?"

Kirsten was already shaking her head. "No. Not at all. Neither of them ever needed to call in a cleanup." To me, she said, "They both dealt in the future. They didn't do spells or charms, nothing that would leave evidence."

"Could they have called Olivia without you knowing about it?" Jesse asked.

"That does sometimes happen, but no. Those two just weren't capable of that kind of magic." Her voice was firm.

"What do you mean, not capable?"

She sighed. "Witches aren't turned into witches, like the vampires and werewolves. We're just ordinary people who happen to be born with the ability to *manipulate* magic. And we have varying strength." She thought for a moment. "It's sort of like being able to sing. There's a whole spectrum of talent, from not being able to carry a tune to being the world's greatest opera singer. But at the same time, there's a question of versatility."

"Like, some opera singers probably wouldn't be able to rap," I contributed, and Jesse flashed me a grin that made my heart ache. Goddammit. Had I really expected him to just wait around for me to be ready to date him? What an idiot, Scarlett.

"Exactly," Kirsten said, but she kept her eyes on me. "Both Erin and Denise were like...girls who go to karaoke bars but only perform country music."

"Limited," he said, trying to catch Kirsten's eye.

I was beginning to feel like the go-between in a middle school fight. *Scarlett, tell Jesse I'm not speaking to him.* It wasn't like Kirsten to be this openly hostile, but at least she was talking to one of us. "But...I don't mean to be insensitive, Kirsten, but wouldn't they, you know—"

"See their own deaths?" Kirsten supplied. She gave me a wan smile. "Even if they looked at their own futures—and every witch I've ever known avoids it—future magic is almost impossible to plan or control, and mostly it works on smaller things that can still be changed. Death is...not small."

"Okay, so they didn't need Olivia for cleanups," Jesse concluded. "But isn't there another way they could have met?"

I thought it over. "The Vampire Trials?" I suggested. Every three years—three being a powerful number for the supernatural—Dashiell holds sort of an open court for the supernatural. Any vampire, witch, or werewolf in the city with a serious gripe can bring it to Dashiell for a ruling. A null—first Olivia, now me—sits with the "defendant" to make sure they can't harm anyone during the proceedings. It's almost exclusively vampire business, though: if a witch or a wolf brings a matter before the court, it's because their leader is too conflicted or too involved to solve the matter in-house. Will and Kirsten deal with almost all of the disputes for their people. Either way, Kirsten would know.

Kirsten was glaring at me, and I realized I probably shouldn't have mentioned the trials in front of Jesse. He was making a point of ignoring the question, but his eyes were jumping around with repressed curiosity. "No," Kirsten said firmly. She broke the glare to look at both of us. "These were not powerful witches. They didn't have enemies, and they *didn't* know Olivia."

"Okay, so what does that mean?" Jesse asked.

Kirsten and I shared a look, but I answered him. "I'm guessing it means that Olivia's *partner* was the one who knew both of the witches. She's helping Olivia kill them, or maybe Olivia is helping her."

"Why 'her'?" he asked.

I hesitated, but Kirsten cut in. "You can say it. If a vampire or a werewolf—or even a human—were going to kill Denise and Erin, they would have done it differently. Olivia is working with a witch. And most witches are female."

"Are we sure that a witch didn't just help Olivia against her will?" Jesse asked diplomatically. He looked at Kirsten. "Do you know if any other witches have died or disappeared in the last two days?"

She shook her head at him, caught up in the conversation despite herself. "That's what I've been doing since three this morning. I called in sick and tried to contact every witch in Los Angeles. If I couldn't reach someone, I used a tracking spell. Everyone is accounted for."

Jesse looked at me with sudden fear. "Wait, that thing you told me about, the mind-control thing, can vampires do that to witches?"

Kirsten answered for me. "Not really. One of the weird things about magic is that it cancels itself out among species. So you can't turn a werewolf into a vampire, you can't change a witch into a werewolf, and you can't really press the mind of a witch. A vampire might be able to press a really weak witch just a little bit, but that would be, like, getting her to lend you a dollar."

"They're like magnets," I supplied, mouth half-full of onion ring. I swallowed and added, "Different...charges. Or whatever."

"All right, well, forget the accomplice for a second," Jesse said. "What do you think Olivia's endgame might be? What does she want?"

"When we speak to Dashiell tonight he may have other insights, but my suspicion is that she wants Scarlett." When Kirsten looked at me, it was chilling. "I've known that woman for more than a decade, and I've never seen anyone as obsessed with anything the way she was with you. But I don't know if Olivia wants to kill you, or maybe toy with you first, or something."

I looked sadly at my empty baskets of onion rings. "Three would probably be too many, right?"

"Scarlett." Jesse's voice was quiet. "This isn't a joke. This is your life."

"And maybe I should just give it to her." When I said it, I was thinking aloud more than anything else, but I turned the thought around for another moment, realizing I was right. They were both staring at me. "Come on, you guys. How many more people have to die—"

"Shut up," Jesse said fiercely. I stopped short. "I never want to hear that crap from you again. If you so much as think about giving yourself up to her, I will know, and I will throw you in jail. I'm still a cop, and I can make it happen."

My mouth dropped open a little. Kirsten was looking at Jesse with a small, amused smile. It was the first look I'd seen her give him that wasn't cold and untrusting.

Reindeer Headband bopped up to our table. "More onion rings?"

Chapter 8

After the meeting with Kirsten, Jesse dropped Scarlett off at home so she could catch up on a few weeks' worth of laundry and run some errands. Jesse was planning to spend the afternoon reading the files for the two witches' deaths and making calls from his apartment: nothing Scarlett could really help with, anyway. Or that was what he'd told Scarlett. Privately, Jesse figured they were both a little raw from the morning's conversations and could use some time apart.

On the way home, he called Glory and asked her to e-mail him the case file for Denise's "suicide," and she promised to do it during her 1:00 p.m. lunch break. He almost asked her to make an excuse for him to his supervisor, Miranda, but remembered that he wasn't actually on duty. Jesse was used to switching shifts around, but it still felt weird, being off from work in the middle of a weekday. Especially since he was technically working.

When he had first realized that Erin's murder was likely tied to the Old World, Jesse had been...well, more than a little excited. The thing was, during the La Brea Park investigation, he'd felt so integral. It had started with him just trying to cover his ass, but then he'd gotten invested, and then suddenly he was playing an important role in finding Jared Hess. And he'd even gotten the credit back in the real world. Jesse had thought his resulting promotion to detective would give him a better shot of keeping that sense of relevancy—he had thought he'd be doing more or less the same thing he'd done with the La Brea Park case, but with human perpetrators and human crimes. Jesse had been disappointed to discover that D1s did nearly as much scut work as the uniformed officers. During all the witness interviews and phone calls and paperwork of the last two months, he'd begun to long for that feeling of knowing you were actually contributing to something.

Now he should be thrilled: he was less than twenty-four hours into a new Old World investigation, and Dashiell had flat-out handed him that same importance. As far as Jesse knew, he was the only cop who had the slightest idea what Erin's death might really be about. And besides, he'd worried about Olivia since she'd first turned up as a vampire; it'd be good to finally be hunting her down. So why did he feel this dread hanging over him, fogging up his thinking? Maybe he was just spending too much time with Scarlett, worrying about her safety and remembering why he'd had such a crush on her. She was beautiful, of course—those bright-green eyes just *got* to him—but he loved her spirit, her attitude. And her attempts to use that attitude to hide how much she was hurting.

He needed to talk to Runa, Jesse decided, and switched lanes to get off the freeway. The files could wait a little longer. He was craving even just a few minutes of the tentative new normalcy they'd been building together. Besides, he needed to talk to her anyway, to make sure she hadn't told anyone about the hand marks on the Jeep. He just had to figure out a way to do that without making her suspicious or giving away anything about the Old World. How do you ask someone to keep something quiet without revealing its importance?

It took him forty minutes to get from Scarlett's home in West Hollywood down to Runa's third-floor efficiency in Venice Beach, which she shared with a one-eyed white cat she'd named Odin and a mountainous pile of photography equipment. Jesse had called ahead, so when he pushed the button for her apartment

Runa buzzed him straight in. She was standing in the doorway when he came out of the elevator, leaning against the frame in a purple tank top and a flowing skirt that Jesse knew was just one piece of fabric draped around her waist and tied in a knot. Her white-blonde hair was parted and pinned back into two little buns, one behind each ear. "Hey, friend," she said merrily, turning her face up for a kiss.

"Hey yourself." Jesse put his hands on Runa's waist, taut from yoga, and backed her into the apartment, craning his neck to plant kisses along her throat.

She giggled. "Oh, boy. Cover your eye, Odin." They both looked at the white cat, who just bared his teeth in response. Cats tended to dislike Jesse, a dog person, and Odin was no exception.

Runa pulled away and took a step backward so she could see him better, her face growing serious. "Listen, Jess, I'm really sorry about your grandmother."

"My—oh. Right. Thank you." There was a reason why he had never worked undercover, Jesse thought wryly. "Thank you, but she was in a lot of pain and it was almost a relief."

Runa nodded, hugging him around the middle again and leaning her upper body back to meet his eyes. "You going to the funeral?"

"No, it's too far. I'm just…well, doing a little work on a couple of my cases, actually."

"That sounds like you," she replied, eyes sparkling.

"What are you up to today?" he asked.

"Oh, today is big. First, I did laundry. Later, I'm getting groceries. And in between…are you ready for this? Get psyched. Are you psyched?" He nodded, grinning. Her cheerfulness was infectious. "Okay. Today is…backup day!"

"Backup day? What, you and Odin drive around town in a convertible, exchanging quips and knocking down doors with your blazer sleeves pushed up?"

"Not that kind of backup, silly. Come see." She led him past her rumpled bed—like Jesse, Runa was not a big bed maker—and to her workstation, which was usually covered in a layer or two of tripods and detachable flashes. Today she'd cleared all that off to make room for two very serious-looking external hard drives. "This," she explained, "is where I back up all my photos. The good ones, anyway. I used to keep all of them, but with digital photography it's just too easy to fill up even the biggest hard drives with data."

The calm that had started to seep into Jesse's chest disappeared again. "This is for your artistic stuff?" Runa was a civilian employee, meaning she only worked part-time for the department. She also taught yoga classes and worked on her own personal photography to sell at shows.

She tapped the two different drives, and Jesse saw that they were faintly labeled, one with an *R* and one with the letters *LAPD*. "Both, the cops and the artistic stuff."

"They let you do that?" Jesse said incredulously.

"Well, I'm not allowed to duplicate, print, or share any of my crime-scene stuff. Not that I'd want to. But you know how the evidence room is, and the department computers. I got paranoid that some of my photos would be lost before a case goes to trial, and the department would blame me for not producing the evidence." She shrugged. "So I back it all up, and delete it after the trial."

"What about the stuff from last night?"

"Yeah, that's here too. Why?"

"No reason." Jesse pulled her back into a hug, kissing the part of her hair. "Listen, is there any way a guy could get a home-cooked lunch around here? I've been dreaming about those vegan teriyaki burgers..."

"Liar!" she teased, swatting him on the shoulder. "You hate my food."

"No, really. I think I might be coming around."

Her face lit up. "Okay, I'll make some lunch today, and you can buy me dinner tomorrow night. Deal?"

Jesse wondered how long it would take to catch Olivia. "The night after okay?"

"Sure." She kissed his cheek. "Make yourself at home, I'll be back in a few." She gave him a strange look as she left the room, sort of speculative and curious, but Jesse was too distracted to worry about it just then. The moment she was gone, Jesse turned back to the computer, unable to believe what he was about to do.

Chapter 9

By 3:00 p.m. I had already done two loads of laundry and been to the dry cleaner's and the drugstore. Jesse and I weren't supposed to be at Dashiell's until 6:00—the sun went down at 4:48 that day—so I should have tried to nap, but I was keyed up, worrying about Olivia and the witch situation. A distraction sounded pretty good right about then. Eli and Caroline were both working at Hair of the Dog, and I wasn't in the mood for Molly, so I called Jesse. My list of friends is not long.

"Cruz."Just checking in. Anything new on your end of things?"

Jesse sighed into the phone. "Nothing we didn't already know. Santa Monica PD believed the suicide story on Denise. Every single detail fits, except for what Kirsten said about the hydrophobia. I can't even really blame them for dismissing her."

"Yeah…" I didn't know what else to say. What did I even want out of this phone call?

But Jesse read my mind. "You're totally antsy, aren't you?"

"Who, me?" I protested halfheartedly. "No way. Cucumbers wish they were this cool."

"Lies," he said solemnly. "Shameless lies. You are antsy in your pantsies."

I couldn't help it: I snorted into the phone. "I can't believe you just said that."

"Come to think of it, neither can I," he said thoughtfully. "But I'm restless too, and I have an idea. I'll pick you up in half an hour. Wear...oh, just wear what you usually wear."

"What does that—" I began, but he had hung up.

An hour later, I was at an honest-to-God shooting range.

Jesse had explained that I needed to know how to defend myself against a human threat, and I didn't necessarily disagree. Besides, I figured learning to shoot was going to be more fun than sitting at home chewing my nails during reruns of crime shows on cable. And I was right—except for the terrible elbow pain.

"Holy crap, this thing *kicks*," I complained, putting the pistol down carefully so I could shake out my arms.

Jesse's voice was calm and instructive. "That's because you're jerking it."

"*You're* jerking it," I retorted. Because I'm mature.

We were in one of the seedier-looking parts of North Hollywood, in a brick building that had once been a shoe factory. The current owner, whom Jesse had introduced simply as Clinton-never-Clint, had converted it to a small shooting range, with ten long aisles and those targets that zoom back and forth. Clinton had also made the excellent decision to offer the city's police a 15 percent discount, which made it a popular place for off-duty cops, especially right after shift changes. It was just before four o'clock, though, and Jesse and I were the only ones in there, aside from Clinton, a clean-shaven guy in his late sixties with one of those man-bellies that would look like pregnancy on a woman. He had greeted Jesse by name and then retreated to a big metal desk near the entrance without another word.

Jesse gave me the kind of long-suffering sigh that my mother had perfected before I turned nine. "Here." He stepped behind me, actually doing that macho thing guys do in movies where they're all *Ooh, let me show you how to do something while simultaneously turning you on with my muscles, ooh.*

I tried to hold that thought up against the more animal part of my brain as Jesse's arms went around mine, and his breath lifted hair off my neck. He wasn't that tall, maybe five ten or five eleven, but he had long, thickly muscled arms that fit all the way around me. He smelled wonderfully of his usual Armani cologne-and-oranges scent, and something else—gun oil? Gun powder? Something mechanical-y.

"You're holding your breath," he reminded me, his voice next to my ear.

"Right." I exhaled and turned my head to face forward. *Eli,* I told myself. *You're...something with Eli. Involved.* Yes, there's a good word. Involved. "This is all so *Beverly Hills Cop,*" I said nervously.

"Look, this is what you're doing," he said. With my index finger still safely on the outside of the trigger guard, he wrapped his own finger around mine and gave the whole gun a quick tug backward toward my chest. "Jerking. Instead, focus straight ahead, keep your elbows loose but firm, and *squeeze,* like this." Demonstrating, he squeezed his whole right hand around my whole right hand. "Got it?"

Work, brain, *work.* "Uh, what about the kick?"

"I'll brace you."

His arms around me loosened a little, giving me more room without moving away. He seemed so solid behind me, I felt like I could take a head-on collision and not so much as rock backward. "Remember," he said, "Breathe in, and squeeze on the exhale."

I managed to wound the diabolical paper target with five of the next six shots. "Good, good!" Jesse said happily. I set the gun down gently on the table and turned my face to his, accidentally grazing his mouth with my cheek. We both froze. I didn't meet his eyes, but a long moment of silence lingered as we both considered the possibility that lay between us. Well, considered it again.

We had gone on one official date, just one. It was right before I left for New York, and the idea was to do something normal.

Human. He picked me up and took me to the ArcLight in Hollywood for a movie and a nearby sushi restaurant for dinner. We talked about the movie and our favorite actors, and he told me stories about his parents' mischievous pit bull. For once, there was no talk of vampires or werewolves or witchcraft or anything else Old World. And it was amazing. I felt guilty about Eli, but he and I had had nothing but awkward work conversations for months, and Jesse...he looked at me sometimes like I was just another person, which no one else had done in the last five years. I couldn't resist it.

At the end of the night, he offered to walk me to Molly's front door, which was sort of sweet. I'm generally more of a one-night-stand girl than a chivalry girl. But when we got there, he reached out and stopped my hand before I could turn the knob. His eyes were troubled, and when he opened his mouth I was sure, just *convinced*, that it was going to be the start of some big "what are we doing" analytical conversation, and I just felt this great rush of...something. I took a step forward, and I kissed him. He wasn't as tall as Eli, and in my high-heeled boots I just had to reach up a little bit and he was right there. His mouth was cool and hesitant at first, but when I didn't resist he took my shoulders and pushed me gently against the door and kissed me *hard*.

It was incredible. It was like I could feel both of us let go of all of it, the Old World and the police and Jared Hess. For just a second there was no weight of history and magic between us. We were just Jesse and Scarlett. I'd never felt like that before.

And then my phone began to play "Bad Moon Rising," which Molly had recently programmed as Eli's ringtone.

I figured it had to be business, since that was all Eli and I talked about anymore, so I stepped a few feet away, still breathing hard, and turned my back on Jesse to take the call. I had been right: two female werewolves had managed to get into a drunken fight at the bar, and Eli just wanted to know what would get blood out of hardwood floors. It was an easy, one-minute conversation, the kind I've had with my brother when he desperately needed to know how many teaspoons went into a tablespoon. But when I slid the phone shut and turned back to Jesse, he was shaking his head.

"I can't do this, Scarlett."

"Because of my job? It was just a stupid bar fight; everyone is fine." I tried to keep the hurt out of my voice.

"Tonight everyone is fine. Tonight it isn't a big deal," he said, sounding sad. "But I can't be around you and listen to you discussing crimes and bloodshed like they're nothing. I'm not...wired like that."

"Jesse—"

"I'm sorry," he said. "I thought I could get past it, but I don't think I can. Every time your phone rings, I'm going to wonder if what you're doing is even legal, or who might be getting hurt because of it." He took my hand, squeezed it gently, and took a step back. "I think we should stop here, before we do some real damage." Then he walked away from me, leaving me standing there with my mouth dropped open.

I went into the house, and for the first time since my parents had died, I cried. And the next time I'd seen Jesse, he was picking me up to take me to Erin's murder scene.

At the gun range, I broke first, turning to face the table in front of me.

"Uh, thanks for doing this, Jesse," I said, in the general direction of the gun.

"Yeah. Of course." He stepped away from me, and I watched him back up to where he'd dropped his duffel bag. "Look, I have an extra gun and holster. I did your paperwork this morning, and I'm pushing it through as fast as I can—"

"Wait. What?" I said incredulously. "Look, I agree that it's good to know how to do this, but I'm not actually going to *carry* a gun."

"Come on, Scarlett. It's a good idea. If you have a gun, and Olivia gets in your...zone, or whatever, you can keep her from taking you down. And even if she's a vampire, it'll slow her down a little, right? What's the problem?"

"I don't...guns just..." Words completely failed me, and I gestured helplessly. Using one very carefully in a controlled environment with an LAPD cop literally at my back was one thing. Carrying one with me in the real world was another.

Jesse saw my panic and held up his hands in surrender. "Okay, let's drop this for the moment. Your paperwork's not done, and I'll be with you for a while anyway. But I do have something else for you." He reached in the duffel and pulled out something long and black. I poked it and saw the little Kevlar logo.

"Merry Christmas." He held it out to me.

"A bulletproof vest?" I said skeptically. "That's completely pointless, Jess. Nothing Old World uses a gun. It'd be like...carrying a homemade machete to a British fencing match. Tacky."

"There were plenty of guns last fall when we took down Jared Hess," he pointed out. "They're starting to think outside the box. Besides, Olivia is coming after you, specifically. She's gonna know a gun's the best way to kill you. It changes things."

That scared me enough to consent. I slid out of my comfortable canvas jacket and let him pull the thing over my head. When he fastened the straps, though, the vest rode way too big, armholes hanging down to the sides of my breasts. The vest's shoulders spiked out a couple of inches past the end of my own shoulders, giving me a Joan-Crawford-from-Hell look. "Jesse, I can't raise my arms. Who does this belong to? Copzilla?"

"Hey," he protested. "It *is* a woman's vest."

"She-Copzilla?" He snorted but let me tug the Velcro straps off. "I can't wear this. And if we don't go now, we're gonna be late."

He frowned at his watch, as if he could glare it into giving us more time, and finally shrugged. "Fine. But I'm getting you a better one tomorrow."

"If we live that long." I put the back of my hand mockingly against my forehead.

He took my tone as intended and gave me a light backhand on the shoulder. "Knock it off."

Chapter 10

The freeway was already crowded when we left the shooting range, which made driving almost *more* dangerous. Instead of an inch-by-inch crawl, the freeway was full of assholes doing that annoying swooping-between-lanes thing. I know, because Jesse was one of them. I didn't say anything, though, just held on tight to the door handle in Jesse's little sedan. As my father had pointed out when I was seventeen and wanted to go to the city by myself, LA driving is not for weenies. We managed to arrive at Dashiell's Pasadena residence at five after six, which counts as on time in LA, where everyone is usually either five minutes early or twenty minutes late.

There is this conception that vampires are loners who live by themselves until they have to go out and seduce a victim to be their dinner, and afterward they come back to their solitary home to…I don't know, brood sexily. But on the contrary, Dashiell and *his wife*, Beatrice, own a gorgeous Spanish colonial mansion—sort of rectangular, with a huge open courtyard in the middle—where there are always people floating around, both with and without heartbeats. There are vampire bodyguards and servants, and plenty of humans too, since when you have as much money as Dashiell does you can afford to have food delivered. Tonight Dashiell's parking area was full, thanks to his usual entourage plus my other Old World employers.

The vampire who opened the door was new to Dashiell's in-house posse. He was on the short side, with that kind of muscular stockiness you see in retired wrestlers, though he'd only been about forty when he was turned. He wasn't registering much wattage on the Scarlett Bernard Power Scale. We hadn't met, but by the way he glared at me I was pretty sure he wasn't a fan of being human again.

"Detective Cruz, Ms. Bernard," he said to each of us in turn. His voice was low and cold as the grave, so to speak, but he gestured for us to come in.

"Jeeves," I replied.

He wasn't amused. "Laurence," he corrected stiffly.

Jesse opened his mouth and closed it again. I was betting his cop superpowers were telling him to ask for Laurence's last name, but by now Jesse knew that vampires rarely use them. The older ones have changed their official last names so often that some of them have actually forgotten the original, and the younger ones don't want to give away how young and inexperienced they are. One of my life dreams is to be in a room with two vampires that have the same name, but somehow it hasn't happened yet. Maybe they add "of Pasadena" or whatever town they live in, like Robin Hood. Or maybe when they meet they have a fight to the death, Highlander-style.

"Are we out on the patio?" I asked, already half-turned in that direction.

"No, the gathering will be in the recreation room. Mr. Dashiell"—I tried not to chortle at the Mr.; I really did—"was concerned about those of you who still get cold." He said "get cold" the way you say "wet the bed." "Right this way," he finished. He turned on his heel and marched down the hall without glancing back to see if we were following. Jesse shot me a grin and mouthed "the *gathering*," before turning to follow. I smiled.

I'd never been in the rec room—frankly I was amused at the thought of Dashiell *having* a rec room—but it looked more like the lobby of one of the classier Holiday Inns than a place where you goofed around and watched television. It even smelled impersonal, like furniture polish and leather. Usually Dashiell has meetings with me out on the patio because the giant oval table is big enough for him to stay out of my radius while technically still sitting with me. Tonight, though, he was throwing caution to the wind and getting inside my personal bubble. I supposed with Olivia running around killing people, we all had bigger things to worry about.

Dashiell was sitting erect in a poufy tan armchair, managing to make the whole thing look dignified as hell. Will and Eli, who was there as the pack's beta, were on opposite ends of a long matching sofa. They were both leaning back into the couch, attempting to look relaxed, but both of their bodies were tight with tension. You could practically see their hackles up, although they both relaxed a centimeter when I got close enough to put them in my radius. Will shot me an appreciative smile, but Eli's gaze was thoughtful, traveling back and forth between me and Jesse. I remembered the feeling of sleeping with him the night before, and then the feeling of Jesse's arms around me at the shooting range, and blushed.

Jesse and I took two of the well-padded upright chairs that had been scattered around the couch set. I waited for a cue from Dashiell or maybe Will, but they were silent, clearly waiting for something. Or for someone. After about two minutes I heard the front door open and close and the sound of high, clunky heels striking the marble hallway floor. Jesse raised his eyebrows at me. "Kirsten," I said quietly. He nodded.

She came in behind Laurence, looking even paler than usual, if that were possible, and weary. Her eyes were clear, but there was a rigidity to her posture that seemed out of character. She looked reluctant to sit, but finally dropped onto another padded seat near the door.

Dashiell allowed Laurence to offer all of us beverages (which we all declined, because there's just something creepy about accepting drinks from the undead), and then waved him away. "Let's begin," he announced.

"Beatrice?" I asked.

"My wife is visiting some acquaintances in Seattle," Dashiell said, and I felt something small and tight release in my chest. One less friend to worry about. At the same time, though, it showed how serious Dashiell was taking Olivia—it's very expensive and complicated for a vampire to travel without a null along. With all the different things that can go wrong or cause delays, they can't exactly fly commercial.

"Thank you for coming," Dashiell continued, courteously implying that any of us had an actual choice when he summoned us. "Recent affairs have now escalated to a point where I thought it important for us to meet. To summarize, based on information gathered by Kirsten and our young police officer, Detective Cruz"—he paused and looked toward Jesse, who did kind of an awkward duck-head-and-wave maneuver—"we now suspect that Olivia has killed, or conspired to kill, at least two witches and two humans in the city in the last week. When I rose this evening I was also informed that she is likely working with a witch." Now Kirsten nodded, still staring stonily at the table in front of her. "Have you figured out whom?" Dashiell asked her.

"No, I haven't," she growled, and Dashiell's eyebrows rose. "As I told Scarlett and the detective, I know all of the witches that used Olivia's services, one way or another, but none of them have the...audacity for this kind of thing." She folded her arms defiantly.

"Well, Olivia can be quite persuasive," Will said mildly. "Vampire or not, if she really set her mind to controlling someone, she'd find a way." His face flushed the moment he'd finished, and I didn't need my null superpowers to feel everyone at the table suddenly *not looking at me.* I tried not to squirm.

"It's not about audacity, or controllability," Kirsten said. "Most of my witches were extremely nervous around Olivia when she was alive." Probably because she was psychotic. "At the time, I thought it was almost helpful, because if they didn't want to have to call her in, they wouldn't risk dangerous spells." She reached up to run a hand over her blonde ponytail, smoothing back nonexistent stray hairs. "But if Olivia approached any of them *now*, as a vampire, they'd turn and run the other way."

"Could that have been what happened to these two witches?" Will wondered aloud. "Maybe she just approached them, and they started to run, so she killed them?"

Kirsten shook his head. "Erin was killed before sunset, and Denise was somewhere she'd never be on her own."

"Someone had to know Olivia," Eli said quietly, causing heads to turn with surprise. He'd been so silent until then that everyone but me seemed to have forgotten his presence. "One of them wanted something enough to work with her to get it."

Kirsten's jaw set, but Dashiell waved a hand dismissively. "Trying to figure out what all of Kirsten's witches might want that badly isn't going to get us anywhere; let's table this line of discussion for the moment."

Jesse jumped in, sounding businesslike. "What about this other vampire she ran off with? Albert? Do we know anything about his relationship with her?"

"I might be able to help with that," Dashiell said. He picked up the telephone that was sitting on a table next to the big armchair. I hadn't even noticed it. "Laurence, please come in here for a moment."

The rest of us exchanged glances. My radar or whatever felt awfully crowded, with a vampire, a witch, and two werewolves, all quite powerful, more or less within my radius. But I still felt it when Laurence crossed the invisible line and became human too. "Yes, sir?"

"You were close to Albert, correct?"

Laurence glanced at the rest of us in turn, looking a little worried. "Yes, sir."

"Were you aware that he was spending time with Olivia Powell?" Even with his humanity, Dashiell's tone was calm, quiet, and absolutely terrifying. Laurence swallowed.

"Yes, sir."

Dashiell leaned back as far as he could without actually bending his spine, gesturing for the other man to go on.

"I don't know how it started, though," Laurence began, already sounding defensive. "I was living in Santa Barbara, and I came down a couple of times to visit Albert and some other friends. Get a drink, talk about old times. During one of those visits Albert was... just different." He trailed off.

"Different how?" Jesse prompted. He was in his element now, eyes focused on Laurence like they were the only two in the room.

"He was...lighter, I suppose would be a good word. I asked him about it over..." He glanced at Jesse and me, "uh, drinks, and he said he had a girl. He talked about her like she was a goddess, even mentioned trying to turn her someday." Laurence glanced at Dashiell nervously. "I know we're not supposed to try to turn new vampires without your permission, sir, but I assumed that he would ask for it."

"Did he?" Will asked Dashiell, frowning.

Dashiell bristled. "No, of course not. Even if it was unlikely to work, there is no way that I would have allowed Olivia to become one of us. Albert was going against my explicit orders." His voice darkened enough for Laurence to visibly flinch. "What else?" he demanded.

Laurence's brow furrowed as he concentrated. "He said...she saw great potential in him."

"What do you mean, potential?" I asked warily.

"I—I don't know," Laurence said. He wiped his hand across his forehead and then held it in front of his face, studying the perspiration like an alien had just sprouted from his hairline. "She had...plans, he said. That could change the way things worked in Los Angeles. I dismissed it as nonsense. I swear, sir, that's all I know about it," Laurence said to Dashiell. He was pleading, and I suddenly understood that Laurence was here in Pasadena to be punished for not telling Dashiell this story right away. Maybe that just meant he had to serve as Dashiell's butler for a while.

Maybe.

"The last time I spoke to Albert was in early September. Until you called me down here I had no idea he was...missing."

Dashiell looked at Jesse, who gave a small shrug. Dashiell waved a hand dismissively, and Laurence did plenty of bowing and scraping as he backed out of the room.

When he was gone, Will said to Dashiell, "But Olivia was a vampire for almost a year before the witch murders. Didn't you know?"

I doubt anyone but Will could have gotten away with second-guessing Dashiell like that, but Will's tone was so neutral and reasonable that Dashiell simply shrugged. "She kept a very low profile for many months, and Albert continued to work here, even after the events of the fall," he said, with a little nod toward Jesse and me. "I didn't find out that she had been turned until Scarlett told me she showed up at the hospital. I never got close enough to ask who had done it."

I jumped in with the question that was nagging at me. "Can we back up a second? We're skipping a really important step. Laurence said Albert was in love with her, and she used him to turn into a vampire." I'd figured as much, but I would bet every penny I'd ever have that she didn't love him back. Olivia didn't love people. She loved owning things. "But Olivia was a null, just like me. So in order to become a vampire, wouldn't she have had to become human first? Is that even possible?"

There was a long, heavy pause. Finally, Kirsten said, "Scarlett, the truth is that we don't know. No one knows all that much about your power. We only know what doesn't work against it."

"What does that mean?"

"You've seen all the old books at my house, right?"

I nodded.

"There are stories in there, plenty of them, about witches trying to cast a spell against a null. Nothing ever worked. Then in the twenties a New York witch became friends with a null, and they did a little experimenting. I can tell you with absolute certainty that there's no spell that even works against you, much less can take away your power. If we physically, permanently change something, you can't undo that, but there's just no active spell that can work against you or around you. We know that much, but we don't know where your power comes from or why it works against magic." Her voice rose with frustration.

I glanced at Will and Dashiell. Will was shaking his head. "The wolves haven't had a ton of interactions with nulls, and we certainly don't have documentation. We just know that when we get close to a null—in either form—we're suddenly normal humans again. Simple as that."

"Dashiell?" I asked. "Any ideas about how Olivia turned?"

He shrugged gracefully. "Don't you think I would tell you if I did?"

I had a few potential answers to *that*, but without warning, Kirsten slammed her hand against a side table. "Enough with the prince of darkness evasion crap," she snapped. "If you'd kept us in the loop from the beginning, this might never have happened. You knew, you *knew* who she was, how crazy she was, and you still let her live in your city after she turned. You let her live, period, even knowing what she did to Scarlett."

I figured this was what Kirsten had been wanting to say since she'd entered the house that night, and she wasn't wrong. As she spoke I felt her power flare again. The feeling was incredible, like I was a socket with a bunch of cords plugged in and one of them suddenly surged. For the first time, I thought I felt whatever was different about me actually push back at something, as though my nullness were saying *down, girl* to Kirsten. And although I felt her magic strain against me, I never doubted my ability to ground it. It was extraordinary, and I had to make an effort to hide my surprise.

Something like guilt flew across Dashiell's face, and then he remembered how to control his human expressions. "I do not answer to you, Kirsten," he said coldly. "You have both"—he turned his head to include Will—"agreed to my leadership in this city. That I would have final word. It was a condition of this little experiment, our working together. If you don't like the way I am running things, you're welcome to try to take what I have built for yourself."

I'm not sure how it happened, but suddenly I was laughing. And then I was laughing a lot, while everyone in the room stared at me. And then I was doubled over with tears of laughter dripping onto my jeans. "I'm sorry," I said when I could breathe. I sat up. Dashiell was glaring at me; the others just stared with their mouths open. I giggled again, until I managed to say, "I'm sorry, Dashiell. Really. It's just a lot of tension, and then you're all 'Grr! My way or the highway!' And I'm just really tired, and you need better dialogue." I cracked up again and saw Will trying to smother a tiny smile. I took a deep breath, forcing myself to calm down.

"I'm going to attribute that to the apprehension, and not insubordination," Dashiell said stiffly. At that, I kept my jaw clenched shut, but I couldn't help the giggles escaping through my lips. "What?!" he finally said, exasperated.

"Did you know, Dashiell, that when you're stressed your speech patterns gain, like, a master's degree? Food for thought," I said as soberly as I could manage. I'd never talked to Dashiell like that. "But more importantly, I don't know that much about how deep Olivia's manipulations go—as Will so helpfully pointed out, I pretty much fell for all of it—but whether or not she planned this, I would bet that she would *love* what's happening right now. Us arguing. Me losing it. All that good stuff."

There was another long silence, and then Kirsten spoke first. "She's right. I'm sorry."

Dashiell tipped his head. "Human emotions and reactions still feel strange to me," he allowed, which was as close to an apology as we were likely to get. To be fair, I did often forget how difficult it must be for the vampires to be around me, given what they are. The wolves retain their human emotions—often, like their metabolisms, they're even revved up—but the vampires seem to lose their grip on feelings over time.

"Okay," Jesse said after a beat. "You've told me what we don't know—who is working with Olivia, and how she became a vampire. So what *do* we know?"

Will said diplomatically, "I think one thing we can all agree on is that there is some kind of pattern or plan here. Olivia is working toward something."

"Kirsten suggested that Olivia wants Scarlett," Jesse said. I had a sudden elementary-school urge to punch him in the arm for tattling. All the eyes in the room turned toward me with speculation, like they were all trying to figure out what Olivia saw in me.

I started picking at a cuticle, my hands hidden under the table. This was probably the most uncomfortable I'd ever been in my life. Everyone at the table knew that I'd been Olivia's puppet, and that I'd fallen for her psychopathic bullshit for years. Not to mention that the two men I had a sort-of thing for were both sitting right there in front of me, aware of each other. I wanted to get up and leave so badly that all I could think about was the route I'd need to take from where I was sitting to the front door. Even if I made it that far, though, I didn't have my van. Jesse had driven us. I fought the urge to bury my face in my hands.

"You're probably right, Kirsten. But if all she wanted was Scarlett, she could have taken her after Scarlett's...injury...last fall. She had the opportunity, and Scarlett's defenses were down. And there would be no need to have an accomplice or kill the two witches," Will said thoughtfully. "There is something else at stake here, as well. I'm guessing that Olivia is saving Scarlett for last."

Jesse said, "My concern is that we won't find our answers until it's too late."

There was a moment of grim silence.

Eventually, Dashiell broke it. "Given what we do know about Olivia's past behavior," he said, "I think we can safely say that Scarlett needs to be protected."

There was a round of agreeable murmurs. *Now?* Now they all decide they're going to get along? Unbelievable. I was thoroughly annoyed, mostly because I had been trying to convince myself that I wasn't pee-your-pants terrified of whatever machinations Olivia had in motion. The last thing I wanted was for everyone to *agree* that I was in deep trouble. And when had they all started discussing me like I wasn't actually a person?

"Scarlett," I retorted, "who is *sitting right here*, by the way, can protect herself from one newborn vampire."

"I agree," said Jesse, to my surprise. I felt a flush of gratitude that he was taking me seriously. But then he added, "Scarlett shouldn't be alone, though, if for no other reason than to trap Olivia when she does decide to come for her."

"Yes, of course," Dashiell said smoothly. He gave Jesse a cool smile. "Someone will need to either kill Olivia or keep her still until I can arrive."

Jesse looked perturbed, but didn't comment, and I felt like I'd missed a chunk of the conversation. Dashiell seemed to be daring him to argue, while the rest of us glanced back and forth between the two of them in bewilderment. Finally Dashiell continued, "It's settled then. For the immediate future, Eli will handle all cleanup problems, except any future crime scenes that relate to Olivia. Detective Cruz will stay with Scarlett for the time being. When you need time away, call one of us at this table to be with her instead." He looked around as he spoke, making eye contact with each of us in turn. "Do not trust anyone else with Scarlett's life. We don't know who else Olivia may have gotten to."

Everyone but Jesse and I simply accepted this pronouncement and began gathering their belongings to leave. Jesse looked confused, his eyebrows knitted in a classic *wait, what just happened* expression, and I sat there sputtering. Dashiell is the cardinal vampire in Los Angeles, but I was a person, not a pet kitten that had to be kept inside while there was a coyote running loose in the city. This wasn't three months earlier, when I had temporarily lost my radius of protection. Olivia—or the witch who was helping her—couldn't lay a fang or a spell anywhere near me now. In some ways, I was better equipped to handle Olivia than any one of them.

I was just mounting a really reasonable and articulate argument along those lines—really, I promise, it was inspiring—when Eli, who had been watching me flail for words, spoke up to stab me in the back. "It's for the best, Scar," he said woodenly, not exactly meeting my eyes. "You'll be safe with Jesse." My jaw may have dropped open a touch. After everything we'd talked about the night before, after I'd let him sleep in my bed sober, he was going all white knight on me? Hell, he was pushing me toward Jesse?

Bullshit.

Chapter 11

As Jesse and I approached the car, he helpfully distracted me by humming the theme song from *The Bodyguard*.

I wanted to smack him, but I settled for a glare. "It's not funny, Jesse. What the hell just happened in there?"

We were still in Dashiell's makeshift parking lot, and he tilted his head to urge me to get into the car to continue this conversation. Fine. I opened the passenger door—and spotted my own gym bag sitting on the driver's seat. I frowned. There was a yellow Post-it note stuck to the strap, secured by a couple of extra pieces of Scotch tape. *Thought you might need this. Molly.*

Jesse leaned forward to peer at the note in the car's dim interior light. "How did she—"

"Dashiell," I said shortly, pissed all over again. "He had her pack up a bag and drive it over at sunset."

"The car was locked," he pointed out. I just shrugged. I'd seen vampires do much stranger things. "But that means...he knew all along we would have to stick together."

"Old World politics," I groused. "Never surprising, yet never predictable."

Jesse looked pensive for a moment, like he was trying to decide whether or not he had been manipulated. Finally he just shrugged at me and started the car. "It's okay," he said. "At least this way I can keep an eye on you. And you were going to help me with the investigation anyway, right?"

I thought for a long moment before answering. I didn't owe Jesse anything—I'd asked around just like I'd promised, and he could no longer threaten to poke around in the Old World, since he'd basically been invited in. But Kirsten...she was another story. I thought about how her power had jumped erratically during the meeting, and how broken she'd seemed at the bar. Then I remembered her brave, trembling smile after she and Eli had taken down Jared Hess to rescue me three months earlier.

Yeah. I owed Kirsten.

"Where are we even going?" I said finally. "I've never been to your place."

"My place is a shoe box with a hot plate." He'd turned the car around and was coasting down Dashiell's driveway. "So let's go to my parents' house. There's more room, they're out of town, and I have to let the dog out, anyway."

I just nodded tiredly. I couldn't believe it was only 8:00 p.m. Maybe it was the lack of sleep, or the stress, or just jet lag, but time was starting to fuzz together for me. Had it really been less than a day since Jesse had picked me up at the airport? And here we were again, with Jesse driving and me falling asleep against the window like it had all been a dream.

"We're here, Scarlett," Jesse said softly. I sat up, blinking in the unfamiliar glare of a motion-sensor security light. We were parked in the driveway of a sprawling two-story house with well-tended landscaping lining the path toward the front door. There was a string of colored lights doodling over the shrubbery, and there were so many delicate white icicle lights lining the roof that for a second I almost believed we were somewhere truly cold. Then I recognized Jesse's parents' house.

"You sure they won't mind?" I said sleepily.

"I'm sure. They're with my mother's people in Hermosillo. Mexico," he added.

I sat up suddenly. "For the holidays, right? Oh, Jesse, I'm sorry. I'm keeping you from them." Honestly, I kind of kept forgetting about Christmas. My parents had made a huge deal out of it every year, but now they were gone.

He shrugged. "It's only the nineteenth. I wasn't planning to head down there for a couple of days anyway. And if I don't make it, I don't make it." Off my look, he said, "Christmas comes every year, Scarlett. And I've missed more than one because of work stuff. It's no big deal."

"I'm sorry."

He waved it off. "Come on in, say hi to the pup."

I brightened. When we'd worked together before, Jesse had brought me to meet his parents' hyperactive pit bull mix, a muscled knot of energy named Max, who had introduced himself by knocking me down in an effort to show his undying love. Not because I was anyone special, but because I was there. I love animals in general, but dogs are the pinnacle of pet ownership, as far as I'm concerned.

This time when Jesse opened the front door, I was braced and ready. The dog shot out onto the porch, ridiculously fast in the poor lighting, and came right over to put his two front paws on my stomach, trying to lick my face. "Goofball," I said, laughing. I scrubbed at his neck and ears with my short fingernails until he dropped down to go greet Jesse.

"Oh, so you do remember me," Jesse said, mock offended. Max's whip-tail wagged hard enough to sting as it hit my leg. Jesse scratched his back for a minute and then bent down to grab a long cord that was fixed to the porch. He ran it through his fingers until he found the metal clasp at the end and fixed it to Max's collar. "Go run, boy." To me, he said, "Come on in."

I hadn't been inside his parents' house before, so I stopped just inside the doorway while Jesse walked to an adjoining wall to hit the lights. The two-story foyer lit up with a warm glow, the light stretching into what looked like a living room on the left and a sunken dining room on the right. "Watch your step," Jesse advised as he led me through the dining room, which featured a huge, ten-foot Christmas tree with a neat row of gorgeously wrapped presents under it. Jesse pointed. "Those are just the fake ones," he said, rolling his eyes good-naturedly. "They took a big carful with them when they left."

"My mother used to wrap empty boxes and leave them under the tree too," I said absently. I stepped closer to look at the ornaments. There were a lot of the nice Hallmark ones—I pressed the button on a Muppets trinket that made Waldorf and Statler holler belligerently—and even more of the homemade kind. I touched a small, neat frame made out of popsicle sticks. There was a picture inside of a handsome, smiling boy of about eight. "You?" I asked.

"Nope, that's my brother, Noah. This one's me." He pointed to another frame a few inches lower. This one was haphazardly glued together, with messy red coloring along one side of the popsicle stick.

"Not much of an artist, huh?"

"Hey," he protested. "I was six! That's damn good for six."

"Remedial," I informed him. "Remedial arts-and-crafts work."

He grumbled, but gave me a few more minutes to study the tree before saying, "Hey, I heard you say something to Corry before, but I forgot to ask. Is it really true that vampires need to be invited into a house?"

I turned around, forgetting the ornament I'd been examining. "Yes."

His brow furrowed. "Why? I mean, what's stopping them."

"Magic," I said briefly, but he made a rolling gesture with his index finger to indicate I should keep going. "Honestly? I have no friggin' clue. Something to do with families and blessings and faith. You could ask Kirsten about it."

He held up his palms in surrender. "Okay, okay. So that means vampires can't come into this house, right?"

"Uh...yeah, that's my bad."

"The null thing again?"

I nodded. "The protective magic forms a bubble around the house, covering every possible entrance—all the doors, the pipes, the vents, the windows, even a damn chimney. It's actually kind of like my radius." I pointed in the direction we'd come from. "But anytime I get within ten feet of an exterior wall, I short that section out. Not the whole thing, it's not built that way, but that specific area that touches my power." Concern had spread across his face. I added, "As soon as your family comes back, living in the house and loving each other, it'll come back, though. Don't worry."

He sighed. "I'm not worried about *that*, Scarlett. Hang on a minute." He looked around the living room, eyes narrowed with concentration, and finally turned back to me. "Wait right here."

"Jesse—" I started, but he'd disappeared back the way we had come. I heard the front door open, and a heartbeat later Max came bounding toward me, panting happily and doggy grinning like he'd just accomplished something amazing. I bent down to sit cross-legged on the floor, and Max put his front paws on one side of me and his back paws on the other, collapsing gleefully across my lap. He had to weigh sixty pounds. I laughed and petted him again, his tail whipping back and forth against a coffee table. If it hurt him, he didn't seem to notice.

Jesse came back a few minutes later with a big armful of pillows and what looked like sleeping bags.

"What are you doing?"

"We're going to have a campout," he announced.

I gave him a dubious look. "Excuse me?"

"Look," he dropped the pile next to Max and me—Max craning his head at an impossible angle to lick Jesse's face, as if not wanting him to feel excluded—and sat down. "We came in the front door, and walked *into* the house. We're not within ten feet of an exterior anything, as far as I know, and the bathroom is farther in still. As long as we stay here, there's only one way they could possibly come in, right?"

"Yeah, but, Jesse, we don't have to sleep on the *floor*. I haven't been in a sleeping bag since, like, high school. My people are not camping people."

He was already shaking his head. "I thought about it. All of the upstairs bedrooms are against exterior walls." He pointed to the couch at the far end of the living room. "That's an exterior wall. I'll move the couch closer, and you can sleep on that. I'll take the floor."

"You really think Olivia's going to, what, dynamite your parents' wall to get to me?" I said skeptically. "Ninja-jump through a second-story window?"

"No, I don't," he said primly, mock offended. "I think that sounds ridiculous. She shouldn't know where my parents live. And I personally don't think she could get within two hundred feet of the house without this mutt"—he pointed at Max, who was still panting and looking from one of our faces to the other like he was in heaven—"sounding the alarm, which is an impressive one. But the two things we know about Olivia for sure are that she's motivated and that she's completely nuts. I don't want to risk it."

"But—"

"Scarlett, for all you know, she could be working with a witch who can cast a spell to get them close to the house without making a sound, and to remove a damn chunk of the building." My mouth snapped shut. That was kind of a good point. I'd once seen Kirsten drop a section of flooring down to rescue me when I was trapped in a basement. "Besides," he overrode me, "I don't want to not be able to sleep all night, imagining her and her crony creeping up on the house. This way they can only come at us from one possible direction, and that feels a lot safer to me than having the whole house exposed."

I sighed and looked down at my lap. "What do you think?" I asked the dog, who focused on my face and wagged his tail hard enough for his butt to wiggle. He licked the air in front of his face a few times, having probably been trained that people didn't want face kisses. I laughed. "Fine. Max says campout."

I went into the bathroom to get ready for bed. To my surprise, Molly had played nice and just packed flannel pants and a gray T-shirt as my pajamas. She ordinarily wouldn't miss an opportunity to dick around with my wardrobe—it would be just like her to pack me, say, a negligee or something involving a thong—but she probably felt bad about being in on Dashiell's plan to shanghai me. Well, good.

When I came out, Jesse was standing in the living room holding a big armful of quilts, with a cell phone tucked between one ear and his shoulder. When he saw me, he said into the phone, "Me too. I'll call you tomorrow." He dropped the blankets so he could hang up the phone.

"The girlfriend?" I said, in what I hoped was a casual manner.

"Yeah." He fidgeted with the blankets for a second, making them into a nest on the floor.

"Is she...upset?" I asked, not even sure how I would feel about it if she was.

"No. I was a little vague on the details, I guess," he said uncomfortably. "I'm just gonna run to the bathroom."

While he was gone, his phone made a little ping, and I impulsively picked it up. New text message from Runa. I didn't open the message, but I couldn't help but see the picture that popped up on the screen for Jesse's new girlfriend. The woman was even more beautiful than I had feared: all white teeth, glowing tan, and white-blonde hair. She was standing on the beach with a camera strapped around her neck and one hand shielding her eyes. The hand was attached to a very tanned, toned arm. She looked happy and lively, just *bursting* with good health and enthusiasm for life.

Of course.

I put the phone back where I'd found it. When Jesse came out we finally got settled, me on the couch and him on the floor with Max stretched on his tummy against one of Jesse's legs. I listened to the silence for a few minutes. It was quieter here than at Molly's Hollywood bungalow, and darker too. You could almost believe we were out in the country somewhere, instead of in the heart of Los Angeles.

"What about her background?" Jesse asked suddenly. "What do you know about Olivia's personal life?"

I blinked at the new topic and hung my head over the couch to squint at him. "Why do you ask?"

His blankets moved in a shrug. "I don't know what else to ask about her."

I lay back and stared into the darkness, thinking it over. "She was married once, but her husband died a long time ago. He left her some money. She didn't really need the job cleaning for Dashiell, but I think she got off on the power. On knowing secrets."

"What else?" Jesse prompted.

"I don't know...she never really talked about her childhood or her family or anything. I got the impression that her parents were dead, and she never mentioned siblings."

"What did she like? I mean, what did she do for fun?"

It took me a long moment to answer. "She didn't care about most of the things people do for fun—drinking, television, hobbies. She liked going out to fancy dinners, I guess, and shopping. But mostly she just liked playing with her favorite toy."

"You," he said softly.

I didn't answer, and after a moment he said, "What? What's bothering you?"

"That couple in the Jeep," I said. "The ones she killed for me."

"Scarlett, that wasn't your fault."

"That's not what I mean...it's just, killing them really doesn't fit Olivia's style. She does everything on purpose, for a reason. Killing those two witches theoretically makes sense, to hide what she and her partner were going to do," I said. "But I don't see the point of killing the Reeds."

"Can't they serve a purpose as a scare tactic?"

"That's just it," I said, getting frustrated. I couldn't explain why, but something about the Reeds' deaths felt *wrong*. "The thing about Olivia is that she doesn't do threats or scare tactics. She's already scary because she just *does* these things. Killing the Reeds, it's like a taunt, but that's all. It's an empty gesture."

"You think maybe they have a different significance? Like they knew Olivia somehow, or knew what she was planning?"

"No, not exactly," I said. "I just...have a bad feeling about this. I think we were supposed to make the connection between Olivia and the witch murders. Then we were supposed to have a big meeting tonight to worry about her. I think she's pulling our attention in one direction, on purpose."

"That's starting to sound kind of paranoid, Scarlett," he said, not unkindly. "And even if you're right, there's not much we can do about it tonight. We should get some sleep."

"Yeah, you're right," I said absently. But I couldn't turn off my brain. This thing we were all apparently doing, where I was the bait or the trap or whatever, that was an awful feeling—after all, how was being a tool for Dashiell any different from being a toy for Olivia?

I rolled onto my stomach, cuddling into the quilt. Olivia had always treated me like I was this vaguely human-shaped piece of clay, and she got to be the master sculptor who made me into whatever she wanted. I was her confidante, her apprentice, her foster daughter, her servant. I've always thought *brainwashing* is a stupid word—this isn't the Cold War—but it was something along those lines.

And I was the perfect plaything for Olivia. She made me start running every day, and fussed over my clothes and my grammar and my food until I could hardly pick between soup or salad without consulting her. It took me years to wake up. It was like one of those Lifetime movies where the wife finds a lipstick stain on the collar and suddenly these pieces fall into place—the late nights at "work," the mysterious phone calls, the sudden disappearances. Then the wife always feels colossally stupid. That was me, only instead of a cheating husband I had a bat-shit crazy homicidal mentor who'd wormed her way into being my only connection to life.

Luckily, when I finally did realize all that, she was dying. Or she was supposed to have been dying. My employers seemed to have dismissed the problem of how Olivia, a null, had managed to get herself infected with vampirism, but it bothered me. No vampire should have been able to get near her without becoming a human again. I was used to not understanding things in the Old World, but I was also used to having someone to ask for the answers I needed.

I thought back to when I'd permanently turned Ariadne. The effort had caused my radius to weaken, leaving me vulnerable to magical attack for a few days. Was it possible that Olivia could do the same thing? No, she'd been way too weak at the end to channel that kind of energy.

Or had she? I'd found out about Olivia murdering my parents about ten days before she'd died, and I hadn't visited her again. I had no idea what her final days had been like.

Suddenly, despite the heavy quilt, I was freezing. I rubbed my hands together under the blanket, but it didn't help. I peeked over the side of the couch again, but Jesse appeared to have drifted off. Max looked up at me with hopeful eyes, slapping his tail against the blankets. Moving as quietly as possible, I lowered myself onto the floor between Max and the couch, with the dog between Jesse and me. He licked my hand happily, and with the dog's warmth against my side, I finally fell asleep.

Chapter 12

I woke up just before seven, for no particular reason other than a stiff neck. As I started to stretch, I realized that my back was up against Jesse's chest, his arm around me. I kept my eyes closed and held my breath for just a heartbeat, feeling what it was like to wake up with his Armani-and-oranges scent around me and his breath on my hair.

Then, of course, my phone rang. The tinny speaker chirped its rendition of "Black Magic Woman." I extricated myself as fast as I could manage without elbowing Jesse in the ribs and crawled forward to grab the phone. He stirred a little, but his eyes stayed closed. As I sat up, I spotted Max's tail thumping happily where the dog lay sprawled across the couch. "Traitor," I whispered to the dog, and then reached for the phone.

"Hey, Kirsten," I said quietly.

"Scarlett?" Her voice was strained and tight, even more so than at the meeting.

"What happened?" I asked immediately.

"She made her move," Kirsten said, a tremor in her voice. "Where are you?"

I felt an automatic twinge of embarrassment, but reminded myself that I had nothing to be ashamed of. Jesse and I were under Dashiell's orders to stick together. "Cruz's parents' house."

"Give me the address. We need to talk *now*."

"Hang on." I poked Jesse with a foot until his eyes opened. He stared at me blearily, and I held out the phone. "Tell Kirsten how to get here. I'm gonna jump in the shower."

I showered quickly and brushed my teeth, pulling clean jeans and a long-sleeved green T-shirt out of my overnight bag. Thank you, Molly. I needed my comfort clothes.

Jesse must have used an upstairs shower, because his hair was as wet as mine when I came back into the kitchen. I noticed a startling lack of kinetic energy in the room and figured the dog must be outside. "Coffee?" he asked.

"You bet."

We heard the barking at 7:20, and Jesse went to let Kirsten and an ecstatic Max inside. She wore a denim jacket over brown cords and a peasant-style shirt, and her hair was neat, but there was something off about her. She looked sort of wild-eyed and desperate, like she'd been the night before when she was yelling at Dashiell, but she seemed more relaxed too. Maybe she was just relieved that the other shoe had dropped.

I was impatient to hear what Olivia had finally done, but Jesse's good manners acted up and he had to offer her a cup of coffee first. "Only if you've got a to-go mug," she said distractedly. "You and I need to hit the road."

"Wait, you and Jesse?" I said with my eyebrows raised. "Not me?"

"No, I'm afraid you can't come," Kirsten replied. She stopped and took a breath, like her brain had just caught up with the fact that she was having this conversation. "Let me sit for just a second."

Jesse found a travel mug in the cupboard and filled it for her. Kirsten thanked him and wrapped her fingers around the mug. "When you're ready," he said quietly.

I was less patient. "Uh, Kirsten?" I waved a hand. "Share with the class?"

"There was a murder last night at Beth Israel, in San Diego. Well, a storage facility near the temple. An elderly rabbi was killed, and something was stolen."

"Okay..."

She looked directly at Jesse, holding his eyes. "Scarlett says that you are a good investigator, and Dashiell seems to trust you to find Olivia. I'd like you to come with me to San Diego and ask some questions."

"Sure," Jesse said mildly. "But it would help if I knew what I was asking about."

"Right." Her gaze shifted to include me again. "How much do you know about alchemy?" she asked.

Jesse and I exchanged a look. "Common metals into gold?" I offered. My dad had been a history teacher, and spent many a family dinner telling stories and theories to my brother and me. As a result I knew a ton of useless facts and historical anecdotes, without having much actual comprehensive knowledge of any one period in history. On the bright side, I was occasionally excellent at Trivial Pursuit.

"Certainly, yes, the ancient alchemists worked on things like that. They were scientists. But in witchcraft the term refers to the creation of magical artifacts. Every once in a while a witch is powerful enough to channel magic *into* an object and have it stay there."

"Why?" Jesse asked. "What's the point?"

"Think of it like a...shortcut. If you want homemade bread, you can go out and buy all the ingredients of the quality you want, then mix and bake the bread. Its quality will depend partly on your ingredients, and partly on your talent. Spells are a lot like cooking that way: you follow certain rituals, contribute the talent you have, and theoretically get what you want." She moved the mug toward her face, then paused with her hands in midair. "Cream?"

Jesse got her some out of the fridge. She nodded a thanks and continued, "With a magical artifact, the goal is to acquire accessible power that is earmarked for one purpose. So instead of following all those steps, you just have what you want ready."

"Like a bread maker," I said, grinning. I earned a weary smile.

"Yes, exactly. Only you don't even have to add ingredients anymore. Just push a button and get bread. That's what alchemy can do." She looked impatiently at her watch. "Detective Cruz, we should get moving."

But Jesse made no move to stand. "Why keep that a secret?" he asked. "What's the big deal?"

Kirsten took a long sip of coffee, like she was delaying. Her eyes jumped between Jesse and me. "Because of nulls," she said finally, and I straightened up in surprise.

"Me? What did I do?"

"Not just you, all nulls. Witches have worked to keep such artifacts away from you, because their power is only borrowed."

"I'm sorry, I don't get it," Jesse said.

Kirsten nodded like she was expecting that and got up. "Watch."

She looked around for a moment and then stepped across the kitchen and out of my radius. Picking up a small saltshaker, she held it against her mouth and whispered something. Holding her hand flat again, the little saltshaker began to rock back and forth on its edges, like it was trying to walk. "Holy crap!" Jesse said, then bit his lip. I elbowed him. "Sorry," he added. Ignoring us, Kirsten took a few steps toward me, the little shaker still rocking. I felt it when she entered my radius; even felt the tiny zing of the active spell shorting out, like a fly crashing into a bug zapper. The saltshaker stilled in Kirsten's hand. Meeting my eyes, Kirsten took a few steps backward, out of my radius. The saltshaker remained still.

"When I come close to Scarlett, my abilities vanish, but when I walk away again they return to me, because the power to manipulate magic *comes* from me. That's what being a witch means. The saltshaker has no power of its own, so when I walk away again it's still dead." She shrugged. "This is just a tiny little spell, but real artifacts take years to build, sometimes using the power of an entire coven. And a null can take that away in *one second*."

"You're saying that I can undo magical objects," I stated. "Permanently."

"Yes. It's happened before. The emerald table in Ireland, Stonehenge."

"Stonehenge?" Jesse said incredulously. "Nulls neutralized Stonehenge?"

"Yes. It was too big to move or hide, and it was really only a matter of time before a null showed up. It might even have been accidental."

I realized then that she'd been politely answering Jesse's questions this whole time. And at the meeting the night before, she had ceased shooting her death-ray glare his way too. Maybe that was just because she was more pissed at Dashiell, but was it my imagination, or was she softening toward Jesse? "That's why you don't tell nulls about magical objects?" I asked, trying to keep that line of thought off my face.

"Yes. There are only a handful of artifacts left in the world that have dangerous power. Some witches believe we should expose all of them to nulls, for the safety of the world. Others believe those objects are part of our history and should be preserved." She shrugged. "Both sides have a point."

"Now explain the part where this connects to the witch murders," Jesse prompted.

"In the car," Kirsten promised him.

"Why can't I come?" I asked, trying really hard not to sound like a whiny kid sister.

"Because," Kirsten said gravely, "there was more than one magical object hidden at Beth Israel. I can't let you get anywhere near the temple without compromising thousands of years of magical history."

"Oh," I said. "That."

"But I'm supposed to be keeping an eye on Scarlett," Jesse objected. "In case Olivia's witch pal tries something during the day."

"Right." Kirsten frowned. "I'm sorry, I forgot for a moment. Okay, both of you get your things. I'm going to make a couple of calls, and I'll meet you out front."

She picked up her coffee and glided back toward the front door before Jesse and I could do more than gape at each other.

Jesse filled Max's food and water bowls while I jerked a brush through my damp hair and rolled it into a bun. We grabbed our jackets and headed outside, where Kirsten was off the phone and waiting for us. "We'll drop Scarlett off somewhere safe," she announced.

"Can't I just go to Hair of the Dog?" I asked with perhaps a little bit of whining in my voice. I was still angry with Eli, but at least he was a knowable factor, unlike whatever hidey-hole Kirsten was going to stick me in. I could hang out with Caroline or something.

She shook her head. "I did try Eli first. There was a big fight at Will's bar last night, among the wolves. No one was killed, but I gather there's quite a bit of blood to clean up. Besides, Hair of the Dog is too obviously a place where you might be found."

Don't worry, we're going someplace very safe." I saw Jesse open his mouth, and she held up a hand to silence him. "Somewhere Dashiell-approved," she added, with a twinkle in her eye. I was very suspicious of that twinkle, but she was giving off a definite don't-ask-questions vibe, so I decided to let it play out. One hidey-hole was pretty much as good as the next, right?

After a moment's discussion, Kirsten persuaded Jesse to drive us in his car so they could use the flashing light on their way down to San Diego. She told him to go toward the 101, and I slumped back in the low car, trying to balance my coffee and missing the White Whale, which was still parked in the garage next to Molly's house. I had gotten used to riding upright, and Jesse's stupid sedan felt like a tilted bed.

Except for Kirsten's directions, we fell into an uneasy silence as Jesse and I waited for the witch to pull her thoughts together and finish her explanation. Personally, I was feeling kind of weird about leaving Jesse and Kirsten alone together to go on their separate adventure. Even if she was being nicer to him, it just felt odd, like having your college friends and high school friends hang out together without you. Okay, I'd only attended a couple of weeks of college, but you get the idea.

At the same time, though, I understood Kirsten's stance on keeping me away from the magical objects. The more I thought about it, the more I suspected that she probably wasn't supposed to tell me about magical objects at all. Would they have to move the items stored at Beth Israel, now that Jesse and I knew about them? I shrugged to myself. Not my problem.

"There is an amulet, on a necklace," Kirsten began suddenly, and Jesse and I both gave a little start. I turned halfway in my seat, my shoulders against the window so I could look at her. She was tilting her head, frowning to herself. "Wait, let me back up. Rabbi Samuel, the man who was killed last night, was the last protector of the Book of Mirrors. It is now missing."

"Wait, wait, I know what that is," I said. "Olivia told me about that. It's a blank book that works like witches' scratch paper, right? Don't all witches have them for notes and stuff?"

"Yes. But this one was special. It belonged to Lilith."

That meant nothing to me, but Jesse suddenly looked hard into the rearview mirror. He said something in Spanish that sounded a lot like "Save us, God."

"Who?" I asked, bewildered.

"Lilith. You've probably heard the name at some point."

"Adam's first wife," Jesse said grimly. "The succubus."

I was turned far enough in the seat to see Kirsten roll her eyes, a very un-Kirsten-like thing to do. "Neither of those things are true. However, at various points in history most of the bad things in the world were blamed upon Lilith, so she's become something of a mythic figure," she said. "Some people in the Old World even speculated for a while that she was a vampire. Actually, though, Lilith was a witch—possibly the first witch, and almost definitely the most powerful in history."

Jesse's shoulders backed down from his ears a little bit. Kirsten opened her enormous purse and pulled out a book with a green cover, some kind of encyclopedia. "I brought this to show you." She flipped it open, turning pages as she talked. "Lilith was known for her *kamias*, amulets. They are the magical shortcuts I was talking about. She was very famous for this one: the Transruah."

She handed the book up to me, and I carefully pulled it through the space between me and Jesse. On the left-hand page I could see the small, penciled illustration: a voluptuous woman in a plain white shift, gazing into the distance. One hand had drifted up to touch her necklace, a simple stone on a leather cord. Jesse glanced down at it too.

"It just looks like a rock," I said bluntly.

Kirsten frowned at me. "It's Jerusalem stone. Lilith is part of Jewish history." She shrugged. "Technically you could infuse any object with magic, but Lilith probably wanted a connection with her heritage."

"What does it do?" I said. "I'm guessing it doesn't make perfect bread."

"No. Transruah literally means 'spirit transfer.' Lilith would kill someone with a spell, and that person's spirit, the essence of their life, would become trapped in the amulet, letting Lilith absorb it. Like"—her hands gestured helplessly in the air for a moment—"like in *Ghostbusters*, they have that machine to trap and store the ghosts. Only this was the souls of living people, and Lilith was the storage container that held all the spirits."

Jesse and I exchanged a dumbfounded look. Although her day job was in the entertainment industry, that had to be the first movie reference I'd ever heard from Kirsten, and it happened to be from my favorite movie. This day just kept getting weirder.

"What could she do with them?" I asked. "The spirits?"

"Well, Lilith was able to live for centuries, which is probably where that vampire rumor came from. If her victim was another witch, she could also absorb their strengths for a time." She shrugged helplessly. "And that's only what we know about. It's hard to say which of Lilith's exploits were because of the Transruah, and which were her own natural power."

"Where is the thing, the amulet?" Jesse said, quite sensibly.

"In the thirteenth century the Knights Templar finally killed Lilith and destroyed her Book of Shadows, her spellbook. Witches have always believed that they destroyed the Transruah as well."

"And now you think they didn't?"

She held up two fingers. "To use the Transruah, you need two things: the amulet itself and the spell to use it. Lilith's spell. The knights were smart enough to destroy her spellbook, but the spell was also written in the Book of Mirrors. It's the only complete spell in the book. Witches like me have been protecting the book, moving it around to keep it safe. If someone went to all the trouble to kill Rabbi Samuel and steal the book..."

"Could someone have just made a new amulet?" I said. It didn't look all that special in the drawing.

"*No*," Kirsten said, with sudden vehemence. "I am absolutely certain on this point. Over the centuries, there have been a few attempts, and it's just not possible. An entire coven of witches as powerful as I am couldn't have re-created the Transruah. It's unique."

"So you think Olivia and her partner got the real amulet somehow, and needed the spell to use it," Jesse said. He looked thoughtful. "That's kind of a leap, though, isn't it? Couldn't the person who took the Book of Mirrors just be a collector or something?"

"I suppose," Kirsten conceded. "But without the amulet, it's just a curiosity, a small piece of history. And more importantly was how Rabbi Samuel died. He was…" She paled considerably, her fingers scrabbling at her neck.

"Drained of blood," I finished, keeping my voice as gentle as I could.

She nodded. "Yes. Sorry. I don't mean to be squeamish, but I considered Rabbi Samuel a friend. I worked very closely with him a few years ago to set up the repository—the collection of historical items."

"You're right, though," Jesse said, nodding his head. "A vampire kill at a location that stores witch history…it's too big of a coincidence."

I was staring out the window without really seeing anything, trying to process all that. The one thing I knew about magic, with absolute certainty, was that you never wanted to mess with the line between the living and the dead. And it sounded like that was this Lilith woman's friggin' specialty. "So wait," I said, closing the history book and handing it back through the seats. "One more time. Say I'm the evil witch who's working with Olivia, and I get my hands on the book and the amulet. What exactly can I do?"

"I could speculate, but we really have no idea," Kirsten said, busying herself with putting the book away so she didn't have to meet my eyes.

"Speculate."

She winced. "Well…in theory, you could live forever. Or bring someone back from the dead."

I leaned back, thonking the back of my head lightly against the window. "Those are some pretty big no-no's, Kirsten."

"You're telling me."

We were driving through a residential neighborhood now. It was 8:00 a.m. in Los Angeles, and while the homeowners were on their way to their jobs, the city's real workforce was beginning to emerge in the world: gardeners, garbage collectors, nannies pushing $3,000 strollers. Sometimes they reminded me of a story my mom had read when I was little, about some elves and a shoemaker. The real magic that kept the nicer parts of the city beautiful and luxurious happened because of these people.

Then I suddenly recognized where we were. "Uh, Kirsten," I said, dread pooling in my stomach, "where *exactly* are we going?"

"The safest place I know of, and somewhere where Olivia wouldn't think to look for you," Kirsten said with a thin smile.

"But this is Pasadena. We're in Pasadena." Maybe the coffee hadn't sunk in, but it took me a moment to put that together. "Are you kidding me?" I asked incredulously. "You're taking me to *Dashiell's*?"

"I don't like this, I don't like this, I really hate this," I chanted as we pulled into the long driveway. I'd never seen the mansion in the daylight, but I wasn't surprised that it still looked gorgeous, all the paint perfect and the windows spotless. Beatrice would pay attention to that sort of thing, even if she couldn't actually enjoy the house in the sunshine. "Dashiell's going to be pissed. Can't I just go to a hotel or something?"

"No, Scarlett," Kirsten said severely. "We know that the witch working with Olivia is very good. She can't perform a tracking spell on you personally, but if she's clever enough she might find a way to track you somehow, anyway. If she chooses to come at you during the day, she would have to kill you like a human would." She gestured at the house as Jesse pulled to a stop. "This is the safest place for that."

We all unbuckled our seat belts, but Kirsten said, "Scarlett, why don't you let me go in first and do the talking? These guys will be less jumpy if there's only one of us."

I wondered if Kirsten was planning to use magic somehow to convince them to be nice to me, but I was more than happy to put off going in there. "Fine with me."

As she rounded the house toward the front door, Jesse said, "These guys?"

"Dashiell's daytime crew," I explained. "I've never met them, but Beatrice told me they're very tough. Ex-military types of guys. They're mostly here in case of daytime attacks."

"Okay," Jesse said, frowning. "Is that what she meant by 'kill you like a human would'?"

I nodded. "She means that the witch would have to shoot me or stab me or whatever. And Dashiell's daytime guys are about the only ones in the LA Old World who use guns."

"Ah." At the mention of guns, I saw Jesse's hand stray down to his own hip.

"Be cool, dude," I advised. "We're basically here asking for help."

He caught himself and relaxed. "Right, sorry."

A few minutes went by, and Kirsten came briefly back into view, waving me inside. "Do you want me to walk in with you?" Jesse asked.

I was tempted for a second, but I shook my head. The whole thing made me nervous, but I didn't really have anything to be afraid of. Hopefully. "No, Kirsten's in a big hurry. I'll be okay."

I leaned into my door to open it, and Jesse caught my free hand. I stilled. "If it's a bad situation, get out of there," he said quietly. "And just call me." He squeezed my hand and let go.

Kirsten was waiting for me at the front door, along with a gigantic, handsome black guy wearing a gun holster over a black polo shirt. I put out my "feelers" for a second, but he was definitely human. He towered over Kirsten, who was only a few inches over five feet tall. "It's all arranged," she said. "This is Mr. Hayne. He and I...well, we go back." She glanced furtively up at Hayne, who just smiled at me with distant politeness.

That was interesting. Hayne was probably in his late forties, but still had bulging muscles and a trim waistline. He reminded me of a British actor with an unusual name, who'd turned up in a lot of action movies recently. As he held out his hand for me to shake, I saw scarring on the inside of his wrist. Puncture wounds, a lot of them. Was Hayne a willing donor, or had he been punished for something? I forced my eyes back to his face as I shook his hand. My hands aren't particularly small, but they disappeared into his.

"It's very nice to meet you, Ms. Bernard," Hayne said with a little smile. "I've heard quite a bit about you."

"Mr. Hayne will explain things to you," Kirsten said hurriedly, taking a few steps back. She reached out to squeeze my arm and promised to call me on the way back to LA. And suddenly I was alone with a large, armed stranger at Dashiell's mansion.

Fantastic.

Chapter 13

As soon as Kirsten got back in the car, Jesse felt a veil of awkwardness suddenly descend over them. He put the flasher on the roof of his vehicle, praying that Dashiell could get him out of trouble if he was noticed by unfamiliar highway patrolmen, and hit the freeway toward San Diego.

"You like Scarlett, don't you?" Kirsten said finally. "I saw the way you were looking at her."

"What? No." He glanced over at the passenger seat and saw Kirsten lifting one side of her mouth skeptically. The gesture reminded him of Scarlett, and, sheepish, he smiled. "I mean, I consider Scarlett a friend, but I'm with someone else."

"Ah."

"You seem to get along with her too," he offered politely.

"I do," she said after a pause. They were being careful with each other, he realized, each weighing every response before they spoke. But that was a lot better than the hostility of the day before. "She's young, but she doesn't play games. She's not interested in politics, or power. It's refreshing."

"Compared to the rest of the Old World?" he said.

She smiled a Mona Lisa smile, not giving him the point. "Compared to the rest of Los Angeles."

Fifteen miles later, Jesse asked, "Do you really think this thing in San Diego is Olivia?"

After a pause, Kirsten said, "When I was a little girl, my mother used to tell my sisters and me the story of Lilith and the Transruah. It was a scary story about a bad witch, meant to frighten us and provide a moral lesson. But I always felt...connected to Lilith. To that story." She shrugged. "From the moment I heard about Rabbi Samuel, I just knew this was something I was a part of."

"You saw the future?"

She held up a hand. "No, that's never been my gift. It's more like...when I got the call about Samuel early this morning, I just understood that the situation was my responsibility."

There was that word again, Jesse thought. "You guys take that pretty seriously, don't you?" Jesse asked. "You feel responsible for the people you lead."

"Yes, I suppose we do. Magic is very, very old, and there are certain attitudes...well. As long as there have been human leaders there has been a connection between power and responsibility."

"So it wasn't just Spiderman, then?"

She smiled, acknowledging the reference. "No."

They stopped for gas and a drive-through breakfast a few miles past Carlsbad. Jesse had pegged Kirsten as one of those organic vegan kind of people, but she took a lusty drink of her Diet Coke before he'd gotten his own straw unwrapped. Kirsten saw his glance and admitted, "I know it's terrible for you, but I can't help it. It's so good." He laughed, feeling for the first time like she was a regular person. She looked down at the cup holders, which both held various paraphernalia from Jesse's work. "Where should I—"

"Oh, let me just clear this crap." Steering with one hand, he reached over to take her drink just as she reached toward him, and Jesse managed to knock the drink into her stomach. The lid popped off and soda splashed across her corduroy pants and white shirt. Jesse pulled the car over and threw it in park. "Shit! I'm so sorry! Should we stop at a bathroom, or..."

"It's all right," Kirsten said calmly. "Just a moment."

She glanced around, and then whispered something under her breath, touching the stain with her index finger. Jesse's jaw dropped open as the brown liquid seemed to adhere itself to the tip of her finger. Kirsten raised her hand, drawing a fat stream of soda into the air, and moved the cup under it. She lowered her finger until the brown stream sank back into the cup. As she settled it carefully into the cup holder, Jesse saw her clothes were clean. She brushed a couple of ice cubes onto the floor and smiled at him, a little shyly.

"That was...that was so cool," Jesse whispered, suddenly feeling outclassed. It was the first actual witchcraft he'd seen, aside from the little dancing saltshaker.

Kirsten gave an elegant shrug. "Saves on the laundry bills, is all," she said modestly.

"I bet." Jesse checked his mirrors and pulled into traffic to get back onto the highway. "If you don't mind me asking, you said you don't deal in the future, but I'm sort of getting the impression that witches specialize in something. So...what kind of witch are you?"

She was quiet for a long few minutes, and Jesse realized she was deciding whether or not to trust him. "I'm sorry, that's probably too personal. Please forget that I asked."

Kirsten was silent for another few seconds, until she said, "It's all right. That's a perfectly natural question, it's just been a long time since I've been asked. I'm what's called a trades witch."

"Trades..."

She picked the resurrected soda up and took another sip. "It's an expression; it comes from the phrase 'jack-of-all-trades.' It just means that I do a little of everything. I don't mess with the future, and I don't read minds. But other than that..." She shrugged.

"I still don't really get it," Jesse admitted. "I mean, I know you explained about being a conduit, but I don't understand how you use magic to fix your clothes or...fly on a broomstick, or whatever."

She looked a little irritated at the broomstick comment but didn't say anything. Jesse suddenly realized he'd put her in the position of being his own personal magical advisor, which was rude. "I'm sorry, is this completely annoying? Am I asking too many questions?"

"No. Well, yes"—she smiled a little—"but I understand why you're asking me. Scarlett doesn't know all that much about magic. Why would she? But it's not supposed to be something that one can understand, not completely. Every culture in every society in history has had its own ways of interpreting the existence of magic," she said. "Greek and Egyptian gods, demonology, Kabbalah, astrology; I could go on and on. It's all one thing, one vast and incomprehensibly complex...thing. We use the word *magic* because it's vague and powerful, but maybe it's the force of creation, God, Mother Nature, mysticism, whatever. Whatever name you give it, however you want to see it, it's always been here."

"Wait, that makes no sense," Jesse objected. "How would these different humans across time and space know the same spells and stuff?"

She jerked her head impatiently, like she'd been waiting for that question, and now that he'd asked he had disappointed her. "It's not about spells. It's not about *how* you manipulate magic, but the manipulation itself. Look at it this way: magic is too big and too wild to be a part of us. Witches need a system, a context, in order to understand it, though it doesn't really matter what the specific system is. How is that different from religion?"

"But..." he sputtered. "If I'm getting this, you're suggesting that a witch in California can say abracadabra and a flame shoots out of her finger, but a witch in Japan can, I don't know, click her heels together and the same thing will happen?"

She held up her hand again, in a *wait, stop* gesture. "You're looking at this wrong. Magic isn't a single trick. It isn't finite at all." She tilted her head and took another sip of the soda, thinking. "Okay, look. If I go to the beach with a gallon bucket and fill the bucket with ocean water, I can do lots of things with that water. I can use it to splash someone who's hot, to build a sand castle, to soak my feet. Now, will that bucket of water that I took make a difference to the ocean, in the grand scheme of things?"

"No, not really."

"What if I brought a hundred of my friends, and we each took a gallon of water?"

"No. The ocean is still too big."

"Right. Now, I have a bucket, but maybe one of my friends has a pitcher, and one has a big plastic baggie, and one has a giant seashell, and so on. It doesn't really matter what we use to transport the water, and it doesn't matter if we wade in and scoop it up, get in a boat and skim the surface, or wait for the tide to come to us. We all have our own methods, passed down from ancestors or completely made up. What matters is what we do with the gallon of water."

He thought about that, and glanced over at Kirsten. She was perfectly composed, sitting with her hands folded and her legs crossed at the ankle. They might have been discussing the Napoleonic Wars or the price of gasoline. "I can see why you're their leader," he said, impressed.

She laughed, a low, musical sound. "Well, thank you."

"Whenever I talk to Scarlett about this stuff, and we get too deep into theory—or get to something she doesn't know, probably—she just says 'It's magic. The smartest people in the Old World don't understand the half of it.'" He realized he was smiling to himself.

"Well," Kirsten said, taking another sip of her soda, "I don't disagree with that, either."

Abusing his police light helped them make record time, and within an hour and a half of leaving Dashiell's Jesse found himself facing exits for San Diego. Kirsten called ahead for directions, and when she hung up she said, "The storage facility is half a block west of the temple."

"They don't keep things on-site?"

Kirsten shook her head. "They used to, but the collection became too large, and safety became a concern. Beth Israel is still a temple, and there are people in and out at all hours. Rabbi Samuel was the one to propose moving things to the storage facility nearby."

"Sort of a hiding in plain sight kind of thing."

"Yes," she said, and added wryly, "For all the good it did." She frowned again. "Of course, we'll have to move everything now. Too many people—especially Olivia—will know about it before this is over."

Jesse squirmed a little in his seat. She was also talking about people like him and Scarlett. Kirsten saw them as a liability, and he couldn't entirely blame her. From her perspective, telling a null and a human cop the location of a warehouse of secret witch artifacts must seem like giving terrorists the key to the president's secret bunker. "Who found him?" Jesse asked, to change the subject.

"His assistant, Alice. The rabbi stayed late last night, which was pretty typical of him, but he was supposed to be in early this morning. When Alice got to the office she couldn't find the rabbi but saw his car was here. She had the sense to see if the storage keys were missing. They were, so she went over there." Jesse glanced over at Kirsten, whose face was suddenly troubled.

"What?" he asked.

"I don't...I mean, I know you know what Scarlett does with crime scenes, that sometimes allowances have to be made to keep our way of life a secret."

Jesse looked at her again, but Kirsten's face was set now, and she stared straight ahead. He understood. "What did Alice do? Did she move the body?"

"No, no." Kirsten was shaking her head. "But she took the key. To the storage facility."

"So the police..."

"Don't know why Samuel was there, no."

Chapter 14

When I was fifteen, years before I had even heard of a null, I got a summer job house-sitting for one of the richest families in Esperanza, the Mycrofts. Every day I would ride my bike the five miles to their house, water the plants, collect the mail, and check that the pool guy had been there and the appliances were all working, stuff like that. It was an easy gig, but I still remember tiptoeing into that huge empty house, feeling its stillness, and terrifying myself with the possibilities of what I might find or what I might do. I could search through all of their things if I wanted to, and no one would ever know. I could throw a pool party, try on all of Mrs. Mycroft's expensive clothes, *steal* something, even. I never did a thing, of course, just did my job perfectly and got a big bonus at the end of the summer, but the thing I remember most about the house is that I always felt guilty when I was in it. Guilt because of what I *could* do.

That was exactly how it felt to be at Dashiell's house in the daytime.

After Kirsten left, Hayne and I eyed each other warily for a moment, and then he turned left into the living room, gesturing for me to follow him. We went into the hall beyond and down a long hallway I hadn't seen before. Dashiell's mansion isn't small, and I was nervous, so after a few minutes of silent walking I lost patience. "So how many daytime guys are there? I've only seen a couple."

He grinned at me. "Enough."

"Have you worked for Dashiell long?"

I'd meant this to be a polite small-talk kind of question, but Hayne gave me a sudden, measured stare as if I'd asked for nuclear codes. Finally he shrugged and smiled, and I let out a breath. "My family has. The Haynes have been working for Dashiell since before he was turned."

It took a lot, but I managed not to giggle over the "Haynes working for Dashiell" thing. This guy would probably not appreciate an underwear reference. "This whole time?" I asked. "Like, generation after generation?"

He nodded calmly. "In each generation one kid has been chosen to serve Dashiell during the daytime. Sometimes more than one of us has wanted the job." I wanted to laugh at the "in each generation" phrasing, but he was just so *serious*. And so very large. Besides, I was too flabbergasted. I knew from personal experience that Dashiell wasn't exactly the world's greatest boss. I would almost certainly never have kids, but if I did I couldn't see myself sending them to Dashiell for work.

"Just...for money?" I asked.

"Not just that. Dashiell pays for training, for college, for health insurance. When my great-aunt got cancer back in the thirties, he turned her into a vampire to save her." Hayne lifted his chin proudly. "Our family's history has been intertwined with Dashiell's for two centuries."

It made sense, when I thought about it. Dashiell had piles of money, but when it came to safety, that wasn't enough: someone who wanted him dead could always just offer more cash. What he really needed in a daytime guard was loyalty, and he'd found a way to earn that. It was actually very clever. "Do the other daytime guys have the same arrangement?"

"Nope," Hayne rumbled, and then grinned at me again. For such a dangerous-looking guy, he was certainly quick to smile. For some reason, it made him scarier. "They're just very well paid, and very loyal to *me*."

Or, I thought, *maybe just very afraid of you.*

We finally reached a door at the end of yet another long hallway, and Hayne took hold of the doorknob. "You can hang out in here," Hayne said to me in his deep voice. I braced myself for a dungeon or empty white cell, but when the door swung open I caught sight of an enormous, sunlit room filled floor to ceiling with books. Of all things.

I craned my head around, stumbling in after Hayne, trying to see all of them. The ceiling was twelve or fifteen feet high, with an astonishingly large skylight to let the sunshine in, and oak shelves covered each wall. The books looked like they were arranged more or less chronologically: the shelves on the west wall held ancient, browning covers with titles I could barely make out, while the south wall books looked all shiny and new. I was so busy looking that I bumped into a thickly stuffed blue armchair in the center of the room. There was another armchair and a matching couch with a coffee table that matched the shade of the bookshelves.

I was in love.

"The library," Hayne boomed behind me. I turned to face him, finally remembering he was there. He was giving me a bemused grin. "You seem to like it okay."

"It's nice," I said noncommittally, but I was thrilled and we both knew it. Hayne and I exchanged a smile. I considered making a comment about feeling like Belle in *Beauty and the Beast*, but wasn't sure how he'd take the implication.

"There's a bell over there," Hayne said, pointing to a little brass bell on the shelf nearest the door we'd come through. "If you need something, ring it and one of the house staff will come. The bathroom is the very next door down the hall, on the right." His face grew stern. "If you need to go anywhere else, ring the bell, and one of the house staff will get me or my men. You do not want to run around this house unescorted." He said the last part with a lot of warning in his voice, and I found myself nodding emphatically. It would just suck if I got accidentally shot.

"Sounds good," I managed. Hayne gave me a nod and turned to go. "Hayne?" I called after him. He turned back. "How do you know Kirsten?"

The guy was reasonably quick with the cheerful expressions, but the smile that spread across his face then was new and sort of mysterious. "She didn't tell you?" he replied. "I was her first husband."

The door clicked shut behind him before I could get my mouth closed again.

When Hayne's footsteps had receded, I plopped down in the armchair and listened to the house. It was wonderfully quiet. I wished I had someone to ask about Hayne and Kirsten—I knew she was currently married to a guy named Paul Dickerson, a normal human who did...well, something with money. I had always sort of dismissed him as just the Darren to her Samantha, and I'd had no idea that she'd been married before. And to Hayne, who looked more than anything like a pleasant-mannered mercenary who smiled a lot. And had bite scars on both wrists.

After a few minutes, though, even the promise of good gossip couldn't distract me, and my thoughts returned to my present situation. The library was gorgeous, but I was still irritated at being dumped in a safe room while everyone else went out and tried to stop Olivia and her partner. What could they be planning with the thing they'd stolen, the Transruah? Was I going to die? Would she just make me her slave, and I'd spend the rest of my life chained in her basement as her pet? I shuddered. That was worse than death. But Jesse would never let that happen...unless she convinced him that I was dead or something. Was it too much to hope that if she took me, he wouldn't stop looking until he found a body?

I pulled out my phone and called Caroline on her cell phone. Obviously the bar is open late, but as the office manager Caroline works a pretty normal 9:00 to 6:00 schedule, so I figured she'd be up.

"Scarlett!" she said cheerfully. Then her voice lowered. "Will told me about Olivia and that car accident thing. I'm so sorry, babe. How are you holding up?"

This is what I love about Caroline: she's just so warm. Everything she says, Molly might say too, but with Molly it's like she's testing the material, trying out a role, or trying to remember what a human should act like. Caroline is just naturally sunny and sincere. Or she's the best actor in a town full of pretty good actors. Either way, there's something comforting about her.

"I'm okay," I lied. "What's going on with the bar? Another fight?"

We chatted for a while about the latest werewolf drama, which involved two wolves getting into a brawl over something neither of them would admit to. "Eli and I have been discussing what the stupidest reason for a fight could be," Caroline confided. "It's hard for us"—meaning the wolves—"to get drunk, so it couldn't be just 'you looked at me weird' or something. I'm thinking maybe local politics, like, school board–type stuff. Eli thinks it's a reality TV show."

I was enjoying the distraction, but the mention of Eli brought me back to my current situation. I wanted to ask Caroline if he'd said anything about our night together, but I couldn't stand how stupid it sounded in my head, much less coming out of my mouth. But she picked up on my sudden silence. "Are you and Eli fighting again?" Caroline said softly.

"Fighting's not the right word," I said uncomfortably. I had absolutely no skill or experience at this kind of girlfriends-sharing thing. I'd been hanging out with Caroline some more, though, and was starting to get the hang of at least trying. "I just...wanted him to understand something, and he just doesn't't."

"Let me guess," Caroline predicted. "It has to do with Olivia."

"Yup."

"And him wanting to protect you."

"Yup." She of all people could understand: as the sigma, Caroline is the least-powerful werewolf in the LA pack, which means the rest of the wolves protect her like a baby sister. She understood the idea of being protected for what you are instead of being loved for who you are. But she didn't pry, which is another reason I love her. "Hang in there, babe," she said sympathetically. "It's all gonna work out."

It wasn't necessarily that I believed her, but like I said, there was just something comforting about Caroline, and I suddenly felt just a little better. "Thanks, Caro." We hung up, and I turned the phone over in my hands. It was weird, having a friend in LA who was so…normal. Of course, it was just like me that my most normal friend was a werewolf, but still, making friends with Caroline had been one of the more positive things I'd done in the last year.

In need of a new distraction, I hopped up and made for the bookshelves. I don't know what I expected Dashiell or Beatrice to read, but the selection on the shelves was surprisingly eclectic. There were a lot of history books, but only involving events before the nineteenth century, which was when Dashiell, anyway, had been turned. Maybe reading about historical events that had happened within his lifetime pissed him off. Or maybe he figured he already knew all of it. There was plenty of fiction, both Pulitzer Prize–type literature and some mass-market thrillers. I noticed that there weren't any horror books, which I suppose made sense for the same reasons the lack of recent history did. Also missing were romance novels and erotica, but pretty much every other genre was represented. The fiction was organized by author's last name, I noticed, but the nonfiction was organized chronologically by subject, so a book on the Black Plague that had been written in 2003 was placed before a book about the Revolutionary War written in 1998. For a second I toyed with the idea of switching around a couple of books, just to mess with Dashiell, but I managed to resist the urge just in case Beatrice was the one who organized the reading material.

I suddenly thought of Kirsten's book of magical history. I had seen dozens of other books on witchcraft and witch history at her house, and it occurred to me for the first time that perhaps Dashiell had an equivalent collection. Had anyone truly written about magic or history from the vampires' perspective? I crossed back to the chronological beginning of the nonfiction section, hunting for anything that looked homemade or cheaply published, or anything with "magic" or "vampire" in the title. I worked my way down the shelves, but it didn't take long for me to realize that if Dashiell collected rare books, he was keeping them somewhere else—there was nothing here that wouldn't be in an ordinary library. With nothing better to do, I kept going, anyway—and was rewarded on the second wall with a single piece of brown paper, folded in half, that had been stuck between two books on the shipping trade in the late 1800s. I pulled it out carefully and took it over to the couch, opening it gingerly on the coffee table. I perched on the edge of the couch so I could lean over to examine it.

The paper wasn't really brown; it was just very old, I realized. I was looking at a large map of the United States that had been crumpled and creased many times, like when you keep consulting the map of Disneyland and then shoving it in your pocket during the rides. The state lines were barely visible, and I squinted at the title at the top of the page. The first few words had been smudged or faded away, so that all I could make out was *Cities, 1910*. Obviously it was United States cities, but most of the ones pictured were along both coasts, and there were plenty missing, so these had to have some significance. There were light circles drawn around several cities in black ink: Baltimore, New York, Chicago. But the City of Los Angeles, as it was called on the map, had a much darker line of ink circling it several times.

I knew that Dashiell had been turned in 1819 in Great Britain, but I had never really thought about when he'd come to the United States. Was this the map he'd used? And if so, why'd he choose these specific cities? I looked closer, and realized that all the cities that had been highlighted—even the ones that didn't touch a coast—were on some kind of body of water. Which meant—

"Port cities," said a voice by the door.

I very nearly fell off the couch. "Thanks, Will. Now I won't need caffeine again. Ever."

The alpha werewolf of Los Angeles smiled apologetically and made his way into the room, inside my radius. He paused to take a deep breath, in and out, and then dropped into the armchair next to the table. "Sorry, I wasn't trying to scare you. Kirsten texted me to let me know where you were, since Dashiell's out for the day." He said "out for the day" like Dashiell had run to a business meeting in Santa Barbara or something. Really he was just dead in the basement, however many stories below our feet.

"And you decided to check on me?" I said, keeping my voice even. I was beyond sick of the let's-protect-Scarlett game.

But Will shook his head. "Not exactly." He leaned over to look at the map. "Nineteen ten, huh? I think Dashiell immigrated here right around then."

"That was my guess. But why these cities?"

Will shrugged. "These are vampire cities."

I looked down at the map, and up at him. "Why?" Then I got it. "Oh. Because vampires had to travel to North America by ship."

"Well, everyone did back then, but yes. Most vampires still travel by ship, if they have to go long distances. Unless they can afford a private plane, like Dashiell." He traced a finger along the East Coast cities. "By default, this is also a map of vampire-controlled cities in the US."

I looked at the browned paper with renewed interest. "Really? Still?"

"Yes. The wolves like medium-sized cities that are close to wild areas—we don't have much use for the ocean. Actually, we don't have a lot of use for controlling big cities, period. The cities that are werewolf-run mostly got that way because the local pack was tired of taking shit from the vampires. Or, in a couple of cases, the witches."

Will had basically just tripled my knowledge of the US Old World scene, and I was momentarily diverted away from finding out why he was there. "Really? There are witch-run cities?"

"Sure." He shrugged and gave me a conspiratorial grin. "But mostly because the wolves and the vampires didn't want them anyway," he stage-whispered.

"Are we the only big city where everyone has a say?" I asked.

"In America, anyway. We're the only place with regular meetings, with a shared cleanup person, with a trial system to keep the peace. We get away with it because LA is such a joke in the Old World." He looked up to study my face. "Olivia didn't tell you any of this stuff?"

I blushed. "Olivia trained me pretty early not to ask too many questions."

Will sighed and looked away. "What is it?" I asked him. When he didn't answer right away, I pushed. "Will, if you're not just checking up on me, why are you here?"

"There's something you need to know," he said. He stood up and began pacing a few feet in either direction, staying within my radius. Pacing is a wolf habit, and apparently it didn't fade even when the werewolf in question was currently human. "I...I owe you quite the apology."

Eli had told me once that Will felt guilty about how Olivia had treated me, like maybe he could have figured out what she was up to and stopped it. "Will, if this is about how Olivia took me in, it wasn't your fault."

"But it kind of was." He sat back down, leaning forward with his elbows on his knees. His head drooped like it was awaiting an executioner's sword. "Dashiell, as you know, doesn't exactly consult Kirsten or me before he does something," he began. "Almost fifteen years ago now, he hired Olivia. He had heard of a cleanup crew in Europe that was run by a null and thought it seemed like a really practical idea.

"I believe he briefly checked her tax returns and didn't find anything alarming, and she did very good work, so as far as Dashiell was concerned, that was that." There was a skeptical tone in his voice.

"But you...didn't like her?" I asked.

He sighed. "You have to understand, I was twenty-eight years old. I had been alpha for all of a year, and Dashiell and I had built this uneasy peace that was unheard-of in America. I wasn't in any hurry to rock the boat."

"But..." I prompted.

"But...yes, she gave me a really bad feeling, just as a person. There was something sort of...*hungry* about her. And empty. Dashiell didn't pick up on it at all—vampires aren't really intuitive. I tried to convince him to vet her better, but he blew me off. It's funny; he's usually very distrusting of humans, but it was like because she was a null, she was on the Old World side of his little us-them line."

"What did you do?"

He spread his hands. "First I tried to ignore it, but I couldn't just dismiss my instincts. So I went behind Dashiell's back to check on her. My dad was in army intelligence. I pulled some strings, paid a little money, and had a background check done. Complete with psych evaluation from her graduate school program, which was not easy to get, believe me." He reached into the messenger bag and pulled out a slightly rumpled manila folder. "This is it."

I managed not to snatch it straight out of his hand, but it was a close thing. "Why didn't you bring this out last night?"

He raised his eyebrows at me to say *are you kidding?* "You saw how tense everybody was last night. Dashiell was about ready to throw down for control of the city, for Pete's sake. I didn't think it was a good time to tell everyone that I'd gone behind his back fifteen years ago." His face drooped. "Or that I could maybe have stopped all of this, back then." Before I could address that, he added, "I tried to find you after the meeting, but you left pretty quickly, and then I had to deal with a fight at the bar."

I wanted to ask him about the fight, but I was afraid if I started another line of questioning I'd stop getting answers, so I held my breath. Literally. I was afraid to move, or I might break the spell. I was finally getting answers.

"Do you know anything about her background?" he asked me. "Before she started working for us?"

"Not really. She did say that she'd once been married and the guy left her money."

Will bobbed his head. "She grew up in Salt Lake City," he said. "Her family was extremely poor. Olivia never knew her father, and her mother, when she wasn't drinking, worked as a maid for a rich family in town." He gave me a small smile. "Well, however rich they get in Salt Lake City, anyway."

I looked down at the map I'd just found. Salt Lake City was a long way from any port cities. "Salt Lake City isn't a vampire town," I guessed.

He pointed at me. "No. Actually, it's one of the few biggish cities in the US that's more or less Old World–free. I'm guessing that's why Dashiell was so willing to hire Olivia—he knew she couldn't possibly have any loyalties within the Old World already. To him it was like…" He paused, looking for words. "It was like a carpenter coming out of his house one morning to find a brand-new power drill sitting on his front step, with nobody claiming it."

"Go on."

He nodded. "Olivia was dirt-poor, but smart—smart enough to leave home at fifteen and put herself through college, grad school, and a PhD program."

I felt my heart sink, but I asked anyway. "What field?"

"Psychology," Will said softly. He dropped the folder on the coffee table, opened it, and fanned the materials out so he could see them better. I was itching to comb through every page of the damned thing, but I held back—he'd tell me what was most important. Also, he was still my boss, and the idea of snatching up all the papers and locking myself in the bathroom to read them seemed slightly unprofessional.

Finally, Will pulled out a Xeroxed packet that had DO NOT COPY stamped all over it. He scanned the sheet. "She was asked to leave the program before she completed her doctorate—I guess there was an incident with some other students and a thesis experiment. It didn't matter to Olivia, though, because by then she'd found what she was looking for."

"New victims?"

He smiled sadly. "One new victim. A husband." He turned the packet around, handing it to me. "According to the psych evaluation, which she took as part of her program, Olivia's big dream was to have a family. A rich family, to be specific."

I looked down the sheet, where the evaluator's handwritten notes read *subject feels an unnaturally strong drive to reproduce, possibly due to death of younger sister.*

"She lost a sister?" I asked, temporarily distracted by pity. I don't care who you are; nobody deserves that.

"When she was fifteen. The little girl was two, and Olivia's mother was driving her to day care. It was eight in the morning, but she was stone drunk." Will looked away miserably. "There's a report in there somewhere, but that's basically the important part. That was why Olivia initially left home, went to school."

I put the psych report down gently, as if that might somehow make the little girl's death less tragic. "And she eventually found a husband," I prompted.

"Right. Or in this case, more of a sperm donor." Now Will pulled a grainy photograph out of the materials. It was a head shot of a smiling man in his early forties. He had an expensive haircut and perfectly white teeth, with a weak chin and watery brown eyes. "Scott Powell. He was a video game programmer who also came from money. Olivia probably figured he'd be a good father, and she went after him hard. They got married when she was thirty-one, and that was right around when she left her doctorate program. She was going to start her family, do the whole fifties housewife thing."

"But nulls can't have kids," I said. Nobody really understood why. Being a null isn't a hereditary trait, like the witches, it's just sort of a random-selection anomaly that crops up here and there in the human species. And for some reason, as long as nulls have been known to exist, they've never been able to conceive or carry a child. Although I still have to deal with periods like every other woman, which strikes me as unfair.

"No. I couldn't get her actual medical files, but I know Olivia underwent all kinds of fertility testing. She wanted a family *bad*, Scarlett. When she found out she couldn't have one...it destroyed her. She was already unbalanced, and this just broke what was left of her mind."

Sudden insight. "How did her husband die?"

I was picturing Olivia pushing him off a cliff or poisoning his cereal or something, but Will said, "That's the thing, Scarlett. He didn't. At least, not then."

Chapter 15

My jaw dropped. "*What?*"

Will pulled out a photocopy of some handwritten notes. "My guy found him hiding out in a little town in the Inland Empire, about ninety miles away. Esperanza. Powell *begged* the investigator not to tell Olivia where he was. He was terrified of her...Scarlett? Are you okay?"

My brain had stopped. Everything had stopped, actually, except my mouth. "What did she do to him?"

"He wouldn't say, just that he threw money at her, got a divorce, and moved to Esperanza without telling her.

"She found him, didn't she?"

Will's eyebrows raised, but he just handed me a newspaper clipping with a familiar-looking masthead. "I found this a couple of months ago, after you spotted Olivia at the hospital." It was an obituary from the Esperanza Herald, the twice-weekly paper my little hometown published. Scott Powell had died of an apparent suicide eight months earlier. I counted back on my fingers. Right after Olivia had "died" and been turned into a vampire. Will added, "I don't know how or when she found him—"

"Years ago," I broke in. I hardly recognized my voice. "Probably seven or eight. But she didn't bother killing him then, because she'd found something else to interest her."

I could feel Will studying my face. "What are you saying?"

I stabbed the clipping with an index finger. "This is my home-town, Will. She came for Scott, and somehow bumped into me."

I didn't actually remember bumping into Olivia or anything. Before I'd come to LA and had it all explained to me, I'd just assumed the weird feelings I got every now and then—my null thing—happened to everyone, the way everyone gets dizzy when they stand up too fast or gets a charley horse when their legs are cramped up. But I could still guess at when she had found me: after all, Olivia hadn't taken me as a child, when I would theoretically have been more docile. She'd waited until I'd turned eighteen and come to LA to take out my parents. I was guessing that meant she hadn't actually found me until late high school or so, and she'd decided to bide her time.

Although seriously, what the fuck did I know?

"Scarlett? Scarlett!" Will shook my arm, and I focused on the room again. When he saw I was all right, he released me right away.

"What did you do?" I demanded.

He blinked in confusion. "Huh?"

I waved my hand over the papers that were scattered across the coffee table. "With all this. You had the fancy background check; you knew she was broken in the head, so what did you do?"

"I—I didn't do anything," he admitted, hanging his head. "The background check set off plenty of alarm bells, from a psychology point of view, but nothing that would convince Dashiell that Olivia was wrong for the job." He scratched the back of his neck absently. "If I had showed him all of this back then, his takeaway would have been 'oh, her mom's a maid, she probably already knows a lot about cleaning.' That's how his mind works." Will looked up to meet my eyes, and probably saw my jaw hanging open. "I'm so sorry, honey," he said very gently, the way you'd talk to a child. "Are you all right?"

I might have been, if he hadn't called me honey. Insistent tears prickled at my eyes, but I blinked them away. "No, Will. I am *not* all right. I am not. And you…you're worse than Dashiell!" His eyes went wide, shocked. "You knew what she was, you knew she was out of her mind, and you had the humanity to care. You had to figure she was a loaded gun of crazy, but you just let her go about her nutjob business. You're right, you could have stopped all of this. My *parents*—"

He held up his hands defensively. "Whoa, whoa! She was crazy, but she hadn't *done anything* yet, then! And I had no idea she was going to kill your parents—"

"Really?" I snapped. "It didn't seem awfully convenient that this woman who always wanted a family suddenly had a cute little null orphan following her around? That didn't raise any goddamned flags?"

I was shouting now, and Hayne came striding into the room. "Miss Bernard, you need to calm down."

"The hell I do," I said, trembling.

Hayne's face stilled, so that only his mouth moved when he spoke. "If you can't calm down, you're going to wake Dashiell, and that would be very bad for everyone," he said, unfazed. "One of the upstairs vampires has already awoken, and she is very confused."

My radius was expanding. Gee whiz, I must be upset or something.

I was breathing heavily, looking from Hayne, with his unflappable expression, to Will, who wasn't meeting my eyes. "I need some air," I whispered. Before either of them could respond, I scooped up the file, jamming it into more of a pile than anything else. I hugged it to my chest and marched down the long hallway. By the time I hit the front door I was running.

"Scarlett," Will called after me. "Wait!" I felt him leave my radius, then enter it again as he caught up with me on Dashiell's porch. Damned werewolf speed. "Goddammit, Scarlett, *slow down!*"

I whirled on him. "You know what this is? This is like those domestic abuse cases where the cops and the friends and the family and the shrink all know he's about to kill her and she can't save herself, but everybody just figures someone else will do something before that happens. Then they're all surprised when she's dead."

That stopped him short. "What can I do?" he pleaded. "How can I make it up to you?"

Without a second of hesitation, I held out my hand. "Give me your keys."

He blanched. "What?"

"Forget Dashiell, forget Olivia, and for two minutes pretend I'm an adult who can make sensible decisions and take care of herself."

He stared at me, both of us breathing hard, and I saw him understand that I knew exactly what I was asking from him. Dashiell had given explicit orders to keep me guarded every minute until Olivia was caught. Will wouldn't go against Dashiell's orders once, when he might have stopped a train wreck, and I was daring him to do it for me now.

He dug in his pocket and dropped the keys in my hand. "Where will you go?" he asked.

I shrugged. "Where she won't think to look for me."

Will drove one of those massive four-door pickup trucks that looks like it could be dropped off a cliff with no damage. In fact, I may have seen that in one of their commercials. It was dark red and well-worn, with nicks and scratches all over the outside and suspicious tears in the inside upholstery. There was one of those big toolboxes welded into the truck's bed, and it was covered in dents too.

Ah, werewolves. Hell on wheels.

The minute I pulled away from Dashiell's, I felt better. It felt good just to be by myself again, for one thing, and to be doing something, even if I had no idea what I was actually going to do. My first impulse was to head to the beach, where I do my best thinking, but I decided that might be too predictable of me. If Olivia's partner really was gunning for me in the daytime, there was no sense making it easy for her. Besides, I'd promised Will I was going to take care of myself, so I would damned well make the effort and stay away from my regular haunts. Which ruled out Hair of the Dog and Molly's house too.

I pulled over a few blocks before the freeway exit to figure out where the hell I was going. What I really wanted, I decided, was to *do something*. Make something happen. I was tired of being the bait. But what could I do that wasn't already being done? Jesse and Kirsten were following up on the witchcraft stuff. I had learned a lot about Olivia's background, but was there anything that would actually help us find her? I looked at Olivia's file, which I'd unceremoniously dumped on the passenger seat. Well, at least that was a place to start. I headed for the nearest coffee shop.

Chapter 16

Jesse had been picturing a storage center like all the ones in LA—a grouping of warehouse-sized buildings that had been divided into large spaces with sliding metal garage doors. But he'd never seen anything like the monstrosity Kirsten directed him toward. Instead of warehouses, it was a single building the size of an enormous parking garage, surrounded by a small, nearly empty blacktop that reminded Jesse more of a moat than a parking lot. There were six double-sized sliding garage doors lined up along each side of the building's exterior, but no indication of where the internal dividers might be, so the building might have been divided into twenty-four identical cubes or any lesser number of units with more than one entrance. The building was also three stories tall, which made Jesse wonder if there were additional storage units on the second and third floors, or if each unit actually needed to be three stories tall. Surely the witches wouldn't need to store anything *that* huge, right?

Right?

"That one, the third door from the left," Kirsten said, pointing, but Jesse could see the crime-scene tape still squared off around a large patch of blacktop. There were three uniformed police officers loitering around, and he recognized the behavior: they were waiting for the all clear to head back to the station.

"Is the lot always this empty?" he asked, feeling conspicuous.

"Every time I've been here. People don't come here to stay very long."

He parked his car a good fifteen spots away from the tape, unbuckled his seat belt, and looked at Kirsten. "How do you want to handle this?"

She bit her lip for a moment, thinking. "Why don't I wait here and contact Alice, and maybe you could speak to the officers about what happened. Then you can ask Alice any other questions you may have."

"I need to see the storage room too," he said firmly.

Kirsten started to shake her head. "I can't allow—"

"Bullshit," Jesse interrupted. "You asked me here. You want my help. I need to see the room that he died for."

Kirsten stared at him for a long moment, but Jesse met her eyes without flinching. Finally she nodded. "I'll go talk to the cops," he said.

Jesse had opened his car door and gotten one leg out when Kirsten grabbed his arm.

"Wait," she said urgently, "you can't tell them that Samuel had a storage unit here."

He pulled his foot back in and closed the door again, holding back a sigh. It was never just easy, dealing with these people. It made him suddenly miss Runa, currently the only person in his life who was drama-free. "Won't they find his name on the rental records eventually, anyway?"

"No," Kirsten said. "Nobody associated with Beth Israel is on any paperwork here. It's a company owned by another company kind of thing."

He stared at her, and she dropped her arm. "Who owns this building, Kirsten?"

"We do," she said, and when he raised his eyebrows she waved vaguely. "The Old World. Let's just say it's Dashiell's equivalent in San Diego."

Jesse felt the balance of power shifting between them. Kirsten now needed something from him as much as he needed information from her. He considered his options. "If you cover all of this up, the people who loved him will never have peace," Jesse said finally. "You know that, don't you?"

Tears trickled down her cheek, though she kept her expression neutral. "I know," she said, her voice miserable. "But if we sent the human police after Olivia, it would only cause more dead bodies that couldn't be explained properly. And some of them would be policemen."

Jesse sighed. This went against every cop instinct he'd developed, but he knew she was right. He would just have to add this to the list of things he had to live with.

The cops on the scene didn't have much information for Jesse, even when they were done teasing him about being pretty enough to be a Hollywood cop. Jesse didn't bother explaining that he worked out of Southwest Los Angeles; he just blushed and gave them a made-up story about visiting a friend of his aunt's who was concerned about the rabbi's death. Jesse was used to the easy gallows humor that homicide cops usually adopted at crime scenes, but to his surprise the three cops seemed genuinely saddened by the murder. Rabbi Samuel had been well-known in the community, they said, and was a great supporter of San Diego PD. He had died of blood loss from a serrated cut across his throat, and there was a lot of blood missing. There were also several new bruises and broken fingers where Samuel had been tortured before his death.

When the senior officer's radio burped out their new orders, Jesse thanked them and walked slowly back toward Kirsten, giving San Diego PD a chance to get out of there. Before he could fill her in on what he'd learned, however, a dark-red Town and Country van drove slowly into the lot, and Kirsten looked up and waved suddenly. "That's Alice. She's going to take us into the collection."

"Is she a witch too?" Jesse asked. Kirsten shook her head.

The van pulled into a spot two down from Jesse's sedan, and the driver rolled down her window. "Hey, Kirsten," she called, in a flat Midwestern accent. She opened the door and climbed down, a fiftyish woman with forty extra pounds around her middle and iron-gray hair. Her eyes were rimmed red, and pink blotches had appeared on her craggy cheeks, but her jaw was set, and she gave Jesse a firm handshake. "Alice Weiss," she said. "You must be the detective."

"Jesse Cruz. Jesse."

"And I'm Alice. Thank you for coming." The older woman glanced nervously toward Kirsten. "Pardon my bluntness, Kirsten, but are you sure...this is okay? To take him in there?

Kirsten looked speculatively at Jesse for a moment, then nodded to Alice. "He's okay."

Alice accepted this without a word and began leading them toward a normal-size door between two of the garage doors. It opened onto a concrete staircase. "We're on the second floor," she explained, without turning her head. Through the door at the top of the stairs was a long concrete hallway, as bare and functional as a bunker. Which, Jesse realized, was exactly what it was. Halfway down the hall Alice stopped them at a heavy steel door with no window. Jesse couldn't help but feel a little excited, as his imagination ran wild with thoughts of possible witch treasures: cauldrons and big, creaky books and stuffed ravens. He was a little disappointed when Alice flicked a light switch and the room burst into ordinary florescent lighting, illuminating an enormous single room with rows and rows of industrial metal shelving. The shelves were stacked with big plastic tubs in mismatched colors. They were the exact same kind that his mother used to store her Christmas decorations.

Kirsten had been watching his reaction, and now she gave him a bemused smile. "You were expecting the Ark of the Covenant?" she teased.

Jesse laughed and shrugged. "Maybe a little."

"They're meant to look boring," Alice said helpfully. "We don't add or remove things very often, but when we do it's in these dull, plastic tubs. Who'd give them a second glance?"

She took off down one row, beckoning for them to follow. Jesse paused to look at the label of one of the tubs next to him. It said only *Romanian artifacts, 1753*. The tub on the shelf above it read *Japanese artifacts, 1752*. He caught up with Alice and Kirsten, glancing at the labels along the way. They were all similarly worded.

Kirsten must have noticed the puzzled look on his face. "They're vague like that on purpose," she explained. "Even the year is just the year that each object fell into the hands of the witches, not when the object was created."

"Are they all Jewish artifacts?"

"No," she said. "But most of the Jewish artifacts the witches control are here."

"Is there a directory?" Jesse asked. "An index of all the boxes?"

Alice shook her head without stopping. "Not here, anyway," she called over her shoulder. "You can see why the vampire needed Samuel's help to find the right place."

The place may have looked pedestrian, but it was huge. Alice threaded them through rows and aisles with no hesitation, and Jesse was grateful she was there. "I've been thinking about that," Jesse said, "about Olivia needing his help." He told them, with as little detail as possible, what the cop outside had said about Samuel suffering before death. "Why would Olivia have to torture the rabbi instead of just pressing his mind?" Jesse asked. Before either woman could answer him, Jesse remembered what Kirsten had said about canceling out magic. "Wait, was he a witch too?"

Kirsten and Alice exchanged an uneasy look that Jesse couldn't interpret, and Kirsten said, "No. There are a handful of male witches, but Samuel wasn't one of us. He was considered a

Friend to the Witches." The way she said it made it sound like a title, but Jesse didn't push it for the moment.

Alice stopped abruptly, pointing forward. "Here," she said unnecessarily. Jesse saw the mess right away: several tubs had been enthusiastically dumped on the ground. Shards of broken glass were scattered on the ground like sequins, and Jesse squatted down and saw bits of dried herbs and battered books mixed in with other unidentifiable wreckage. He looked up at Kirsten, whose face was stricken. "I didn't move anything," Alice volunteered. "I wanted to clean up, but you know...I watch TV."

Jesse nodded absently. He was staring at the wreckage, wishing Glory was there to help him understand what he was looking at. There were definite trails in the glass, like Olivia had dragged Samuel back toward the door when she was finished. They weren't neat, though, so Jesse thought Samuel must have been struggling.

"So Olivia was just torturing him for the hell of it?" Jesse asked. "I know she's nuts, but that seems sort of risky, given how public Beth Israel is."

"It's possible," Kirsten said hesitantly.

He straightened up to meet her eyes. "But...?"

She sighed. "The witches keep certain things private. Certain things we can *do*, I mean. One of those is to create protection amulets." She gave Alice a meaningful look, and the heavyset woman pulled a long chain out of her button-down shirt. Jesse saw a locket at the end of the chain, in the shape of a stylized Star of David. She held it in her palm as Jesse stepped forward to get a better look, but he instinctively knew not to touch it.

"Alchemy again," he said, looking at Kirsten.

The witch nodded. "Alice, like Samuel, knows about and deals with this repository," she said. "The handful of humans who know have protection amulets. They cannot be pressed by vampires, nor can they be turned." Her face was grim. "Although they can be killed, as you can see."

"Would Olivia have known about these?"

Kirsten bit her lip again, thinking. "Probably not," she said at last. "I created these myself, and I'm very careful about who knows about them. Honestly, I'm not even sure if Dashiell knows about these. It may have frustrated Olivia, that she couldn't press Samuel, which might be why this was so violent." She stared at Jesse, and he got the message. *Keep it to yourself.*

Alice put the locket back under her blouse, shifting nervously from one foot to the other. Jesse realized *he* was making her nervous by being there. She wasn't used to outsiders, and she had said she wanted to get the mess cleaned up. Jesse took one more look around and stood up. "We should let you get back to work," he said kindly to Alice.

Her shoulders slumped in relief. "There's so much to do," she murmured, distractedly. "I need to call his brother and sister-in-law in Montana, and speak to the board..." She headed back up the aisle in the direction of the door, still muttering under her breath. Kirsten gave Jesse a questioning look—*did you get what you came for?*—but he just shrugged and tilted his head to follow Alice. He didn't want to talk in front of the older woman in case there were things she wasn't supposed to know.

When they were almost to the door, Kirsten stopped in her tracks. "Wait," she said urgently. "I have to check one other thing."

Alice called a question after her, but Kirsten had spun on a heel and was hurrying down one of the labyrinthine corridors. Alice looked at Jesse, but he just turned and followed along in the witch's wake. Kirsten completely ignored both of them, scanning the tub labels and hurrying from one shelf to the next. Finally she found the tub she wanted and ripped it from the chest-high shelf. Jesse made a move to help her lift it, but she shook her head without looking at him. Dropping it on the floor with a hollow thud, she tore the lid off and looked inside. Jesse leaned forward to see, but the only thing in the tub was three empty glass jars. There was nothing overtly special about them—in fact, Jesse thought, he had seen similar jars at Target. But when he looked up at Alice, she was as pale as she'd been when Jesse told them about Samuel's injuries. He opened his mouth to ask, but Kirsten had sagged down on the floor next to the tub, head in her hands. "We've got a problem," she said to the concrete floor.

Jesse touched her shoulder, trying to be patient. "What is it? What was in the jars?" he asked gently. He peeked at the side of the tub, but the label just said "Spices." No date, no country.

Kirsten looked up at the two of them, and from the corner of his eye Jesse saw Alice shaking her head *no*. Kirsten's gaze landed on him as she pulled herself up using one of the shelves as balance. "I'll tell you in the car," she said to Jesse, and Alice's eyes widened.

"Kirsten, you can't—"

"I can," Kirsten interrupted. "Thank you for all your help, Alice. Please let me know when Samuel's funeral arrangements have been made, so I can come pay my respects." Her tone was crisp and formal, and Alice shrank back as if reprimanded. Jesse felt sorry for the woman but still had no idea what was happening. He clenched his jaw, trying to keep his questions until they got to the car.

Chapter 17

I claimed a table in the back of a coffee shop near Dashiell's house, Kalista's Koffee, and then spent the first few minutes trying to reorganize the papers into a more or less chronological timeline of Olivia's life. I scanned through the early stuff—there wasn't a lot that Will hadn't already touched upon. There was, however, a transcript of an interview with Olivia's husband, Scott Powell.

Interviewer: Mr. Powell, what can you tell me about your marriage to Olivia Richards?

Powell: I really don't think I should be talking to you. I think you should go. She can't find out where I am, you see?

Interviewer: Mr. Powell, I promise you, there is no reason for Olivia to ever know that you and I spoke. This is purely for background information regarding a sensitive employment position.

Powell: You mean like with the government or something?

Interviewer: Something of that nature, yes.

Powell: Is it a shrink thing—I mean, a psychiatry job? Because you should know she was asked to leave the program.

Interviewer: Is that how you two met, at graduate school?

Powell: At first, yes. I was getting my doctorate in computer science while she was working on her PhD.

Interviewer: Did anything about her strike you as odd, when you first met?

Powell: No...I mean, except for the fact that she was interested in me. She was—is—gorgeous, you know? So I figured she might just be into my family's money...

I skipped ahead a few pages, past Scott Powell's description of their early life together, when he thought she was perfect. I already knew about Olivia's ability to seem perfect. The investigator Will had hired was pretty good—he was able to get Powell past his fear of being found within a few minutes. Or maybe he'd just realized that Scott Powell was *dying* to talk to someone about his ex-wife.

Investigator: You said you "woke up" to what she was doing. What did you mean by that?

Powell: It was like...she'd been training me, the whole time we were together. Changing who I was. At first I figured, well, a lot of guys feel like that when they get married. But this wasn't just, like, buying me new clothes or making me get a haircut. A few months after the honeymoon, she was sort of...isolating me. She cut off my contact with my family, with my friends. She didn't want me going anywhere without her—I worked from home, even then, so I was expected to be with her twenty-four hours a day, every day. If I tried to resist, she got real quiet, like I'd broken her heart, or she ran guilt trips, or she used... you know.

Investigator: Sex?

Powell: Yeah. It was like she had a box of tools, and she pulled out whichever one she needed to keep me in line...

Ouch. I flicked that page aside. I remembered the box of tools too.

Investigator: So how bad did it get before you asked for a divorce?

Powell: Well, first of all, I didn't *ask* for a divorce. I begged her. *Begged* her. But that was later, after all the fertility testing. When Olivia found out she couldn't have kids...look, I don't want to talk about those days.

Investigator: Okay.

Powell: I mean, I wanted kids too, always did, so I said well, let's adopt. No big deal, I had plenty of money for lawyers or whatever. But Olivia screamed at me; she said her kids needed to have something of her in them or they wouldn't be hers.

I closed the packet. It was interesting, no doubt, filling in the blanks of Olivia's inner life, but it wasn't getting me any closer to finding her. Or to figuring out how she'd been turned into a vampire. I checked my watch: almost noon. What else could I do? I flipped impatiently through the file. Will's investigator may have been good, but the timeline ended fifteen years ago, when Olivia had gone to work for Dashiell. There was no mention of me or the Old World, much less anything about her final days, when she had presumably planned her "death."

Her final days.

That set off a bell in my head, but I was still chasing the thought when my phone buzzed on the table. I picked it up. Jesse.

"Hello?" I said absently. Something had been on the tip of my brain-tongue. What was it?

"Death spices?" Jesse yelled. "You decided that I didn't need to know about *death spices*?!"

Oops. He had my attention now. I automatically glanced around, even though nobody was going to hear the yelling over the phone. Luckily, Kalista's was more or less abandoned—everybody had gotten their coffee to go, so they could get back to their week-day jobs. The artsy-looking girl behind the counter raised her eye-brows when she saw me looking around, but I just gave her a brief smile and a thumbs-up. All good here. No refills needed.

I took a deep breath. "Uh, it was need-to-know basis, and you didn't need to know?" I tried. But I could practically feel him seething on the other end. I couldn't even blame him.

"Scarlett?" Kirsten's voice rang out. "You're on speakerphone; we're on our way back to LA."

"Oh, good," I said, but my voice was limp.

"I tried to explain to Jesse that you were acting under standing orders not to talk about the herbs," she said meaningfully, and I could picture her staring pointedly at Jesse as he drove.

"Yes. That's right," I said lamely. To be fair, no one had told me specifically not to tell Jesse about the Big Three. But I'd sort of figured out on my own that knowing that kind of thing could put his life even more at risk. And then by the time I had started to trust Jesse, it was too late to tell him without pissing him off that I hadn't said anything right away.

During the seventeenth century, when witches were more or less hunted for sport, the vampires and werewolves had refused to help them. So the witches did the only thing they could: they started exper-imenting with their magic. And they discovered something very dan-gerous: the nightshades. Just as magic clung to the evolutionary lines of humans, it clung to a class of plants, as well, and those plants had a chemical reaction with magic. The whole subspecies was loaded with magic, which the witches began using in everyday spells, but there were three in particular that were treacherous: *Atropa bella-donna*, *Mandragora officinarum*, and *Lycium barbarum*, which eventually became known as wolfberry. Belladonna, it turned out, was poisonous to vampires—you needed a lot to actually kill them, but a little bit worked as a paralytic. *Mandragora*, or mandrake root, was used by the witches in the really dangerous spells, the ones that toed the line between the living and the dead—a huge no-no in witch circles. And ingesting wolfberry caused the werewolves to completely lose control of their shifting, and often their minds.

When the witches discovered all this, there was a very quiet, very horrible war. Finally, in the twentieth century botanists tinkered with all three plants, and they'd all but eradicated the specific strains that had magical properties. You could now buy perfectly safe, nonmagical belladonna at a farmers' market in Wisconsin, if you wanted to. But those original strains still existed, and it was illegal for anyone in the Old World to even possess them. I'd been to a lot of crime scenes in my five years working for the Old World, and I'd never even *seen* any of the nightshades. Even Dashiell, Will, and Kirsten supposedly didn't keep any, though I could see how it might be valuable to, say, paralyze a nutty vampire. The Big Three, as they so cleverly were called, were just too dangerous. Which was exactly why I'd kept Jesse from even knowing about them.

The fact that Olivia now had all three strains...that made this a whole new ball game. It was pretty much the equivalent of that scene in *Jurassic Park* where they realize that in addition to all their other problems, the velociraptors have now escaped.

There was a long, pregnant pause while Kirsten and I both waited for Jesse's reaction. Finally he muttered, "We'll talk about this later, Scarlett."

So looking forward to that, I thought. Meanwhile, if ever anyone needed a subject change, it was me. "Um, what did you guys find out in San Diego?"

Kirsten filled me in on the basics: that Rabbi Samuel had been tortured for the location of the amulet, which had been stolen along with a box's worth of the Big Three. Then she'd dragged him to the parking lot and drained him, dumping the body on the lawn.

We had wandered back into my field of experience. I tried to picture the crime scene, something I've had plenty of practice with. "Why drag him downstairs?" I asked, keeping my voice low. I probably didn't need to bother—in this town anybody who overheard would probably assume I was running lines for my CSI audition. "Why not kill him up in the storage room and leave the body? It would have delayed anyone finding the body, and made a lot of trouble for the Old World in trying to explain what happened."

Kirsten was silent, but Jesse piped up. "I thought about that. I think she did it for two reasons: first, she was trying to disguise the fact that she stole those...herbs. She made a big show of violence near where the amulet had been kept, but the area by that box looked undisturbed. If Kirsten hadn't thought to check there, no one would have known they were missing."

"Okay," I said, processing that. "And the second reason?"

"Well, not to put too fine a point on it, but I think she's fucking with us," Jesse said. He explained that Olivia had drained Samuel's blood and then gone to the trouble of covering up the wound. "You told me once that the Old World gets involved if a crime doesn't look human," Jesse added.

I nodded, and then remembered that he couldn't actually see me nodding. "Yes. There's a cleanup person like me in San Diego. He's not a null, though, and I haven't met him."

"Well, Olivia didn't even try to hide the fact that she murdered Samuel and drained his blood, but she still went to the trouble of shredding that spot on his neck with a serrated blade, to cover the bite marks. It's like Olivia wants to shove this murder in Dashiell's and Kirsten's faces, teach them that they can't protect their own.

She would know how much that would bother them. At the same time, though, she doesn't want anyone else to be *too* motivated to hunt her down."

Kirsten's voice said, "You think she's just trying not to piss anyone else off, besides us?"

"Something like that," Jesse said. "She's deliberately poking you and Dashiell, though. If nothing else that thing with the Reeds would have made it clear that she was starting something."

"It's all misdirection," I said softly, and Jesse asked me to repeat myself. "She's jerking us around. We look at Erin; she does the Reeds. We look at the Reeds; she steals the amulet."

"So?" Jesse asked.

"So the question isn't what's the next logical step in the investigation, Jesse. The question is what are we *not* paying attention to?"

There was a long pause, and my gaze wandered down to the file. Her final days. I hadn't been paying any attention to the week or so between the last time I'd visited Olivia and her actual death. But there was somewhere I could go to find out. "I gotta go, Jesse."

His voice was immediately on alert. "Why? What's wrong?"

"Nothing's wrong." I frowned. How much to tell him? If I didn't explain that I wasn't at the mansion, they were going to make a wasted trip out there, and that would just piss him off more. Then again, if I did tell him I'd left, he would yell at me until I explained where I was. But he would do that whenever he found out I'd left. I might as well save them the trip to Pasadena. I asked to be taken off speakerphone, and Jesse switched me to his hands-free thing so we could talk somewhat privately. "Listen, Jesse, I'm not at the mansion anymore," I started, then rushed to add, "but I'm safe, and I'm not anywhere I go regularly."

There was a very long silence, and I held the phone away from my ear for a moment to make sure I hadn't dropped the call. Still had the signal. "Hello? Jesse?"

"We're here," Jesse said flatly. "But I wish you hadn't done that."

"I know. I had to."

"Did something happen?" he said, his voice concerned now.

"Not the way you mean. But I've gotten some background information on Olivia, and I'm going to follow up on something by myself."

"You can't just do that," he protested. "Dashiell said—"

"Jesse," I said tiredly, "since when do you give a shit about Dashiell's orders?"

There was a pause, and then to my surprise, he laughed. "You know, you're absolutely right. You're a big girl. Just tell me where you're going to be," he said. "No, wait, don't tell me."

I blinked. "You think she bugged the phones?" I said skeptically.

"Hey, you're not really the person to accuse anyone of paranoia."

"Fair enough," I admitted.

"Just promise me it's somewhere really safe."

"I promise," I said. "Lots of cameras, lots of people, security guards. Won't take more than an hour. I'll be fine."

"Call me after?"

"You bet."

Even in the strange car, my body remembered exactly how to get to the cancer ward at UCLA's Medical Center. On autopilot, I took a ticket, got a parking spot, and trooped up to the same floor where Olivia had spent months getting treatments. You could practically follow the sense of grief to find the place: sadness lingered on this floor like a bad decoration. The staff overcompensated by garnishing every flat surface with cheerful holiday decor. If I hadn't just seen similar decorations at Kalista's, I would have assumed that everything red and green in the city had escaped and taken sanctuary here on the oncology floor. There was even a twelve-foot Christ-mas tree, trimmed like a damn magazine photo, just before the nurse's station. I didn't stop to look at the ornaments or read the names on the presents under the tree. It would just make me sad.

Instead, I beelined for the nurses' station, and only had to loiter next to a nearby drinking fountain for about three minutes before I spotted a nurse I recognized: a thin black woman in her sixties with a half-inch Afro and a perpetual look of busy concen-tration. She hadn't been Olivia's favorite, but she'd been mine.

"Sadie?" I said tentatively.

She looked up sharply, and her face broke into a pleased smile. "Why, Scarlett!" she cried, rushing around the counter to throw her thin arms around me. "How you doin', sugar?"

"I'm good," I said lightly, returning the hug and taking a step back when it was polite to do so. I'm not really a hugger.

Her face creased in concern. "Sorry about your mom, sugar. I'm sure you had a tough year."

"Yeah." When she'd started treatments, Olivia had told the hospital that I was her daughter, so I would be able to visit during non–visiting hours. Or that was what she'd told me, and at the time it had made perfect sense. Silly Scarlett. "I know I wasn't around, that last week," I began, with an apology in my voice. I had a per-fectly good reason for blowing off Olivia during her last days as a human—I had found out about her murdering my parents. But I couldn't exactly explain that to Sadie.

The nurse just waved her hand like she was getting smoke out of the air. "Don't even worry about it. I have seen every reaction a per-son can have to death. Disappearing for a week or so is nothing new."

Even though I hadn't done anything wrong, Sadie's forgive-ness was kind of touching. "Listen, I know how busy you are, but would you have a few minutes today to talk about her last week? There are just a few things I wanted to know…you know, with the holidays coming and all." I gestured helplessly at the decor. Okay, maybe working undercover was not my best skill. But people took stock of their lives at Christmas, right? Or maybe New Year's?

Sadie nodded sympathetically. "Of course, sugar." She checked her watch. "I have a break coming up anyway. Why don't you go sit in the chapel? I'll meet you there in a few minutes. You know the way."

"Yeah, I know the way."

After the busy decorations in the hallway, the cancer ward chapel seemed plain and refreshing. There was no religion in here, so no actual decorations, not even a cross or Star of David. Instead, the small room had a simple stained-glass window, an empty altar, and two rows of short wooden pews. The room was always empty, except when it was needed. In my experience, though, when it was needed, it was *really* needed. I had personally spent hours here during Olivia's last months, praying for some kind of a miracle, which was funny, since Olivia more or less got one.

I sat down in the back-row pew, my usual seat. It had only been a year or so since Olivia had "died," but it felt like ten. I felt like a different person from the girl who'd prayed in this room. My parents had been regular churchgoers, but my brother and I were raised to make up our own minds whether or not we believed in God. It had taken me a few years to sort out my feelings, but I'd eventually decided I believed in God but didn't believe in religion. I would keep faith on my own terms. It's funny, but finding out that Hollywood movie monsters were real never shook my convictions. If God could create a platypus, why couldn't he create a vampire? If AIDS could exist in God's kingdom, why not lycanthropy?

No, it took Olivia to really make me wonder if there was a God.

My thoughts were interrupted by the sound of the pressure-controlled door opening and closing. Sadie settled into the pew beside me, reaching over to pat my hand.

"Thanks for talking to me, Sadie."

She patted again. "Don't worry about it, Scarlett. You're not the first relative to come back after it's all over, wanting answers to more questions. Our perspective of death, of our family member's death, it changes with time."

You got that right, Sadie.

"Did you ever see a guy with Olivia, at the end?" I asked. "Average height, sort of weaselly looking?"

Sadie blinked at me, and there was suddenly a glint in her eye. "You found out about Al, did you?" she said coyly. "I figured you might. They tried so hard to keep it secret." She shook her head. "I always figured they were just getting a kick out of that, sneaking around. Wasn't like you'd mind, that your mom had a beau in her last few months."

I had been right—Albert had been visiting Olivia at the hospital. I had about a thousand questions, but no idea where to start. "Was she...did she say how they met?"

Sadie frowned. "I never got a full story on that, but I assumed it was through the radiology specialist, Dr. Barton. Did you meet him?"

"There were so many specialists..."

"He stood out, though—had a scar going down his lip, right here"—she touched her lower lip like she was making a vertical mark on it. "Fell off a motorcycle, he told me once. He's a very big deal in experimental oncology, though he's based in New York, usually."

A vague image of a sandy-haired guy with squinty little glasses came to mind. "I think I met him once or twice. Albert...Al...he knew Barton?"

"Worked for him, I think." She shrugged. "At any rate, every time I saw Dr. Barton, Al was with him. Stayed real close, like he needed to hear every word Barton said."

Or like Barton needed to hear every word Albert said. Albert had found a specialist for Olivia and pressed his mind to get her the treatment. "What did Barton do for...my mom?"

Sadie shook her head sadly. "He gave her some new experimental drug...Domincydactl, I believe it was called. It was a Hail Mary pass, sugar, and it didn't work. They've discontinued the drug since then. Didn't work for anyone, I guess."

"Why didn't I know about this?"

"Your mom asked us to keep it private. She said she didn't want you getting your hopes up about a one-in-a-million chance."

Or she didn't want me to know what she was planning. Had she suspected that I was on to her? Or was she just hedging her bets in case it really didn't work? Whatever this drug was, it had either turned her or made it possible for Albert to turn her. It had honestly never occurred to me that nullness could be tempered chemically; I had assumed Olivia's transformation had had something to do with magic. We all had.

"You okay, Scarlett?"

My attention had wandered. I worked to focus back on Sadie. "I think so." I groped for something to say. "I'm...glad she found someone to be with, at the end."

"So am I, sugar." She patted my hand one more time and stood up. "Just remember, Miss Scarlett, your momma loved you. She was just devoted to you. I'm sure wherever she is now, she's at peace."

Not fucking likely.

Chapter 18

When Scarlett hung up, Jesse had looked at the phone in confusion for a moment, until Kirsten said, "Well, that was abrupt."

They had hit a patch of traffic on the way back to LA, and he didn't feel comfortable using the siren this time, since they were sort of at a loss for their next step. "Yes. I hope she's not in trouble."

"Hayne will look after her," Kirsten said, with perfect confidence. Jesse decided not to mention that Scarlett had escaped from Dashiell's mansion. "Do you think Scarlett was right," Kirsten asked, "about Olivia trying to distract us from something?"

"Probably," Jesse said grimly. He was lost in thought, half hypnotized by the brake-gas-brake-gas repetition of the traffic. "I do think we're missing something big. We've been running around trying so hard to catch up to Olivia, we haven't stopped to think. Scarlett suggested as much last night, but I thought she was just being paranoid."

"Well, let's go over it all again," Kirsten suggested.

They started with Denise's death, what little they knew about it. "I read the police file," Jesse said. "Witnesses saw her packing up her things on the Promenade just before one in the morning. We—the police, that is—didn't find any of it on the Promenade or the pier, so she must have loaded it in her car."

From the corner of his eye, he saw Kirsten nodding. "She had a special permit to park at the mall off the Promenade, I think."

"Right. Olivia—I'm assuming it was Olivia, because she would've had the strength—must have taken her at the car."

"Wait," Kirsten objected. "That doesn't make sense. Olivia is a vampire; she wouldn't have wasted good blood, not when she could make it look accidental."

"Maybe she needed it to look like a suicide. She didn't want to attract any attention yet."

Kirsten was shaking her head emphatically. "No, there's a method for that, which vampires just love. They put the victim in their bathtub, drink most of the blood, and let a little bit run into the water to turn it red. Hardly anyone who commits suicide that way is actually a suicide."

Jesse was temporarily distracted. He glanced over at Kirsten. "Really? Wouldn't the medical examiner realize a lot of blood was missing?"

She shrugged. "I've never heard of anyone catching it. They do this fairly often." She wrinkled her nose. "Think about it. If you were going to commit suicide, wouldn't you rather just shoot yourself, or take pills?

Jesse started to answer that, but remembered the actual point of the discussion. "Anyway," he said, gesturing for them to get back on track.

"Right. You read the police report. Did Denise have any major cuts? Specifically at the arteries?"

Jesse thought back. Denise's body had been nearly pristine, he remembered, except for some minor bites from fish. No major arteries. "No."

"Then maybe it wasn't Olivia," Kirsten said. "Maybe it was the witch."

"Denise weighed a hundred and fifty pounds," Jesse said skeptically. He didn't mention that that was her weight *after* the fish had nibbled on her—Kirsten didn't need to know about that. "And she would have been fighting like crazy, and maybe screaming for help, and terrified of the pier. If we're talking about one witch, a woman…I just can't see her being able to get Denise that far. Could someone have…hypnotized her?"

"A reasonably powerful witch could," she said thoughtfully. "But although we can technically perform spells on each other, we're naturally a bit resistant to other witches' magic. And Denise's mind would have dug in its heels, metaphorically speaking, about going out over the water. Hypnosis is like that; it's hard to make the subject do something that goes against her deepest feelings."

"Are there any other spells, though? For, I don't know, mind control?"

She shook her head. "Neuromancy, witchcraft that deals with the mind, is an extremely specialized and difficult area to work in. I know a few witches who could put her in a trance, or maybe take a few seconds of memory, but to get her to the pier and then over the side…" She shook her head. "It doesn't really work like that."

They were both quiet for a long moment, thinking that over. Jesse could understand why the Santa Monica PD had ruled Denise's death a suicide. It was just too neatly done. "Okay, let's put a pin in that for the moment," he said at last. The car had finally made it to the source of the traffic—a multicar fender bender that had forced the police to close off two lanes of the freeway. Jesse nodded to the highway patrolman directing traffic around the cones, and was momentarily grateful that he'd never signed on for highway patrol. "What happened next?"

"I knew about Denise's death, and I was suspicious right away," Kirsten said. "But there wasn't anything I could do, really. I just thought…I don't know what I thought." She slumped back in her seat, biting on a cuticle. It was obvious that Kirsten was blaming herself for not acting after Denise's death, but Jesse didn't bother pointing out that it wasn't her fault. She *knew* that; she just didn't feel it, and Jesse understood. He'd felt the same when Jared Hess had taken Scarlett.

"Then Erin died," he prompted gently. "What do you know about that?"

Kirsten told him about being unable to reach Erin, about using a locator spell and sending the substitute cleaner to her apartment. Jesse was still itching to know who had helped Scarlett get rid of the body, but Kirsten didn't use the cleaner's name, and by her sidelong glance Jesse could tell she knew not to tell him. *Dammit, Scarlett*, he thought. She must have warned Kirsten.

Jesse was still a little pissed about the cleaner taking Erin's body, but he did realize that Kirsten wasn't the person to take it out on, so he pushed ahead. "Was there anything else that the cleaner mentioned?" he asked. "Anything else he noticed while he was there?"

Kirsten held up a hand. "Let me think." She sat silently for a few minutes, and Jesse figured she was trying to figure out what he should and shouldn't know. That pissed him off again, and he was about to say so, when Kirsten said, "Two things. First, he said it looked like the body had been crushed, evenly. Not like it had been beaten and bones were crushed, but the whole thing at once."

That matched what the crime scene techs had said about the bloodstain. "And the second thing?"

She shrugged. "It's probably nothing, but he said there was a bit of an earthly smell. Like dirt, but sort of…processed."

That rang an alarm bell in Jesse's brain. He had forgotten about the dirt being at both Erin's apartment and the Reeds' crime scene. "Wait. I gotta stop for a minute," Jesse said. He took the next exit off the freeway and pulled into the parking lot of an In-N-Out Burger. Kirsten began to ask him a question, but he shook his head. "Hang on a second," he told Kirsten, and pulled out his cell phone. He turned off the Bluetooth and dialed Glory at the lab.

The phone was answered by one of her underlings, a bright Asian twentysomething with a Mohawk whom Jesse had met a few times. He informed Jesse that Glory was working nights this week, and Jesse immediately felt stupid. Of course she was; that was why she'd been at the Jeep crime scene to begin with. He hung up and dialed Glory's cell, glancing over at Kirsten. The witch was calmly playing Angry Birds on her own phone.

"Jesse?" Glory's voice was sleepy and irritated. "This better be really good. The kids are in school and I was finally sleeping."

"Listen," Jesse began, "did you test that weird dirt you found in the Reed Jeep?"

Glory sighed into the phone. "Of course I did." Jesse grinned to himself. "It was something called...wait, let me remember this right...industrial plasticine. It's mostly used to make full-size models of cars before they go into production, to see how they'll look when completed. I just figured maybe Mr. Reed did something like that for work." She yawned into the phone. "I was gonna call you about it when I woke up."

"What's it made of?"

"Basically? It's man-made clay."

"Thanks, Glory," he said. "That was a big help. Go back to sleep."

He hung up the phone and relayed the information to Kirsten. "I don't know if that helps us any, but it's something," he finished, but Kirsten had frozen in her seat, eyes big and round. Her phone slipped from her hand onto the car floor. "What? What is it?"

"It can't be," she whispered. She was shaking her head. "Jewish magics...Jewish artifacts...God, I'm such an idiot."

"*Kirsten*," Jesse said impatiently, and the witch's gaze snapped over to him.

"It was the witch, the one who's working with Olivia," Kirsten said. "She's made a golem."

Jesse was a child of the movies before anything else. "Like...
in *Lord of the Rings?*"

"No, no. A golem is a creature, made from clay and shaped
like a man. The witch uses magic to animate the clay, sort of like
Dr. Frankenstein's monster." She rubbed her face with her hands
like she was scrubbing something away. "I don't know why I didn't
think of it sooner."

"Is it...alive?"

"I've never seen one—as far as I know, no witch has created
a golem since the sixteenth century. But think of it more like a
windup toy. The witch builds a humanoid statue out of clay and
funnels magic into it. That's the windup. She then gives it a task,
usually something simple, like 'take this heavy box and carry it
until I tell you to put it down.'"

"Just to play devil's advocate here, how do you know that's
what this is? Aside from the bits of clay we found at the scenes?"

She shrugged. "It just fits. Clay is very heavy, and I understand
the weight of the spell makes a golem heavier yet. It could easily
have crushed Erin to death." She straightened up in the seat, as if
she'd just thought of something. "And in dim lighting, with a long
coat and hat, it could pass for human for a few minutes. If the witch
and the golem surprised Denise at her car, the golem could easily
have carried her to the end of the pier and thrown her over. They're
incredibly strong."

Jesse tried to picture it. A shadowy figure in a long coat and
fedora, marching straight down the pier with a struggling woman...
it didn't fit. "The Santa Monica Pier is crawling with homeless people," he objected. "Wouldn't someone have noticed?"

"I told you, there are spells for taking away a few seconds of memory. Or for creating a small distraction, or helping people to sleep..."

Jesse held up a hand, a little frustrated. "Okay, okay, I believe
you." He was beginning to understand why witches made Scarlett
a little uneasy. At least with the other Old World creatures, you

knew what they wanted and what they could do. He wished Kirsten could just hand over trading cards with all the witches' stats. "We operate under the conclusion that it's a golem. But what exactly could you do if you had a golem, the Book of Mirrors, and Lilith's amulet, all at once?"

"Oh, God." Kirsten said. "I hadn't even gotten that far. I have no idea; there are too many variables, and it depends a lot on what kind of witch you are...death magics," she said suddenly, paling in the midday sun.

"What?"

"A golem to be your henchman, and possibly take the lightning strike if something goes wrong. The Transruah, which collects the energy of life." Jesse got the feeling Kirsten wasn't entirely aware of his presence anymore, and fought the urge to hurry her along. "With the right magics, the right specialty, you could live forever, like I said before...kill someone remotely...even bring someone back from the dead..."

"Slow down," Jesse said, before she could speculate any further. "This is getting too big, and there's too much we still don't know about what Olivia and this witch are planning, or when. What do we focus on first?"

"The golem," Kirsten said immediately. "That's their muscle. If we could dismantle the golem right away, it would cripple them and make the witch much more hesitant to begin the Transruah spell."

"Okay, how do we kill the golem?" Jesse asked, feeling like an idiot as the words left his mouth.

He looked across at Kirsten, who was frowning. "I'm not sure... I need to consult some texts. A golem is one of those creatures that has many different legends and stories. Most of it is folklore, some of it is truth."

Jesse couldn't resist. "You mean like witches?"

She smiled. "Touché." The smile faded from her face as quickly as it came, and she gasped with a sudden realization.

"Kirsten?"

"It's tonight," she said solemnly, turning in her seat to face him. "Whatever Olivia and her witch are doing, it's going to happen tonight."

"Why?"

"Because it's the winter solstice," she said, as if that explained everything.

"The longest night of the year, right? What does that have to do with anything?"

Kirsten gave him an incredulous look. "You don't...the solstice is a holy night for many religions and pagan rituals. I usually have a big party for all the witches, sort of like a multi-holiday party. I canceled this year because of Denise and Erin."

What did a canceled party have to do with the bad guys' plan? "Does that really matter for Olivia and her partner?"

"It could," Kirsten said, excitement in her voice. "The solstice has particular relevance for Lilith, and for the connection between life and death, though I don't know all of the specifics. Jewish magic has never been a specialty of mine. But if I were summoning power for a big spell, using Lilith's amulet, involving the dead, and I didn't have a coven to back me up...yes, this is the night I'd do it."

Jesse tried to follow this line of thought. "You're saying it'll make the witch even more powerful?"

"Yes," she said simply.

"Can you narrow down the time frame any, based on those rituals?"

Kirsten chewed on her lower lip as she considered his question. "If she were worried about us finding her, she'd go a little early, like ten o'clock, to throw us off. But I'm guessing this witch wants every bit of power she can grab. She'll cast at midnight."

Jesse checked the dashboard clock. It was barely noon. "So we've got twelve hours." He restarted the car and turned it back toward the freeway. "Does knowing it's a golem help us find the witch who made it?" he asked.

"I don't know," she said distractedly. "Animation magic is a very unique specialty, and animating and controlling a golem would require an enormous amount of power. I'm not even certain that I could do it. I certainly don't see any of my witches having that kind of...muscle."

She sounded so trusting when she talked about her witches, and Jesse raised his eyebrows. "Would you necessarily know?"

Kirsten snapped to attention, looking across the seat at him. "A very good question. A few weeks ago I would have said yes, of course, I know all my witches. But now..." She turned up her palms in a helpless gesture. "I don't know. If one of them really wished to, I suppose she could be hiding her level of power from me."

They drove in silence for a few minutes. Jesse was trying to process the new information. This golem thing sounded like a cop's worst nightmare. Even assuming Kirsten could figure out how to kill it, they had to find it first. And if they couldn't find Olivia, and they had no way of figuring out which of Kirsten's witches was secretly helping her..."Scarlett," Jesse said aloud.

"What?"

"Scarlett can gauge power." He took his eyes off the traffic long enough to meet Kirsten's. "She told me once she gets a sense of how powerful the vampires and werewolves are, when they come into her...aura, or whatever. I asked her about you guys"—Kirsten gave a short nod, understanding that he meant the witches—"and she said...how did she put it? That you all have a low-level buzz when you're not trying to use magic, and when you do use it the buzz flares up. She said your buzz is stronger because you're more powerful than the other witches she's met."

"But how does that help us?" Kirsten asked sensibly.

"If we could get the witches together in one place, and if we put Scarlett among them, she'd be able to tell who was hiding power," he said excitedly. "And she'd be able to neutralize the witch at the same time, and we could use her to find Olivia."

"That...could work," she said slowly, her face creased in concentration. "It's a bit of a long shot."

"I know," Jesse admitted, "but the only other things I can think of would be to dig through Olivia's background to see if we can find a witch connection, or run background checks on all your witches. And we'd need more time for either of those options."

Kirsten's mouth turned down at the words *background checks*. "Let's do it."

"Do you have any way of getting the witches together?" Jesse asked. "Do you guys have meetings or something?"

"Not until the first weekend of next month. I could *call* an emergency meeting, but then whoever it is might just not show up."

"If she thought the meeting was about something else?" Jesse asked. "Like, you say there's news about the killer, or something?"

He glanced at the witch and saw that Kirsten's face had brightened. "I have an even better idea," she said, with sudden cheerfulness. "I'll just uncancel the party."

Chapter 19

I let Sadie hug me again before I left the hospital. As soon as I got out of the building, my cell phone began to ring, the regular old *ring-ring* sound that meant it wasn't one of my bosses. I didn't recognize the number.

"Hello?" I said cautiously.

"Oh, thank God. I've been calling and calling. Is this Scarlett Bernard?"

I glanced back at the hospital building. I'd forgotten that I couldn't get reception inside.

"Yes, this is Scarlett."

"I have a—a problem? Is that the right word?"

I frowned. Most of my cleanup calls happened at night, but a daytime crime scene wasn't unheard-of. "You're calling about my cleaning services?"

"Yes, I'm Esther, there's this vampire and..." She took a sobbing breath. "I think he might be dead."

I opened my mouth to say that she should call Eli and give him the job, but then I remembered he was dealing with a big cleanup at Hair of the Dog. I shrugged to myself. There wasn't anywhere I needed to be just then, and it *was* still my job. "Give me the address. I'll be right there."

As soon as I had entered the address in my GPS and was on my way, I started to call Jesse to tell him where I was going. I had his number highlighted on my phone's screen and everything, but then I abruptly pushed END and tossed the phone into my work duffel on the passenger seat. Vampire or not, this was a dead body. Jesse would feel obligated to call the police and turn it into an actual investigation; he was dense like that. I couldn't involve him.

Then again, I wasn't an idiot, either, and I knew this might also be a trap designed by Olivia. I doubted it, as the sun was still up. Whenever she unleashed her evil plan, she would do it at night, so she could see its horrors reflected on my face. But still…if I got killed because I didn't tell Jesse where I was, I was going to feel really stupid.

I thought about it a moment, then pulled over and sent him a text that I would be delayed for a work errand. Then I called Molly's cell phone and left her a voice mail: "Hey, babe. If there isn't an 'all clear' voice mail on here when you get up, something bad has probably happened to me. Call Jesse and tell him I went to two five four Spring Boulevard in Silver Lake. Oh, this is Scarlett."

Problem solved. I pulled back onto the road.

The address that Esther had given me was for a small, weathered-looking cottage on the outskirts of Silver Lake, currently one of the city's trendiest neighborhoods. Wait, no, maybe that was last year. I can't keep track. At any rate, Silver Lake had once been one of LA's most dangerous areas, then had gone through urban renewal or whatever, so now it was a mix of excessively developed residential areas and neighborhoods that hadn't quite gotten the memo about cleaning up their act. Spring Boulevard was somewhere in the middle: two blocks from a Coffee Bean but shabby enough to have bars on every window of every building, even the upper floors.

I don't know what I was expecting Esther to look like—maybe a teenage runaway from a Lifetime movie, with big eyes and an artfully dirty face—but she wasn't it. When the cottage door opened, the woman inside was plain, skinny as a rail, and bald as Daddy Warbucks. A dark-pink cotton scarf was wrapped around her head, and she didn't have eyelashes or eyebrows. She looked like she was pushing fifty. Oh. I suddenly understood the situation.

"Thank you so much for coming," she said, a little cough clutching at her words.

"Of course. Nice to meet you," I said, holding out my hand. She shook it with a frail grip. Esther was one of the human servants who had hooked up with vampires in hopes that they would turn her. She was dying. Which also explained why she looked so miserable—if her vampire had died, she was out of luck. "Tell me what's happening."

"I'm a—well, I don't know what you call it, but I sort of help out a, a vampire?"

A human servant. With the habit of ending every sentence with a question mark. This was just what my day had been missing. "What can I do for you, Esther?"

Her voice broke. "Well, he's—he's dead? I mean, he's *really* dead. I just came over and he was here and I didn't know that they even *left* bodies; I thought they went to dust or something—"

She kept rambling, so I broke in, trying to sound soothing. "It depends on the vampire, Esther. When they're killed the magic leaves them, the years catch up with them, and their bodies revert to where they should be. So very old vampires do turn into dust, just like in the movies. But new vampires may just look like a slightly rotted dead body, and so on."

When she answered her voice was very small. "I didn't know that."

"Can you take me to the body?" I said gently.

"Oh. Right. This way." I followed her into the cottage, which was barely furnished at all: a couple of folding chairs and a cheap TV in the living room, a card table in the kitchen. There was no refrigerator, no signs of food. "I don't eat much," she said, catching my look. "He's—the body is down here."

She opened a door in the kitchen, revealing a set of wooden stairs. A basement. Great. Vampires have a talent for finding the few houses in LA that actually have basements. *It doesn't necessarily mean this is a trap*, I told myself. I certainly didn't feel anything Old World in my radius. But I motioned for Esther to go first.

The downstairs was the opposite of the first floor: wall-to-wall carpeting, gorgeously framed art prints on the walls, a flat-screen TV, couches. Everything was well kept but comfortable looking: someone spent time here. Esther continued toward the back wall, where another door led to a tiny bedroom. I could see the dead body lying in the doorway. "That's him," she said unnecessarily.

The body had a sort of mummified look: most of the flesh had wasted away, but a few tendrils of hair and skin still clung to the skeleton—male, judging by the clothes. He was wearing a simple button-down men's shirt and dark slacks that weren't new but still contrasted heavily with the decrepit skeleton. He'd also been wearing black loafers, but they'd fallen off when his body shriveled up and were lying on the floor near his feet. In the middle of his chest, a gaping hole had ruined the nice line of the shirt. I looked closely and saw the little wood splinters. He'd been staked. Vampires die when their heads are detached from their bodies, or when their hearts are destroyed, or by fire. You don't technically need a wooden stake to destroy a heart; that's just something that worked well in the Middle Ages. We have better weapons now, but the stake is a classic, and a lot of people believe that its long history makes it more powerful.

I looked around, but didn't see anything stake shaped. I didn't really smell him, just the faintest whiff of old decay. The vampire had been a vampire for a couple of years, at least. I was pretty confident now that this wasn't a trap, but I was still glad when Esther hovered near the stairs, staying in my line of vision. I dropped my oversize duffel bag of supplies and crouched down, balancing on my heels as I pulled out a thick, disposable plastic body bag and my surgical gloves. "You found him like this?" I asked. "You didn't pull the stake out?" Vampires don't die very often in LA, and when they do, Dashiell has to know about it. If it had been after sunset I would have called him immediately after my first conversation with Esther, but since he'd be unavailable for a few more hours I'd have to remember all the details myself and fill him in later that night.

"No, I think she took it with her."

"She?" I said. "Do you know who did this?" Excellent. I could simply tell Dashiell and be done with the matter.

Esther nodded, biting her lip. "I think so. I think it was his... friend. She's a vampire too, but she gives me the creeps." She shuddered and wrapped her stick arms around herself.

"Know anything else about her?" I asked, mostly focused on spreading the body bag out next to the corpse.

"Just her name. He introduced her as Olivia."

Chapter 20

Olivia's name hit me like a slap, and I lost my balance, toppling over onto the carpet. Fully seated on the floor, I stared at Esther, and then back at the desiccated corpse. The shape was right, but just in case, I asked her for the vampire's name.

"Albert," she whispered. "His name was Albert."

So Olivia had killed her accomplice. One of her accomplices. I had no idea what to say next, and I suddenly couldn't stand being in the same room as the corpse. "Can we go up to the kitchen and talk for a second?"

Shrugging and biting at a fingernail, she led me back up the stairs. I sat down at the card table and nodded toward the other chair. Esther sat.

"How did you find me?" I began. "How did you know where I'd be?"

"I didn't. But Albert gave me your phone number in case of emergencies. He said if something happened to him, I should call you."

That seemed odd. Jesse had said that Albert was off the grid, on the run from Dashiell. Why would Albert direct Esther to call me, one of Dashiell's employees? Unless..."Did Albert suspect something might happen?"

Esther hesitated, thinking it over. "I think...I think he loved Olivia? For whatever reason. But he didn't really trust her."

"Okay. Who owns this house?"

"Albert did. It wasn't in his name, though. He said it used to be one of his former human servants?"

"And why do you think Olivia was the one who killed him?"

Her shoulders hunched. "It just seems like something she would do."

Couldn't argue with that. "Did they both live here? Albert and Olivia."

"Sort of. Albert lived here all the time, in that room where his"—she winced—"his body is. Olivia has a room here, but she used to come and go when she wanted. When she was here, I tried to be somewhere else."

"How come?"

"Like I said, she gave me the creeps. Albert and I, we weren't, like, romantic, you know?" She seemed to be waiting for a response on that, so I nodded. "It was more of a business thing. But one time he let her feed off me, and she was...not gentle. And now Albert's gone, and he promised to turn me before..." She swallowed hard, seeming to struggle with it. I could see her eyes filling. "Before I die." Esther was crying openly now. "What am I gonna do?"

Awkward. I felt sorry for these people, the vampire hangers-on who just wanted to be able to live, on whatever terms necessary. Who knows, maybe I'd have more sympathy if I were the one dying. But you shouldn't become a vampire out of fear of death. If anyone should become a vampire at all, it should be because that's what you want to be. I felt like I should tell her I was sorry or ask how much time she had left or something, but I'm not good at that kind of thing. Besides, I had bigger fish at the moment. "Can you show me her room?"

"It's in the basement too," she sniffled. "But it's locked."

"Is she *in there* now?" This stupidly hadn't even occurred to me. What if I was in the same house as Olivia? A flood of emotions ran through me: fear that she would get me, relief that she might have been found, and, of course, the urge to run away very quickly.

But Esther shook her head. "The lock is one of those heavy detachable ones, and it's on the outside. She can't be in there."

I looked out the window, reassuring myself that the sun was very much out. Then I told Esther she could stay where she was and descended back into the basement. In the main living room, I turned in a circle until I spotted the skinny door against the back wall. The door and the handle had both been painted the same white as the sheetrock around it, which would have been pretty good camouflage if it weren't for the heavy silver padlock dangling from the doorframe. I approached it cautiously, paying close attention to the edges of my radius, just in case. If Olivia was in there, she was currently dead, but proximity to me would bring her to life, and she was still plenty dangerous as a human. By the time I got to the door, though, I was satisfied that unless the room turned into a huge tunnel, there was nothing Old World inside.

Behind me, I heard Esther climbing partway down the stairs, where she sat down to watch. I ignored her and looked at the padlock. It was shaped like the kind you see at the gym, but three times the size, and I didn't think even my heavy-duty bolt cutters could gnaw through it. I went back to my bag of tools and pulled out a simple flat-head screwdriver. There was no way I was getting that padlock off without a blowtorch, but the two metal loops that it locked together were another story: they were just screwed into the door and the doorframe with ordinary screws. Rookie mistake. I could have taken the time to take out all the screws, but instead I poked the screwdriver into the U of the bolt and levered it back. I put my weight into it, and was finally rewarded with a splintering snap as the whole setup came fumbling into my stomach. "Hey," Esther protested, but her voice was even weaker than it had been. I dropped the padlock onto the floor and pulled the door open.

Dark. Lots of dark. I felt around both sides of the wall but couldn't find a switch. Trying not to think about what else I might find, I flailed my hand into the air a few steps into the room. Esther probably thought this looked hilarious. Finally, my fingers closed around a thin piece of string. I tugged.

There are some who might say that I screamed, but I maintain that it was more of a womanly bellow. Esther shrieked behind me. I jumped back a few feet, and when I finally got my breath, I stepped back in, letting my eyes adjust to the dim light and to the shock.

Every inch of every wall in the low-ceilinged room was covered in photos of me.

There were a few older shots—me in my high school graduation robe, a couple of shots of me running on a track. I'd only been on the cross-country team my junior year of high school, which was probably about when Olivia had found me. But most of the pictures were from the time of Olivia's death onward. Me at the grocery store, me at a bookstore, me lying on the beach with a hat over my eyes. There was even a whole series taken through the windows of Molly's house: me watching TV, making supper, napping on the couch with a spilled water glass on the floor next to me. I winced. No moment of my life was too mundane or too private for her to capture.

"They're all of you."

The voice was only a few inches behind me, and I jumped, half expecting to hit my head on the ceiling like a Looney Tunes character. "Jesus, Esther, don't do that." I turned around, and that's when I saw the back wall of the room. This one wasn't covered in pictures. There were just four big eight by tens, hung neatly, two on each side of the door. Each shot was of the person walking on the street, completely oblivious. Molly was captured at night, talking on her cell phone and throwing her head back to laugh. My brother Jack was walking with a slice of pizza in his hands. He was wearing his scrubs and an anxious look on his face, like he had to get back to work. Jesse was leaning against an unmarked car, reading from a file and chewing on his lip. Eli was wheeling a dolly stacked with boxes into Hair of the Dog.

You will not cry, I told myself. *You will not run screaming. You will not stop breathing.* I had gotten used to the idea of Olivia being obsessed with me, and while all those shots of me were creepy, they almost had an inevitability to them. But the pictures by the door were different. She had pinpointed the four people I cared about most. Had she left those out so I would know she was coming for them? I pulled my phone out of my jacket pocket and stared at it stupidly, as if I didn't know what it was.

"I think I'm gonna go," Esther said behind me. "Um, good luck with everything." There were footsteps, and then a heavy silence behind me. Smart girl, that Esther.

I don't know how long I sat there, staring at my phone, watching it tremble in my shaking hands. Eventually, I was able to dial.

Eli got there first, as planned. I had closed the door to the Scarlett room and was sitting outside on the front steps. Hugging my knees again. He got out of the truck in a hurry, then slowed down when he saw me. I didn't say anything as he crouched into my eyeline. He was wearing jeans and a dark-red T-shirt with Hair of the Dog embroidered on the left breast.

"I'm sorry, I didn't mean to make you leave work," I said woodenly.

"It's fine. Will's there today. There was a fight last night, but I finished cleaning up half an hour ago." Eli had that barely contained look he gets when he wants to touch me. I kept my eyes on the sidewalk. I had forgotten all about the other crime scene.

"The stairs are in the kitchen. The body's at the bottom of the stairs, straight ahead. You need to get it out of there as fast as you can, because Jesse is on his way. He can't see it." My voice sounded dead even to me.

"Okay..." he said cautiously. "Are we switching vehicles? I can pick up the truck later." He held out his keys expectantly.

"No. You'll have to put the body in your truck. It should be light. Squish it down in front of the passenger seat. Whatever. I don't care."

He stood there for a moment, hesitating. I didn't bother explaining that I didn't have the White Whale with me. "Just *do it*, Eli," I snapped. I didn't look up again.

He disappeared from my vision, and I heard him step into the house. I didn't move. After a while he came out carrying a surprisingly small plastic garbage bag, which presumably held the disposable body bag I'd left down there earlier. He loaded it in his truck without a word, but then came back to squat in front of me again. "It's done," he said quietly. "Scarlett, what is it?"

"You should go," I said. "Jesse will be here."

I thought he flinched when I mentioned Jesse, which gave me an idea. "We're going to handle the case together," I said. "I don't need you." He stood up, staring down at me, looking confused. "Jesse and I will be together," I repeated. "Just stay away." I flicked my eyes down so I didn't have so see his reaction.

Eli disappeared from my line of sight, and a moment later I heard his truck start up. I didn't move.

It took Jesse another fifteen minutes to get there. He had probably had to drop Kirsten off at his parents' house. He pulled up in his personal car, a navy Corolla, and came straight up to the steps, standing in front of me. "I checked the records," he said. "The place is owned by a woman named LuEllen Schaub. She was found dead in a hotel room last year. No heirs, and the courts haven't gotten around to figuring out what to do with this place."

"The stairs are in the kitchen," I repeated. I felt like the animatronic guardian of a theme park ride. "Take a hard left at the bottom of the stairs. Skinny door painted to match the wall around it."

Jesse paused, confused, but just shrugged and went into the house. He was in there for a long time. When he came back, he sat down on the stairs next to me, looking out at the neighborhood. It was midafternoon, and we watched a school bus deposit a dozen kids at a corner across the street. Their parents divided up the herd and split off in different directions. Jesse started to speak, but then he shook his head and remained silent. Finally, he said, "I think we should just stick together from here on out. This learning things separately business is obnoxious."

I didn't smile. After a few seconds, I felt Jesse staring at me, and finally looked over.

"What?"

"Olivia is not your fault, you know," he said.

"I know."

"No, you really don't seem to."

"Thanks, Robin Williams. I appreciate the after-school-special moment, but we both know that if I wasn't around Olivia wouldn't be on the rampage. Maybe it's not my *fault*, exactly, but I'm still the cause."

"We don't know for sure what her agenda is," he argued.

"You saw the pictures by the door?" I asked. He nodded. "She knows about you. She's gonna come after all of you. It's the same thing she did before; the exact same thing. Take away the people close to me. Take me."

"You really think that's her plan?" he asked, turning his body to study my face.

I nodded. "It makes sense. She's not just an asshole; she's completely boring. She's the Elmer Fudd of trying to kill me." I fought to keep my head from sinking onto my chest. I was so tired. In every possible way.

His voice was so dangerously soft that I barely heard it. "You're not still thinking it'd be best to give yourself up?"

I managed to raise my head and look over at him. Jesse was watching me with his guarded cop face, but there was tension in his jaw and shoulders. "Um, I was threatened very specifically to think no such thing."

"Just spit it out, Scarlett."

"Fine." I made a point to focus on the road in front of us. The kids had cleared away now, and it seemed surprisingly deserted. "I'm not a nutcase; I do have a reasonable line of thinking. She hasn't taken a run at me yet, right?"

"Right."

"And I haven't exactly been hiding. I think she's saving me for last, which means she's going to do something else before she gets to me. Based on that room down there, I'd put good money on her trying to kill someone I love. If I surrender, I could cut out the middle part, the part where people I love die. Tell me you wouldn't do the same thing, Detective."

"That's different. I took an oath to protect and serve, and if I could exchange my life for a citizen's, I would. But I can't just walk up to a gang leader and say, here, kill me so you can stop killing all these other people."

"Why not?"

He made a frustrated sound. "Because who's to guarantee that they really will stop? Not me, because I'd be dead. And because... you don't just let the bad guy win."

"You're being theoretical. I'm being realistic. Olivia isn't a gang leader, she's a crazy evil vampire with a metaphorical hard-on for me. Besides, who's to say I'm not one of the bad guys too?"

"I do."

I snorted. "No, you just don't want me to be. It's not the same thing."

"Just stop it," he snapped. "Stop talking about killing your-self—no, letting yourself die, which is even worse because it requires nothing of you—in this reasonable tone, like it's no big deal. It's a big fucking deal, Scarlett. And this everyone would be better off without me bullshit is tired."

You will not cry. You will not *cry.* I started to shake with the effort, and he put his arm around me. "I'll be fine, Scarlett," he said softly. "We all will." He smelled like Giorgio Armani aftershave and orange peel. We sat there like that for a long time, my thoughts drifting around like butterflies in a fog bank. I felt the house behind me like a presence, as though Olivia had marked it as her territory and some part of her had actually seeped into the walls. Jesse's warm arm around my shoulders seemed like the only thing keeping it from swallowing me.

Finally, I sat upright and pushed loose strands of hair behind my ears. I turned to face him. He looked troubled. "I know you're worried about me," I said. "I know you don't want to leave me. But there's something else I have to do, and I can't have you with me to do it. Do you understand?"

I could tell by his face that he was going to argue, so I cut him off before he got the chance. "I swear, Jesse, you can be around me every second if you want to, but there's something I have to do first. I'm asking you to trust me. I need you to trust me."

He searched my face for a long moment and sighed. "It's three o'clock now. The sun sets around five. If I pick you up at four thirty, will that give you enough time?"

"Six."

"Scarlett—"

"I'm not going to be home; she won't be able to find me. And I need the sunset. *Please*, Jesse."

The "please" did it. "Okay, okay," he said reluctantly. "What about that?" he asked, nodding back toward the little cottage. "What do you want to do?"

"I'll take care of it."

"I could help you—"

"*I will take care of it.*"

He looked at me for a long moment, and I saw him understand. Then I saw him resign himself. "There's something else you need to know," he said. He told me about Kirsten's party and what they wanted me to do.

"The party's at seven," he finished. "Can you do it?"

I was beyond decision making, so I just nodded. I ignored the deeply concerned expression on his face. He looked like he wanted to say something else, but after a moment of hesitation he just stood up.

"I'll pick you up at six," he said, and left.

I waited until the Corolla had turned the corner, and then I counted to a hundred. I got a few things from the toolbox in the back of Will's truck and headed back into the basement.

Then I burned the goddamned house down.

Chapter 21

"Molly. Molly!" I shook her shoulder gently. Then a little harder. Finally, her eyes opened.

"Whaaat?" she said irritably.

"Wake up. I need you."

She looked at me for the first time and sat up, swinging her long legs over the side of the bed. She wore pink flannel boxer shorts and a Hello Kitty shirt, with Hello Kitty dressed as a goth punk. Vampire or not, her blonde hair seemed to rumple adorably. "What happened?"

As quickly as I could, I told her about the house in Silver Lake—the photos of me, the pictures of her, Eli, Jesse, and my brother.

"You have a brother?" she asked incredulously.

I sighed. Whoops. Molly was a decent friend to me, but anything I did or said could easily end up getting back to Dashiell, so I'd never told her about Jack. But that horse was already out of the barn—Dashiell had given Jack a job specifically to remind me that he could fuck with my last remaining family member anytime he wanted to—and I had bigger problems right now, anyway. "Yes. We're not really...close. But I need your help with something. I'll explain on the way." I hopped off the bed and turned toward the door.

"Uh, can I get dressed first?"

"Oh. Right." I turned to face the wall, which made Molly giggle, as usual, while she donned jeans and a long-sleeved thermal shirt that read *Spanky's House of Pain. How may we hurt you?* I chose not to comment.

I hadn't talked to Jack since Thanksgiving, when we'd gone out to dinner at the Stinking Rose, a garlic-lovers' restaurant on La Cienega. (No, it wasn't a big anti-vampire statement or anything. I just really like garlic. And restaurants that are open on Thanksgiving.) Things were weird between us: Jack didn't know that our parents had been murdered because of me. I always cringed with guilt when I saw him, which made him think he was doing something wrong, which usually just snowballed into awkwardness and stammering. But we'd managed to pull it together for one night, at least. We'd avoided talking about Thanksgivings past, sticking to his job, movies, and current events. For once, things between us were actually kind of okay.

And now I was about to ruin it.

Jack lived in the Valley, in one-half of a tiny duplex on the outskirts of Sherman Oaks. I knocked on his door at 5:00 p.m. on the dot, praying that he'd be home. There was a wreath hanging at eye level, and while I waited for him to answer I leaned forward to smell it. The fresh scent of pine needles hit my nose and traveled straight to wherever my memories are kept. He'd gotten a real wreath with a red velvet bow, just like our mother always had. If they didn't wither away at the end of every winter, I could swear that this was the same one.

Get it together, Scarlett.

My brother is a few inches taller than I am—five eleven, with our father's dark-red hair. Unlike our dad, though, Jack keeps it buzzed close to his head. He has my green eyes, a narrow build, and the snow-white complexion that comes from being inside all day. If he's not working full-time for Dashiell's hematology laboratory, he's taking med school classes at night. When the door popped open with a weather-stripping hiss, he was wearing sweatpants, a Chicago Bears T-shirt (our dad had been a fan), and a dish towel over one shoulder. "Hey, Scarbo," he said with some surprise. In the three months Jack had lived in LA, I had never initiated contact. "Um, who's your pretty friend?"

"Jack, this is Molly. Molly, this is my big brother, Jack."

He suddenly noticed the dish towel on his chest and snatched it down, blushing. After wiping his hands, he held one out to Molly. "You must be Scarlett's roommate. She's told me a lot about you."

Molly shook, arching an eyebrow at me. "Really? Wish I could say the same."

I ignored her. "Can we come in for a minute?"

"Of course." He stepped back, ushering us into the dining room. He didn't comment on Molly's shirt. Good for him.

I took the seat nearest the window and pulled the shades down. Jack gave me a funny look but didn't ask. "I was just finishing the dishes. I gotta be back on campus for study group at seven, so dinner was early tonight."

"You look tired," I said, seeing dark circles under his eyes.

"I was at the premed library all last night," he explained. "Trying to finish up some stuff for the holidays."

"About that, Jack," I began. "I have this problem."

"What can I do?" he said, instantly concerned. I almost rolled my eyes. Everywhere I went, I seemed to trip over protective men.

"Well, I'd actually love it if you took a little trip. To visit Mom's cousin Rhys in Scotland. He's lonely, and really wants to meet up with some family. For the holidays."

"Mom didn't have any cousins," he said, looking confused. "Besides, I thought we were gonna get together for Christmas."

"It might be second cousin, I'm not sure. But you can have Christmas with him," I said, too brightly. Rhys is one of the other five nulls that I know about in the world. He lives in Scotland (there's a theory that evolution has spread the nulls out deliberately to give us maximum effect, but that's another story), and though we'd barely spoken in the past, when I called to explain that Jack was in danger he'd agreed to do this for me. I'd tried to talk him into taking Molly too, but he'd refused to host a vampire over the holidays. Which was kind of okay, since Jack's last-minute international ticket cost almost every penny in my already pathetic savings account.

"Scarbo," Jack said, glancing at Molly, who remained quiet. She was waiting for a cue from me. "I can't just do that. I have study group, and work—"

"I already cleared it with Dashiell," I said. That was technically a lie, but I was certain that once Dashiell woke for the night, he'd okay it. Mostly certain. Okay, I was just hoping. "He's giving you all the time you need."

"But what about you?" Jack protested. "You can't be alone on Christmas!"

"I've been alone on Christmas before," I reminded him gently. This was a cheap shot. The year after our parents died, Jack was still so grief stricken that he couldn't stand to be around me. Of course, I was too guilt stricken to be around him, so it kind of worked out.

"Which is exactly why I shouldn't leave," he said promptly.

Backfire. "Look, he already sent you a ticket, for tonight," I said, handing it over with a weak little flourish. "It's nonrefundable. It would be awful if Rhys wasted all that money."

But Jack didn't even look at the ticket. He was looking straight at me. "Don't use Mom guilt on me, Scarbo. What's going on?" he said. "Why are you so anxious to get rid of me? Are you and I... not okay?"

Shit, shit, shit. I checked my watch: 5:10. It was rush hour in LA, and I had less than an hour before Jesse would come for me. If I wasn't there, he'd probably swear out an arrest warrant. I sighed and made eye contact with Molly. "I need to use the restroom." She nodded at me.

"Uh, okay…" Jack said, confusion still in his voice.

I got up and trudged toward the hallway. When I felt Molly leave my radius, I went a few steps farther and turned to watch them, keeping tight against the wall. Guilt folded my stomach in on itself. Molly was smiling at Jack, her face suddenly radiant, her hair brighter. Even her clothes seemed to perk up when she became vampire. She reached across the table and took Jack's hand, forcing eye contact. I couldn't see his face from that angle, but he didn't pull away.

"Jack," Molly began, still smiling. "You're going to go to Scotland for Christmas."

"Yes."

Molly didn't seem to be doing anything special, at least not from where I was, but I'd never heard Jack's voice so empty of life. Tears spilled down my cheeks, but I couldn't look away. I had caused this. I owed it to Jack not to hide from it.

"You're excited to see Rhys, who is your mother's favorite cousin."

"Yes."

"You're grateful to Scarlett for setting all this up, as a Christmas present."

"Yes."

"You're not at all suspicious or worried about the trip. Are you?"

"No."

With one last smile, Molly let go of his hand and looked over to me. She nodded. I brushed tears away with my sleeves and went back to my spot near the window. Molly readjusted to mortality.

"Hey, Scarbo," Jack said cheerfully. "Thank you, again, for setting all this up. This is the coolest Christmas present ever!"

"No problem," I said, trying to keep my voice even.

"Oh, hey, since I'll be gone next week, let me go grab your present," he said, racing off toward the bedroom.

I felt Molly's eyes on me, but I couldn't look at her. "I just did what you asked," she said quietly.

"I know. Thank you." I heard her sigh. "What about you, Molls?"

"Me? I'll be just fine."

"I'm so sorry."

"Don't start with me, Scarlett."

"This is the second time this year you've had to leave town because of who I am."

"Oh, please. The self-blaming thing is boring. Besides, I'll be having a great time. I'm going—"

"Don't tell me where you're going," I said, too sharply.

"Right." She didn't falter. "Just do me a favor and kill that disgraceful bitch. For all of us."

When we left Jack's, I was wearing his present—a deep-green scarf, chosen to set off my eyes ("I just asked the saleslady to match it to mine," Jack had said, blushing again)—and Jack was calling a cab to take him to the airport. I would have liked to march him right up to the security screening—hell, I wanted to close the door of the plane myself—but he promised to text when he had boarded, which would have to be good enough. I broke about twelve traffic regulations on the way home and made it to the house at 5:57. Molly made for the staircase, up to her room to pack. After a moment of thought, I went up after her and knocked on her doorframe.

"Hey, Molls, can you do one more thing for me?"

She looked up from an expensive-looking leather duffel bag. "What's that?"

"Can you call Dashiell, fill him in on Olivia and the party tonight? Just so he's updated?" Kirsten would never let vampires actually attend the party, but he'd want to know what we were doing.

A smile spread across her face. "Already done."

Sometimes it can be useful, living with a spy.

Without really thinking, I stepped forward into her room and wrapped my arms around her slender frame. "Thanks," I said into her hair.

Surprised, she hugged me back. "You're welcome."

We managed to avoid the whole when-to-pull-away issue, because the doorbell rang. I trotted down the stairs. Remembering my idiocy from the day before, I focused on my radius for a moment before opening it, but there was nothing Old World nearby. I checked the peephole anyway, and then let Jesse inside.

"Oh, good, you're ready to go," he said, eyeing my jacket and scarf. I did the classic look-down-at-what-you're-wearing double take. "Uh...I guess so," I said doubtfully. Then I saw a smear of ash on my jeans leg. "Wait, just a second."

I trotted up the stairs, hearing Molly exchange a few pleasantries with Jesse as I went, and burst into the room. What do you wear to a witch's party? Not red or green, because it wasn't Christmas oriented, and probably not a dress, in case I had to run toward or away from something. Someone. I pushed the thought aside and tried to focus on the problem at hand. Clothes, I reminded myself. The problem at hand was clothes.

After Olivia died I had mercilessly thrown out all of the clothes she'd bought me, all those brand-name dresses from Nordstrom and the fancy heels she'd taught me to walk in. I wasn't anyone's fucking puppet anymore. But that meant my wardrobe pretty much consisted of what I'd worn in high school, a supplement of jeans and T-shirts I'd chosen for comfort, and whatever Molly had forced me to buy via her famous excessive-whining torture method. I finally settled on clean jeans, silver flats, and a lightweight black V-neck sweater. Witches always appreciate black, right?

"Scar?" There was a light knock on my door.

"Come in."

The door swung open and Jesse shuffled a few steps into the room with his hands covering his eyes. "You decent?"

I laughed. On our last case, he'd accidentally walked in on me while I was close to naked. "Yeah, I guess." He took his hands down and gave me a warm smile. *Don't blush, Scarlett,* I told myself sternly. *You're better than that.* But the awkward silence unnerved me, and finally I looked down at what I was wearing. "What? You think it's wrong?"

"No, I think you look great," he said earnestly. "Do you ever wear your hair down?"

I stuck out my tongue and blew a raspberry at him. "What is this, a teen comedy in the nineties? If I just take off my glasses and take out my ponytail, I'll be instantly pretty?"

"You don't wear glasses, and you're already pretty," he said matter-of-factly. Then his voice softened. "You're beautiful."

I flinched. I never had learned how to take a compliment. Impatient, I turned back to my mirror and jerked the ponytail holder out of my hair. "Yeah, well, so's your girlfriend," I snapped. I reached up and braided my hair upside down, twisting the pony-tail holder onto the end and letting the long braid settle down my back. "Happy?" I asked, turning back to him.

But Jesse's face had stiffened. "I have something for you," he said. He picked up a large paper bag from the hallway floor and thrust it toward me.

I immediately felt like an ass. Why couldn't I ever say the right thing, just once? I reached into the bag and pulled out...a small, black bulletproof vest. "Uh...you shouldn't have...?" I said uncertainly.

"There's more."

I peeked into the bag and saw a black leather cup with a snap-ping lid, the size of my two hands. "What is it?" I asked, pulling the thing out. Jesse didn't answer, but I figured it out myself. I looked up to meet his face. "Jesse, this is for a gun," I said stu-pidly. "This is a holster for a *gun*."

"I know." He reached around his back and pulled out a small chunk of black metal. "It's the same model we used at the shooting range," he said. "I think you should take it along tonight."

I dropped the holster on the floor and backed away, as though it had burned my fingers. "No way. I am not carrying that. Put it away."

"Scarlett..." He sighed. "Look, sending you into that party was my idea, okay? And Kirsten won't let me come in and keep an eye on you. I'll be all the way out in the car, by the street. Just do this for me, okay? I'll feel better if I know you can defend yourself."

"*No*," I said. "No guns."

"Scarlett—"

I shook my head. "*No guns.*"

He tried a few more arguments, but I just shook my head and waited him out. Finally he threw up his hands. "At least tell me why not," he said, frustration all over his face.

I swallowed and tried to figure out what the hell to tell him. I didn't actually disagree with anything Jesse had said. Being armed seemed perfectly logical when you were going up against a vampire who'd been crazy before she'd turned undead. But still..."Look, Jesse," I began. "What I do for a living—and what I just *am*— it's all about undoing damage." I held up a hand, warding off his next words. "I know, I know, you think erasing crime scenes is *causing* damage. But that's just not how I see it. I undo things that were done in violence, whether it's cleaning a crime scene or humanizing a werewolf or vampire. But guns...what they do is forever. There's no unshooting someone. And accidents happen, and I might miss, and it's just so permanent." I took a deep breath. "So shut the hell up about the gun, okay?"

I met his eyes for a long, searching moment, and something in my stomach turned over. Finally he relaxed, sighing. "Would you at least wear the vest?" he asked.

I smiled. "Fine. But I've got to change again."

It took a while to find a top with a high enough collar, but when we finally left Molly's I was wearing the vest under a purple crewneck sweater Molly had reluctantly lent me. After a moment's thought, I'd discarded the flats in favor of my knee-high leather boots, which were reasonably noncasual, but better for running or getting dirty. I couldn't wear my beloved coat-o'-nine-pockets over the whole situation, which meant I had to leave my Taser at home. That was somewhat deflating, but at least I was bringing along my very own armed police escort.

At any rate, I figured I had better not get shot, because vest or no vest, if I got bullet holes in her cashmere sweater Molly would probably just finish me off. Or I could ask Jesse to shoot me as a mercy kill. Either way.

Chapter 22

Kirsten's house in Sherman Oaks isn't a mansion the way Dashiell's is, but it's big and perfectly kept: expansive manicured lawn, beautiful landscaping, white picket fence that's really only decorative. The whole neighborhood is like that, and in my darker moments I've wondered if it's a witchcraft thing: Could she be using magic to keep her street planted firmly in perfect fifties suburbia? Probably not...right?

I didn't want to miss anyone who came and left early, so we arrived half an hour before the party was supposed to start. Jesse found a good parking spot on the street where he could see Kirsten's front door without being completely obvious about it.

"You've got your phone? Battery charged?" he asked before I stepped out.

I rolled my eyes. "Yes, Mom. Cab fare too, in case my date drinks too much."

He shrugged unapologetically. "Are you sure you don't want to take the gun?"

"No. No way."

Jesse nodded, resigned, and reached over to squeeze my hand. "Good luck. I'll be right out here."

I got out of the car and walked briskly up to the front porch, wiggling a little at the itchy bulletproof vest. *Damn, I should have put a tank top on under it instead of just a sports bra*, I thought, but it was way too late to go back. It was a cool night, but between the vest and the sweater I was comfortable.

Kirsten's front door was framed by a decorative pillar on one side and a porch swing on the other. As I walked up I winced when I saw the swing—Eli and I had once had kind of a moment there. I was so distracted by the memory that I completely missed the witch sitting placidly behind the decorative pillar. I didn't even feel him enter my radius.

"Uh, boo?"

The voice had been quiet and mild, but I was still so startled I almost fell off the porch steps. When I spun to face him, the witch stood up, grinning at me. He was a balding man in his late forties with a small paunch under his sweater-vest and slacks and one of those affable, saggy faces that was not handsome but instantly likable. "Hi," I said, clutching my chest and trying to still my breathing. "You scared me."

"Sorry about that. I'm Kevin." He looked like a Kevin. "You must be Scarlett." He held out a hand, and I shook it without thinking. I gave him a friendly smile and concentrated on my radius. He was a low-level witch, not particularly powerful. I suddenly felt a spark of magic come from him, and I let go of his hand, raising my eyebrows. He grinned again.

"You felt that, huh?" he said sheepishly. "Sorry, I was just trying a simple wind spell. I've never met a null before."

"Well, I've never met a male witch before," I said without thinking. "So we're even."

His head bobbed up and down. "We're a rare breed, aren't we? There are only a handful in Kirsten's organization."

"You're on bouncer duty tonight?" Either that or he had a serious thing for scaring the shit out of people.

"Yup. I do it every year."

"Is that…" I hesitated. I had learned a lot about the mechanics of witchcraft in the last couple of days, but I still didn't know the social conventions. Asking a werewolf how they were changed was a really personal question. Was asking a witch about their talents the same? *Screw it*, I decided. I wasn't here to make friends. "Is that part of your specialty?"

His cheerful expression didn't waver a bit. "You bet. I can sense intentions. Nothing specific, just whether or not people are hoping to have a good time, planning some trouble, dreading the whole party. That kind of thing."

He has so little power, though, I thought, but I managed not to say that aloud. "Couldn't another witch just...cast a spell to hide their plans from you?"

Kevin shrugged. "Sure. But it's better than nothing, right?"

"What are you supposed to do if someone has bad intentions?"

His smile dropped off his face for the first time since "Boo." "Call Kirsten. Or call the police directly, depending on how bad it is."

I thought that over for a second, and then pulled out my cell phone. "Let me give you my number too. I can be here quickly, and I can stop the magic, at least. What's your phone number?" He told me, and I called his cell, letting it ring just long enough for me to hear it buzz in his pocket. He agreed to call if someone scary showed up, and I turned back to the front door.

Before I went in, though, I paused and turned back to Kevin. "Does everyone know I'm coming?"

"Nope." A man of few words, was Kevin.

"Can you keep it to yourself?" He hesitated, shifting his weight uneasily, and I waved a hand. "Don't worry, I'll ask Kirsten to come tell you the same thing."

Kevin bobbed his head again, looking relieved, and I went inside.

My jaw dropped open at the threshold. The front door opened into a typical entryway: stairs straight ahead, a living room on the right, hallway to the bathroom, and kitchen on the left. And every single surface was covered in candy. Enormous candies made from foam or plastic hung from the walls and ceiling. Big, brown ginger-bread-men cutouts were attached to the walls, looking like they'd step forward at any second and challenge me to a footrace. Every table had at least one bowl of brightly colored M&M's or Skittles on it. I looked down at my feet. I was standing on a bright-green plastic square. It was part of a long path of colored squares that led off to both my right and left.

I felt a familiar buzz of serious power as Kirsten appeared from the hallway. She was dressed in a long, white-and-ice-blue strapless gown and had put some sort of blue rinse or dye through her light-blonde hair, which hung loose on her shoulders. A light-blue plastic crown perched on top of her head, completing the look. She smiled at my confused expression.

"There are so many religious and spiritual beliefs and customs tied to the solstice, and I don't want any fighting. So every year I pick a random, secular theme for the party." She gestured at the decorations. "Do you get it?"

For a very brief moment, I pictured the witch from Hansel and Gretel, the one with the house made out of candy. But no, Kirsten wouldn't be that crass. "Um...diabetic shock?"

Kirsten chuckled. "Nope. Welcome to Candy Land."

I looked around again. "*Ohhhhh.*" That explained the plastic squares. I took another look at Kirsten too. It had been a long time since I'd played Candy Land, but there was one character card that I'd always hoped to get, just because she was so pretty. "You're Queen Frostine."

Kirsten curtsied, which would have looked ridiculous on me, but she made it look kind of regal. "You did all this with six hours' notice?" I asked incredulously.

She straightened, shrugging modestly. "I had all the supplies already, and some of my witches came to help." She pointed to the hallway. "They're still here, setting up in the kitchen. Let me show you where I think you should hang out."

I asked her to talk to Kevin first, and she nodded, grabbed a handful of candy from a nearby dish, and popped out to the front porch. She returned a second later with empty hands. "He understands. He won't mention you." She frowned as she started down the hallway. I followed. "I suppose someone at the party could text their friends who aren't here yet, and one of those friends could be Olivia's partner. But I find it hard to believe the conspiracy is that big."

I shrugged. "There's also the thing where none of us had any better ideas."

"Yes, there's that."

I followed Kirsten down the hall, past a small den with a fireplace, and through the dining room. I felt a couple of low-intensity hits on my radius as we passed the kitchen. Nothing to worry about there. Whatever the witches were making did smell wonderful, though: sort of like cupcakes and almonds.

Finally, Kirsten stopped at a patio door that opened onto a sunken sunroom. The space had been done up like Queen Frostine's kingdom: rolls of white cotton hung over tables, bearing an uncanny resemblance to snow. Paper snowflakes dangled from the ceiling, and tufts of silver garland, like the kind you put on Christmas trees, dangled from a slow-moving ceiling fan. It was beautiful.

"We usually gather in here to talk," Kirsten explained. She pointed toward a sofa that had been covered in a white sheet with blue embroidery. "If you hang out there, everyone who comes down the stairs into the room should pretty much pop into your radius, I think."

"Let's try it."

We did a bit of experimenting with Kirsten coming in and out of the doorway, and ended up moving the sofa six inches farther into the room. When she was satisfied, Kirsten nodded to herself and moved back toward the doorway. "I need to get back to hostessing duties, but I'll try to make sure everyone heads in here at some point. Usually people like to see all the decorations, so it shouldn't be a problem."

"Are you keeping track of who doesn't show up?" I asked. Kirsten nodded. "Okay, then."

She vanished back into the kitchen, and I plopped down on the couch, wishing I had a magazine or something. Now that I was here, this plan was beginning to feel rather stupid. Yes, I could tell how powerful witches were, especially with Kirsten around as a litmus test. But we were counting on an awful lot of luck too: that the right witch would show up, that she wouldn't hear about me being here, that she'd come close enough. On the other hand, there were only a few more hours until midnight. We were fresh out of better ideas.

People began trickling in, carrying appetizer plates and chattering. Kirsten was right—just about everyone came into the sunroom to admire the decorations. Most of them were women, but a few of the women had brought their husbands along. Some of the guests were dressed fairly casually in street clothes, like I was, but plenty had turned up in costume: either Candy Land themed, like Kirsten (I saw one detail-intensive Gloppy costume, which I hoped to drive out of my memory someday), or as famous witches: Harry Potter was a popular theme, as was *Wicked*, and I saw two witches who'd dressed up like Tilda Swinton from the Narnia movies.

As they came and left the sunroom, I stayed where I was. As long as nobody tried to use their magic, I was pretty much invisible. A few people sat down on my couch and made small talk for a few minutes, but it was obvious that everyone there knew everyone else, and after a few minutes the small talker always wandered off to find someone more interesting. Kirsten popped in to hand me a plate of hors d'oeuvres and a soda at some point, and I took my time working through the snacks, watching the witches talk and laugh. A few of them seemed troubled rather than celebratory, and I figured they were probably talking about Erin and Denise.

In two hours, I only got caught twice: once when a young red-head in green Elspeth makeup tried to demonstrate a levitation spell, and once when a middle-aged witch in a perfect Grandma Nut costume tried to clean up a spilled glass of wine with magic instead of paper towels. Both times the witch looked around, confused, and spotted me curled up on my couch. I met her eyes, challenging, and got a glare before the other woman looked away. If I was here, Kirsten knew I was here, and that meant I was invited. None of the witches in Kirsten's society were going to question her in front of everyone.

By 9:00, no more new people seemed to be arriving, and I was getting bored and restless. Jack had texted to say he was waiting at the gate, so at least that was one less person to worry about. But tonight's mission was tanking: there was nobody at Kirsten's who was anywhere near powerful enough to challenge her, much less muck around with animation spells. We were wasting time that we didn't have. I kept checking my phone for texts, figuring Jesse must be getting even more impatient out in the car. At 9:15 I stood up, stretched, and headed for the sunroom doors. It was time to find Kirsten and figure out a plan B. Maybe she knew of some witches who hadn't shown up at the party, and Jesse and I could go track them down. That seemed even thinner than this plan, but at least we'd be doing something.

I never made it back to the dining room, though. On my way up the stairs from the sunroom I ran smack into a pretty young witch with white-blonde pigtails. She was wearing an intimidating-looking camera on a strap around her neck, and when we collided it hit me in the chest. The blow was softened by my bulletproof vest, so we were both looking at the camera first, checking for damage, before we met each others' eyes and I realized who I had just run down. We were frozen for a long moment as I put some puzzle pieces together, and her gorgeous blue eyes widened with apprehension. Almost without my knowing, my hand darted out and grabbed her upper arm. "You and I need to talk," I snapped.

"I'm sorry, have we met?" she asked nervously.

"Knock it off, Runa." This was not what I needed right now, but I couldn't just ignore it, either. "Are we talking right here in front of everyone, or do you want to step outside?"

The blonde witch looked around for help, but I'd managed to keep my voice low, and no one had noticed us. Finally she nodded, resigned, and pointed toward the sliding door in the sunroom. "Let's go out back."

I followed her through the glass doors and down a little hill to Kirsten's wide backyard. I hadn't actually been back there before, but even in the dark I could tell it was just as landscaped as the front. Runa sat down on a little bench next to a birdbath. I grudgingly perched myself on the other side.

"How did you know who I was?" she asked.

"I saw a picture on Jesse's phone," I said, fury in my voice. "I'm guessing he doesn't know you're a witch."

Her voice was low and miserable. "No."

Anger was making my head swim. I took a deep breath of the cool night air before I continued. "Please tell me you're not dating him just because Kirsten ordered you to. Tell me you're not part of some half-assed undercover thing to keep an eye on Jesse Cruz."

Her shoulders hunched down, but she looked up to meet my eyes. "I wish I could. But that's how it started. Then I—"

I held up a hand. "Stop. Spare me the then I fell in love with him crap. Of course you did, because he's a good and honest man. And you've been lying to him *this whole time*." Okay, I admit it. Part of me was rejoicing inside, because this meant Jesse wasn't taken after all. *He can be with me now*, the voice said. But this wasn't how I wanted to win him over. And I'd seen the goofy look on his face whenever he talked to this girl. I suddenly wanted very much to hurt her. "You know, you're just proving everything he hates about the Old World," I spat out. I was working hard to stay away from name-calling. "He doesn't *do* this political crap, with the secrets and the backstabbing. He's better than all of...this." I'd almost said *all of us.*

"You don't understand," she burst out, her face hardening with passion. "Kirsten, she's my cousin. She brought me to LA, let me live here for months while I figured things out. I owe her everything. I couldn't just say no! And she was so worried, after you brought him into our affairs—"

"Wait, stop," I interrupted. "She called you because of me? Because I brought him into the Old World?" I really, really wanted to be yelling at Kirsten. I'd known she was powerful, and I'd known she was capable of playing politics with Dashiell and Will. But I hadn't expected something so underhanded. Not from her.

Then I thought of her and Jesse going off to San Diego that morning, and how her attitude seemed to have changed. "Wait," I said. "What happened yesterday? Why did Kirsten suddenly want to work with him?"

"He passed a test," Runa answered, her voice almost a whisper. "He erased my crime-scene photos from the car accident. Then we—then Kirsten knew he was for real."

Of course he was for real. Kirsten just hadn't been willing to take my word for it. I thought of how she'd guilt-tripped me into partnering up with Jesse for the investigation and felt my hands clenching together. I took a deep breath and tried to relax them.

"Why you?" I said. "You're not powerful, so what's your specialty? Seduction?" Believe it or not, that was the more polite version of that question.

Her lovely face soured. "Locator spells. I'm great with finding people or things. If I know the person or I've handled the object, I can even do it without a focus." She straightened herself with pride. "Not even Kirsten can do that."

"I get it. You're human LoJack, which—wait, can you find Olivia?" I asked, momentarily distracted.

She shook her head. "Kirsten had me try months ago, when Olivia attacked you. But I'd never met her, so I needed a focus, and everything we could find of hers was from when she was human. The magic…stalled out at finding her as a vampire."

I sighed. Of course it couldn't just be that easy. "But you knew Jesse, so you could keep track of him. Which made you a great spy. Did you give any thought to how this might affect him?"

"More and more every day," she said softly. Tears slipped down her cheeks, and all of a sudden the fight went out of me, and I couldn't hate her anymore. I just felt tired. Dammit.

She bit her lip, and then asked, "You're not going to tell him, are you?"

I smiled grimly. "Nope. But you are. Right now. " I stood up. "He's parked in front of the house."

'I can't!" she cried, wringing her hands. "I'm not ready."

I sighed. That was the ironclad argument of every single person who'd ever done something bad and kept it a secret. *I'm not ready.* "When do you see yourself being ready, Runa? When he asks you to move in with him? When he proposes?"

The witch hung her head, suddenly silent. Dammit, Scarlett! *Stop feeling sorry for this person*, I thought. I couldn't help it, though. I'm such a softie. I dropped back down onto the bench. "Could you…I don't know, choose him somehow?" I asked gently. "Tell Kirsten you want to be with him?"

"If I went against Kirsten, I'd have to leave the society," she said mournfully. "They're, like, my home. Nobody leaves, once you're in."

I rolled my eyes at that particular *Godfather*esque comment, but something about it made a little spark in my brain. Runa began to say something else, but I held up both hands like a traffic cop. "Wait. I may be having some kind of thought here." *Once you're*

in... "I need to go," I said suddenly. "I need to talk to your cousin."
I gritted my teeth. "About a couple of things."

Before I could even step forward, my cell phone rang, the ordinary *ring-ring* sound again. I dug it out of my pocket, but it was already silent. Who calls and only lets it ring once? I checked the display.

Kevin.

"Oh, *shit*." I broke into a sprint, Runa yelling a question behind me, but I hadn't even made it around the corner of the house before I heard the screams.

Chapter 23

I had made it about six steps around the house when I pulled up short. *Think it through, Scarlett.* Jesse was out front; he would have heard the screaming. He was probably approaching the front of the house right now, gun in hand. If I burst into view, I was going to distract him, and if I wasn't close enough to cancel out the witch's magic right away, she'd have the perfect opportunity to hurt him. If she hadn't done so already. Choking on my frustration, I reversed direction and raced back toward the sunroom door. If I could come up behind the witch, I could neutralize her, and Jesse could cover her with the gun. Simple.

As I raced toward the sunroom doors, witches were pouring out, and I had to shoulder them aside to push my way into the house. It wasn't like the mob stampedes you see in the movies: some of the witches weren't running with the others; they milled around asking questions, halfheartedly letting themselves be pulled toward the doors. Nervous laughter mixed in with shouts and screams. "What happened, though?" someone hollered. "Where are we all going?" It felt like I was pushing against water out of a fire hose. And then I heard another witch yell, "Vampire! It's a vampire!"

Olivia. She was here.

Of course, there was the possibility that the whole supervillain team had shown up: Olivia, the witch, and the golem. That didn't feel right, though. They'd worked separately this whole time, with

Olivia doing most of the legwork, and if they really didn't know I was here, this wasn't their big endgame. No, it had to be Olivia alone. I knocked over one of the Narnia witches but didn't slow down to apologize. I headed straight for the front of the house, desperately wishing I knew where Jesse was. The little fireplace room had emptied, as had the kitchen and the entryway—but the front door stood open, and a man lay sprawled half in, half out of the house. There. I skidded to a stop as I recognized Kevin, the bouncer witch—and saw the spreading pool of blood below him. I crouched to check his pulse, but I wasn't very surprised when I felt none. His eyes already stared upward, his face completely blank. *Too late, too late.* I heard a crunch as I shifted my weight, and I looked down and saw bits of his cell phone under my boot. She had crushed it.

Instinctively, I rose and threw myself against the wall next to the front door, panting. I could hear shouts outside, but I couldn't make out the words or voices—there was music playing somewhere in the house, and still plenty of screaming. I closed my eyes, took a few deep breaths, and concentrated on my radius. This was it, my first real test. I felt for the edges of my circle. It took longer than it had before, but eventually I was able to hold it all in my mind. I breathed in, breathed out, and thought *expand*.

And then all hell broke loose, because the first thing my circle found on the porch was Kirsten.

The second I felt her, I opened my eyes and dropped the expansion, but it was too late. I stepped awkwardly over Kevin's body and burst onto the porch just as Jesse began firing at Olivia.

I took it all in in an instant. I'd made the wrong call. Olivia must have been on the porch when Kirsten came running out. The witch had managed to hold Olivia in place with a spell while Jesse advanced on her from the street, presumably to try to put handcuffs on her until I arrived. When I'd expanded my radius, I had killed Kirsten's magic and cut the cord holding Olivia still. And the first thing the vampire had done was race farther away from me—and straight toward Jesse.

"The heart," I screamed. "Shoot the heart!" Jesse's face was frozen in concentration as he emptied his gun at the vampire—but she was too fast. She veered away from her direct course toward Jesse, and I saw bits of skin explode on her arms, her abdomen, her thigh. She had reached the line of cars when his gun clicked empty, and Olivia paused, a wicked smirk spreading across her face. Why was she pausing? Jesse moved to reload, and Kirsten started toward Olivia, probably trying to get far enough away from me to freeze Olivia again. I tensed to throw myself backward to get Kirsten out of my radius faster, but Olivia's face changed again, and her hand moved into the nylon jacket she was wearing.

And I just...knew what she would do. Somehow.

"No!" I screamed, and lurched forward again. And as fast as everything had happened up until then, it sped up even more. I took the two steps it took to close the gap between Kirsten and me, and I grabbed at her roughly, getting a handful of her hair and one shoulder. I pulled her backward with everything I had, moving around her left side to cover her just as Olivia began firing the gun she'd pulled from the jacket. I heard two bursts, and in the same instant my back seemed to explode, and I was on the ground with Kirsten under me.

"Scarlett!" Jesse screamed, and everything went spacey for a moment. I hadn't had the wind knocked out of me since I was a little kid on the playground, but I recognized the sickly frozen feeling as though it had been yesterday. Seconds passed, or maybe minutes. I heard the police sirens wailing toward us, and then Jesse was rolling me over, off of Kirsten. I was gulping for air, unable to do too much to help him move me—but as I finally flopped onto the ground I could feel the horrible lifelessness of Kirsten's body.

"Olivia's gone?" I gasped. My back ached with an agonizing, rippling pain that made it hard to think. I stayed where I was, with it pressed into the cool ground. Jesse nodded. "And Kirsten?" Jesse was frantically pushing loose strands of hair away from my eyes so he could search my face. As though there might be pieces missing. "I'm fine, check her," I managed to say to Jesse. He ignored me until I added. "It hit the vest." I wiggled a little so my back wasn't against the ground. I'd never been shot before, but it felt like a major-league pitcher had fired a baseball into the muscles next to my spine.

Jesse met my eyes again and nodded quickly, shifting his attention to the witch next to us. I stared at the streetlight for a second, rejoicing in my now-working lungs, until Jesse reported, "She's been shot in the side. I can't tell how bad, but the ambulance will be here soon. She bumped her head when you tackled her, but it doesn't look too bad. Maybe a minor concussion."

"Is she gonna live?" I asked, panicked.

"I think so," he said, using his professional cop voice. "But you need to stay calm. You did everything you could."

"I should have come running around the outside of the house instead of running through it."

Jesse gave me a sharp look. "And you were supposed to know that how? *Olivia* shot Kirsten, Scarlett. Not you. You took a bullet for her."

I managed to roll myself over, onto all fours. I dug my cell phone out of my pocket and checked the screen. The little LCD face had a crack through it, but when I started pushing buttons everything else seemed to work fine. Beside me, Jesse was applying pressure to the bullet hole on Kirsten's side. Blood covered his hands and stained the torso of her beautiful gown. It seemed like a really good time to call Dashiell.

He picked up immediately. "What's happened? Did you get them?"

"No." I told him about Olivia showing up at the party instead of the witch. "She brought a gun; she was prepared in case I showed up. Dashiell, you've gotta get people over here to press minds," I said. "There's a dead body, and Kirsten's been shot, and some other witches may have been hurt, and the police are gonna be here in a second—"

"Scarlett, you're babbling," he said with exaggerated patience. "Don't worry about Kirsten. I'll come myself."

I sighed with relief. That was kind of what I'd been hoping for. Dashiell was arrogant, pushy, and controlling, but this was exactly the kind of situation that made me glad to have him around. "Thank you."

"I'll talk to you more when I arrive. For now, just don't say anything to the police." He hung up.

I looked over at Jesse. "Dashiell's on his way," I said—thus speaking to the police. Then I groaned. "Oh, shit."

He looked up from Kirsten in alarm. "What? Are you hurt somewhere else?"

"She shot Molly's sweater. Molly is gonna kill me."

He looked at me, and we both sort of...giggled. Before I could say anything else, though, three police cars came screaming up to the house, and I froze. I'd seen this in the movies a thousand times, but it was still kind of terrifying when you were the one lit up in the headlights. "Just be still," Jesse murmured. "Keep your hands visible."

I'd just been shot in the back. What was I gonna do, run a five-minute mile? "No problem."

The cops from the first squad car, a man and a woman, came boiling out of the car with their guns drawn, just like in the movies. They began to shout at us, but Jesse shook his head and yelled, "Detective Jesse Cruz, Southwest Homicide. My badge is in my inside jacket pocket. I don't want to move my hands from this wound."

The uniformed officers exchanged a glance, and then the female cop holstered her gun while the male kept his trained on us. Jesse and I held perfectly still while she approached and reached into the pocket of Jesse's leather jacket, pulling out his identification. She nodded at the male officer, and they both relaxed visibly. "She's with me," Jesse said, tilting his head my way. I waved limply.

The three of them began to chatter at each other in cop codes, which I made no effort to sort out. After a few minutes, the other cops went inside to check the rest of the house. The ambulance arrived and two female EMTs jumped out, beelining straight for Kirsten. One of them was older, maybe sixty, with gray hair cropped short. The one who'd been driving was younger and moved with more energy. She had a ponytail pulled through a baseball cap with the name of the ambulance service printed on it. I scooted back a few feet so they could work, and Jesse was finally able to lift his bloody hands off Kirsten's side. I looked away. I could handle the sight of blood, but there was no point in giving myself this memory of Kirsten.

"She's waking up," the older EMT reported. She leaned forward with a little flashlight, checking Kirsten's pupil dilation. "Ma'am, please try not to move. Do you know where you are?"

Kirsten blinked against the light. "Yes."

There was a wave of bustling activity, and Jesse helped the two EMTs get Kirsten onto one of those backboard thingies, and then a gurney. I managed to get to my feet while they were folding the wheels and getting her in the ambulance, although it probably didn't look very graceful. By the time Kirsten was settled in the ambulance, she was out again. "Her too," Jesse ordered, pointing at me. "She needs to go along and get checked out."

I don't know why I was surprised. "Me? I'm fine. The vest caught it."

"She got shot in the back," Jesse explained to the younger EMT.

The woman with the ponytail went around to my back and unceremoniously lifted the sweater. "Hey," I protested mildly. At least it was a woman.

"I've got a bullet here," the ponytailed woman yelled to her colleague. To me, she said, "He's right, Miss. You need to come with us. There could be internal bleeding or cracked ribs."

One of the uniformed cops opened a downstairs window and stuck his head out. "We've got a few more injuries in here. You guys want to take a look now or call for another bus?"

The younger EMT raised her eyebrows at the older woman, who said, "She'll be stable for a few minutes. Run and look quick so we can at least give them a heads-up."

The young driver nodded briskly and jogged inside, letting a cop guide her around Kevin's body. Poor Kevin. Even in death, he was just a backdrop.

"Come on, I'll help you climb up," Jesse said, taking my hand and steering me toward the back of the ambulance.

"We don't have time for this," I protested. He ignored me, and I pretty much had to allow him to pull me along. Digging my heels in would hurt too much.

"We're making time," he said, and I knew from his tone that further arguments would be pointless. Jesse helped me climb carefully into the rig. I scooted around the older EMT, who was working over Kirsten, and settled down in the seat across from the witch.

"You should get back in there," I called to Jesse, who was still on the ground. "Dashiell will be here any second." I gave him a meaningful look that I hoped said *and you guys have to figure out what to tell everyone.*

"I want to stay with you," he said simply.

"I know, but—" Before I could finish that thought, I saw the younger EMT walking around the outside of the house leading a young woman with a long, ugly gash on her forearm. Runa. "Oh, fuck me," I said out loud. I had forgotten all about her.

"What?" Jesse said. He turned around, following my gaze, and saw his girlfriend being led away from the witch party. The coward in me was glad I didn't have to see his face just then. *"Runa?"*

he said incredulously. "What are you doing here?" He must have taken in the camera that was still hanging around her neck. Even from twenty feet away I could see the cracked lens. "Was this, like, a gig, or something? What happened?"

Runa looked at me briefly, and back at Jesse. "I sort of got pushed, cut my arm on the edge of the fountain," she explained, her voice weak. "And, um, I think we need to talk."

I almost laughed. That was an understatement. Before either of them could speak, though, the younger EMT said, "It's not that deep, but we should take her in for surface stitches." She turned to address Runa. "Miss, the next ambulance is going to take you to the hospital. Please wait here with the detective until it arrives."

"Oh, hey, she looks way more hurt than I am," I protested, starting to stand up from my stretcher. It hurt, but the pain was already less than it had been a few minutes earlier. "And this is her cousin," I added, pointing at Kirsten. "I can drive myself to the ER." Jesse glared. "Or wait for the next ambulance," I said contritely, before he could yell.

The EMTs exchanged another look, and then the older woman shrugged. "Fine by me."

Runa came over to the ambulance, and I stood up to climb down. Before I could move to the edge, though, Kirsten's hand waved weakly. "Scarlett?"

"Kirsten!" I took her hand. It was very cool.

"We need to get going, Miss," the older EMT said, but I didn't bother to look at her. I was focused on the witch.

"Kirsten?" I said again. Her eyelids fluttered, but after a moment her deep-blue eyes found me again. "I know you're hurting, but I have to ask you something." She nodded slightly. I looked up at Runa and gave her a look. She understood and began engaging the two EMTs in a question about types of stitches.

I took a deep breath. "There was nobody at that party stronger than you, Kirsten. I'm sure of it. But this whole time we've been looking for a witch *inside* your union. What about the witches in LA who didn't want to join you? Could a powerful witch be operating in the city without you knowing?"

Kirsten mumbled, "I'd know. Go talk to them. Ask them to join us." Her last two words slurred together.

I frowned. "But witches have said no before, right? Have you ever been turned down by someone very powerful?"

For a moment, Kirsten's eyes cleared and her eyebrows furrowed. Then her face relaxed, and her head seemed to sink a little farther into the gurney. "There was someone once. Years ago. But she died. There was an accident. Olivia..." She gasped, and both EMTs' heads swiveled our way in alarm. Kirsten's face couldn't get any paler, but her hand squeezed mine.

I leaned forward so only Kirsten could hear. "Olivia got rid of the body," I said quietly. Kirsten nodded, a tiny, urgent movement. "Only she didn't."

"I should have...I should have..." Her eyelids fluttered again. "Mallory," she whispered, and her hand relaxed in mine.

"Kirsten? What's her last name? Where does she live?" But her eyes were closed again.

"Miss," the driver said firmly. "Come down here. Now."

When the ambulance sped off with Kirsten and Runa, Jesse turned on me. "Did you know?" he asked in a soft voice. "About Runa?"

"I found out about ten minutes ago," I said honestly.

"Was she...was she sent? To be with me?"

I sighed. "I think so. But you should really talk to her." I saw Dashiell's expensive car pull up to the nearest curb spot, and I nodded at it. "Dashiell's here." I held out my hand. "You still have the best parking spot, though. Can I sit in your car until the ambulance gets here?"

He automatically dug in his pocket, still dazed, but froze with his keys in the air. "Swear to me that you won't try to drive yourself to the hospital," he demanded.

I nodded. "I swear I won't drive myself to the hospital. I just want to sit down for a second, Jesse, I promise. But I don't want to sit on the porch by...the body." And I didn't want to sit on the ground, because getting up off of it had not been fun the first time, but I didn't feel the need to mention that.

He searched my face for a long moment, saw that I meant it, and dropped the keys in my palm. "I'll meet you at the ER," he promised.

"Oh, Jesse?"

He raised his eyebrows at me.

I told him about the name Kirsten had remembered. "Mallory," he said thoughtfully. Then he looked back over his shoulder and sighed. "Let me take care of this first." He took off toward Dashiell.

I limped toward Jesse's car, feeling the pain in my back. I opened the passenger door, which was closest to the curb, and sort of fell into the low seat. It was better than the ground, I figured. From that spot I could see Jesse confer briefly with Dashiell, keeping his eyes away from Dashiell's gaze. I felt a silly burst of pride. He was taking care of himself. Jesse talked to some uniformed officers, who began spreading crime-scene tape around the house's exterior now that the wounded had been cleared away. I leaned back and closed my eyes.

How had everything gotten so messed up, so quickly? The plan had been for me to go to the party in order to identify Olivia's witch partner. Instead, Olivia herself had shown up and...shot at Kirsten? The gun itself didn't surprise me; I could see Olivia carrying one on all her recent missions on the off chance that I might show. But unless I'd completely misjudged the angles, it had really seemed like Olivia was *aiming* at Kirsten, not me, and certainly not Jesse.

Kirsten hadn't had a picture on the basement wall, though. I had been so sure Olivia's next move would be to come after someone I loved. Was I completely wrong about Olivia's plan? Or was

Olivia's plan just on hold until after the night of the solstice? Maybe they were focused on what this other witch, Mallory, wanted, but if that were the case, why come here and kill Kirsten? To keep her from interfering? That seemed awfully random, given that Kirsten was clearly busy and distracted tonight. She hadn't exactly been about to pound on Mallory's door.

I rubbed my face in frustration, feeling the muscles in my back cry out from the movement. Tonight was supposed to be about getting answers, and all I had was more frickin' questions.

I was distracted by my cell phone, which was vibrating in my pocket. I heard the dim strains of "Werewolves of London." Will. I dug out the phone, wincing at the pain as I leaned sideways. I felt a flash of guilt. He was probably calling about his truck, which was parked on the street back in front of Molly's house. I'd kind of forgotten all about it. I held the phone to my ear.

"Hey, Will, listen…" I began, but my voice trailed off as I listened to the unmistakable sounds of glass breaking and screaming. Then Will's voice came on the line, so suddenly I jumped in my seat. "Scarlett!" he screamed. "Get here now!" There was another crash and then a tangle of words, but I could only make out one.

"*Wolfberry.*"

Chapter 24

So I stole a cop's car. It seemed like a good idea at the time.

I didn't bother to tell Jesse what I was going to do. He would either insist on coming with me, which would be dangerous for him, or insist that I needed to go to the hospital first, which would be dangerous for everyone at Hair of the Dog. And there was no way in hell I wasn't going. Eli was at the bar, and if it was Will calling instead of him, then Eli had probably ingested the wolfberry.

As I drove I tried to remember what Olivia had told me about the effects of that strain of nightshade: it caused the werewolves to completely lose control of both the human and the wolf sides. They couldn't keep from changing back and forth, over and over, which was excruciatingly painful. They attacked humans at will, which was out of character for both real wolves and the shapeshifters, who preferred to hunt deer and rabbits. Most wolves who ingested wolfberry had to be shot. The lucky ones just lost their minds and spent years recovering. The good news was, all of that was caused by werewolf magic interacting with the herb's magic, so if a null like me could get close enough, he or she could stop everything. Olivia had once said that the only two ways to stop a werewolf who'd ingested wolfberry were a null or a silver bullet.

Olivia. She had done this. I didn't know how yet, but unlike the scene at Kirsten's house, this felt like classic Olivia: a big, messy strike at someone I loved, designed to cause maximum damage with no regard for bystanders. *I can hurt you whenever I want*; that was the message. *No one is safe from me.* I worked to keep my breathing even as I drove. I had to stay calm. I had to be able to get in there and do this. I wasn't going to help Eli if I couldn't keep my shit together. I bit down on a burst of hysterical laughter, my back aching from the effort. I was so past keeping anything together.

I blew through the traffic and only stopped for a single red light, because I wanted to take the opportunity to dig through Jesse's glove compartment. I was rewarded, though: I found a great big bottle of extra-strength Advil and shook out four pills. I swallowed them with a flat soda that was in Jesse's cup holder, and then sped on to the bar.

I parked right out in front without bothering to see if it was even a legal spot. As I ran to the entrance, I saw a thin figure on the sidewalk in a defensive crouch, like she expected someone to run up and shove her over. I squinted against the streetlight and recognized Anastasia, an African-American woman in her late twenties. She was a werewolf and one of Will's part-time bartenders. He must have stationed her out here to let me in and keep everyone else out.

That made sense, but she was shaking like a leaf. I crouched, very carefully touching her wrist. "Ana?"

Her gaze met mine for an instant, and then she looked away. "Will ordered me to stay out," she said, her low voice clouded with shock and grief. "My girlfriend's in there, but he said I had to leave, and I couldn't…I couldn't stay."

Ouch. I understood that she was being literal. She *couldn't* go in. As the alpha, Will can control the wolf half of his pack members, but he's a good guy and doesn't usually push them. This was probably the first time he'd flexed his power over her, and she wasn't taking it well.

"Who's in there, Ana?"

She swallowed. "Some customers. Will. And Lydia."

"Which wolves?" I said, trying to keep the impatience out of my voice. "Who took the wolfberry?"

"Eli," she said. "And Caroline."

I didn't wait for further explanation, just rose carefully—the Advil was already helping, but my back was still stiff and tender—and stepped past Anastasia, into the bar.

The door opened into a tiny alcove, a few feet away from the main bar area. As soon as I stepped all the way into the alcove, I froze and looked down. I was standing on a human hand.

I managed not to yelp but lurched backward, almost slipping in a long smear of blood. When I was steady I pressed my back against the door, which had closed behind me, straining to see in the dim bar lighting. There was a body taking up most of the alcove, a woman lying on her stomach, pointed toward the door as though she were trying to leave. I recognized the short, dark hair, the sweeping, tilted nose. Caroline. A strangled sob escaping my throat, I bent at the waist, spotting at least two bullet holes in her back. Silver bullets.

"Scarlett?" Will's voice whispered.

Later, Scarlett. Mourn for her later. I held my breath and stepped around Caroline's corpse into the main room of the bar. Hair of the Dog was in shambles. There was broken glass *everywhere*, from dozens of framed pictures that had exploded off the walls. It looked like someone had swept an arm around the room, knocking everything violently to the floor, and then rolled around in the broken glass and shaken like a dog. Which was probably more or less what had happened. The smell of blood was overwhelming, and I saw that the dark-colored floor was shining in places. A lot of places. I counted four other bodies on the floor, that I could see.

Against my usual instincts, I ignored them. They were either dead or in need of help, and that wasn't coming while there was a crazed werewolf running around. I looked at Will, who was holding a huge revolver in his right hand, his left hand flat and out in a "calm down" gesture. They were both pointed toward the back corner of the bar, which I couldn't see yet. I stepped up next to him, trying to keep as quiet as I could, and rounded the bar to see an enormous wolf—Eli—growling in the back corner of the room. The wolf's fur was raised all along his back, and his huge teeth were locked around the neck of a young woman in her midtwenties. She was pale, drenched in blood and tears and wolf slobber, breathing in a rapid pant with little whimpering noises. My own breath caught in my throat.

I had seen pictures of Eli's wolf, but they didn't do him justice: he was gorgeous, colored in blurred shades of silver and black, with white tips on the bottom of each paw. I couldn't get over the *size* of him, either—wild wolves are big, but werewolves weigh as much in wolf form as they do in human form. Eli had to be around two hundred pounds, most of it muscle, and the wolf was the same. His eyes, though...there was unmistakable madness in them. I'd seen werewolves from this distance before, and I'd once seen a rabid dog in our neighborhood when I was growing up. But I'd never seen the two combined.

The woman was scrambling to hold her own weight upright on the slippery blood-and-glass floor so she wouldn't just be dangling from the wolf's enormous jaws, while simultaneously trying not to jar the wolf. It was obvious that she was tiring, and with nothing to gain purchase on, she was beginning to slip downward. I tried to swallow, my mouth suddenly bone-dry.

Will must have seen me in his peripheral vision, but he gave a tiny head shake. *Don't move yet.* I stayed a step behind him, keeping the wolf's attention on the bigger man. "Eli," Will crooned softly, "let go of her, okay? She's a friend." The wolf didn't move, just continued to growl. "He's shifting about every two minutes," Will said in the same soothing voice, and I realized he was talking to me. "He's got maybe a minute and a half. If he starts to change, he'll bite down. I *will* shoot him before that happens."

Will's voice was firm and calm, but when I chanced a sideways look I saw tears rolling down his cheeks. "Silver?" I asked briefly, though I knew the answer. Will was the one who had shot Caroline. *Later, Scarlett.*

"Yes."

"Let me try," I whispered, as calmly as I could.

For the first time, Will took his eyes off Eli's wolf to glance at me. "He can snap her neck before you can get a single step forward—"

"No time to argue," I said. Moving *very* slowly, I pulled Molly's sweater over my head, keeping my eyes away from the wolf's. I spotted a tattered gray bar rag hanging out of Will's back pocket and reached forward to tug it out at the same speed. "You have to let me try, Will. It's *Eli*." I tried to keep my voice as calm as Will's, but when I got to Eli's name I couldn't keep the desperation out of it. The wolf heard it and snarled in his throat, ears flicking in my direction.

"If he so much as starts to twitch—"

"Shh. I know." Wearing only my bulletproof vest on top, I slowly lowered my body to the floor. At least we wouldn't have to worry about Will shooting me in the back by accident.

A cornered wolf was one of the most dangerous creatures in nature. Still, all I had to do was get close enough to get him in my radius, which meant I needed to move maybe fifteen feet. I wanted to try my new expansion trick, but it had backfired on me at Kirsten's, and besides I just couldn't trust my ability to concentrate, not now. I dropped the sweater on the floor and put my right hand on it. I kept the bar towel covering as much of my left hand as possible, though my finger pads got cut almost immediately. My hands more or less protected, I got down on my hands and knees. Ignoring the pain in my back, I kept my lips closed and my teeth covered as the Velcro on the bulletproof vest rustled softly. My gaze focused on the floor, I made my first "step" on all fours toward Eli's wolf.

The wolf growled again. I had changed the rules of behavior. I cringed a little but kept going. "It's okay," I said softly, keeping my eyes on the floor. I kept my body low, so my face and my imaginary tail wouldn't appear to be any higher than the wolf in front of me. The struggling woman had started making involuntary whimpering sounds, which probably wasn't helping Eli calm down any. "I'm a friend. It's okay." I kept going, crooning nonsense in the same calming tone Will had used. The bar towel was already soaked through with blood, though none of it was mine.

I flicked my eyes up for the briefest of seconds, to check on the wolf's reaction. The fur had gone down along his spine. He was still growling, but there was a note of uncertainty in it now.

"My mom was an veterinary tech at an animal hospital," I said to no one in particular. I just wanted to keep talking, keep the calming sound going. "She worked with abused dogs a lot, crazy dogs."

"Thirty seconds, Scarlett." Tension had crept into Will's voice now. I gave a very brief nod without looking back and kept going. Just eight more feet.

"I know you're not a dog, Eli, but I'm really hoping the same rules apply," I added, keeping my voice low. Five more feet. The wolf's low-throated growl changed slightly, to something that sounded more like whining. His tail, which had been standing perfectly straight and stiff, wilted a bit into a more relaxed pose.

"It's gonna happen, Scarlett," Will whispered urgently. As he said it, the wolf made a sudden cry of pain and began to flinch, cringing inward upon himself like he'd been viciously kicked in the stomach. The woman cried out in fear. Without thinking, I dropped and rolled as fast as I could, sliding in the slippery mess. Blood-covered glass fragments cut into my jeans and the bullet-proof vest.

There. I felt Eli enter my radius, and faster than my dizzy eyes could follow, a naked man dropped suddenly to the floor in place of the wolf. The woman gave a full-out scream, but I skidded right past her through the blood, to Eli's side. He was unconscious. I shifted to kneel next to him and checked his pulse, held my cheek in front of his nose. Alive. I sighed with relief and looked back up.

The woman had run toward Will and was clinging to him, her body shaking with sobs. Behind her, Will nodded at me, a complicated expression of relief and misery clouding his face.

Will walked the bloody woman over to a bar stool and propped her on it. Her upper body collapsed down onto the bar's surface, and she stayed there, sobbing into her arms. Will moved his hands like he might try to comfort her, but then reversed direction, disappearing for a moment into his office through the back door. When he came back there was something in his hand, but I didn't see the syringe until he'd stabbed it into the bloody woman's upper arm.

I gasped. "Will—"

"It's okay," he said levelly. "It's just a sedative." *A lot of that going around*, I thought. The woman's body went limp, and he picked her up from the bar stool and lifted her whole body onto the bar, which was much cleaner and safer looking than the floor at the moment. "She's going into shock, but I need her to stay here until I can get some of Dashiell's crew here to erase her memory. I just called him, from the office."

"Is she going to change?"

He frowned. "I can't tell. His teeth punctured her neck, but only slightly—I think the rest of the blood on her is from the glass and the other...the other..." *Victims*, I thought, but neither of us wanted to say it. "And you were here, which might have slowed the magic. I'm just not sure." He shrugged. "We'll erase her memory, but we'll keep an eye on her."

"What *happened* here?" I said bluntly, unable to keep it in. "Caroline...?"

Without answering, Will crunched across the glass toward the nearest body lying on the ground. It was a man I'd never seen before, around thirty, wearing one of those tacky bowler shirts under a lot of blood. I couldn't see his actual injuries from where I was sitting, but Will checked for a pulse, checked for breathing, just as I had with Eli. Then he shook his head. "Dead," he said briefly, and moved on to the next body. I looked away. Part of me felt like I should get up and help him, but I had no idea if leaving Eli would cause the wolfberry's effects to start up again.

"It was cookies," Will said matter-of-factly, and I looked up at him. He was answering my question. "Small businesses like ours, we exchange gifts with a lot of our vendors. Gourmet chocolate, nuts, microbrews, that kind of thing. We got a big tin of Christmas cookies delivered here a couple of hours ago. I was at the bar, but Caroline was in the office, and Eli was back there eating his dinner at my desk. They both had some."

"Olivia."

He nodded, bitterness on his face. He checked another pulse, shook his head again. "It hit Caroline first. She started screaming, and I saw the change take her. Usually I can control their wolves, help them stay in human form if they start to lose it before the full moon. But with the wolfberry...I was helpless."

"And then Eli..." I prompted.

Will nodded. "And then Eli," he said grimly. "He's strong, and he fought it, harder than I've ever seen anyone who wasn't an alpha. But in the end I think that made it worse." He shook his head. "When he finally went, there was no sense to him. Just... madness.

"Caroline's wolf knocked a bunch of shit off the walls, glasses off the bar. She bit a woman, but then she made for the exit. She wanted to get out, into the wild. I'd gotten my gun by then, but I was between the two of them." He shrugged miserably. "I couldn't let her leave, and I couldn't follow her while Eli was here killing people. So I shot her."

"I'm surprised you didn't shoot Eli too," I said without thinking.

His smile was wry and a little sheepish. "I tried to. I got off four shots. I think I grazed his pelt once. He's so damned *fast*." Will shook his head. "I had him cornered when you came in. That was going to be the killing shot."

He looked down at the woman in front of him. "This one's alive," he said. She was small and Asian, with a vine tattoo snaking its way along the outside of one arm. She had been curled into a ball behind a couple of barstools, maybe trying to hide. Will bent to look closer at the woman's face, and his shoulders relaxed a few inches. "She's Anastasia's girlfriend. I don't remember her name, though."

"Lydia," I said.

"That's right." He looked down at her like he was memorizing her face. "At least she won't be alone."

"She's going to change?"

Will nodded. "She's the one that Caroline bit on her way to the door. Her wounds are closing fast. She's starting the process." There was a lot he wasn't saying in those words. For some years now, the werewolves and vampires have had trouble reproducing. Sometimes the process still worked, but much more often the victim simply died. If Lydia's wounds were closing, she was going to be one of the few new wolves who survived. That didn't exactly make her lucky, though. It takes three excruciating days for a werewolf to fully transform. But, like Will had said, at least the girl wouldn't be alone in it.

"The other three?" I asked, nodding at the other bodies. Will shook his head. Dead.

Will went to the door and called Anastasia to come in. She looked at her fallen girlfriend and burst into tears, dropping to her knees to cradle Lydia in her lap. I looked away. Will spoke softly to Ana for a few minutes, until they both stood up and Will lifted Lydia into his arms.

"I'm going to put them in the janitorial room to give them some privacy," he told me in a low voice. He carried Lydia past me, not even shifting his grip when he lost his werewolf strength in my radius, and down the hall to the tiny room across from his office. I'd peeked in there once and knew the room held only cleaning supplies, a heavy-duty safe, and a single cot where Will let the werewolves camp out every now and then, when one of them needed a place.

After a couple of minutes, Will returned and slumped against the bar.

"What about Eli?" I asked, looking back at the unconscious man beside me. His chest was rising and falling, but he hadn't so much as shifted his position since I'd gotten close to him. I concentrated on him for a moment, feeling out at him with whatever it is that makes me what I am. I blinked in surprise. "He feels *wrong*. Twisted and sick."

Will rubbed his face. "Physically, he's going to be fine. The wolfberry won't hurt him in human form. The pack knows a doctor, in Orange County. I called him right after I called you. He has a...well, it isn't really an antidote, but it's a sedative designed for werewolves. It'll knock Eli out until the wolfberry leaves his system."

"You don't keep it here?" I nodded toward the woman who was still collapsed at the bar. "Like that sedative?"

He shook his head, with some bitterness. "He won't let me. It's...well, let's say it's a controlled substance. A lot of the ingredients aren't legal."

It sounded like there was a story behind all that, but I was in no mood to ask for it. "Is Eli going to wake up before the doctor gets here?"

Will eyed the man on the floor. "I would think so. I'm not exactly sure what made him pass out, unless it was just the shock of changing so fast after all those other changes." His gaze moved over to me. "Um, Scarlett..."

"What?" I said, narrowing my eyes at him.

"You look like a horror movie," Will said simply. I looked down at myself. My hands were fine, except for the cuts on my left finger pads. But every other part of my body was coated with blood. My bare arms were covered with scratches from the glass, some of which was still in my skin. The bulletproof vest had protected most of my middle, but it was riddled with little holes where larger bits of glass had punctured the Kevlar. My jeans were the same. Will was right—I looked like I'd barely survived an encounter with Freddy Krueger.

"You know, when Bruce Willis rolls through glass, it's like water off a duck," I said casually.

Will just looked concerned. "I'm not kidding, Scarlett. That looks really bad."

Suddenly, Eli shifted a little beside me. A faint smile flickered across his face.

"Scar?" he murmured, and then his eyes opened. He looked at me, then at Will a few feet away, and his face instantly caved in on itself. He remembered. "No," he moaned. "*No.*" He curled into a ball on the side, either not seeing or not caring about all the glass. "Will, did I...are they..."

"Yes, Eli," Will said, his voice empty. "They're dead."

"How many?"

"Three."

"No." Eli curved even tighter into the fetal position, his face pushing down into the glass. "Not again. You should have killed me first." There was no accusation in his voice, just a sort of quiet lifelessness. I tried to keep the surprise off my face. Not again? Had Eli killed someone before? This wasn't the time to ask.

"I tried, my friend," Will said quietly. "I knew you wouldn't want this. I'm sorry."

"Shoot me now," he whispered to Will. "I don't want to be this thing anymore." His body began to shake. "I don't want to hurt anyone else."

Will looked at me for a moment and said very quietly, "It might be better—"

"*No.*" I was not going to let Will shoot Eli. There had been enough damage tonight, enough lives lost. Olivia had already taken too much away from me. And maybe that was selfish, but I'd work the ethics out later.

I glared up at Will, but the alpha werewolf was focused on Eli. "We'll talk about this when you're well again," he said at last.

Eli's body spasmed with grief, dry sobs escaping his throat in a desperate, wild sound that was more wolf than human. I had no idea what to say, so I put my hands lightly on his shoulders, trying to calm him down—but he didn't seem to be aware of me anymore. His arms went above his head, instinctively protecting it as he sobbed and sobbed. I looked up at Will, tears in my own eyes. "Give him the sedative," I demanded.

Will checked his watch. "The doctor won't—"

"Not that one," I snapped. "The one you gave that girl." I nodded toward the woman sleeping on the bar.

Will hesitated. "The doctor will be here in a couple of minutes, then he can have the really serious stuff—"

"*Look at him,*" I shouted. "Give him the goddamned sedative." My jaw trembled, but I didn't look away from Will as he stared at me. He may have been in human form, but he was still the alpha. He wasn't in the habit of taking orders, especially from a human employee. After a moment, though, he looked away. I had won the staring contest. Bully for me. Wordlessly, Will disappeared into the back office again. When he returned he was carrying a first-aid kit the size of a carry-on suitcase.

"Hold him still," he said grimly, and I leaned onto Eli's jack-knifing body.

"Shh, Eli, it'll be okay," I soothed, but Eli was too far gone to even look at me. Between the two of us, we were able to hold him steady long enough for Will to get the needle in, and a moment later Eli's whole body went limp under me. I hadn't realized until then that he'd been straining every muscle he had.

I looked across Eli's body at Will. "Thank you," I said sincerely. My voice must have sounded calm, because I think we were both surprised when I burst into tears.

Chapter 25

I cried for a long time. I cried for Eli, who was broken. I cried for Caroline, who was dead, and Kirsten, who was hurt. I cried for Ana and Lydia, whose lives were changed forever just because they knew someone who knew me. I cried for me, for the person I should have been instead of the person who Olivia had made me. I cried for all of us. I couldn't seem to stop.

While I was crying, Will disappeared for a moment, then came back and pulled me carefully to my feet. He rummaged in the first-aid suitcase and came up with a pair of scissors. I stood there sobbing as he cut away the bulletproof vest, and didn't feel anything when he gently picked glass bits out of my arms and stomach. He walked around to my back and cut the strap of my sports bra vertically, so the bra straps slipped off my shoulders. A sprinkle of glass bits fell onto the ground with the fabric. He carefully took the ponytail holder out of my braid and fluffed at my hair. There was another muted sprinkle of glass.

I was trying to get control back by then, but it was a losing battle. Will stayed behind me, minding my privacy, and I felt him slip clothing over my head. I let him put the oversized Hair of the Dog T-shirt on me, and I didn't move or struggle as he knelt in the glass to cut off my jeans and underpants. I didn't feel the pain of the scratches or the sting of the glass being pulled out. The moment should have been creepy, but Will was being so gentle, and I was crying so hard that it didn't even occur to me. When he finally stood up, I was wearing only the T-shirt, which reached my midthighs, and my knee-high boots. It was a weird look.

By then I was working on breathing deeply, trying to calm down. When he saw me finally coming back to myself, Will handed me a clean pair of men's boxer shorts, a bar towel that smelled like detergent, and a glass of water. He turned away while I put the shorts on under the huge bar T-shirt. I drank deeply, and then dipped the towel into the glass and washed my face. Will pulled out a chair from the table next to Eli and brushed it off, then made me sit down and take my boots off to shake out any glass fragments. There were some in my socks, so I took them off, and Will gave me a clean pair from the stash of spare clothing he keeps around for the werewolves, which was probably where the T-shirt and boxers had come from too. The leather boots had held out against the glass, God bless 'em, so I put them back on over the new socks. There were bloodstains on the leather, so they would have to be tossed by the end of the night, but for the moment it was comforting to have them. I gulped in air, completely spent.

Will sat down in the chair across from mine, looking as exhausted as I felt. Neither of us had said a word since I'd thanked him for giving Eli the sedative. I don't know how long we sat there—time seemed to fuzz away from me for a long moment, and then suddenly someone was knocking on the back door at the end of the little hallway. I looked a question at Will.

"The doctor," he assured me. "He always comes to the back door."

Will went back there to let him in, and I stared at the floor, absently tracing a circle in the glass with my boot. The shock was beginning to fade again, and I realized I had no idea what to do now. I checked my watch: 10:50 p.m. And Olivia was still out there. Jesse was safe, surrounded by a legion of police. Molly and Jack were hiding. Kirsten was in the hospital. Dashiell was busy taking care of cleanup—doing my job, I supposed—at Kirsten's and then here. I had no one left to lose, but I also had no one left to help me. And whatever Olivia and Mallory were going to do, they were going to do it in just over an hour.

I was alone.

Will and the doctor returned from the back door. I had been picturing someone older, maybe a guy in his late fifties with nefarious horn-rimmed glasses, like the evil Nazi in *Raiders of the Lost Ark*, but I was wrong again. The guy who followed Will back toward Eli and me was forty at the most, carried a briefcase, and was movie-star handsome, with a perfect cleft chin and warm eyes that were almost as green as my own. He was wearing navy-blue scrubs, and he looked for all the world like one of those doctors on prime-time soaps, the ones who spend more time sleeping around than practicing medicine. "*You're* the doctor?" I said, not bothering to keep the skepticism out of my voice.

He grinned and eyed my T-shirt-and-boots ensemble. "You're the null?" he countered.

I glanced down at the outfit and shrugged. "Touché."

"Scarlett, this is Matthias. Matthias, Scarlett."

I considered a comment on his ridiculous name, but I didn't exactly have a leg to stand on there, either. "Can you help him?" I said instead.

"Yes." Matthias squatted down next to Eli, checking his pulse. He opened his briefcase, rummaged around, and pulled out the biggest needle I'd ever seen. Syrupy-looking pink fluid sloshed inside. "This is going to take a little finesse, though."

He directed me to walk away from Eli, to whatever I thought the edge of my radius might be. I complied, and he got the mammoth needle into position at the vein on Eli's arm. When he nodded, I took the last two steps away from Eli and felt him leave my radius. Matthias quickly drove in the needle's plunger, injecting the pinkish fluid into the vein. I hovered, half-expecting it to not work. I wanted to be ready to leap back toward Eli. But the unconscious man didn't even stir, and Matthias checked his pulse and nodded to himself. "Keep him out of your range for the next four hours or so," he said to me. "These drugs would kill a human pretty quickly."

I nodded and took a few steps back, just to be sure. "Mind if I sit in your office a minute?" I asked Will. I wanted to be away from the carnage, and I had no interest in seeing Will and Matthias handle the doctor's payment. Will nodded. I leaned down and carefully extracted my wallet, Jesse's keys, and my phone from the bloody pile that used to be my jeans, hoping to find a plastic bag or something for them in the office.

Will's office was unpretentious and comfortable: a solid old wooden desk and matching chair, a bulletin board with pictures of Will, his family, the pack. There was some debris in here too, from when Caroline had first changed: papers and office supplies scattered over the floor, trash cans upturned. It wasn't nearly as bad as the bar, though. Her first instinct had probably been to get to a more open space.

Caroline. Caroline was gone.

I pulled back the chair, which seemed to weigh a hundred pounds. I was so tired. Before I could even sit down, though, my phone buzzed in my hand, making me jump. I looked at the screen cautiously. Unlisted number. I answered it. "Bernard."

"Scarlett, darling," Olivia's voice cooed. "Did you get the cookies I sent?"

Now I did sit, my body dropping into the office chair without me really noticing. "Where are you?"

"Oh, come on, baby, where are your manners? Didn't I teach you anything?"

I felt a familiar little sting for the briefest moment—*I had disappointed her! I hadn't followed directions!* As soon as I registered that thought, however, it made me even angrier. I was not a little girl. I was not her Barbie doll. And I didn't have to play her games. "Where are you?" I repeated, through gritted teeth. Then I remembered the psych report and the background we'd collected: Olivia wanted a family. She wanted me with her. "I—I really want to see you," I added, letting my voice break with emotion. "I don't know what else to do." Well, that was honest.

There was a pause. "I'm afraid tonight's not a good night, darling. Plans, you know. But we'll get together soon," she said coyly. "You can count on it."

I moved the receiver away from my mouth so she wouldn't hear me taking a deep breath. That was bullshit. She'd called me, she *wanted* me to see her fingerprints all over the wolfberry. She wanted me to know she was still in control, still the puppet master—and she wanted me to see her finest hour. Whatever she was planning with Mallory, she wanted to show it off, or she wouldn't have called tonight.

She wanted me to beg for her. Fine. I could beg. "Please, Livvie?" I pleaded. In a very small voice, I said, "I don't know where else to go anymore." *Thanks to you, you deranged harpy.*

Another long pause. I was still calming down from my earlier crying jag, and I made no attempt to hide my jagged breathing.

"Well…maybe it's a good night after all," Olivia said, her voice a little smug. She had won, and she knew it. "Things are going to change now, Scarlett. The way this whole city works is going to change. Would you like to see it happen?"

I waited a beat, and simply said, "Yes."

"Everything's going to be better now, Scarlett," she said soothingly. "We'll be together again. I have so many new things to teach you." She rattled off an address. "But you must come alone," she added.

"I will."

Olivia hung up without another word. I set the phone down on Will's desk. She didn't actually care if I brought backup or not—in her mind, there was nothing that could stop her and Mallory now. Kirsten would have been the biggest problem, and Kirsten had been shot. But it didn't matter—I wasn't going to bring anyone with me. Olivia was not going to hurt anyone else.

I was going to stop her first. Or die trying.

I looked around the office, and spotted Eli's jacket hanging on the back of Caroline's chair. I dug in his pockets until I found his keys. He wasn't going to need his pickup anytime soon, and I was guessing that Jesse's car had the GPS-LoJack thingy. And apparently it was my day for cruising around in half-borrowed, half-stolen vehicles. After a long moment of indecision, I picked up the handset of Will's office phone and dialed Jesse's cell phone number. He didn't pick up, which was a relief, really. I waited for the voice mail tone.

"Hey, it's Scarlett," I began. "Listen, I know where she is, and I'm going after her. By myself. Nobody else is going to die because Olivia wants me, and I'm not going to spend one more day as a bargaining chip, or a toy, or bait." I paused. "I know you think I'm just going to surrender and let her kill me, Jesse, but I promise, I'll fight. You...you make me want to fight. So thank you for that, I guess. I...I'm sorry it didn't work out between us." I rubbed my eyes, thinking about the broken werewolf in the other room. "I'm sorry about a lot of things. But not about this. Good-bye, Jesse."

I picked up Eli's keys and my wallet, started for the office door, and stopped again. I turned in a circle. The safe was in the janitorial room with Ana and her girlfriend, but Will had only been in and out for a second, and he wouldn't have wanted to be puttering with the safe while he was trying to give the women privacy. I went back to his desk and started opening drawers. I found the big revolver in the right middle drawer, next to a bottle of very expensive whiskey. Will must have been planning to put the gun away later. I picked up the gun and clumsily popped out the thingy that stored the bullets. I hadn't handled a gun like this before, but I'd seen plenty of Westerns with my grandfather when I was little. I counted two bright silver shells and snapped the thing shut again. I checked all the drawers one more time, but the extra bullets, if there were any, must have been locked in the safe. It was better than nothing.

My only real play here was to go the simplest route: get the bad guys in my radius and kill them. Mallory, whoever she was, couldn't use any kind of spell on me, including her big clay toy, so the greatest danger was that one of them would be carrying a gun. I didn't have my vest anymore, but I was guessing—well, betting my life, actually—that nobody was going to shoot me on sight. Olivia would try to convert me first, to get me on Team Evil. I just had to play along long enough to get close to both of them, shoot them, and be done. I took a deep breath. Piece of cake.

I looked down at myself, in the boots, T-shirt, and boxers. Where the hell was I going to put it? The boxers were too loose to hold the massive gun up, and my boots were too tight for it to fit inside. I sighed, wishing I'd kept the holster Jesse had given me. Out of ideas, I finally got a roll of duct tape from the desk and taped the gun to my lower back with a big X of tape. It hurt to bend my arms that way, and pulling the gun and tape off of my back would require an even more awkward position, but you couldn't see the gun while I was moving around in the T-shirt.

And besides, it had worked for Bruce Willis in a movie once.

I left my cell phone on the desk and stepped toward the hallway, pausing in the doorway to listen. I could hear the low voices of Matthias and Will still talking in the other room. Just across the hall, Anastasia was crying softly next to her unconscious girlfriend. I turned the other way, walking straight out the back exit and into the night.

Chapter 26

"What do you mean, she never got here?" Jesse Cruz asked the intake nurse, seething with frustration.

The nurse flicked a few keys on her keyboard with long, scary-looking red nails. "I have no record of anyone with that name coming in this evening," she reported. She gave him a professionally help-less look. "I'm sorry, Detective. There's nothing else I can tell you.

Jesse fidgeted, unwilling to move away from the counter despite the three people in line behind him. He had hitched a ride with a squad car to get to the hospital, irritated but unsur-prised that Scarlett had decided to drive herself to get checked out. When he'd finally arrived at the hospital, he'd been so *angry*, his thoughts focused on Runa and her betrayal, replaying all the con-versations they'd had to see what he might have given away. After he'd learned that Scarlett never arrived at the hospital, though, the rage had suddenly drained away, replaced by worry.

Just then the doors to the emergency room exam area began to open on their hydraulic controls, and Runa herself walked through them, her left forearm wrapped in a bandage. Her eyes were unfo-cused, distracted, and she nearly ran straight into Jesse.

"Oh. Hey." Her voice was uncertain and almost afraid.

Jesse looked her over. Even now, she was beautiful, with corn-silk hair falling out of her braids and sadness in her blue eyes. Jesse felt a sudden rush of grief for the person he had thought she was. He had been so wrong. "You got a second?" he asked. "I think you owe me a conversation."

She nodded, and they trudged over to the ER waiting room. Runa sat down first, looking exhausted, and Jesse took the seat opposite her, half-afraid that if he sat too close she'd somehow... what? Lure him back?

Once they were seated, though, he didn't know where to begin. "It's been over an hour," he said finally. "It took this long just for stitches?"

"I wouldn't let them stitch me until I knew what was happening with Kirsten," Runa explained. "She's my cousin."

"Oh." Jesse leaned back, digesting this. "Is she gonna be okay?" he asked.

Runa nodded cautiously. "They think so. The bullet didn't hit anything major, kidneys or lungs or whatever, but she'll probably lose her spleen. Which I guess you can live without. She's in surgery."

She added, "I called her husband. He was at a Christmas party in the Valley. He's probably with her by now."

"Good." Jesse felt his left knee jiggling up and down and made an effort to stop it. "So it's true? She sent you to spy on me?"

Runa looked around with concern, but the only other people in the waiting room were two young men discussing something feverishly in the opposite corner. They wouldn't be listening in. Runa relaxed an inch and met Jesse's eyes, her voice even. "Yes. At first."

"Did she tell you to sleep with me?"

Runa looked away, her strength already crumpled. *Different from Scarlett*, he thought.

"I deserve that," she said. "But no. I was just supposed to get a job as a police photographer and keep an eye on you. Be your friend."

"Explain to me, then, how you ended up being my girlfriend." *How you made me fall for you* was what he wanted to say, but he had a little bit of dignity left.

Runa smiled ruefully at Jesse, wrinkling her nose in that way that he loved. Had loved. "Kirsten actually thought you were too in love with Scarlett to make a pass at me. We were both surprised when you first asked me out." She began to lift her hands to gesture, but winced and settled her injured arm back onto her lap. "I wasn't, like, this evil Bond girl out to seduce away your soul and betray you, or anything like that. I was just supposed to keep an eye on who you talked to, whether you seemed to be investigating the Old World on your own, if you were keeping lists of us, stuff like that. It was clear to me a while ago that you weren't interested in exposing or arresting us, and I sort of...relaxed into our relationship."

Jesse thought that over for a moment. "Then why didn't Kirsten come to me right away when the witches began dying?"

She shook her head. "*I* trusted you, but Kirsten didn't. She could tell that I was...that I was falling for you." Runa took another deep breath. "We argued about it. Scarlett said something that helped convince her, and then she and I set up a little test for you, at the Jeep crime scene."

"Wait," Jesse said, confused. "What happened at the crime scene?"

She waved her good hand in front of her face, as if shooing a fly. "Not at the crime scene itself, but the next day. I had all those incriminating pictures of vampire activity, just right there for the taking. Kirsten thought you'd steal those shots, keep them as some kind of leverage against Dashiell." She beamed at him. "But you erased them. You helped cover up an Old World secret. I knew I could trust you."

"You could trust me," Jesse said flatly, "but I couldn't trust you, could I?"

She frowned, uncomfortable. "You have to understand what was at stake," she began, "what the witches have worried about for centuries..."

Jesse held up his hand. "Runa, I just spent the last hour help-ing a vampire control the minds of my brother officers. It's killing me, but I also know it was the right thing to do. I think I'm capable of some big-picture perspective."

She was silent for a moment, and then she said very quietly, "For what it's worth, I'm sorry."

Jesse was at a loss. He had loved this girl. And he was sup-posed to be a detective. How had he been so oblivious? How was it possible to love someone when you didn't really know them at all? He leaned forward, resting his elbows on his knees. "I'm sorry too," he said. "But you understand why I can't see you anymore, right?"

Tears filled her eyes. She would be one of those women who cried beautifully, he saw. When she nodded, they leaked down onto her cheeks. She lifted her good arm to wipe them off with the back of her hand. "Yes."

He stood up. "I should get going. I think Scarlett is missing, and we haven't caught Olivia or Mallory yet."

Runa frowned. "Scarlett is missing?" she asked.

"I'm not positive that it's anything big. But she's not answering her phone, and this isn't really the night for her to do that." He studied her face. "You don't know where she is, do you?"

"No...wait. What is she driving?"

Jesse smiled ruefully. "She took my car. I suppose I could always report it as stolen, but—" He slapped his head, feeling impossibly stupid.

"What?"

"I'm such an idiot. I have LoJack."

He made the calls, pacing a few feet away toward the waiting-room windows so he could get better reception. Runa looked up when he returned. She showed no signs of getting up from her wait-ing room chair, and he figured she must be sticking around for Kirsten.

"The car is at Hair of the Dog," he said.

"That's good, right?" Runa asked. "She probably had a cleanup job there or something. And Will will keep her safe."

"Yeah, I guess." But something felt wrong, he decided. He scrolled through his phone and found the right number. "I'm gonna call the bar." He went back over to the seats by the windows.

It rang forever. When someone finally picked up, the line was shockingly quiet. Every other time he'd called there, he'd had to shout over loud music to be heard. "This is Will," said a tired voice. Jesse identified himself and asked for Scarlett.

"Yeah," Will said heavily. "She's here. We had a...well, she can fill you in, I guess. I don't have it in me to talk about it. Hang on, I'll go have her pick up the line in the office."

There was a long pause, and Jesse found himself listening to a horrible Muzak cover of "Tainted Love." Then "I Want to Run to You." Just before the final chorus, Will finally picked back up. "Detective?"

"Jesse," he said automatically.

"Jesse. She's um...she's not here. I left her in the office, but she must have walked out the back door. Her wallet is gone, but she left her phone here."

"She couldn't have gotten far," Jesse objected. "My car is still parked there, or it was five minutes ago."

Will coughed. "I actually went outside and checked. If your car is a blue sedan, then yeah, it's here. But Eli's truck is missing. His keys are gone too." Will paused, and finally added, "I...um... think she's gone rogue."

Chapter 27

I drove south, blasting the heater in Eli's truck. I was shivering in my borrowed T-shirt and boxers, but there just wasn't time to stop at Molly's for a change of clothes and the White Whale, not if Mallory was really going to perform her spell at midnight. I was going to have to face Olivia just as I was, bloody boots and all.

She had given me directions to the San Mateo Clinic in Redondo Beach, which was a small, modern outpatient facility that had closed down in the mid-2000s. The once-prestigious clinic had grown famous for a perfect storm of controversy: within eighteen months, a corrupt chief of staff had set up an elaborate insurance scam and escaped the country, a huge sexual harassment lawsuit had been filed against a cardiologist on behalf of the support staff, and a little girl had died in a freak accident when she'd been climbing too quickly down a set of fire stairs. The clinic might have survived any one of those incidents, but not all three at once. The building's owners got tangled up in legal repercussions, and even years later San Mateo stood vacant while the court battles raged on. It wasn't much to look at: a squat, lonely brick building with a parking lot in back and faded *No Trespassing* signs to deter vandals and homeless people. Or, now that I thought about it, perhaps the deterrent was that anyone who wandered in would be eaten by vampires. I had to admit, it was an excellent choice for an evil lair.

I pulled Eli's truck around the back of the clinic building, as instructed, and saw no signs of life: no lit windows, no cars in the lot, no sound from the building's heating or air-conditioning systems. Cautiously, I followed the sidewalk to the clinic's enormous loading dock and climbed up the short ramp that led to a human-sized door beside it. I knocked twice.

After only a second, I felt a vampire enter my radius from the other side of the door. Olivia had been waiting for me. Even though I'd walked into the situation of my own free will, I still felt cornered when the door swung open and she stepped forward. "Scar-bear!" Olivia cried gaily. "You made it!"

Like we were at a goddamned brunch.

I allowed myself to be enveloped, and even managed to hug her back. "Hey," I said helplessly.

She took a step back, and her smile faded to a disapproving frown. "What on earth are you wearing?"

"Um, my clothes got shredded. Long story."

"I see. Are you all by yourself?" Olivia asked, peering around behind me. She was a human at the moment, so her night vision wouldn't be any better than mine, but I understood she had to make a show of it.

"Yes. Just like you said."

"Wonderful!" she said, beaming. We were back to brunch mode. "Follow me, please."

When the door had closed behind me she paused to type a code into a little numeric pad by the door. An alarm system. Her back was to me, and for a second I thought about just shooting her right there in the doorway. *Could I do that?* I wondered. *Just shoot her in the back, cold-bloodedly?* It didn't matter: I still needed to know where the witch was and what they had been planning. I followed her into the clinic building.

There was still a bit of emergency lighting, and I was able to make out a couple of long hallways and a big waiting room with an empty aquarium. Olivia led me through the waiting room and into the center of the building, where patients had been treated. There was a long corridor of exam rooms and then a big, open nurses' area with empty desks and metal file cabinets. This was where the vampire and the witch had set up shop.

There was no emergency lighting here, but a small portable generator hummed on one side of the room, and some lamps and extension cords brightened the cavernous area from almost pitch-black to bar-lighting dim. There were also candles set up all over the place, which contributed both to the lighting and the creepy sense of atmosphere. As my eyes fully adjusted, I realized the candles were set at all the corners of an enormous pentagram that had been painted on the open floor space. There were symbols and characters within the pentagram, but nothing I recognized with my limited experience. I shivered, suddenly unnerved.

"I don't like this," said a cold, hard voice behind us. I spun around, caught between Olivia and the new voice. I squinted and made out a woman silhouetted against the doorway. She'd been waiting for us, and now I was truly trapped.

"You must be Mallory," I said, still trying to make out the woman's features. I needn't have bothered—she stepped forward, into the light—and into my radius.

I gasped, hit by two perceptions at once. First, that this woman practically vibrated with power. She was as strong as Kirsten, maybe even stronger. At the same time, there was something about her magic that felt different from Kirsten's—darker, somehow, or more...decaying? There wasn't really a good word for it. I'd never felt anything like that.

As the light hit her, I also realized that she was horrifically scarred. She had long, gorgeous black hair, and her eyes, nose, and forehead were perfect, but all the exposed skin on her chin, neck, and chest looked like it'd been burned. Somewhat ironically, it looked like those parts of her skin were made from wet, flesh-colored clay. The scarring disappeared into her button-down shirt, which she wore under a traditional white lab coat. She leaned on some kind of cane, favoring her right leg. That was why she'd sent Olivia to take care of Rabbi Samuel. Samuel was a friend of the witches and a Jewish historian; he might have recognized the golem and known how to stop it. And Mallory couldn't overpower a grown man by herself. They made a good team, the vampire and the handicapped witch.

"So Kirsten figured it out, finally. Well, good for her," the woman said, nodding to herself. "I suppose it doesn't much matter at this point."

"Why not?" I asked, trying to keep my voice casual. Just having a little chat between us girls. They were both in my radius; it was time to make my move. My right hand drifted toward my back, but I paused. *Think it through first, Scarlett.* It would take a few seconds to pull up the long T-shirt and unstick the gun from my back. Another second to get the safety off. Olivia and Mallory would both realize what I was doing as soon as I lifted the T-shirt— did either of them have their own gun handy?

"Because Kirsten's going to die," Mallory was saying. "As are you."

Fuck it. I had to try.

I was just shifting my weight to reach for the pistol when, with no warning, Olivia's fist drove into my stomach. I gasped, doubling over so fast I lost my balance and fell on the floor, which jarred my aching back. Had Olivia seen the outline of the gun? I peered up at her, but she just smiled broadly. She'd been human, but she'd been so *fast.*

"What...was that for?" I panted.

"Sorry, darling," Olivia said, with a sympathetic smile. "I know Mallory sounds scary, but you'll actually be just fine. Better than ever."

I didn't answer, because for the second time that night I was struggling to remember the mechanics of breathing.

Mallory was looking at Olivia too. "It's eleven thirty already. Are you *sure* this can't wait until afterwards?" The way she said it made it sound like this was an argument they'd been having right before I arrived.

Olivia was too close to me to be a vampire, but she still bared her teeth in a feral, angry gesture. When she spoke, though, her voice was neither angry nor bubbly. "This was my condition," she said simply. "I want her with me. I want her to be a part of this. You knew that."

"Fine," Mallory sighed. "I'll prepare the IV. It'll take a bit for the radiation machine to warm up."

"*What?*" I gasped, but they both ignored me.

"How would you like her restrained?" Mallory asked Olivia, in a perfectly polite tone, like she was asking how Olivia wanted her eggs.

"The golem, of course."

"Of course. I'll go fetch it." Mallory leaned on her cane and took a few steps away from me, toward one of the exam rooms. I felt her leave my radius. As she went I saw her pulling something from her lab coat pocket that looked like a paintbrush or a small stick. I was still too weak to care much. I managed to roll myself onto my butt, head between my knees, trying to figure out how to uncurl myself and get to the gun. But Olivia crouched down right in front of me, eyes searching my face, and I froze, shivering with cold and nerves. Would she see it on my face? Dammit, I was *terrible* at this. Bruce would be ashamed.

There was some mumbling from the exam room, and then Mallory reemerged, brushing her hands together. The stick had disappeared back into her lab coat pocket. I opened my mouth to say something—no idea what—when I heard the thudding steps coming from just behind her. And the golem emerged.

It was shorter than I would have expected—maybe five foot six, only an inch taller than Mallory. It was gray and clumsy looking, with thick, long fingers, and it had been dressed in enormous baggy scrubs that strained against its wide body. A surgical cap was perched on its head, which turned slowly in my direction. Suddenly the pain in my midsection seemed awfully unimportant. Mallory had sculpted a crude nose onto it, probably so it would appear human from a distance, and she had gouged in bizarre flat holes where eyes should be. *Does he need to see where he was going?* I wondered. But she hadn't bothered giving the golem a mouth, which was the creepiest thing about it.

I imagined a halting Frankenstein walk, but the step that it took toward me was fluid and natural, if a little slow, like it was counting out paces. A bit of gray dust sprinkled down as it moved. The next step was the same. And the next. There was an aura of careless brutality about it. I wouldn't have been surprised if it suddenly picked up a kitten and snapped it in half. Now, I decided, would be an excellent time to actually friggin' do something. Shooting it wouldn't work, but I was still a null. I closed my eyes and concentrated on the outlines of my power, expanding my circle slowly until it reached the clay man. I felt the buzz of the spell enter my radius—

And the golem kept coming.

My eyes popped open. Had I done it wrong? A few steps later, he was inside the limits of my regular radius, and I narrowed my eyes at him, forgetting everything else and concentrating on the buzz of magic. It felt strange too—sort of detached. From magic. Like instead of a spell, a small generator had entered my radius.

And the golem kept coming.

Sudden laughter startled me, and as the thing continued forward I saw both Olivia and Mallory chuckling happily at each other, exchanging a look of "we got her!" like I'd fallen victim to a sorority prank. More quickly than I had expected, the golem closed the distance between us, and I felt crude fingers wrap around my left upper arm. I had expected the thing to be made of *wet* clay, given that it was moving, but its fingers felt dry and cold against my skin. It lifted, dragging me to my feet, and the strength of that movement was petrifying. There was no give to it, no fleshiness, no jerking. It was one smooth move, like being pulled up by the Terminator. "What the *hell*?" I demanded, forgetting that I was supposed to be playing Meek Scarlett. "How is this possible?"

Olivia frowned at me. "I believe we've talked about language, Scarlett."

I bit back what I *wanted* to say and forced my voice to sound contrite. "I'm sorry, Olivia. I just don't understand why her spell is still working."

"Isn't it phenomenal?" Olivia asked, beaming at me. "She's found a loophole."

The golem shifted around behind me, grabbing my other wrist. He shifted his grip to lock both of my wrists tight against my body with his cold hands, his fingers long enough to hold my hips still along with my arms. I gasped. *Handcuffs*, I thought, and fought a wave of terror. Breathe, Scarlett. Breathe.

"What kind of a loophole?" I choked out, wanting a distraction as much as I just wanted to know.

Across the room, Mallory rolled her eyes and strode off to another exam room. But Olivia *loved* lecturing me. "The golem isn't a normal movement spell," she explained smugly. "Animation magic is a lot closer to physically changing an object than it is to simply moving it. Mallory uses magic to bring the golem to life, as it were, and give it a task. Then the golem is animated in its own right, until the task is done.

"Giving the golem instructions counts as magic, but completing its current task does not." She gave an elegant shrug of her shoulders. "Like a windup doll. Your aura could stop her from winding it up, but once the windup has happened the little doll goes on its way regardless of what happens to its master."

"A windup doll," I repeated, dazed. The solid *wall* of clay behind me did not feel like any kind of children's plaything.

Experimentally, I tried throwing my weight back against it. It hurt like hell, both on my sore back and with the gun digging into my spine. Not only did the golem not rock backward, it didn't even sway a little.

Fantastic.

Olivia's voice rang with laughter. "Not to worry, Scar-bear," she assured me. "It's just going to hold you still for me."

"What are you going to do?" I asked. I couldn't keep the nervousness out of my voice. She patted my upper arm reassuringly.

She circled me until we were face-to-face and began smoothing my hair away from my ears, straightening the locks. "Do you know where our—where your—ability comes from?"

"Magic?"

She gave me an indulgent look. "Of course. But magic and science, they're permanently intertwined. And as it turns out, nullness is intertwined with a particular part of the body. A particular *system*." She paused. "You really have let this grow out, haven't you? Do you get regular trims?" She picked up a loose strand, examining the ends.

I knew she was baiting me on purpose, but I couldn't help but take it. "Please, Olivia, what do you mean by system? Like, circulatory and digestive, that kind of thing?"

"Exactly." She stepped back, spreading her hands. "If you think about it, it makes perfect sense. Your aura fights magic, fights to keep you normal and healthy and untouched by outside infection like vampirism or lycanthropy." She looked at me expectantly, but I just shook my head. Behind Olivia, Mallory had returned wheeling an IV stand. A bag of unidentified fluid with a long IV tube attached hung from one of the pegs at the top, and Mallory had already hooked two more bags on the opposite peg. She was making her way toward us, pulling the stand as she hobbled along on the cane.

Olivia was shaking her head, and I turned my attention back to her. "You never were a very good student. It's the immune system," she announced. "Your immune system suppresses invading disease, and your null aura suppresses invading magic. They're tied together." I'd spent months hanging around the cancer ward; I knew what the immune system did. I also knew that many cancer treatments—specifically chemotherapy and radiation—killed the immune system along with cancer cells. It was why cancer patients had to avoid being around sick people or little kids. "And when you *abandoned* me"—her eyes darkened—"I just happened to make a surprising discovery."

My mind raced.

"Domincydactl," I said softly.

Olivia took another step back to examine my face. She looked a little annoyed, like I'd ruined her punch line. "Perhaps you're not such a bad student after all," she said airily.

Mallory finally appeared at Olivia's elbow. "I have to begin in fifteen minutes," she told Olivia sternly.

My old mentor waved her hand dismissively. "You're all prepared, it'll be fine."

Mallory's mouth set in a frown, but she nodded and began tying a small rubber tube around my upper arm.

And it finally hit me. Olivia wasn't planning to keep me around as her pet, and she wasn't planning to kill me. She was going to do both.

She wanted to make me a vampire.

Chapter 28

"What about Eli?" Jesse asked, desperation seeping into his voice. "Does he know anything? Can I talk to him?"

Silence. Then Will said, "Eli is unconscious. It's a long story, but he'll be out at least until morning. I'm sorry; he can't help."

Jesse thought that over for a second. "Maybe you better tell me the long story."

When he hung up a few minutes later, Jesse realized he was sitting down again, his head in his hands as he stared absently at his cell phone. What was Scarlett thinking? Scratch that, he decided. He knew exactly what she was thinking. In that moment, he realized that the little voice mail icon on his phone's screen was blinking. Jesse frowned. When had that happened? His reception was terrible in the hospital, so it must have popped up when he'd finally gotten close to the windows. He pressed the screen and listened to the message.

"Shit!" he yelled, not caring that the two arguing men, the clawed intake nurse, and his newly minted ex were all staring at him. He couldn't believe she was really going to just hand herself over to the vampire. Jesse jumped up and beelined for Runa. "I need a car," he said bluntly. "You're staying here with Kirsten and her husband, right? Can I borrow their car?"

"Did you find her?" Runa asked, without moving.

He shook his head. "She went after Olivia by herself. I have to go look for her."

Runa raised her white-blonde eyebrows. "Do you know where she is?"

"No." He shifted his weight, anxious to be moving.

"So you're just going to drive around aimlessly and hope you find her?"

"Do you have a better idea?" he snapped.

"I might." Runa gave him a strange, speculative look. "Does *she* have a car?"

"She's driving Eli's."

"The bartender at Hair of the Dog?"

Jesse was surprised. He'd been under the impression that the different Old World factions didn't mix much. "You know him?"

"Kirsten does." She stood up from her seat, dug in her pocket, and dangled her keys. "I have a spare key for their car. You can drive. But I'm coming along. I can help."

His brow furrowed. "I'm not trying to start a fight, but how can you possibly help me?"

She straightened her back, squaring her shoulders. "First of all, I was the one who spent all afternoon researching the golem for Kirsten. She delegated to me so she could get ready for the party. I explained everything to her while we were making the appetizers, but I'm guessing she didn't have time to tell you or Scarlett before everything went to hell."

"No," Jesse said sheepishly. "Um, is there a second of all?"

"Second," Runa said, with sudden confidence, "I think I can find her."

Within a few minutes, they were speeding down the freeway to Santa Monica, where Eli had an apartment a few blocks from the beach. Christmas songs played on the radio in Paul Dickerson's

BMW, but Jesse was too distracted to pay attention. He had called and gotten Eli's home address from Will. Runa was texting Kirsten's husband to let him know she'd taken the car.

"Explain this to me again," Jesse said, glancing over at Runa. "I get the thing about you being good at finding things, but I thought you couldn't use that kind of spell on a null."

"I can't," she replied, looking up from her phone. "But I can find the car. This would be easy if I'd ever actually touched it myself, but because I haven't, I need a focus."

"Which is like a smaller part of what you're trying to find?"

He saw her nodding out of the corner of his eye. "With a person, a stranger, I need something of theirs. Hair or fingernails work the best—that's how Kirsten does it—but I can use pretty much anything they've owned and cared about for a long time."

"Wait," he objected. "So we can't just use one of Eli's T-shirts, or something, because that would just lead to Eli himself, right? What exactly are you planning to use as your focus?"

"A spare key," she pronounced. "The key might belong to Eli, as does the whole car, but a key is also *part* of the car itself, at least in the eyes of the spell. They belong together. It's a little different from ownership, but what should happen is I'll get two locations off the key: one for Eli, one for the car. And we already know where Eli is."

"What if he doesn't have a spare key? What if we can't find it?"

"It's LA. Everyone has a spare car key. Don't you?"

"Well, yeah," he said. "But still..."

"Look, it's better than driving around the city, yelling Scarlett's name out of an open car window like she's a lost puppy."

"Fair point," he conceded. They drove in silence for a second, and then he couldn't help but ask. "So you, like, never lose your keys, huh?"

When he glanced over, she was smiling. "You don't know the half of it," she said demurely. "Think of what I could do with a missing murder weapon."

"Whoa," he said, eyes wide. *Stick to tonight's problem,* Jesse told himself. "Okay, so what do I need to know about this golem thing?"

He felt Runa looking at him. "What did Kirsten already tell you?"

"That the golem is animated by a witch, and then runs on her commands," he recited.

"Right."

"And Kirsten said it was indestructible. If you chop it into bits, the bits would keep trying to complete the command."

She nodded. "And that's assuming it will hold still and let you chop it. Golems have incredible strength, and if the witch commands it, they can hurt or kill anything that comes between them and their goals. Besides, this is a *massive* chunk of clay. You could take an ax to its arm and only make it halfway through on your first swing."

"But wouldn't the golem just fall apart when it gets near Scarlett, anyway?" He was really hoping Scarlett's radius, as she called it, would encompass the witch, the vampire, and the golem, leaving him to face down just two humans and a pile of dirt. That seemed doable.

But Runa was shaking her head, looking solemn. "This is important. Scarlett won't be able to neutralize the golem."

"*What?* That's...how is that possible?"

She sighed. "I don't completely understand it. Something about animation as a permanent change, rather than a temporary spell. Think of it like...a loophole."

"That must be why Olivia wanted to work with Mallory in the first place," Jesse concluded. "Because she knew Mallory had a way around Scarlett's ability."

"Yes."

He thought that over for a minute. "You said 'if the witch commands it.' So it's sort of about careful wording for the commands?"

"Exactly. If the witch says, 'Go get me that banana,' the golem will go over to the banana and pick it up. She would have to specifically instruct it to bring it back to her. And, if she were so inclined, she'd have to tell it to destroy anyone who gets in its way," Runa said. "That's the really tricky thing about the golem magic. Once the clay is animated, there are plenty of witches who have the juice to push a command like 'Bring me Denise Godfry' into the golem. But only a really powerful witch can hold the golem long enough to give it a complicated command like, 'Bring Denise Godfrey to the end of the Santa Monica Pier and throw her in the water. Keep her quiet and still the whole time, and kill anyone who gets in your way,' or something like that."

Jesse tried to concentrate. He needed to ask the right questions. "So if I can't destroy the golem physically, how do I stop it?"

He glanced at Runa. "That's the interesting part," she said, tucking loose strands of blonde hair behind her ears. "Channeling magic is all about symbolism—this stands in for that, this spell symbolizes that activity. A golem needs more than just words in the air. It needs a word on *itself*."

"You lost me."

Runa reached up and touched her own forehead. "Here. The witch carves a word in the clay right here, and it's like the stamp of the command spell. In the example I used before, the witch would carve the word *banana*. If the task is directed at a person, it's a name, like Denise or Scarlett. The word is the permanent change; it's what allows the golem to act even in Scarlett's radius. If everyone is standing next to Scarlett, Mallory wouldn't be able to give the golem a new command. She needs to channel magic for that. But if she gives the golem a command outside Scarlett's radius, the golem can follow through within it."

"Unless I remove the word?" Jesse said.

"Exactly. Take away the word, you take away the command. No command and no magic means no golem. In theory the thing would just...collapse."

"In theory."

"Just keep in mind, the thing is made out of hard clay that's dry on the outside. You can't just rub your hand across it a couple of times."

"Okay."

"I think we're here," she said abruptly.

Jesse checked the GPS on his phone. "You're right." He parked the car at a legal spot on the block next to Eli's, and the two of them got out and walked casually toward the outdoor stairs that led up to his place. "Will said it's on the third floor," he said quietly to Runa. "There's an interior door into the building, but you need a key to get in."

"This is so weird," she whispered back. "I've broken into my friends' houses before, with a hide-a-key or whatever, but never someone I haven't actually met."

"Me neither," Jesse growled. He was getting more and more nervous as they climbed the stairs. He was a *cop*, for crying out loud. It helped a little that he knew Eli would approve, if he were conscious, but that would still be hard to explain to the Santa Monica patrol cops. A West LA detective committing a B and E at 11:00 on a school night didn't look good, no matter how you spun it.

"You sure you want to do this?" Runa whispered, reading his expression.

He nodded. "Let's just get it over with."

They finally reached the right door, and Jesse peeked around, seeing no obvious witnesses. There was a bit of noise from some clubs on the next street over. He glanced at Runa, who nodded that it looked all clear to her too. Then Jesse pulled the minicrowbar out of his jacket sleeve.

It was a nice, solid chunk of metal that they'd purchased at a twenty-four-hour convenience store along with two candy bars, a hammer, and some nails to divert suspicion. Jesse fitted

252   *Melissa F. Olson*

the crowbar into the crack of the door, closest to the lock. They didn't have time for finesse. He nodded at Runa, and she began knocking. "Eli?" Jesse called. "It's Jesse, man, you around?" The noise from the knocking and yelling almost masked the sharp *crack* of the wooden door as it splintered open. Jesse and Runa slipped in quickly, closing the broken door behind them, and Jesse turned on all the lights. He immediately wiped the crowbar on his shirt and dropped it on a chair near the front door. If they got caught, he would simply say the door had been broken when they'd arrived.

The apartment was more or less one big room, with two doors jammed in the back. Jesse figured they probably led to a bedroom and bathroom, not the kind of places where one usually kept a spare key. "If you were a spare key, where would you be?" Runa mused.

Jesse checked the walls and tables nearest the door, in case he kept it conveniently in plain sight. No such luck. Eli had decorated the walls with bits and pieces from the ocean, shells and starfish and things, and the main wall space near the front door was taken up by an enormous surfboard. "Usually people go for a kitchen drawer or desk drawer," he said absently, taking in the rest of the room. It was sparse: a couch, an armchair, a television, and a small card table that was covered in some sort of woodworking project. Runa peeked into the two doors at the end of the room. "No desk," she reported.

The kitchenette was tiny, but he gestured that way with a nod. "Let's start there."

They worked quickly through the drawers and cupboards, shifting through utensils and hard plastic dinnerware that looked like it could take a bullet before cracking. Eli must not eat in very often, Jesse thought, or he only ate sandwiches and fruit, because there weren't enough dishes for real cooking. In this case it worked to their advantage: less stuff to go through.

Runa checked the freezer, rummaging around behind boxes of microwave dinners. "Saw it in a movie," she said sheepishly, as she closed the freezer door.

Jesse dropped into a folding chair, fidgeting. "We might be way off about this. He might not even have a spare key. Or he might have given it to a friend for safekeeping. Hell, *Scarlett* might have it."

"Don't give up yet," Runa soothed him, patting his shoulder. "We still have the bedroom and the bathroom."

Jesse looked up at her. He still felt the vestiges of love, and the grief, but something had changed fundamentally between them. It was like she'd torn off a mask. He didn't even know this Runa, who was committing a major crime with him to stop a couple of nutcases she'd never even met. "I don't want to go in there," he confessed. "It's too...personal." And he didn't want to see where Scarlett and Eli had slept together.

"Okay, let's stop and think this through," she said thoughtfully. "You're Eli. You lock your keys in your car, which is parked illegally downstairs. You're running late for something, so you wouldn't want to have to track through the whole apartment to find it."

"It's not in the kitchen, and it's not on a hook by the door," Jesse added.

They stood like that for a moment, and Jesse felt the beginnings of despair. If they couldn't find Scarlett...

"The surfboard," Runa said suddenly. She was eyeing the giant board by the front door.

"What about the surfboard?"

"Look, there's something behind it."

Jesse followed her line of sight. There was a very narrow closet door set in the wall just behind the surfboard. They moved at the same time; Jesse pulled the board aside so Runa could grab the closet doorknob. It opened with a jingle. There were three sets of keys tacked to the back of the door. Someone had taped a piece of masking tape over each one, labeling the sets *Car*, *Apartment*, and *HotD*.

"Hot Dee?" Runa said, confused.

"Hair of the Dog," Jesse said. He snatched the car keys off the hook and thrust them at Runa. "Let's do it."

Runa looked around the room, and finally went over to the carpeted area in front of the TV. She pulled a piece of chalk out of her skirt pocket. "Other witches do this differently, but I've always liked working within circles," she explained, drawing a large one on the carpeting. She didn't completely close the circle, leaving a gap of four or five inches. "It helps me focus."

Jesse shifted his weight uneasily. "Do you need me to leave?"

"No, just be quiet and don't let anything cross the line." She looked around. "And I don't have a map, so I'll need to do this with a pen and paper."

"That I did see in the kitchen," Jesse said, and he retrieved a chewed-up pen and a pack of Post-it notes for her. "How long will it take?" He tried not to sound as anxious as he felt.

Runa shrugged helplessly. "Five minutes? Ten? Usually I do an elaborate circle with candles and stuff to help get me in a trance, but this is the quick-and-dirty version. Just try to be patient."

He nodded, and she stepped into the circle, sitting cross-legged with the paper and pen and key in front of her. She picked up the chalk again and closed the circle, then exchanged the chalk for the car key. Jesse sat down in the folding chair again, not wanting to crowd her by taking the sofa or armchair. He was expecting her to start chanting in Latin or something, but to his surprise she closed her eyes, took in a deep breath, and let it out in a single humming note. Jesse had attended a couple of her yoga classes when they'd first started dating, and this was not unlike the *Ommmmmm* sound she used at the beginning and end of each class. She had a nice voice, and he found the tone sort of pleasant, rather than annoying.

That went on for a few minutes, until Jesse felt the tiredness overtaking his body. He'd been running on adrenaline since his stakeout at Kirsten's, and he hadn't exactly slept well on the floor at his parents' house. Now that his body was still, he was beginning to feel it.

Suddenly the hum stopped, and Runa did begin to chant, but not in Latin. It was a singsong, lilting language Jesse didn't recognize. Kirsten was Swedish, wasn't she? If they were cousins, maybe this was Swedish? Finnish? Something Scandinavian, surely. Runa's upper body tilted forward, and her right hand crept down to the floor, picking up the pen. She scrawled something on the Post-it note, and Jesse had to restrain himself from running over to break the circle and snatch it up. Instead, he sat impatiently as Runa went through a couple more minutes of the humming tone, and then she opened her eyes. She shook her head a little, focusing on him, and looked blearily down at the note.

"Oh, here." She ripped the top sheet off and handed it to him. He squinted to make out her tiny handwriting: *Dayton and Freight St., Redondo Beach.* "Do you know where that is?"

"I think so," Jesse said. "I know Freight Street, anyway."

"Then you should go."

He took a step and hesitated. "What about you?"

Runa smiled sadly. "I'm going to call a cab." She brightened suddenly. "Oh, wait." The witch dug in her other skirt pocket and came out with a tiny bag on a long string. "I grabbed this for you from Kirsten's car. She keeps a couple just in case."

He took the little bag, looking at her face. "Protection amulet?" he asked, surprised. He'd been under the impression that only certain people were given these.

She nodded. "It's not elegant, but it's the quick-and-dirty version again," she said. She reached over and tapped the bag. "This one is for protection against witches."

"Not vampires?"

Runa shrugged. "You can only wear one at a time, for it to work. From what Kirsten told me, Olivia will stay pretty close to Scarlett, which means the witch will be the one at large. This will prevent her from spelling you."

"Thank you." He hung the long string over his head, tucking the bag into his shirt. Looking around, he also picked up the crowbar and hid it back in his sleeve. Just in case.

"Remember," Runa added, "as soon as you get close to Scarlett, that amulet will short out. So make it count, Jesse."

He met her gaze and found a whole unspoken conversation there. She stepped forward and gave him a gentle, brief kiss on the lips. "Go," she whispered.

He went.

Chapter 29

The second I realized what Olivia was planning, the panic took over. Even though some rational part of my brain knew it was useless, I kicked backward against the golem, forcing it to hold my weight so I could use both legs. Nothing happened. The damn thing didn't even have to adjust its grip, and my kicks were completely ineffective. I braced my feet back on the ground and slammed my head backward, hoping to startle it, but the golem didn't have pain sensors, and although I did feel a tiny bit of give as I dented its nose, all I really ended up with was a minor headache.

Olivia had simply taken a small step back while I did all this, a bemused, taunting smile on her face. "All done?" she said cheerfully. I didn't answer. "Very well." She nodded to Mallory, who shuffled forward, bent a little, and pinched at a vein in my left hand. The pain was surprising and sharp, and I felt involuntary tears spring to my eyes. I'd had an IV before, but real nurses actually tried *not* to hurt you. The needle went in, and Mallory held it in place with one hand while she peeled a line of surgical tape off her opposite arm. She taped the needle roughly to my hand, and then straightened up to fiddle with something on the IV pole. The clear liquid—the Domincydactl—flooded down into the tubing.

Mallory took a hobbling step back, admiring her handiwork. She looked at Olivia. "Good?" Olivia nodded, and Mallory checked her watch. "I'm going to begin," she announced. Mallory hobbled away, toward her pentagram. I felt it when she tugged out of my radius.

The needle was in. The chemo had begun.

I was too stunned to make any kind of comment. Part of me had been counting on Jesse to burst in at the last second, shoot the bad guys, and somehow destroy the golem. That part just couldn't believe it hadn't happened.

They were really going to kill me. And then bring me back.

The possibility had honestly never occurred to me, and it was taking a long time to sink in. When I found out about the Old World, I thought I had guaranteed immunity from becoming a vampire or werewolf. Even when I'd learned Olivia was a vampire, I hadn't really considered the implications. God, I was an idiot.

What would happen after? Best case, maybe I could escape from her, somehow, and go live with Molly again. We could be like morally questionable sisters, or something. But vampires had some sort of power over their progeny. Molly had hinted about it at some point, but I hadn't asked more questions—it wasn't like I would ever need to know personally, right? But what if Olivia could order me to do anything she wanted?

And even if she didn't...I just didn't want to be a vampire. I didn't want to only live when the sun was down. I didn't want to hurt anyone. And I would miss the beach, and running in the sunlight, and oh my God, *food*...

I struggled to get hold of myself. I had promised Jesse I would fight. I didn't want to break my last promise as a human.

Olivia disappeared from my line of sight for a second, then returned pushing a wheelchair. She parked it next to the golem, put the brakes on, and settled herself into the chair, crossing her ankles demurely. We watched as Mallory puttered about her pentagram, reciting chants and sprinkling herbs around. She picked up something that had been resting on the book's open page and hung it over her head. As she bent forward, I saw an ordinary-looking rock swinging back and forth on a leather thong.

"Exciting, isn't it?" Olivia sighed. When I didn't answer, she looked over at my stunned expression. "Oh, relax," she said dismissively, waving a hand. "It'll probably take several doses before your aura dies. We're not really sure, as I had already completed a number of treatments before the Domincydactl worked." She added brightly, "But we'll just keep trying until we figure out the formula. This clinic has all the equipment. That's why I was so eager to get your treatment started, in case it takes us a few tries." She patted my upper arm again, then frowned at my hair. "Of course, I'd hate for you to lose all that gorgeous hair, even if it does need a trim." She smoothed her own dark bob. "I was one of the lucky ones who didn't lose hair with chemo, of course, but I don't know if you'll be so fortunate."

I searched for words, completely at a loss. Olivia's plan, anyway, was clear to me now: she had threatened and scared and hurt my loved ones just enough so that when she called for me, I would come. Like a dog. Then she could turn me into her little vampire pet. But what the hell was Mallory doing?

Also, if I lost my hair from the chemo, would it grow back, or would I be a bald vampire?

"What," I began, and had to swallow past my dry throat. "What is she doing?"

Olivia looked at me to see if I was being sincere, and she decided to answer me. "She's completing a spell she began almost a decade ago," Olivia whispered conspiratorially. "That was how we met. The spell failed the first time, and the golem she had at the time took most of the lightning strike for her." Olivia gestured to her own face and chest. "It still managed to hit Mallory, though."

I was beginning to feel a little woozy, but I was trying to tell myself I might just be tired and sore. I'd lost a reasonable amount of blood too, back at the bar. Maybe that was all I was feeling. "I don't get it. If she was able to almost complete the spell the first time, why did you guys have to go for the big guns? The Transruah? The mandrake?"

Olivia gave me an approving look. "You *have* been doing your homework, haven't you?" She stretched luxuriously in her chair. When I didn't respond, she pouted a little. It wasn't as much fun if I didn't beg for it. "Mallory had help the first time," she explained. "Another witch worked with her, someone of no consequence. I'm absolutely useless with magic, of course, so this time Mallory decided to get all her ducks in a row before she would make her move: the Transruah, the solstice, and the mandrake root, which she's using now." Olivia nodded toward Mallory and her herbs. "She doesn't even need her golem, with all of that." She patted my hand, saying warmly, "I'm so pleased that you get to be here for this." Like we were at a brunch again.

"But why?" I asked, trying to keep my voice mild. I *had* to know what was behind all of this. All those deaths. "I mean, does this big spell even do anything?"

This was meant to taunt her a little, and it worked. She gave me another disapproving look. "Of course it does," she said severely. She turned her focus back to the pentagram. Mallory was seated now, her cane abandoned outside the ring of candles. An enormous, tattered book sat open in front of her, and she was reading aloud from it. The Book of Mirrors. A good man had died just so that book could be in this room. "There are two parts, now," Olivia whispered. "First she needs to restore herself, physically and magically. That's what the mandrake is for, to gather life that she can channel into her own body."

"She's going to heal?" I asked. I don't know why I was surprised.

Olivia nodded smugly.

"Where does it come from? The...life...she uses to heal herself?"

Olivia waved a hand. "Oh, the air, perhaps, I don't know. She's not stealing a whole life for that, so a sacrifice is not necessary, not with the arsenal she's got."

Okay, I thought. *So far not so bad.* "What's part two?"

The smug look again. "When she is whole, I'll escort her to the hospital, to Kirsten's bedside."

"Kirsten?" I echoed, startled. "What does she have to do with any of this?"

But Olivia held up a hand. "Shh. This is my favorite part."

I felt like we were at an outdoor barbecue, watching the cook flip burgers in the air. Mallory went silent, her eyes closed, and a wind seemed to pick up in the enclosed room. The witch's long hair whipped around her head, and the lapel on her white lab coat fluttered. I couldn't feel any sort of draft, though, and the candles weren't flickering.

I had to at least *try* to do something. If I could just get the Transruah in my radius, I could shut it down permanently, and the spell with it. I closed my eyes and concentrated on my radius again, trying to expand it once more, but I couldn't find the edges. It was still intact, still there, because I could feel Olivia within my radius, but I just couldn't focus on it.

"Is there something else in this IV?" I mumbled.

Olivia smirked. "I wondered if you'd notice." She patted my hand again. "The chemo can be quite painful, so I had Mallory add a little bit of morphine. Just to help with the first dose."

I'd had the drug before, when I had my wisdom teeth out in high school, and the thrown-for-a-loop-de-loop feeling was awfully familiar, now that she mentioned it. I also thought that I might pass out. Olivia had an expectant look on her face, like I should be thanking her, but I couldn't even collect my thoughts enough to decide if the morphine was a good thing or not. Had she really given it to me to help with pain, or had she figured that morphine would scramble my thoughts enough that I wouldn't be able to focus on my radius? Was that too paranoid? Could you *be* too paranoid, on a morphine drip?

My eyelids slid shut. A few minutes went by, or maybe more, and then I felt Olivia nudge me.

"Watch this," she whispered next to me, and I struggled to open my eyes. The wind inside the pentagram was dying down, and Mallory's hair went still. Her head was slumped over, her chin resting on her chest. As she lifted it, both Olivia and I gasped.

Mallory's face was *flawless*. The scarring was completely gone from her neck and chest too, and the skin looked white and brandnew, which it was. She met Olivia's eyes and gave her a sharp nod, then stood up swiftly, testing her weight on her right leg. Then Mallory broke into a brilliant, victorious smile, and for just a moment I couldn't even hold it against her. Almost a decade of those injuries, and now they had been wiped clean.

In that moment, if Mallory had announced she was planning to stop right there, retire from witchcraft, and move to Flagstaff to raise purebred French bulldogs, I would probably have wished her luck and offered her some gas money. Then I remembered Eli and Caroline, not to mention Erin and Denise and the rabbi in San Diego. And Denise's daughter, Gracie.

And Kirsten. *She wants to hurt Kirsten*, I reminded myself.

But you're kind of mad at Kirsten right now, my inner monologue said. *For Jesse?*

Yeah, not that mad.

Goddamned morphine.

Mallory took the Transruah off and set it carefully on the Book of Mirrors. She left both of them in the center of the pentagram and came over to us. When she hit my radius it felt blinding, like when you walk out of a dark movie theater into bright sunlight. If my arms had been free, I might even have shielded my eyes from it. As strong as she had felt before, now she was supercharged.

And yet…my radius still made her human again. She was strong, but my ability to neutralize her was stronger. I would have felt a teensy bit smug about that if I hadn't been receiving unnecessary chemotherapy in the arms of an invulnerable clay robot man at the moment.

"Are you ready to get moving?" Mallory asked Olivia, still smiling her joyful smile. "I'm feeling very energized. The time is right."

Olivia rose from the wheelchair in one graceful move and looked doubtfully at me. "Will she be okay?" she asked Mallory. "I don't want anything to happen to her." She eyed me speculatively, like a valuable painting she had purchased and now had to store.

"She'll be fine," Mallory assured her. "The golem will keep her in position. I'll switch the IV bag before we leave." She came up to Olivia and put one hand on her shoulder. "Everything we've worked for is finally happening, Liv." Olivia patted Mallory's hand on her shoulder.

I blinked with surprise at that. I'd never seen Olivia sincerely accept a comforting gesture before. Hell, I'd never seen her treat anyone like an equal, ever. I wasn't getting any kind of romantic vibes between them or anything, but was it actually possible that Olivia had found…a friend?

Maybe it was the morphine, but I almost giggled. The psychopathic monster vampire had a friend. Then I remembered what they were about to do.

"Why go after Kirsten?" I asked Mallory bluntly. Way to form a question, Scarlett! Keep going! "You've got all this power, why waste your time on another witch? Why not just…do what you've been wanting to do?"

Mallory raised her eyebrows at Olivia, who shrugged like I was a puppy that just wouldn't stop begging. Might as well just give her the treat. Mallory advanced on me until our faces were inches apart. "Stupid girl," she said. "Killing Kirsten *is* what I've been wanting to do." She glared at me. "Years ago I wanted to kill her with magic, to prove that she was nothing special. And I thought it would be elegant to force the Old World to take care of the cleanup for me." She tilted her head at Olivia. "But now I'll be able to not just kill her, but take what she has for my own." The witch turned away from me.

Her power. Mallory was going to use the Transruah to steal Kirsten's power. "But why?" I blurted. "What did she ever do to you?"

Mallory stopped and spun on her heel. "You people," she hissed with frustration, glaring at me. Olivia was tense beside her, looking from me to Mallory and back again, but she stayed silent. "You think you're—what, a government? With your rules and your procedures? You think you can regulate magic, tell witches what they can and can't do?" She spat at my feet. Which could probably only help my boots at this point, I figured. Olivia twitched, like she was ready to get between us. "We are better than all of you. We have fought longer and harder for what we can do, and *Kirsten* dares to call herself a leader to us. When all she really does is hand out muzzles and teach the other witches to be grateful for them."

I only had one move here, I decided. I had to stall the two of them, to buy Kirsten as much time as I could to get her strength back, and to try to push Mallory's timetable so that she wouldn't have the solstice to aid her. It wasn't much, but it was the only play I had left. The only problem was that I was having a little trouble holding my head up at this point. It kept threatening to loll forward, which probably wouldn't look very dignified. I decided it was time to bring out my personal superpower: insolence.

No more Meek Scarlett. *Fuck* Meek Scarlett.

But by the time I had put that string of thoughts together, Mallory had turned away again. "So wait," I said in a thoughtful, conversational tone. "You're saying it's *not* just because she's prettier than you?"

Mallory whipped back around, seething, and slapped my face. I tasted blood in my mouth, but didn't feel any actual pain. I had no idea what the usual chemo treatments felt like, but I was beginning to think someone could make a killing selling a Domincydactl and morphine cocktail on the street. Olivia shot me a glare but stepped in between the two of us. "I can't have that," she warned Mallory. "She is mine to protect, mine to strike."

"I meant now, by the way," I interjected. "Obviously you were a total dog an hour ago, but at least your face had some character. Now you look like plastic that melted and got re-formed all wrong."

Mallory looked from me to Olivia, incredulous. "You heard what she—"

"She is trying to annoy you," Olivia cut in smoothly. "She wants you to focus on her so you'll stay away from Kirsten. Don't fall for it." Damn. I had forgotten that as well as I knew Olivia, she knew me too. "Change the IV bag, and let's go collect our witch," Olivia said to Mallory. To me, she said, "I must thank you, by the way. My intention was to wound Kirsten and bring her with me, but I got overzealous. If you hadn't stepped in front of that second shot, I might have accidentally killed her." I stared at her. "Of course, my poor heart almost stopped again when I saw you get hit," she added, as an afterthought. "I'm so glad you had the vest."

She poked me in the stomach, provoking a surprised little grunt from me. "Not wearing it now, I see. Good to know." I felt my IV line swaying as Mallory disconnected the now-empty first bag of fluid. She tossed it to the floor and hung the next bag in its place.

Before she could connect the tubing, however, every lamp in the room went out. The generator had ceased its buzz. The only light was from the candles that still burned around Mallory's pentagram. "What was that?" Mallory asked, annoyed. I felt her drop the IV tubing in disgust. "I can't see a damned thing," she snapped.

"The generator went out," Olivia said. "It's probably nothing."

But Mallory's voice was suddenly in front of me again, her breath hot on my face. "Who did you tell?" she growled at me. "Who knows we're here?"

"Calm down, Mal. She didn't tell anyone."

"How do you know that? How can you know for sure?"

I felt a familiar hand begin to caress my hair. "Because her greatest fear is that someone else will die for her. I threatened her loved ones. And attacked her favorite, the werewolf. She wouldn't take any risks that I might hurt one of them here."

That was it. I wanted to maintain control, but I couldn't help myself. I turned my head and bit Olivia's hand and hard as I could, drawing blood. She gasped with surprise, tearing it out of my teeth, and I felt my face getting slapped again, and for a moment I saw stars.

And then something happened. Maybe it was getting hit, or the morphine, or the chemo, but inside my head I felt something just *shift*. It wasn't like something had changed in me, not exactly. It was more like a door sliding open on oiled hinges. I felt the edges of my radius again, instantly, and more strongly than I'd ever felt them before. The circle—no, the sphere—was defined perfectly, and I felt what I could do, the nullness, flood in to fill it, like pouring a can of paint into an aquarium. For the first time in my life, I *understood* it. I could call to it. I just wasn't sure what I could get it to do. Not yet.

But I lost the thread of that thought pretty quickly, as more pressing matters required my attention. Olivia had been saying something, like she was announcing some sort of a plan. "I'll go restart the generator," she said to Mallory. "Then we—"

"Quiet!" Mallory hissed suddenly. "I heard something." All three of us froze, listening to the dark, but there wasn't anything to hear.

"Let me get away from her," Olivia whispered. "I can't do anything if I can't see." She moved away from my side, presumably to get out of my radius, where she would have excellent night vision.

"Neither can I," Mallory grumbled. "I'll restart the generator." She patted the golem's arm, almost affectionately. And then every candle in the room went out at once.

Chapter 30

Let them be by her, Jesse prayed as he crept down the hallway. He'd seen Eli's truck parked outside the clinic building—if they all survived this, it was going to take a ridiculous amount of driving to get everyone's cars back to the right owner—and driven right past it, parking on the complete opposite side of the building, near the main clinic entrance. The door, when he came up to it, was wired with a serious-looking alarm. Not knowing what else to do, Jesse had called Dashiell on his cell phone and explained the problem.

"I don't suppose you would wait until I arrived to go in?" Dashiell had asked.

"Not a chance." Kirsten's house was at least half an hour away, and if he'd returned to Pasadena, Dashiell was even farther.

"Fine. Give me two minutes, and then break whatever you have to," Dashiell said. "I'll be on my way."

Jesse had actually timed out the two minutes on his watch, and then used the minicrowbar to shatter one of the waist-high windows near the entrance. He had thought the window would cause less of a racket than the full-length glass doors, but the shattering glass still seemed terrifically loud. If they were in the heart of the building, and Scarlett was close enough to neutralize Olivia and Mallory, they might not have noticed. Maybe. At any rate, there hadn't been any sort of alarm. Dashiell really was scary like that.

Jesse crept through a big lobby area, grateful for the emergency lighting that gave him some sort of path to follow. He'd brought a flashlight, but the second he turned it on he'd give himself away, so he kept it off until he finally came upon a small wall map for the clinic's interior. Holding the flashlight close to the map, he'd studied the exits and building interior and taken a guess at where Mallory and Olivia might be holed up. Then he did his best to follow the bright red pulse of the exit signs down the right hallways.

At last, Jesse heard voices. He froze, holding his breath as though that might give him away. The voices didn't pause, however, and he figured Olivia, at least, must be inside Scarlett's circle. He used the toe of one shoe against the heel of the other, working his shoes off, then crept forward silently in his socks.

When he peeked around the corner of the doorway, he could see them: Scarlett and two dark-haired women, on the opposite side of a large, open area where there must once have been desks for nurses. On the wall closest to Jesse, there was a small generator humming. Beyond that, an enormous pentacle had been painted on the floor, with a book and amulet left in the middle of it. Beyond *that*, he could just make out the women. Scarlett was talking but not moving, and it took a second of staring for Jesse to make out the shadow behind her, holding her wrists tight against her body. The golem.

He pulled his head back into the hall and thought for a moment. A direct assault wouldn't work—Olivia might still have her gun. If he burst in there with his own weapon drawn, she could just step behind Scarlett and lift the gun to her temple, creating a classic hostage standoff. Instead, Jesse got down on his hands and knees and crawled into the room, toward the generator. He was grateful for his dark clothes and for the very dim candle lighting on this side of the room. If he stayed low, he had to be pretty much invisible to them.

Now he could make out the conversation on the far side of the room. They were talking about Kirsten, about going to her hospital room. One of the women was nearly shaking with anger as she talked about Kirsten, and Jesse figured this must be Mallory. She and Olivia were focused on Scarlett, their backs to the rest of the room. Scarlett said something in a low voice he couldn't make out, and Mallory slapped her in the face. Jesse flinched, but a slap wouldn't kill her, and he needed to stay focused. Then he heard something about an IV bag and squinted in the darkness again. Sure enough, there was a long silver pole standing next to Scarlett and the shadowy golem. Whatever they were giving her, it couldn't be good: Scarlett's head was lolling, and her words had a slight slur. *Shit.* He'd been counting on her to be able to help him fight as soon as she was free. Now he needed a new idea. Unconsciously, he reached up to touch the little bag around his neck. Runa was right: he knew what Olivia wanted, and she'd stay close to Scarlett. Mallory was the wild card. He needed to draw her out first.

Jesse looked around quickly and crawled to the nearest candle on the pentagram, a thick four-inch-tall votive in a simple glass jar. He slid it to the side very carefully and slowly, inch by inch, so that he could slide his upper body forward in the pentagram. He was holding his breath, not daring to look up at the women in front of him. Scarlett was talking again, so hopefully the other two still had their backs to him. He leaned farther and farther until his fingers touched the edges of the large spellbook. Jesse wanted both the amulet *and* the book, but when he lifted the book to slide it toward him the Transruah rolled soundlessly off the page and onto the carpet. He hesitated, but it was too much of a risk. The book would have to do.

He slid backward again and scooped up the candle he'd moved earlier, shielding it behind his body. He crawled back into the hallway, where he set it on top of a cheap fake-wood desk that had been abandoned against a wall. As quickly and quietly as he could, Jesse climbed up onto the table, lifted up one of the ceiling tiles, and shoved the Book of Mirrors on top of neighboring tiles. He replaced the tile he'd lifted, hopped down so fast he almost landed on his ass, and sneaked back into the room, crouching next to the generator. Jesse waited by the generator, tense, until the witch disconnected the old bag from the IV, and then he flipped the switch.

The lamps on their side of the room snapped out, as did a couple of floor fans and an alarm clock. The room went silent for a heartbeat, and then Olivia and Mallory began asking questions. Jesse scooted back into the hallway as fast as he could, climbed onto the desk in his sock feet, and lifted the candle above his head, toward the little sprinkler spigot.

Jesse knew sprinklers didn't work like in the movies—you didn't automatically get a building full of active sprinklers just because heat registered under one of them. Usually the only sprinkler that went off was the one that had detected heat. This was a medical clinic, though, and on the building map Jesse had seen the little symbols that indicated this was a zone-sprinkler building—if you set off one sprinkler, all the sprinklers in a designated zone would follow. He was just praying the hall spigot was part of the same zone as the nurse's area. And that the emergency system was still working, period.

Ten, fifteen, twenty seconds ticked by, and even the spigot he was under remained dry. Jesse began to worry that the system was too old, or perhaps it had been turned off, if that was possible—and then the water began. And a moment later, the screams.

Chapter 31

When the sprinklers went off, I knew immediately that it was Jesse, despite my not-unpleasant drug haze. He had found me. I felt a great swell of joy that he was there, but a simultaneous panic too. My chances of getting through this had probably increased, but this was also exactly what I *didn't* want: risking someone else I cared about. I needed to *wake up*. I tilted my head back to let the rancid-smelling water splatter on my face, hoping it would clear my head a little. It wasn't coming down like rain so much as misting all around us, and my arms were immediately as wet as my face. Which gave me an idea.

Olivia and Mallory had both shrieked when the water began—for a second I entertained a brief hope that Mallory, anyway, would start melting into a puddle, but no dice—and then started screeching at each other. I ignored them and focused on my wrists. They were definitely bruised where the golem had been clutching them, but he wasn't tightening his grip any. I wiggled my arms experimentally. *There.* If I could just get them a little wetter, I might be able to slip out of its grip.

"You're the vampire, go do something!" Mallory was screaming at Olivia. The sprinkler system was *loud*. I felt the massive buzz of her magic swell and spark with her frustration. "Kill him!"

But Olivia had seen me wiggling my arms. "I'm not leaving her, not while your little pet is getting soaked!" she shouted back.

"He'll stay on task," Mallory began, but Olivia shook her head stubbornly. She had her prize and wasn't going to walk away from it. Mallory threw up her hands and stalked away into the dark drizzle toward the opposite end of the room, where the generator was. I heard her stumble and swear before she left my radius, and I couldn't help but laugh at that. Then she let out an anguished cry, and Olivia called a question at her.

"The book!" she screamed. "He's taken the Book of Mirrors!" There was a rustling of feet and water as she ran in Jesse's direction, and then Olivia and I didn't hear anything else.

I could only see about two feet in any direction, but Olivia pivoted to face me, her eyes inches from mine. "This is your doing, I suppose?" she said coolly.

"Actually, I had—" I began, but she was coming at me now, leaning forward to pinch the skin on my upper arm, *hard*, and twist it. I cried out in pain.

"What is *wrong* with you?" she exploded. "I gave you a home, a job, beautiful things, and then you betrayed me. Despite all of that, I came back to give you this *gift*"—she released me and gestured openly with her arms—"and you spit it back in my face. All the planning, all the work I put into you! You ungrateful little brat." She hit me again, a backhand. It slid off my wet cheek, but I still felt a spurt of blood in my mouth.

I laughed in her face. Couldn't help it, didn't want to. Olivia stared at me, shocked, like I'd just peed on her rug.

"Let me make something clear, *Liv*," I snarled. "And I want you to listen, because this is critical. You. Are. Not. My. Mother." I spat the blood in her face, and even though the water washed it right off she took a step back, shocked. "You aren't anyone's mother, and you never will be, thank God, because you are so incredibly unhinged that it's a little funny. You're a psychotic parasite, and I am not your goddamned Barbie doll."

She was fast, but she was still human, and she telegraphed the punch. I saw her rear her arm back, but I was already moving, pulling my wrists up and free through the wet golem's hands. I ducked just in time, and Olivia's fist drove into the golem's face.

Wet clay or not, it had to hurt, because she cried out, backing up a few steps and clutching her right hand with her left, unaccustomed to pain. That's what you get for trying to punch a null. I had a new problem, though: the golem was wet but not dead. His orders were to contain me, and he was going to keep coming. I slipped away from his first lunge and side-checked the off-balance Olivia, who slid on the carpeting and went down.

I ran.

Chapter 32

Jesse dashed back through the hallway and into the nearest corridor where the sprinklers hadn't come on. He ducked into the first open doorway—an office. He'd just drawn his gun when he heard Mallory rushing into the hallway. Jesse took a deep breath, in and out, and stepped out of the office with his gun drawn. He switched the flashlight on as he went, holding it against the gun and shining it directly into her eyes. "Police. Don't move," he said levelly.

Mallory blinked in the sudden light. Her hands had been fussing at her neckline, but now she raised them slowly, the way everyone who has ever seen a cop movie knows to do. Then she began to mutter something, and this time Jesse recognized the language—it was Hebrew. He thumbed the safety off his weapon. "Stop. No spells, or I shoot now and try to figure out what the hell you were saying later."

The witch closed her mouth, a murderous look in her eye. "So what's your plan?" she asked in English, her voice a little out of breath from running. "Are you going to arrest me?"

"You killed two people, and were an accomplice in at least two more murders," he pointed out.

Her smile widened. "True," she allowed, "but we both know that the human courts won't see it that way. And you work for them."

She was extremely pretty, with thick dark hair plastered to her head, and might have been anywhere from thirty to fifty. She looked very small and wet all of a sudden, and the two of them stood there staring at each other. "I've been doing a lot of research lately," Jesse told her, "and my guess is that you poured a lot of magic into that thing in there"—he nodded his head back in the direction they'd come from, where the golem was trapped inside Scarlett's radius—"which hopefully means you don't have much to burn right now."

An insidious smile spread across Mallory's face. Her hands didn't move, but all of a sudden the neckline of her blouse jumped, as if someone had plucked at it. Jesse leveled the gun. "Stop it!" he yelled.

She took one small step closer to him, and Jesse tensed, standing his ground. Suddenly every light in the room flickered on, even the ones without light bulbs. The miscellaneous bits of trash and office supplies that had been scattered around the corridor suddenly rose in the air and began a whirling dance, like they were trying to form an invisible braid of energy. Jesse felt the gun tug and jump in his hand, and he dropped the flashlight and clutched the gun tighter, with both hands. "You were wrong," Mallory called to him over the rustling of papers and junk. "I still have plenty of magic to burn." And her blouse jumped again. The Transruah lifted out of her shirt and settled on her chest. She must have snatched it up when she came after him. *Shit.* "And I'm not just an animator," she finished, her voice smug. "Now. Where's my book?"

The gun began to spin slowly, twisting out of his grip. "I'll shoot," he yelled amid the chaos. He was about a second away from having to decide whether to release the gun or have his fingers broken.

"No you won't," Mallory said. He squeezed the trigger, but it was too late—the metal had crumpled, mangling the barrel. Yelping, Jesse released the weapon—which came flying straight at his head. He ducked the chunk of metal the first time, but it came right back at him, and Jesse took a hard blow to his temple, his ears ringing and his vision fuzzing over for a moment. Before he could really see what he was doing, Jesse lurched forward, missing the chunk of metal's third effort to brain him. He tackled the witch, who merely laughed at him—until Jesse got his hands on the Jerusalem stone at her neck. He pulled hard, but the stone was on a leather string, not a chain, and Jesse took several more blows from flying objects before he was able to wrestle the leather thong from around her neck. Everything that had been flying around the room suddenly stilled, wavering in the air as Mallory tried to sustain the flow of magic without the Transruah to aid her. With no other ideas, Jesse gritted his teeth and lifted the witch to a seated position. And then he hit Mallory, a quick uppercut that snapped her head back. Her eyes went distant, and suddenly everything in the room crashed to the ground. The lights went out again.

Chapter 33

As it turns out, you can't hide from a golem.

He didn't bother trying to cut me off or dodging to get to me; he simply beelined toward me, wherever I went, and I wanted to stay in the part of the clinic where the sprinklers were going. Whatever direction I ran, the clay figure followed me, his surgical scrubs and hat plastered with mud. His face had mostly washed away now, and whenever he got close enough for me to catch glimpses of him I was newly inspired to run. I was much faster, since the golem couldn't really run without slipping on muddy feet, but I was also high on morphine and sick from chemo and injuries. And the golem couldn't tire.

Olivia was after me too, and I desperately wanted to buy myself one minute to get the gun that was still taped to my back. But this proved impossible with the golem chasing me, Terminator-style. For a while there, it was the world's dumbest Benny Hill sketch. Then Olivia caught on to the golem's uncomplicated plan—follow Scarlett anywhere—and positioned herself to circle around to where I *would* be, instead of following me. Then she just had to wait for me to come to her, a triumphant smile on her face.

But she had miscalculated, either because she'd gotten used to vampiric powers or because she'd gotten used to me submitting, or both. Instead of allowing her to push me into the golem's arms, I took the offensive. I had no training in martial arts or self-defense, but I did know that Olivia had had a knee injury in college. I kicked out with my right leg and hit the side of her left knee as hard as I could, slipping in the process but managing to remain on my feet. Olivia cried out with surprise and pain, falling on her butt and clutching at her leg. By now the golem had caught up with me, though, and it wrapped one hand around my upper left arm, just as it had before. The generator started suddenly, and the room was filled with dim lamplight, even as the water from the sprinklers began to slow. I didn't pay attention to any of this, though. I knew if it caught my other arm I was screwed, so I flailed wildly, working to evade the golem's searching hand.

Olivia screamed again, only a few feet away now, and I managed to turn my head to see Jesse clutching a handful of her hair. He must have turned the generator on so he could see what the hell was happening. Olivia had gotten to her feet and pulled her gun out from somewhere, and Jesse had his other hand on hers as she tried to keep the gun from his grasp. His arms were longer, though, and one big hand was wrapped around hers where it clutched the gun. I heard two shots fire into the ceiling, but I had my own problems—the golem had wrapped his free hand around my entire upper body, trapping my whole right arm instead of trying to grab my wrist. I cried out in pain as it squeezed me in place like we were hugging. The air reeked of stale water and industrial clay. It was like being in a pressured mud bath.

"The head," Jesse yelled at me. "You have to rub his forehead—" His voice cut off in a strangled yelp. Olivia had bitten him on the forearm.

That sounded ridiculous, but I wasn't exactly suffering from an abundance of planning. Before the golem could do anything else I *wrenched* my left arm with everything I had, feeling it almost pull out of the socket. I felt the wet clay give a little, gritted my teeth, and did it again. I heard myself scream with the pain, but I managed to slip my left hand free. I reached up, pushed the scrub cap backward off the golem's head—and could just make out a word carved into its forehead. My name. I flailed my arm, throwing the golem and myself off-balance as I tried to avoid his grasp. We began to tip backward as I scrubbed furiously at the writing with the heel of my hand. Suddenly all I could think of was Erin, and the way the heavy clay and the weight of the magic had crushed her. My back hit the ground—tilted to the side a bit rather than straight on, thank God—and I had one second to brace myself to be crushed. Instead, though, a few hundred pounds of loose wet clay crumbled gently around me, filling in the spaces between my limbs, coating my hair and face. The golem was dead.

I found myself in a pile of mud just as the water from the sprinklers trickled into a drip. There was a metallic thud, and I turned to see Jesse pulling Olivia's arms behind her back in the classic handcuffing-a-suspect position you see on television. She was facing me, and her expression was terrifying: wild-eyed and hungry. She actually lunged in my direction, but Jesse was ready for it and caught her weight easily.

"Settle down," he said sternly. To me, he said, "Scarlett, are you hurt?"

"Not as much as I will be when this morphine wears off," I said truthfully.

Jesse frowned. "Morphine?"

I shrugged. "Long story. Mallory?"

"Dead."

"Did you…"

Jesse shook his head. "I took off the amulet, and then I tried to just knock her out, but it was like her body had just…emptied."

"Kirsten would probably know why," I said. "Maybe she OD'd on magic or something."

"You're mine," Olivia snarled at me, completely unaware that we had been talking. Spittle flew from her mouth as she spoke. "Wherever you go, whatever happens to me, you will always be mine. I made you."

Without being particularly conscious of it, I had started wriggling my way out of the pile of clay and backward, away from Olivia. "I've got her," Jesse assured me. "Just stay close enough to keep her human."

That got through my momentary panic, and I stopped backing away. Jesse glanced around for a moment, and then frog-marched Olivia a couple of feet to an examination room with a long metal handle on the door, shaped roughly like a staple. He did something quickly with the handcuffs, and when he stepped back Olivia's hands were cuffed together in front of her, through the door handle.

Jesse slumped down to the floor a few feet away, leaning against the wall. He looked as tired and beat-up as I felt, which was quite an accomplishment. I was campaigning pretty hard for most fucked-up looking.

"What do we do with her now?" I asked.

Jesse sighed, looking miserable. "I have no idea. She should go to prison, but a human prison can't hold her. Dashiell said I should call him when I caught her, and he's probably on his way here anyway. But he's just going to kill her."

Olivia suddenly went half-limp, clutching the door handle like it was the only thing keeping her out of deep water. She was still staring at me, but her eyes had gone baby-deer soft, and tears began to slide down her cheeks. She slid down to the floor, letting herself dangle helplessly from the cuffs. "Scarlett, you won't let them kill me, will you? After everything we've been through together? Everything I taught you?"

I looked at Jesse for a long, foggy moment that felt siphoned off from the rest of the night's timeline. And then I finally understood. If he turned Olivia over to Dashiell, in his own eyes, Jesse would be killing her. He'd be haunted forever, knowing that he'd compromised his deepest beliefs about order and justice and let a murderer die lawlessly. And in that way, Jesse would become another one of her victims.

I was not going to let that happen. I lifted Will's revolver, which I'd retrieved from my back as I scrambled away from the pile of clay. And I shot Olivia twice in the chest.

It was *loud*. I dropped the gun and squeezed my eyes shut, listening to the ringing in my ears. I hadn't looked at Jesse, and I was afraid to open my eyes and do so. I knew exactly what expression was going to be on his face—shock and disappointment that I'd let him down, that I'd demonstrated my complete lack of morals, ethics, or character yet again. I'd seen it before, and I didn't even blame him, really. I just...wasn't ready.

I don't know how much time passed, but eventually I could hear again. The only sound in the room was a slow drip-dripping of water, probably coming from sprinkler heads. Then I felt a warm hand touch mine, and I opened my eyes. Jesse was crouched in front of me, turning my hand over to press a wad of paper towels into my palm. "They're wet," he said softly, "but they'll work."

I lifted my hands. They were shaking. "I—can you—"Jesse nodded and began wiping clay and blood from my face. I shivered with cold, wincing a couple of times when he found one of my new bruises.

"Why did you do that?" Jesse asked me quietly. "Why shoot her?"

I shrugged. "Bitch deserved to die. Dashiell was going to do it anyway, so I figured I might as well have the privilege." My teeth chattered as I spoke. When had it gotten so cold?

Jesse sat back on his heels and studied my face. "You're lying," he said simply. "You did it for me."

"Pshaw," I said scornfully. "That doesn't sound like me at *all*—" And I stopped talking then, because he was kissing me. His lips were warm, and as he pulled me into his lap I discovered that the rest of him was too. He smoothed my wet hair from my face, and I moved past the surprise and kissed him back with a hunger that would have scared me if I was anywhere in the vicinity of my right mind.

Chills spread through my chest, but I wasn't cold anymore. The kiss went on and on. I couldn't get enough of him. Our first kiss, on Molly's porch, had been like a bubble bursting, tension breaking into passion. This was something else, though. This was...connection.

Then I heard a familiar voice behind us. "I believe the word you humans use is *ahem*."

We broke apart, gasping for breath. Dashiell stood in the same doorway Jesse had come through, leaning against the doorframe and looking amused. Goddamn vampires. I scooted off Jesse's lap, trying to keep the embarrassment off my face.

"Hey," I managed.

Dashiell raised his eyebrows. "I found a dead witch in the hallway. Would that be Mallory?"

"Yes," Jesse said. He climbed to his feet, putting one hand against the wall to steady himself.

"Ah." Dashiell came forward and looked down at Olivia's body. It hadn't yet rotted the way a vampire corpse usually does as it dies. She had been human when I'd shot her, and died as a human. We all go back to human in the end. Dashiell looked at Jesse. "I see you managed to take care of Olivia."

Jesse opened his mouth, but I spoke first. "Yes." I stood up shakily. Dashiell didn't need to know that it had been me. He'd respect Jesse more if he thought Jesse was secretly ruthless. "I can get her to my furnace guy, if someone can help me load her in..." I realized I didn't have my van and stopped short, uncertain of what to do. I felt myself swaying.

"Scarlett," Dashiell said, the amused tone back in his voice. "You're about to pass out, and you look like you just crawled out of the grave during a downpour. I think you can have the rest of the night off." He looked around, taking in the clinic with a newly focused eye. "Consider this one on me."

"That's nice," I said, a little loopy, and sagged against a counter.

"Detective Cruz, I trust you can get her out of here?" Dashiell asked. Jesse nodded and came over to put my arm around his shoulders. He walked me down the hall without another word to my boss.

There was no sign of the witch's body in the hall, so Dashiell must have already put it in a car. We paused briefly so Jesse could put his shoes back on, and then began plodding forward again. "You can't drive like this, you know," Jesse said in my ear.

"Of course I can," I protested. Then I stopped in my tracks. "Jesse, the Transruah...if Dashiell gets it, it could start this whole big thing—"

"It's okay," he said. He reached into his jacket pocket and showed me the little piece of Jerusalem stone on its leather cord.

I turned it over in my hands, shocked. I must have shorted it out when Jesse had come in to help me fight Olivia and the golem, but I hadn't even felt it. "Jesse, you brought it too close to me. You shorted it out."

"I know," he said, taking it gently and putting it back in his pocket. "I made the decision. I'll take the responsibility." He grinned. "Or I'll just tell Kirsten it was unavoidable, and she'll have to understand."

My mouth was working like a fish's. "It was too powerful, Scarlett," he said gravely. "I'll return the book and the amulet tomorrow, and the witches can keep them as historical artifacts. But no one should have that much power. Think what would have happened if Olivia and Mallory had made it to Kirsten."

I shuddered and nodded. I wasn't really opposed to shorting out the Transruah, I was just...surprised. It was a bold move.

We made it outside, finally. Jesse took my keys and went around the side of the building to pull Eli's truck up so I wouldn't have to walk any farther. As soon as he was gone, though, I stuck my head back inside the building. "Dashiell?" I called. There was a flash of vampire speed, and then Dashiell hit my radius and walked toward me casually.

"Yes?" he inquired.

I took a deep breath. "There's someone I still need to talk to. I need an address, and I would *appreciate*"—I chose my words carefully—"if I could get it from you, no questions asked."

"Whose address?"

I told him. "Just to talk, right?" he asked warily.

I nodded. "I swear."

He met my eyes for a long moment, judging, and gave me the address.

It took almost ten minutes to convince Jesse I was well enough to drive. But we had two cars at the clinic, and Jesse still had to go back in for the Book of Mirrors, and…what can I say, I whined my way into it. Finally Jesse reached over to hand me back the keys. As I took them, he leaned forward and kissed me on the mouth, gently. "I'll call you tomorrow; we'll figure out getting the cars back," he told me, and I just nodded.

Chapter 34

Jesse watched Scarlett pull away, making sure that the truck's headlights were on and it was moving in a straight line. When she was finally out of sight, he trudged back into the clinic.

He headed for the desk he'd climbed on to hide the Book of Mirrors. It would only take a moment to retrieve the book from the ceiling tile. He would turn the book and the dead amulet over to Runa the next day. She'd know what to do with them.

Before he climbed up, though, Jesse sat down on the desk, intending to rest for just one second. He knew if he thought too hard about the events of the day, much less the last few days, his brain would melt into a puddle. Only a few days ago, Scarlett had been out of the picture, Runa had been his girlfriend, and his biggest problem was that his dream job wasn't quite as challenging as he'd wanted. And now...he shook his head, trying to clear it.

Then, too tired to look for him, Jesse simply called, "Dashiell?"

The vampire was suddenly *there*. "*Dios*," Jesse muttered, grabbing his heart. "I had forgotten about that."

"Did you need something else, Detective?" the vampire asked politely, but Jesse thought he saw a twinkle in Dashiell's eye. Maybe startling humans was just the kind of thing that never got old. Or something.

"We need to talk," Jesse said.

"What about?"

"Your system," Jesse said frankly. "This way that you have, of covering up crimes and crime scenes and then getting the police to cover what Scarlett misses. It's not working for me."

A look of annoyance flickered on Dashiell's face. "Continue," he said shortly.

"Right now, you're trying to have it both ways," Jesse began. "You're trying to work outside the law but also use the law—including me—in illegal ways, whenever you think it's useful. What I'd like to discuss is the possibility of streamlining this a little more. I think there may be a way that the police force can be involved in Old World crimes without you having to press a lot of minds or bribe anyone."

Dashiell stared at him for a long moment, and Jesse fought the instinct to look away, to protect himself from having his mind pressed. After Scarlett left he had found one of the vampire amulets in Kirsten's car, and he was prepared for that eventuality. But let Dashiell think that Jesse was just brave enough to face him.

They stayed like that for a long moment, until the amusement left the vampire's face and he tilted his head slightly, as if considering Jesse for the first time.

"I'm listening," Dashiell said at last.

Chapter 35

I stopped at Molly's house for a quick shower and to get dressed in a clean T-shirt and jeans. I was now delighted that I hadn't been able to wear my favorite canvas jacket to Kirsten's party. It greeted me, whole and unstained, from the back of a chair, where I happily shrugged it on. The T-shirt and boxers I'd taken off went directly in the garbage can, but I was sorry I had to throw away the boots, an old birthday gift from my mom. At least Molly would have fun making me shop for new ones. While I was thinking of it, I called and left her a voice mail to let her know it was safe to come home.

I followed Dashiell's directions all the way east to the Palisades, until I found a tiny stretch of beach with a small house that faced the ocean. It was after two in the morning, but I knocked hard on the back door and then went over to lean against the porch railing to wait, giving him time to get dressed and come out. I felt, rather than saw, when the man came up to lean against the railing next to me.

"Beautiful view," I commented, although it was hard to make out much in the dark besides the flash of white water in the breaking waves.

"It is."

"Kind of a long commute, though."

"True."

I turned around to face the house, leaning my elbows against the rails and turning my head to look at him. "Dashiell gave me your address, in case you were wondering. He knows that I'm here."

Hayne frowned. "Miss Bernard, you say that like you think I'm going to murder you."

I shrugged casually. "Just letting you know."

"I see." He looked back out at the ocean. "What is it you wanted to talk to me about?" he asked calmly. Which I suppose was a lot more polite than "What the fuck are you doing at my house at two a.m.," which would have been my reaction.

"I've been on this case," I began, "and I don't know how much you already know about it, but it's kept me awfully busy the last few days. I had this little thought sometimes, though, at the back of my mind, and every time I tried to chase it down it just escaped me. Then today I realized it was actually a question." I looked at him and waited until he turned his head to meet my eyes. "How did Olivia and Mallory know where to find the Book of Mirrors?"

Hayne flinched. It was small, but it was there. He looked away again, without speaking. That was okay. I could do the talking for both of us. "After all," I said, "Mallory was never really part of Kirsten's society. And I doubt Kirsten told any of her witches about a secret that big, because that's just not what leaders do. You don't give the governor of Hawaii the code to the nuclear weapons stash, for crying out loud. But if you had to be traveling back and forth to San Diego and you had to explain your absence to, say, a spouse..."

"Miss Bernard," Hayne said, and then sighed. There was a long silence, and we stared at the ocean some more.

When Hayne showed no signs of speaking again, I said, "Okay, I'll keep going. At the same time, I couldn't help noticing the scars on your wrists." Automatically, Hayne turned his hands palms-up, looking down toward the old puncture wounds. I couldn't see them in the dark, but maybe he could. "It didn't seem like Dashiell's style to feed off his daytime security guy, not when he has regular volunteers for that. But I figured, what the hell, maybe he does it to keep you in line or something.

"If that were the case, though, why are those scars so old? Why wouldn't he still be feeding off you? There's more than one bite there, so it wasn't just some weird initiation ritual or something. You were fed on, a bunch of times, a while ago. And not by Dashiell."

When he still didn't speak, I opted for a more direct route. "Tell me, Hayne: Why did you and Kirsten split up?"

After a beat, Hayne finally answered me. "It wasn't Dashiell, though I imagine that's what anyone would think. He's a lot of things, but he knew I was in love with her, and he didn't stand in our way. She met him because of me—that's how she was able to campaign for the witches to have rights, to share a cleaner, all of that." His voice had a tinge of pride.

"It was Kirsten who eventually...she just couldn't accept that I trusted Dashiell, that I wasn't worried that he'd kill me or feed from me." He gave me a sidelong glance. "I knew that he pressed me sometimes, you know? I'd overhear a phone call, or he'd have secret guests over, or whatever, and he'd take the memory from me. It didn't bother me, but it drove Kirsten crazy. She offered me a way to protect myself, protect my mind from him, but I refused." He shrugged. "Eventually it came down to a choice. I loved her, but... anyway."

"And the bites?" I prompted.

He sighed heavily. "Yes, the bites. We split up, and she eventually got remarried. I was in a rough place. I let my guard down. And then Albert asked me for a favor, just delivering some package to his friend on my way home from work, at sunset. No big deal." Hayne stared down at his hands, miserable. "Olivia didn't take all of it, all of the memory. I was there too long for that. And I think she and Mallory enjoyed having me know that I'd given up secrets—I knew some of Kirsten's and some of Dashiell's, you see. If I'd said anything to Dashiell about it…"

"Didn't Dashiell see the marks?"

He nodded. "I told him I'd met a lady vampire at one of Gregory's parties and things got out of hand. I was so messed up about Kirsten, still, that it made a lot of sense."

Gregory was a creepy, powerful vampire who threw weekly parties for the vampire hangers-on. I had to agree, it was a great place to go for some recreational self-destruction.

Hayne went quiet for a few minutes, and I let him stew.

"You're going to tell him now, aren't you," he said. It wasn't a question. "He's gotta know that Olivia and the witch know things."

"They're dead, Hayne," I said. "Both of them. And Albert was killed too. There's no one left to know what you told them."

He stared at me without blinking, for so long that I was beginning to worry. Finally, he said, "And?"

I looked at him levelly. "And Dashiell and Kirsten aren't stupid. When the dust settles it may occur to them to ask questions. For now, though, I'm planning to keep it to myself."

He eyed me warily. "In exchange for what?"

I shrugged. "You've seen *The Godfather*, Hayne, you know the drill. 'Someday I may call upon you for a favor' and all that. You owe me one."

"I won't betray any confidences," he said stubbornly. "Not again."

I shook my head and stepped off the porch. "Hayne, my man," I said over my shoulder, "I wouldn't ask you to."

By the time I left the little beach house, I was so tired my bones felt rubbery, and the morphine had completely worn off. I hurt everywhere, and it seemed like too much trouble to try to remember any of the specific injuries. My night still wasn't over, though, not yet. There was one more thing I had to do, and it couldn't wait.

I called ahead, and Will met me at the front door of Hair of the Dog. He looked exhausted, but still smiled at me the way he always does, part pleasure at being human again and part general good cheer at seeing me. I followed him through the bar and toward the back hallway.

"Ana took her girlfriend back to my place," he explained as we went. Will had been busy since I'd left: the bodies, glass, and blood were gone, and the floor was still slick with cleaner. It was a little funny that everyone was cleaning up crime scenes today except for me. "I turned a spare bedroom into a secure room for my wolves a few years ago. Lydia will be safe there."

"Has he woken up yet?" I asked.

Will shook his head. "I check on him every few minutes. The wolfberry is long gone from his system, according to Matthias, but I think he's still sleeping off the aftereffects from the sedatives." We arrived at the door to the little janitorial closet, and Will unceremoniously flipped the light switch.

Eli was laid out on the cot, dressed in a clean-looking pair of sweatpants that had been cut off at the knees, and nothing else. The room was warm, and he didn't even stir when the light went on. I concentrated on my radius. I knew how Eli's magic felt better than anyone, and the sense of wrongness had vanished.

"Is it okay if I stay with him tonight?" I asked Will.

He nodded immediately. "Of course." He checked his watch. "If you're here, I'm going to go home and catch a couple of hours of sleep. I'll come in an hour or so before opening to finish the cleanup." He looked up. "But, Scarlett, call me if you need *anything*. Or if he wakes up and wants to talk. Don't hesitate, seriously."

I nodded dully. I was already shrugging out of my jacket. Will waved and took off, turning off all the other lights as he went. I went over and closed the door, but left the lights on, in case one of us had nightmares. I untied my Chuck Taylors and took them off too.

The cot that Will kept in the janitor's closet wasn't very big, but I did the best I could to shove Eli over and make room for myself. Instead of lying down, however, I sat cross-legged at the foot of the bed, looking at Eli. Expressions danced across his face in his sleep, and I felt a little guilty when it reminded me of a dog kicking its legs as it dreamed. When I was sure I was calm and relaxed, I closed my eyes.

And this time, when I called, the circle was *there*. No searching, no grasping at edges. I was immediately relieved—some part of me had worried I'd need to be high to do it again. Then I concentrated, not on the circle, but on Eli and his magic, the magic that bonded to his blood and made him a werewolf. It was blocked from him while he was in my radius, but it wasn't blocked from *me*. It was there, waiting for Eli to move away from me. Or, I finally realized, waiting for me to do something with it.

I called the magic to me. Or at least, that's the best way I can describe it. I called the magic past the part of my radius where it was waiting, closer and closer until I could feel it come into *me*. I held it for a moment, in perfect balance, and there was potential there, potential to do...something? It wasn't important. Instead, I let Eli's magic dissolve slowly, bit by bit like sand through my fingers, until it was gone. When I finally opened my eyes, Eli no longer pulsed with magic.

I couldn't bring any of Olivia's victims back to life, including the people Eli had killed. I couldn't save him from that memory, either, or the knowledge that he had taken lives. But I could give him this gift instead: the promise that it could never, ever happen to him again.

Because he was human.

I checked my nose, but there was no blood this time. And I managed to curl up against Eli's side before I blacked out, which was definitely progress. My last thought before sleep wasn't of Jesse, or Eli, or the things that had happened between both of them and myself in the past week. No, even though I knew it was temporary, even though I knew there would be much to face the next day, my last thought was of peace.

Acknowledgments

During the writing and editing of this book I spent months in bed with hyperemesis gravidarum and other fun pregnancy ailments, and I'd like to take this opportunity to thank my friends and family who provided vital support, help, and love while I was sick. I especially want to extend my gratitude to my parents, my forgiving and often saintlike husband, and my elder daughter, who will hopefully not be scarred by the months of excessive television privileges. All my love to Molly, who was born perfect anyway, and who is definitely *not* named after the vampire in this book. I promise.

I don't live in Los Angeles anymore, so I definitely owe a big thank you to Tracy Tong, who served as my LA advisor on this book especially. She's the person I can count on to know what parts of the city wouldn't have graffiti and what brands of dresses Olivia might have worn. Thank you to my old friend Brian Frederick, who probably didn't attend medical school just to answer my bizarre questions, but who was always gracious enough to answer them anyway, and to author Lori Devoti, whose class at the UW-Madison School of Continuing Studies was a major contributor to the structure and first chapter of this book. I can't tell you how much your support means to me.

Thank you to my sister Elizabeth, who was always around with compliments when I doubted myself most, and who was willing to contribute her marketing and graphic design expertise despite my inability to pay for it. Much appreciation to Kari Harms, who enlightened me on how Candy Land could be an excellent party theme, and Krista Ewbank, who suggested that an abandoned theater might be a good place to cast some dark magic. Thank you, also, to my followers and friends on Facebook and Twitter, who remind me every day of why it's so much fun to write books.

Finally, I owe many thanks, once again, to my hardworking team: Alex Carr and Patrick McGee at 47North, my editor Jeff VanderMeer, my agent Jacquie Flynn, and my copy editor Deb for her outstanding attention to detail. Someday I will get a version of Microsoft Word that isn't almost a decade old, and I'll have fewer typos, I promise.

About the Author

Melissa F. Olson was born and raised in Chippewa Falls, Wisconsin, and studied film and literature at the University of Southern California in Los Angeles. After graduation, and a brief stint bouncing around the Hollywood studio system, Melissa moved to Madison, Wisconsin, where she eventually acquired a master's degree from the University of Wisconsin–Milwaukee, a husband, a mortgage, two kids, and two comically oversize dogs—not at all in that order. She is the author of *Dead Spots*.